The Complete War in Heaven Trilogy

Angel Story Saga Books 1-3

By

Julius St. Clair

Table of Contents:

Angels of Eden (Book #2)

Angels and the Ark (Book #3)

End of Angels

Book I

PROLOGUE:

I am Immortal.

I know how that must sound...

Tempting...

Desirable.

Impossible...

But it's true...

And I have known nothing else.

No matter how hard one may try to impose it upon me

I will never taste the finality of death...

But do not be fooled by my words

This does not mean all is well

That Immortality by definition equals

Perfect.

Unregrettable.

Bliss...

And I will tell you why.

My name is Lysander,

And I am an Angel of the most, high God...

"Behold, I send you forth as sheep in the midst of wolves: be ye therefore wise as serpents, and harmless as doves.

– Matthew 10:16

"Fear them not therefore: for there is nothing covered, that shall not be revealed; and hid, that shall not be known. What I tell you in darkness, that speak ye in light: and what ye hear in the ear, that preach ye upon the housetops. And fear not them which kill the body, but are not able to kill the soul: but rather fear him which is able to destroy both soul and body in hell."

– Matthew 10:26-28

CHAPTER 1: In the Beginning...

Something scratched my foot.

I sprung up from the grass and sat at full alert, because I'd never felt such a sensation. For no particular reason, I thought it might have been caused by a small animal of some kind, but I quickly dismissed the thought for it was impossible. Nothing of that nature had been created yet. In actuality, it was an angel trying to win over my hard-earned attention. He had to be no bigger than a large dog, and the way he hunched his shoulders and pawed at my feet, he must have been very disoriented and unaware of his surroundings. No one in their right mind would be acting that way, unless they were playing...but even then, it was usually customary to at least learn someone's name before popping their personal bubble.

I wanted him to stop. But I couldn't say anything, even with his strange behavior. The view around us was far too captivating, and it pulled me into its hypnotizing calm with ease as the angel before me whimpered. The universe all around me, a vast network of diverse stars, planets and phenomenon orbiting the negligible, small, floating island in which I resided. A peninsula hovering in the midst of space. With nothing else on it besides grass and a few other angels, star gazing was becoming an increasingly popular pastime - one that I had long ago mastered. You would think I would be tired of the monotony, but I had come to find out that beauty had the strange ability to renew itself, no matter how many times it was seen. And with a dazzling view at our express disposal, I was often engrossed in its splendor...

Okay...maybe an angel mauling your foot like you were a cat's scratching post was a little more distracting...

"I don't recognize you," I said to him abruptly, trying to break him from his clawing frenzy. The angel ceased his assault and hung his head low, shaking it fiercely - the wings on his back coiling and shooting out like they were on springs. It looked strange, but I interpreted his body language perfectly, for I too had been in a similar predicament. Not the scratching, that was new. But I understood the rest of his dilemma and figured he would adapt to the loss he had just experienced soon enough.

"I'm new here," he said shyly, before being consumed by the aquarium-like view walling us in. His voice trailed off and I kept silent, letting him indulge, chuckling to myself over his sudden fascination. It was hard not to be engaged with such a presentation, and within seconds, I was enchanted anew.

I didn't even hear someone sneak up behind me. And I wish I had, because it was his favorite form of greeting someone and unquestionably the opposite of mine. Before my senses could kick in, I was already in a headlock.

"So this is why you left us?" a familiar voice laughed as its source freed me from his personal prison. I shuffled around to get a good view of the first angel I had ever met, Cadence, towering over me.

A tall and slender angel with wings as lanky as his frame, he often stood out due to his bulky armor, which looked like it was two sizes too big. A dull silver and gold plated his shoulder pads and gauntlets, and he held a bronze-colored, trashcan-looking shield in his hand like it was his security blanket. No one knew where it had come from, but there had to be some explanation as to why he was born with it. Perhaps it was identification. That was assuredly my guess because when I had first met him, his face was so plain, it had struck me as immediately forgettable.

"I told you I was going off to stargaze," I said innocently. "Besides, the group was just prattling along...brainstorming the perfect adjective to describe the grass...I was getting tired of that conversation."

"Lysander, every spot on this island transmits the same view. There isn't a place you can't stargaze. There is literally *nothing else*," he said, walking in front of me, but out of the way of my new guest - now infatuated with the grass beneath him. "How is going off to look around by yourself any better than staying with us and doing it? At least we'd be together."

"I was hoping to see something new. We never move from our meeting spot on the island, and we hang out there so often it's like our home...so much so that I've got cabin fever. Some travelling could do me some good."

"What difference does it make where you're looking out from? There are zero new events out there. It's the same animated painting plastered on the universal wall. Look, there's the blue steam planet, the red and purple cosmic dust, and the yellowish-green-blue nebula. Oh, and that protostar. Nothing's out of place."

"The protostar is new," I said matter-of-factly, pointing toward it.

"What are you trying to say?"

"That there are new developments from time to time."

"Like what?" he said casually. "A rock flies by? That steam planet rotates?"

"No...but that protostar wasn't there before."

"I'm sure it was," he said flatly, refusing to take a closer look. I rubbed my eyes vigorously.

"New events do occur, Cadence. They're just rare or relatively small. If you gazed out as much as I do, you would have noticed them yourself, emerging at various times and locations."

I was surprised I had been able to keep the conversation going for so long, especially with Cadence along for the ride. Usually if he was fed up with a topic, he would end the discussion on the spot.

"Looks the same to me," he said stubbornly.

"You're so complacent," I sighed.

"How long did it take you to come up with that word?"

"Complacent AND dismissive," I yelled at him, feeling more confident by the second. "You didn't even bother looking back at the star because you're so stuck in your ways. No wonder you think nothing changes around here. You refuse to accept it, even when it taps you on the shoulder."

"Change? Really? Change? Out here?!" he exclaimed, waving his hands out like he was balancing two plates.

"About as much change as there is in a fishbowl," another angel remarked, gliding down beside Cadence. Her name was Alessa, a moderately-sized angel with the royal color of purple gracing her from head to toe. Streaks of it were lined into her silver hair. Splashes of it were spread across her slender but durable gray armor. Strands of it were even found mingling amongst the fibers of her unimposing, average-sized wings. She made it known to us on a consistent basis that she was important, but thankfully Cadence reminded her often that she was stuck here just like the rest of us, so how special could she possibly be? Seeing her ego deflate was a rare and satisfying form of entertainment.

"There was no point in leaving, Lysander," she scolded. "And Cadence, you took too long to get him. Now Farah's going to tell her story from the beginning, and you know how I can't stand it when she does that. One interruption and it's the end of the world."

"I like her stories, even when they're reruns," I admitted. "They're...epic in scale."

"You mean exaggerated," Alessa retorted. "Like the one where she broke through the barrier, grabbed a star and pulled it out of orbit. C'mon, that didn't happen. Trust me, we would have noticed."

"It could have happened. We weren't there to say otherwise, and I did notice that star number thirty-three had veered off to the right a bit."

"You numbered them all?" She gave me a face like I had just eaten a cockroach.

"Is there something wrong with that?" *Didn't everyone count the stars?*

"It doesn't matter," she exhaled heavily. "The point is that Farah is making all this up. Did you notice how she can't break through a second time? I asked her what was the point of coming back if she had made it out. Do you know what she said? She said that she wanted to tell us what had happened, like she couldn't get our attention from outside the barrier! All she would have to do is fly in circles until we noticed! This island is not that big!" Her talking was building momentum and her hands were flailing all around her like she was trying to rap in sign language. I struggled to keep up but before her ranting got too intense, she stopped abruptly and waited for a response.

"I believe you," I winced, cupping my left ear. "What you just said...about getting our attention."

"If she did it before, why is it so hard all of a sudden?" she yelled, unaware of my discomfort. "I'm telling you, her story is false."

"It might not be impossible..."

"You're so gullible," she huffed, and looked away from me to Cadence. He was staring at the brand new angel, still in awe at the so-called "animated painting" in the distance.

"He's new, isn't he?" Cadence asked, very serious, and I smiled back at him.

"First one since we arrived."

"You mean since you arrived," Alessa corrected.

"Right, right," I said, stretching my wings and trying to compose myself. "I see what you're implying - that you have some kind of seniority. But you may not be much older than I am. For all we know, we could have been created at the same time, just released sparingly. Think about the number of angels on our island. There's no more than thirty, but something tells me there's a multitude of them, probably in Heaven right now."

"Do you honestly think so?" Alessa asked hopefully. Her change in attitude perplexed me, but I soon realized that Alessa may never have come to this conclusion herself. The very idea was thrilling to consider – that there were more of us on the other side and Heaven was more than an empty city we may see someday.

"Even though we can only think about what is given to us, whether it be what we see or what's in our minds…" I said, staring off into space, "I have no doubts that there's more out there, and not just other angels. The landscape hasn't been altered much, but occasionally I will see the birth of a new moon in the distance, or a comet streaking across our ceiling. And in that moment, I know this can't be it. Eventually, God will take us away from here."

"I wonder why we can't go yet," Cadence muttered under his breath, but Alessa already had an answer in the queue.

"God has His reasons -" she said.

"- I was talking to myself."

"Maybe He's preparing a place for us there, or maybe the entire construction of Heaven isn't done yet–"

"- it was rhetorical. It was a comment that didn't need answering."

"Either way; we know this for a fact: Heaven exists," Alessa enunciated happily, ignoring Cadence completely. "Our mental database tells us so."

"It's true. We're bombarded with the images whenever we look it up," I said in agreement but Cadence started sighing loudly and obnoxiously.

"Are we really going to have this debate again?" he groaned.

"Did I say we were?" Alessa, of course.

"I only ask because every time you or Marcus bring it up, we start arguing forever about whether it's real or not - whether the concept was just planted in our minds to make us think it's real. I'm over the subject."

"So what do you think then?" I asked him. "Does Heaven exist?"

"Didn't I tell you already?"

"No," Alessa said. "Whenever we want your opinion, you get all defensive and act like you're deaf."

"I'm pretty sure I've said this already, but in case you weren't listening, I'll tell you one more time. *I don't know*. Yes, the database says Heaven exists, but that doesn't mean we'll get to experience it...I just want to wait and see what happens for myself. What's the point in talking about it over and over?"

"What else can we do? It's not like we have a lot of options," Alessa replied as Cadence's face sagged and his shoulders dropped wearily. It was true that we would go crazy if we kept our curiosity to ourselves, but Cadence's mindset was also appropriate for the situation we were in. We had to be patient, especially since there was no timetable on when we would be able to leave our beautiful penitentiary. We all had tried, especially Marcus, to fly off into space - to touch one of the numerous anomalies that littered our sky - but there was an invisible barrier of some kind preventing us from going too far. Marcus tried breaking it with his fists once every few hours, and the whole island watched in anticipation when he did, but in the end, his excessive failures only confirmed that we were stuck until God decided to release us. If He had put us here, only He could get us out.

"Honestly, I would rather talk about God," I said, picking myself up off the grass, and standing right between them. "There is no debate about His existence."

"No, I guess not," Alessa agreed and Cadence nodded.

"At least we would be doing more than speculating," Cadence said. "To be honest, God takes up more of my thoughts than anything else."

The new angel suddenly produced a surprised yelp, noticeably coming out of his daze and eagerly jumping into the conversation, hopping up and down like he was going to explode.

"You know God? Where is He? I want to see Him again!" he chirped, his teeth greeting us for the first time. We all looked at him with a mix of envy and pity, for the situation wasn't yet known to him. But neither of us could deny the faint embers of excitement glimmering within us at the mention of God - for we too, had experienced the joy that came from being in the presence of our Father. No child could forget.

And slowly, my mind could not help but wander, from the present to the past - to when we had met for the first and last time...

This may come as a surprise, but when I was born, it was nothing like that of a human's, for in that instant, I was fundamentally whole. I possessed all of my limbs, my wings, and dexterity. Even my stature was one of an adult and not one of an infant. I did not see these appendages and extensions of my body outright, for like any newborn, I had yet to fathom my sight. But I noticed the way my limbs moved – swimming freely from my torso like they were in the midst of their own interpretive dance.

Of course, I was unaware of what "life" had entailed before my birth, but after I had dusted off the cobwebs of my consciousness, it was like coming out of a deep sleep. As if I were an ancient computer being booted up after centuries of dormancy. My body came alive, and it swelled and compressed, my imagination soaring with thoughts of staggering awareness.

I was not a blank slate. There was no tabula rasa.

I knew everything I was supposed to know. Nothing more. All that was required of me - programmed into the core of my soul, unfiltered and disorganized. I'm sure you can only imagine how disconcerting that was – to be born and have instant knowledge of nearly everything – even concepts that had yet to have significance: like how to extract sap from a maple tree, how pepperoni pizza burned the roof of one's mouth when neglected to be blown upon, or why wind is invisible to the naked eye. A people called Israelites, a city called Babylon, a place called the Garden of Eden. Baseball, spaghetti, sleds, planets, Jerusalem, solar flares, Jazz, toilet paper, automobiles, Heaven, money, bracelets, electricity, toaster ovens and hair extensions...all these foreign objects, places and things tumbling around my head like they were in a washing machine.

I was completely stimulated, and it felt like my mind was going to collapse with the influx of information bombarding me. In that sense, I guess I was like a baby – barely moving, taking my time to open my eyes and encompass my surroundings. It was far too overwhelming to go from none to all, and if I must confess, I wanted to cry.

Crying - my mind computed, startling me with its alarming responsiveness: to weep, to utter sounds associated with grief or suffering...I listened to the definition attentively. Yes, that sounded about right. Suffering, I was. But where was the solution in making it stop? Could these definitions alleviate my distress, or were they there just to tell me what I was feeling?

Thankfully, this pain, this suffering, would not become my first memory – for the discomfort lasted for less than a millisecond, though it felt significantly longer. I suppose the agony I felt must be just like what a child experiences psychologically, coming forth from his mother's womb and given no time to process his birth. Like a whisper heard from a mile away, I wasn't even sure of what I had just experienced, and with new sensations flaring up around me – the pressure was already forgotten, like I was working on an assembly line, already moving on to the next product. With the vexation gone, I felt something come near, something I could not feel when my database had been downloaded into my spirit.

This something embraced me, wrapping me up in what felt like strips of soft white linen, swaddling me, soothing me.

It was not the frostbiting cold that every human baby feels when they are taken from their mother's warmth. That abrupt disconnect from the womb in which he must suddenly face the harsh truth: that from this point on, he is an individual – that he is utterly alone in the unforgiving world.

It was not a machine to pump the fluid from my lungs, the weeping of a relative upon my advent or the cheering of a fellow angel welcoming a companion into Heaven.

No one and nothing greeted me – but Him.

My Father.

God Himself.

It is very hard to explain what it's like to be in His uninhibited, unadulterated presence. If I had not been made of a spiritual composition, I imagine I would have been obliterated into dust and my ashes cast throughout the cosmos, like ripples spreading across a pond. But I survived, and I was able to assess Him, if only superficially.

His love is what surprised me most. It was suffocating, but in a good way – filling my thoughts, my emotions, my every desire with great respect and admiration. It swept through me like I was transparent; pouring into me once it arrived, transferring its unconditional architecture – filling an empty shell longing for sustenance. Yet even this is not what held my attention.

I could not see Him in His entirety, though we were both of a spiritual nature…but He did allow one aspect of Himself to be visually accessible.

It was the light – that is what grabbed me. A radiant, all-encompassing brilliance that stretched my vision to its breaking point - just right on the edge of strain. Its warm, cozy illumination wrapped itself around my being like a hug, causing little fires to erupt simultaneously all over my spiritual skin. It was like the sun itself had sent an armada of ultraviolet rays to pierce through me, but they were unable to harm - only to kiss my skin in wisps to the border of pleasure and pang.

For what felt like eternity, I floated in that aesthetic light, devouring it with my senses, saturated in its wonder. There was nothing but God around me as I basked in perpetual delight – a new womb to replace my old dark husk in which I had been clueless of my existence. No words were spoken and no thoughts were exchanged. We had become one and the same, our souls inseparable and divinely interwoven by an unspoken agreement.

And then it was gone.

And I was alone again.

And all I cared about – all I desired, all my soul craved, was to feel that episode of complete euphoria once more.

I almost went into a frenzy of madness and despair, until a voice interrupted my descent.

"Open your eyes."

The voice gave a command – and I obeyed desperately.

I opened my eyes, and I saw a man before me – no, not a man, for man did not yet exist – an angel. I gasped, thirsty for God's quenching embrace, but the angel had no remorse for my agony.

"Open your eyes," he said, "and try to get up."

My wings were quivering and my mind was disoriented. I could barely see, and the little I could was too much to handle. There were too many colors and objects to focus on, and the angel before me was still trying to converse.

"You're a mess," he chuckled, placing both of his hands on my shoulders and forcing me to sit back down. "Maybe you're not ready to get up just yet....I have to say, I've never seen an angel get this discombobulated from God's presence. You can't even concentrate."

I took a gulp and waved my hands all around me in fly-swatting motions - vertigo manning the helm of my motor functions. Eventually, my hands brushed up against the fluffy grass beneath me – yes, it was fluffy - and I began to calm down, rubbing it between my fingers back and forth like I was moving a computer mouse, and discovering an interesting sensation when I swept my face across it.

By now I sensed that the angel had sat down beside me and I abruptly stopped my embarrassing episode. I lifted my head with eyes wide, swiveling back and forth, unsure if he was the only angel there, or if there were others near me, silently watching. With him being so close, it was hard to take in the area, but I couldn't muster up the words to tell him to back away. In the end, I just thanked God he didn't try to rub my back or touch me in any way to comfort me. I was having enough trouble reaching beyond the cloud of overstimulation to even hear his words.

"My name is Cadence," he said soothingly. "Listen, I know what you're going through. I was taken from God's presence not too long ago myself. It's not a...pleasant feeling, but I figure there has to be a reason for it. Not that I know what that is, so don't bother asking, but - I decided one day, that if He loved me so much...He'll be back for me. What I'm trying to say is that you shouldn't worry. Save yourself the heartache and come to this conclusion: God will be back, and until then, you'll have a number of friends here to help you."

I didn't thank him for his kind words. I couldn't, for I was still too wrapped up in my own desires, and a peek beyond my eyelids was the equivalent of running on a field of land mines. But he stayed by my side, despite my miserable company, and waited silently for me to come around. I don't know how long it took, but he never complained. He would simply look out at the galaxy before us and whistle, or copy my grass-brushing technique, laughing at me whenever I saw what he was doing and whipped my hand away, refusing to touch the grass again for three more seconds. Eventually, I came around enough that I felt comfortable engaging him in conversation, but by then, the others had arrived to see where Cadence had disappeared to. It was the first time I met Cadence's friends: Alessa, Farah, and Marcus.

Marcus stood out the most, and my first impression of him was more of fear than awe. To this day, I remind myself the two should not be interchangeable if I want a mutual friendship with him, especially since his look hasn't changed. His hair was cut low and spiky. His face was chiseled and rigid, complementing his gigantic size which was struggling not to explode through the armor he wore. His armor - a monstrosity bathed in crimson red, had silver streaks running across it like stripes on a zebra. Unlike the rest of us, he had no gauntlets or defensive artillery on his arms. His limbs protruded from his shoulders like elephant trunks, flexing and swaying with dominion, biceps almost as big as my head. His wings were folded behind him, but I could already tell they were as large as his arms were and looked just as heavy. How he could fly, was beyond me.

Farah was the exact opposite of Marcus. Small, petite, and muscleless, she wasn't intimidating at all. She had dull green armor that looked like flimsy plastic, and it hugged her like it was a second layer of skin. Her long, lightning green hair veiled half of her tiny baby face, and her wings were like a dragonfly's, translucent and blurry, producing a low hum that was barely audible. She was so tiny, I instantly knew I would remember her forever.

But it was Alessa, whose personality superseded them both, and I quickly realized she was not an angel to be taken lightly. When I met her, the first thing she did was grab Cadence by the side of his armor and practically lift him off the ground.

"Cadence, you can't keep babying every single angel that lands here. They'll get attached."

"Like all of you?" Cadence snapped back, swiveling his head toward her like it was a weapon. "I don't hear any complaining about how I helped each of *you* back then." Alessa's eyes widened in horror, but she easily let Cadence down, recollected herself and pointed a menacing finger at his forehead.

"Don't patronize me, skeleton. You know full well that I adapted on my own. I wasn't a child."

"I realize that, but you still didn't deny my company."

"Just because you helped a couple of us out, it doesn't mean you have to become a missionary and go on goodwill missions."

"I'm not."

"Then why do you have to console each one that appears?"

"I'm doing exactly what I've done from the start – being there for the new arrivals. Nothing more. I don't see the problem. I never imposed myself on any of you, and I would have walked away if you had told me so, but no one ever did - because you needed the support. Imagine if I had left you alone. You would all be Absent right n…" His voice trailed off as he replayed a distant memory. "Never mind, it's irrelevant. What's important is we're together. A lot of the angels who came before us…they don't talk to each other like we do, and it affects them. We have to be different."

"Be strong," Marcus agreed in a deep, slow, resonating voice.

"Yes, Marcus," Cadence replied, his attention not yet completely in the present. "We must."

With Marcus's words at the forefront, and the notion of strength reinforcing the group, I finally was cognizant enough to take a glance at the armor that provided me my angelic clothing. Each component shone with its own lightning blue tint, almost rippling in animation. The gauntlets on my wrists were solid krillic - a durable material that my database told me existed only in Heaven. They extended slightly over my knuckles to give my hands extra protection, and I could only wonder why they were designed for function and not fashion. When would I have to use a gauntlet? There was simply no real animosity where we were.

And if there was to be violence, I didn't know how I would fare. My sad excuse for a breast plate was flimsy and thin in material, feeling more like fabric than krillic, diamond or gold…but I let this flaw go in order to examine the rest. There were barely any allotments on my legs, and even my forearms were naked. I couldn't see my tern-like wings entirely, but I could tell there was a set of fore and back wings - very silky and lush, with many layers upon layers of featherweight material. They weren't very big or wide in and of themselves, but they were a little more than half my body in volume.

I flittered my back wings over my fore wings, playing with their flexibility while the others waited for me to finish. I was having too much fun twisting my wings into knots and rolling them up like large towels, letting them explode open and snap at the air.

The group was so charmed by my display that they all laughed at my playfulness for over five minutes. At first, I was appalled, but when I realized they meant no harm, I laughed too. Reflecting back on that day, I realized it told me just how long they had gone without amusement. And I would find out why soon enough.

Nevertheless, from that moment on, I was a part of the group. And it didn't matter that it had been Cadence's sole decision to help me and accept me. They all treated me like I was a member.

The island was exciting at first - the panoramic galaxy making up the ceiling and our walls, the number of new angels to talk to and laugh with, the playing...and reminiscing about God. Because we needed nothing for survival per se, we used our stay on the island to wonder, or to talk about what new file we had pulled from our mental database – asking each other what a carrot was like since we had never seen or tasted one, or even knew if we had taste buds to begin with. In short, conversations usually got superfluous and out of hand, because there was no way we could come to a concrete conclusion for any of them. Yes, they were nothing but theories and hypotheses, but talking was all we had.

Most of our evidence-gathering sessions were about a shining city called Heaven. Ingrained in us were two major places: Heaven and Earth. No one debated against the weighing importance our mental database placed on Earth, but whenever we tried to study it, most lost interest, because we were under the impression that it was a distant concept. A place that would have great significance but was nowhere near our immediate future. Therefore, Heaven was the popular topic, for we saw images of angels, like us, flying to it. Maybe not in it, but definitely to it. The general consensus was that it was irrevocably a home for angels, and with nothing more than a small island to live on, we were eager to go there, especially with recent talk that if the current ratio of new angels to the island's size continued, it would soon be crowded. But until we saw a way out, we abided, and waited in our holding area, hoping that one day, it would all be over.

"Where is God?!" the new angel cried again, and I came to. Cadence and Alessa both glanced at me and each other, smirking in unison at how easily we had become lost in our thoughts.

"I'm sorry," I said to him. "You may not see Him for a little while, but He will be back."

"When?" he whined, his body beginning to tremble in anxiety. I took both of my hands, and pressed down on his shoulders, forcing him to sit - the nostalgia hitting me like a sweet smelling savour.

"Soon enough," I said, and Alessa snickered behind me. I could feel Cadence glare at her, even with my back turned.

"So should we ask him if Heaven exists?" Alessa offered, but I rolled my eyes and ignored her. "Calm down, Lysander. I was joking."

"Let's take him with us," Cadence said, but the angel shook his head violently.

"NO!" he snapped at him. "I'm staying right here until God comes back!"

Cadence didn't hesitate to plop down on the grass beside him, folding his arms over his legs.

"Cadence, c'mon," Alessa whined, but she knew where the situation was heading.

"I said NO!" the angel cried once more. "I'm not leaving!"

"Then I will be here until either He shows, or you come with us," Cadence stated adamantly, and I knew by the tone of his voice that his mind was made up. Alessa groaned a little to herself and started to protest, but she decided against it and immediately took flight, back to where Marcus and Farah were. Cadence didn't bother saying goodbye as he began staring off into the distance. The new angel sulked and wept silently, knees on the ground and his face planted in his palms. It was a familiar sight I had no interest in reliving.

"Do you want me to stay?" I asked Cadence, who shook his head "no" and nodded toward the angel.

"It might be a while before he comes to terms with this," he stated emotionlessly. "But I will be here for him, when that time comes."

"There's cosmic dust over in the northwest quadrant...turning into what I think will be a stellar nebula. I'm going to look at it for a little bit and then I'll come join you both."

"There's no rush," Cadence smiled toward me. "We have the time."

"No argument there," I said solemnly, and I spread my wings.

It took a heartbeat to get to my favorite spot on the island. I could have easily seen the cosmic dust from where Cadence and the new angel were, but honestly, I wanted to be alone, to contemplate why God gave us such a beautiful view, and not just blank walls. It had been a project of mine for months, and even with little progress, I was still habitually searching through the database for clues. Whenever I found some possible evidence, I matched them up to my own beliefs, seeing if there was harmony between the two, a little peace to ease the forlorn hope that God would soon return.

But it looked like I would have difficulty concentrating this time. Someone was already there, sitting exactly in my favorite spot. Since he had gotten there first, I didn't make a fuss about it, but my face definitely twitched when I saw him...if that's possible.

I gently floated down to where he sat and stood idly next to him, figuring that he wouldn't mind if we watched together. It's not like there was any privacy on the island, and I didn't plan on talking. Besides, I had work to do, so where was the harm?

But after the silence ensued for hours, the lack of initial greetings was making the air awkward, and I soon found it strange that he didn't even acknowledge my company. I looked down at him out of the corner of my eye and saw that he was staring at the cosmic dust like I had been, but with disturbing, listless eyes - his wings folded and tucked uncomfortably beneath his posterior. His face was worn, as if a shadow had been cast upon it from an upward angle and his jaw drooped like oatmeal coming off of a spoon. He didn't look like he was interested at all in what he saw and I finally understood what he was. It was a little frightening to be so close.

But I got over it. Since I had already been standing next to him for a good couple of hours, I figured it wouldn't be harmful to ask what he was engrossed in with such fervor, and while I was at it - see if he wouldn't mind a partner. Whenever I asked Cadence to help in my investigation projects, he usually said he had more important things to think about. Alessa and Farah had found it boring the couple of times they had ventured to join my studies, and there was no point in explaining it to Marcus. The instructions usually took hours alone. So in short, I was more than willing to pick up an assistant. I had heard his kind were tapped into the database at all times, lost in the infinite surge of information. If I could bring his mind back to the present, he would make an excellent partner, and who knows? I may even make a friend.

I was just about to touch his shoulder when someone grabbed my arm, so fast, it was like it had been there all along. The imposing hand was strong and firm, squeezing my forearm to the point my eyes began darting back and forth, my body trembling, paralyzed under the pressure.

A being stood before me, but its physical characteristics were shrouded. It was like trying to describe someone while only being able to see out of your eyelashes. I knew someone was there, but that was the extent of my analysis.

"Do not touch him," the being said in a deep, authoritative voice, squeezing extra hard to get the message across. "He is to learn this lesson on his own. He will come back in time."

"What lesson?" I asked, my fear subsiding and my stupidity rising. I was acting like this being had not just half-crushed my arm.

"A lesson you have already learned, Lysander."

I reached forward to grab the being but he was already behind me, like he was an extension of my own shadow. It was a dumb move, trying to touch him and confirm he was real, but I was so grateful to see a new, albeit scary authoritative presence speaking to me, I was past formalities. He was nothing like God, but he could have had some news on where I might find Him.

"Where is God?" I asked, but he didn't even attempt to answer my question.

"There is a purpose for this wait," he said. "That wait is now over. You have learned the lesson."

"I don't understand. What did I learn?"

"You will realize it momentarily, but for now, prepare your mind. You are going to be taken to Heaven."

CHAPTER 2: Sweet Sorrow

"In precisely one hour," the being continued, "you will be brought to an angel named Raphael. He will guide you into the next stage of your development. Until then, you are not to speak of this appointment to anyone. They are to seek out the answers of their own volition. Now...are there any inquiries before I depart?"

"Why me?" I asked, very confused. "What about my friends? Are they going too?"

"If they have learned the lesson."

"How will I know?"

"You won't. Not until you arrive in Heaven."

"What is this lesson you speak of? How could I have passed it when I have no clue what you're talking about?"

"Do not worry, Lysander. All will be revealed in the end. You have one hour – starting now. Farewell."

The being vanished and I was left alone with the creepy worn-out angel who seemed to have lost his mind. Whoever the mysterious being was, he was clear in his message – I was going to Heaven...but how could that be? I had gotten so used to being on the island...I had never thought about how it would feel to leave, especially without the group...one hour – how was that enough time to say good-bye without being able to say good-bye? And I had relied on Cadence for so long; I couldn't bear the thought of venturing out on my own. Why did *I deserve to make it into Heaven?*

I wearily glanced down at the angel next to me, who was still in a daze, and wondered if he would still be in a stupor if he had heard the message I just received. He probably would be downright healed, for now I was being relieved from the very predicament that he and so many others suffered from. And I could have easily been in their number, if not for the group. If not for their love and assistance. How could I repay them? Perhaps if I stopped dwelling on the past, and all they had done for me - maybe leaving them would get easier. After all, it was Cadence who had brought me in, and not necessarily the others. Sure, he would miss me on some level, but the rest would move on. I was sure of it.

And the longer I stood there, thinking of myself as the odd man out, the easier it became to believe it. Of course I wanted to belong, and to pretend that I always had, but that wouldn't make my trip to Heaven any easier. There was no guarantee they would make it, so I had to distance myself – to make sure the separation was easier for all of us in the long run.

But I couldn't just disappear either. They would search for me all over the island and it wouldn't take long before they'd conclude I was gone. Speculation and sorrow would set in. They would wonder why I was chosen and not them. The group would separate and in despair, turn into the very angels we promised to never become – the Absent.

"No," I said aloud to no one. "That won't happen." Maybe there was a way to let them know where I was going so that they wouldn't be depressed when I left - prevent the offset of becoming an Absent.

As long as we have each other, there is hope. That's what Cadence used to tell me in the early days, and it was the only advice I had ever gotten. Hearing his words echo back at me, I resolved to spend my last moments on the island with them. Until my departure, I would leave them with some good memories, make them understand that I didn't abandon them outright.

It didn't take long to get to them. I figured they would be in the meeting area - a slightly brown-green patch of grass that was easily identifiable amongst the rest. With the rest of the field immaculately trimmed, it was easy to spot the outcast. And our group, more unique than any other on the island, gravitated toward it like dust under a vacuum.

I started missing them as soon as I floated down to the patch for they were in full lovable entertainer mode. No one could capture an angel's attention like they, and despite the apprehension of many to join our group, they couldn't help but watch whenever we got together and started playing around or showcasing our next verbal sparring match. I didn't have a clue as to why no one had joined us after my arrival. Maybe angels had started giving up – I did notice the Absent increasing in number lately.

But it was nice to see a few still in their right mind hanging about, watching my friends embarrass themselves from a distance. And what a sight it was. Marcus was head-butting the invisible glass ceiling, wincing with every consecutive blow as Farah, that little bird, used all her mini-might to wrap her arms around Marcus' neck and thrust it upward, causing his head to slam harder into the barrier. It was so hilarious to watch, all I could do was burst out laughing as I half-stumbled, half-floated down to where Cadence and Alessa were watching in awe, shaking their heads rhythmically.

"Where's the new angel?" I asked Cadence, who was captivated by the circus act up above.

"Absent," he said calmly. He was used to these things.

"Already?"

"Unfortunately. You saw the way he was acting. It didn't take long."

"I see…"

A loud thump echoed from above, and I let the subject of the new angel go, to focus on the ridiculousness that was Farah and Marcus.

"How long has this been going on?" I asked, afraid of the answer.

"About twenty minutes," he said slowly, partly paying attention.

"There was one smash in the beginning where it looked like they might break through," Alessa said. "I started cheering and making a fool of myself, but then Marcus rubbed his head and fell down to the ground, clutching it like it was going to pop off."

"If God placed the barrier there," I said, "I don't see how this is going to work."

"Well, Farah said if God let her do it once, she can do it again. Who are we to say she can't, right?" She winked toward me and I crashed backward onto the grass to get the best view. Farah was getting frustrated, and was now plowing Marcus' head into the barrier with great fury, bonking it every two seconds. Marcus' limbs were starting to resemble cooked spaghetti.

"I don't think Marcus is going to make it." I said. "He's not aware of what's going on anymore."

"The knucklehead will be fine," Alessa replied, and then turned to Cadence. "I said that correctly, right? Knucklehead? Is that the word?"

"I don't care," Cadence responded in a monotonous tone.

"What are you two talking about?" I asked. She turned to me.

"I've been going through the database, studying slang. It's words that have an exact definition, but they are used to infer another. For example, knucklehead means someone who is hard-headed or stubborn in slang, but one could assume the real definition means he has a head that literally looks like a closed fist. See what I mean?"

"Of course," I said. "Look at the way his hair is cut short and made of tiny spikes. He definitely has a knucklehead."

Alessa snorted and giggled while Cadence sighed again.

"Another waste of time," he said, bored. "Slang."

"Oh, c'mon," I said, sitting up. "We all know you search through the database for fun."

"You have no proof."

"Everyone does it."

"Okay, and that sounds logical to you? That's your evidence?"

"Why wouldn't you do it? We have all this knowledge to sift through, and you're telling me that you ignore it?"

"If there's a reason I need it, then yes, I'll access the library. If not, then I forget about it."

"You're so boring," I laughed. Alessa slapped a palm on his forehead playfully. He ignored it and closed his eyes, probably searching the database for ways to kill an angel.

"I heard that," a voice said behind me. I swiveled my head to see a very intimidating Marcus puff up his chest. His nostrils were flaring like a bull's and he stuck a meaty finger in my face. The scary part was that it almost touched me on the lips.

"I heard that," he repeated, but I played dumb.

"Heard what?"

"Knucklehead!" he yelled at me angrily.

"Are you calling me a knucklehead?"

"No..." he paused. "You call me knucklehead."

"That's not very nice... but okay. Knucklehead."

"No. You call me knucklehead."

"I just did. You want me to call you it again?"

"No!" he roared. "CALL ME KNUCKLEHEAD!"

"OKAY, MARCUS!" I screamed at him, struggling to keep the corners of my mouth rising. "KNUCKLEHEAD!!!"

"NOOOOOOOOOOOO!!!!" he bellowed and Cadence cut him off at the pass. Using his trusty shield, he blocked one of Marcus' fists from colliding with my face. Cadence pushed Marcus back gently and led him away, patting him on the shoulders and talking to him in whispers.

Marcus kept looking my way, past Cadence, but after a few seconds, he focused only on what was being said. Thankfully.

"I can't believe you, Lysander," Farah said in a motherly tone, her hands on her hips, but then she suddenly burst out laughing. "I tried. I tried. I just couldn't keep a straight face. That was hilarious! Good job!"

She extended a hand up and I gave her a high-five. Marcus was usually trying so hard to incite fear in others over his size, that she loved it when he was taken down a notch. Being Marcus's very own immortal, pesky housefly was one of her self-proclaimed hobbies, and she had become an expert in a very short amount of time.

"I didn't know you could do that," she mused, hands on her hips again, a big smile plastered on her face. "I thought Marcus scared you, to be honest. You tend to clam up around him."

"I guess I'm feeling courageous. Feeling like I should try new things," I said with my best smug voice. Farah raised an eyebrow and chuckled again.

"Well, keep at it. We have to keep the big guys nice and humbled."

I felt warm from her compliment and I immediately wanted more. I could probably count on one hand how many times I had received one. But despite this, I decided to put my comedy act on hold and quit while I was ahead. Good memories of Lysander in Farah's mind – check.

"So I need to loosen up more?" I asked to no one in particular.

"Yes," Alessa said with added emphasis, "it's better than being a loner who's scared all the time. And look at how natural you were too!"

The compliment felt weird coming from Alessa, like it was caked with sarcasm.

"Okay," I said, looking down at the grass. "Maybe we should change the subject. So…who's idea was it to use the hardest substance in the universe to crack the barrier?"

"Marcus," Farah giggled. "It was all him. The whole idea sounded crazy the moment he said it but of course I didn't tell him that. He was actually happy when I volunteered to help him get ahead, if you catch my drift."

"I think we do," Alessa giggled as Marcus and Cadence came over to rejoin us.

"Marcus has something he wants to say," Cadence announced. Marcus scrunched up his face like he had caught a whiff of rotten eggs.

"Sorry. Tried to hit you," he muttered.

"I accept," I said. "And I'm sorry for calling you a knucklehead."

"I'm not," Alessa said boldly, standing up to face him directly. "You think bashing your head against the barrier would actually cause damage to it?"

"Don't know," Marcus replied, rubbing his head idly. "Bored."

"There has to be a better way," she huffed. "Right, Cadence?"

"Whatever," he yawned, stretching out on the grass.

"Some leader you are," Alessa muttered and then made a "gather around" motion with her hands. "Listen up, we need to be smart about this. Instead of sitting here debating about Heaven, or bashing our heads against invisible walls, we should put our heads together."

"But Alessa, we already used our heads," Farah giggled, winking at Marcus, who frowned and clutched his brow in fear.

"No more heads," Marcus agreed.

"Dummy, I mean we should access our databases and work on how to break the barrier from there. We talk about getting to Heaven a lot, but we never focus on the real problem – that we're stuck here. By removing the barrier, we'll be free to go."

"You don't think there's a reason it's in place?" I asked, and Alessa snapped her head back, appalled.

"And what reason would that be?"

"What if we break through and we disintegrate? Like, we can only survive within the island's parameters."

"Farah broke through. She's okay," Alessa said matter-of-factly as Farah nodded in approval.

"You don't even believe her story!" I cried out and Farah pouted in response. Alessa refused to turn her way.

"She said she did it!"

"You don't believe me?" Farah whimpered, but Alessa wouldn't let up her defenses.

"I think it's worth a try," Alessa stressed, swatting at Farah who was creeping closer to her face.

"I'm tired," Marcus stated. Cadence sighed heavily.

"As long as everyone stops talking about it," Cadence said, "and Marcus joins in...I'll help with your search – but only about the barrier. If we start getting distracted, I'm out."

Hearing Cadence agree to investigate a matter was a once-in-a-lifetime opportunity and Alessa wasn't about to let it pass by.

"Marcus is joining us," she volunteered for him happily, "because we're a team."

Marcus sneered in response but Alessa patted him on the back and rubbed his forehead, which soothed the beast. The four of them sat down in different spots approximately two feet from each other, closing their eyes and beginning to delve deep into the knowledge God had given us. I didn't bother participating. I had to keep a close watch on my deadline or else I would be trying to find a way through the barrier myself. With their eyes closed, I didn't think they would notice my absence of effort, but I soon discovered that being alone, even with the group present, brought on a whole new form of sadness.

I couldn't bear the fear of forgetting them – of not knowing whether my life would go by and they would become nothing more than buried memories. When I got to Heaven, would I laugh? Would I easily make new friends? Dwelling upon Heaven's analysis, there were certainly visions of angels flying toward it, but no snippets of laughter or angels celebrating along the streets were seen in the slide show. Heaven didn't equate to total happiness for us since we lacked the evidence to make that assumption. But it was something new and different, and that was enough to look forward to it. It was what kept us moving ahead, but what was the point of going there if you couldn't share the experience with your family?

I looked over to the left, back at the red and purple cosmic dust, which was now beginning to take shape at an accelerating rate - the two sides or crests of the mass crashing into each other gently like an oceanic wave, culminating into a spray of fireworks that separated only momentarily, before being pulled into the center. It was a star, enduring its growing pains.

But the display was merely a large distraction from the main show. I noticed that not all of the cosmic dust returned to the center, joining its proverbial brothers and sisters for centuries to come. Some of it became collateral damage in the crash, thrust from the gathering and out into the blackness of space, sprinkling amongst the planets and rocks and ice. It settled, and did not move again. And suddenly, I interpreted our interactive mural, our animated painting. For God would not leave an elaborate show of that caliber without purpose.

I understood the lesson completely...who represented the cosmic dust that became the star, and who were the granules being cast away. Our group and the Absent. Those who maintained their sanity – fought through the hardship, the crash of the waves, and those who gave in, and were discarded.

But this revelation didn't relieve me. It disturbed me.

Because Heaven and its mysterious ambassador had somehow gotten it all wrong. I had just gotten the lesson, not a second sooner, and I could barely give myself credit.

The only reason I had survived this long was because I had Cadence and the others to string me along and give me some strength. I could have easily become one of the Absent inhabiting the island, hopelessly staring at the same cosmic dust, looking for answers and slowly declining mentally as my frustration increased.

So where was the justice? What did it matter if I made it to Heaven, while they were forced to remain? Why? What was the reason they had to stay on the island? To assist new arrivals? That was the only logical explanation, but it was still unfair to them. I had done nothing to warrant Heaven's welcome, and the more I thought about it, the angrier I became. So I made a decision.

I would say no. That's right. I would decline the offer, until all of us made it in. Unless...I was just an angel for them to mentor, to assist in my development until I got the lesson on my own...was that my ticket into Heaven? And the mysterious angel simply knew this would happen ahead of time? Had Cadence and the others been available during my time on the island because they were here to push me along to this moment? Did they really need me, after all? Or was I a passing student?

"There better not be any barriers in Heaven," Alessa muttered under her breath, and a nervous chuckle escaped my throat as I hoped to see Farah slam Marcus's head into the barrier one last time. An accusing eye burst onto the scene, and glared at me suspiciously.

"You weren't searching with us, were you?" she accused me, her body relaxing as she opened both her eyes and scrunched up her eyebrows into an upward V.

"No. I wasn't," I whispered sheepishly as the rest began stirring themselves back to reality, giving me strange looks.

"Why not?" Farah asked. Cadence leaned in for an answer.

"I was thinking."

"We're all thinking," Cadence said in a fatherly tone of voice. "Thinking about how to break the barrier. It's what was decided on...not that you're forced to participate. But we need you with us on this."

"Why?"

"Because the more of us there are working on this, the faster we'll come to a solution. I didn't want to do it either, but since it's productive, I chipped in, and Marcus too! That doesn't happen very often."

"No, I mean why don't I have to participate?"

"You're an individual. You can do what you want, Lysander," Cadence replied. "All of us can."

"No, you're misunderstanding me. I mean, why isn't it a big deal if I participate or not? You were going to jump in only if Marcus did. No one asked what I thought. Why is that? I have nothing to contribute?"

"What are you so worked up for?" Alessa's voice began to rise. "This isn't a big deal. I just got the feeling that this was something worth working on and I wanted to see if the group could help."

"A feeling?"

"Yes. A feeling...I don't know. It was just a feeling. What does it matter?"

"Lysander," Farah said sweetly, "why don't you think you contribute?"

"I don't."

"None of us do."

"That's not true. We all look to Cadence for direction —"

"- for what reason, is beyond me," he yawned, laying back on the grass, hands behind his head. "You're blowing this participation thing out of proportion. Think about it. The only reason you all look up to me is because I was here before you. That's it. The order could have easily been different."

"There's more to it than that," I said, but Cadence cut me off again.

"Marcus doesn't contribute. Especially not in the database department. We all know that. Farah entertains us with tall tales and Alessa opens her mouth. Do you understand what I'm telling you? We don't have skills. We don't have talents. We're just a misfit ensemble of children waiting for their Daddy to come home. We just keep busy in the meantime so we don't go insane and become one of the Absent. So you're asking us what you contribute? Nothing, and that's perfectly fine, because we all provide the same...nothing. Does that answer your question?"

"More like raises some," Alessa said, standing over Cadence with hands on her hips.

"I knew I took a risk talking about you," Cadence muttered but Farah laughed it all off.

"He's right, you know," she giggled. "We're not special at all."

"You're agreeing with him?!" Alessa yelled, turning to Farah.

"Why not? He's telling the truth."

"He said all I do is open my mouth!"

"It must be tired," Farah said and sped off into the air, gone in a blink. Alessa pursued her in rage, screaming the entire flight about how if Farah was ever going to break through the barrier a second time, now had better be it. Their chase continued over to the other side of the island, and I was sure it wouldn't stop in a timely fashion.

"We like you," Marcus grunted abruptly, making me jump up to a standing position. I had been watching the chase so intensely, I was unaware that he and Cadence had been left behind too.

"We like you," Marcus said, "because you funny."

I didn't know what to make of his description, whether it meant I was a comedian or a joke. I assumed the latter at first, but I gave him the benefit of the doubt in the end.

"What Marcus is trying to say," Cadence began, "is that sometimes you do strange things that make us laugh."

So much for benefit of the doubt.

"My intention is not to make you self-conscious, Lysander. It's just that you're entertaining in your own way. Like how Alessa never shuts up. We get irritated occasionally, but most of the time, we're curious about what she'll say next, and that provides its own level of amusement. Yes, it may be a little perverted to think of it as entertainment...but still, we all laugh at each other from time to time. And it's always out of fun, not maliciousness."

"You laugh at me?" Marcus asked and we couldn't help but chuckle into our palms.

"Marcus, you're hilarious," I said to him, and he beamed with pride.

"Thank you."

"So what was all that about?" Cadence asked me casually. I could see that this question had been on his mind for the past few minutes.

"What?"

"The whole participating thing. Where did that come from?"

"I was feeling like I didn't belong here with the rest of you."

"Why's that?"

"I can't say..."

I had decided earlier to stay with my friends on the island, but for motives I could not explain, I was having second doubts. Cadence had given an excellent rendition of our lack of importance on my account, but it didn't alter my perceptions. I felt like I was a solid line, trying to break into a complete circle. No matter how hard I incorporated myself into their activities, something was missing. Maybe Heaven would give me what I needed.

"It's because you're leaving us," Cadence blurted out, "and you want to fit into Heaven easily without having to worry about us. Am I right?"

I stared at him in horror while Marcus shifted to the right nervously. How could he have known? Had he been watching me?

"You don't have to say a word, Lysander. I figured it out on my own."

"You must be one great detective."

"I get it. If you feel like you've never belonged here - there's no attachment, no emotions invested. Makes for an easier transition. Listen, I'm not going to tell you what to do, but as your friend, I can give you some advice: next time you want to try causing division to make your options easier to manage – don't. It's true I like helping the new angels, but at some point, I let them make their own decisions. Most don't stick around. Some become Absent, others survive alone, but we rarely get a new family member. Because everyone thinks they can make it on their own. Maybe you can, but it all depends on if you want to take the risk. You could have left us for good whenever you wanted."

"Any time I was by myself, you or Alessa would show up looking for me. I would hardly call that respect of one's privacy."

"It's because we wanted to make sure you wanted to be alone *for you* - that you had weighed all the consequences and made a decision on your own. But you never refused us. And whenever we came looking for you, you came right back...willingly."

"I think I was just scared."

Cadence let a smile loose for once. It was so eerie, I wasn't sure if it was real or fake.

"Scared of me? What am I going to do? Beat you up with laziness?"

"You're not lazy."

"Listen, whatever decision you make is yours. But don't hurt others in the process, that's all I'm saying. It's about principle."

"You're really not going to try to persuade me to stay here...or to go?"

"Why would I? All I have are opinions. It's yours to take or trash."

"Then this could be the last time I see you."

The words came out before I realized. Apparently, my inner desires had leapt out and made a decision. Heaven was where I ultimately wanted to be, even if that meant I couldn't enjoy my friends' company any longer.

"Then I'm happy for you," Cadence said, giving me a sudden, big hug. The display of love overwhelmed me with squirmy uneasiness. I almost decided to stay again.

"Take care, my friend," he said solemnly and stood up to give me a hand to my feet. I accessed my database for a quick check of the clock.

"Cadence, do you mind telling the others what happened? It looks like I can't if I'm going to keep my schedule."

"Of course," he said as I turned to Marcus. I punched him in his gigantic chest playfully and followed up with a soft right hook to the jaw. Marcus placed a meaty palm on the crown on my head and rubbed my hair.

"Do well," he said, and I was more surprised by his endearing good-bye than the fact he understood my conversation with Cadence. What went on in that head of his?

"Until we meet again," I said, walking away from them for good. I gave a half-wave and flew off, worried about the future, uncertain about my life to this point. Without the support of my friends, I only had myself to rely on...oh, and God, wherever He may be...

CHAPTER 3: Alternative Darkness

"Are you ready?" the shroud spoke as I descended from the air. It was hard to see if he was looking at me or the view behind me. Maybe it was my imagination, but his head seemed to be pointed upward, or his hood...or whatever it was. The closest similarity my database could rustle up was a stereotypical picture of "Death," with a hooded cloak, scythe and all. I wouldn't say the mystery angel was that scary, but his lack of definition did make me uneasy.

"Am I late?"

"Two minutes are left on the clock. You have until they expire."

"I know why I was given an hour," I said. The shroud didn't speak. "It's because I needed to grasp what I had learned, understand the importance of the lesson for myself. Without that hour, I would be second-guessing myself the entire time in Heaven."

"So are you ready?" he asked and I scowled at him. Did he hear a word I just said?

"Yes, I'm ready," I said flatly and he extended his shadowy palm out toward me. I grabbed it.

"Then welcome to Heaven," he said.

Instantly, it felt like every atom of my body separated and was swept up into a rushing mighty wind. It was so jarring that I lost all of my senses and yet, in a strange way, they were also heightened in intensity. I spiraled throughout the cosmos, too fast to appreciate its beauty, but slow enough to know that I was traveling across a massive universe that stretched out to an unfathomable distance.

Before I hit the end, I saw it...I saw it...I saw Him!!!

The light.

My Father.

I ran into the light like a freight train and my atoms dispersed on impact to soak in His love, like each piece was a child being hugged by its parents. My entire body was mesmerized and entranced, having no desire to speak or to even think. I slept in His comfort, forgiving His absence entirely.

Angels are unable to sleep since there is no need to, whether physically or psychologically, but I promise you...I slept. And when I awoke from my warm, divine cradle, I wept like a ravenous baby for nourishment. And I was fed once more with pure, complete love. It warmed me and made me feel cozy, like I was wrapped in a soft blanket on a chilly winter day, staying inside next to a crackling fire – my cheeks becoming rosy and my face full of happiness and contentment.

For three earth days, this exhilarating cycle repeated itself: sleeping, waking, "eating," then going back to my rest. In truth, it felt like seconds, but I was grateful for the confirmation that God existed, that I hadn't lost my mind...

After the last minute of the third day, I was cast away, for I still had to learn about the world beyond the island. And just like waking from a dream, I woke out of my slumber shaken up and confused, uncertain as to where I was and if what had transpired had been real.

My body was tremulous, and my vision was strained from looking into the light of God for so long. The area I found myself in was lit up adequately, but dim by comparison, and it would take time for my sight to adjust to this relative darkness. I was on my hands and knees, scrambling for an object that could instill an ounce of familiarity. A boot of some kind eventually met my right hand.

I craned my head up and saw an angel standing over me. The room was still in a type of smoky haze but the angel was as clear as glass. His eyes were of a bronze tint with a half-circle the color of magenta placed on the left of each of his retinas. His hair – if one could call it that – was wild and stretched in all directions, including skyward. His nose was small, and his face – boyish but chiseled at the jawline. He was toned, not too big or too small, but still at least twice my size. An immaculately polished breastplate adorned his chest, with the same material protecting his forearms, shoulders, stomach and legs. My mind informed me that he was a force worthy of respect and I desired to give it. But even respect could not satisfy my renewed insatiable hunger.

"Where is the light?" I asked him, my first words dripping with selfishness, my focus only on his answer and not on our location. I used his presence as an anchor to reality for I had been in this state before. Focusing on something specific, even words, were already beginning to help me adapt.

"I will explain all in time," he said in amusement, extending a hand toward me. I grabbed it with the little effort I could muster and he lifted me to my feet with ease. His touch was nothing like that of God's light, which shocked me, considering I was supposed to be in Heaven. As a matter of fact, no luster emanated from him at all.

"Where is the light?" I repeated timidly, my head down as the angel shook his head and his bottom lip wrinkled humorously.

"I find it interesting you keep saying 'light' when it was, in fact, God."

"Where is He? Where did He go?" I whined. This relationship was beginning to turn borderline abusive in my eyes.

"Why, He's all around you."

My head swiveled left to right, refusing to examine the room itself but searching for the sensation that drove me. I cringed in frustration.

"No, He's not here," I told him through a clenched jaw, feeling a little betrayed. Wasn't Heaven the place where God lived? Or was it another type of confinement? I wouldn't be able to maintain my composure if I was told I had left my friends on the island for a lonely substitute. The angel placed his right hand on my shoulder to cool my kindling rage.

"You have just begun to understand the universe around you, Lysander. Your senses are dull. Do you not feel that He is still here?"

"Where am I? Will my friends be here?" I asked him frantically. I didn't entertain his last comment simply because of all the turmoil and pain that speculation had caused on the island. Until I actually felt God's Spirit for myself, I couldn't say He was here.

"Where am I?" I demanded and he chuckled at my attempt to sound courageous.

"You're in Heaven...of course," he stated slowly, "although we are currently inside my home – one of many buildings that make up its infrastructure. Your database offers you specific images to Heaven's layout, and I assure you that you will see it in its entirety, but you must be patient. As for your friends, it is not in my power to say what their fate will be."

"When will I get a real answer?"

"In time, young one. But do not be surprised if you find yourself making some new acquaintances in their stead. If you concentrate, you can see that there is more to behold than my impressive residence."

He swept a hand into the air, allowing me to examine the room. We were in a hall colossal in length – about three football fields, though the diamond ceiling was only a few yards above our heads, reflecting sharp arrows of light throughout the room like a prism - all the colors of the spectrum lighting up the walls like a disco ball. The walls were made of solid krillic and metallic purple adorned the drapes hung across the horizontal walls, which extended to the entrance - where it all came to an arch. I could see something darting back and forth outside and as I squinted to get more details, the lights in the room ceased their theatrics and allowed me to interpret what I saw. The angel before me explained my curiosity.

"They are angels, like you – traveling to and fro. You will join them soon."

I barely heard him. My mind was still concentrating on God's light...the general sensation was fading, and I could no longer feel its warmth. If I was to be separated from God, what was the point of having me commune with Him, not once, but twice?

"I see it all over you," the angel said thoughtfully. "What you're feeling is natural. I don't blame you. It was difficult enough leaving Him the first time. However, we have our duties, Lysander. And no matter how hard you try, you cannot escape your role in His plans."

Role. Plans. Duties. What could I offer God?

"I was the same way when I was created," the angel affirmed, "but within seconds of our separation, I understood that I was not made to bask and play before Him for all of eternity. This epiphany may have contributed to my early release from the island, I might add. You see, we were not destined to be spectacles or mere entertainment. We were given great potential. And it did not have to be so. We could have been mindless drones, with specific abilities designed only for His amusement. But this is not true of us. The fact that you can reason, that you have your own desires – it tells you that we have been chosen for a greater calling."

"What are my duties?" I replied instantly, letting emotion subside and logic reign. If I would never see my friends or God ever again...then I would keep my mind busy, if for no other reason than to keep my thoughts from wandering to places they shouldn't. The angel was slowly starting to make sense, and once I was done with my internal tantrum, I realized that my mental database had been trying to talk to me the entire time, confirming that I had a job to do. And what that duty was – could only be explained by the angel in front of me. His name was Raphael – and I knew this, but I had been too involved in my own greed to let the knowledge come forth. Raphael knew what happened the moment I stopped sulking.

"There you are," he said cheerfully. "Now we can have a real conversation."

"Sorry about that," I said sheepishly. "It's just so cold and lonely now."

"I understand it's hard to pull you away from God so abruptly. You might even say it's cruel, but we cannot allow you to be with Him for too long. The longer you are there; the harder it will be to remove you."

"Then why do it at all?"

"We must let every angel experience His presence whenever they are transferred to a new location – before any other greets them. It's essential that He stays at the forefront of your mind at all times."

"But why? It would've made more sense to whisk me away directly from the island. Putting me back with God was so…addicting. I didn't want to leave."

"I know, but that's what God wants. He needs you to not only be able to function in Heaven and carry out your purpose, but to remember His power and glory as well. If we were to just let you traverse around Heaven without ever knowing your Father, there would be a disconnect, even upon your inevitable meeting - a disjointed relationship. So you're given quality time with Him upon each transfer – enough to remember Him forever, even when you may feel He is absent. You see, most of the time He is invisible to us. We may be spiritual in composition like He is, but we are still unable to grasp Him completely. Those moments, those few instances we are with Him, sustain us for an interminable amount of time."

"Invisible or not, how can one forget?"

"You would be surprised…but enough of that. We must begin our training – to learn how to fight. My name is Raphael, and as you may have surmised, I will be your instructor."

Fight? I knew the meaning, yet it made no sense. Even my database turned up no search results on why an angel would have to learn combat skills. In Heaven, there was no such thing as war. Even if two angels disagreed on a matter, it never got to the point where they would duel each other seriously. Also, God was undeniably in control. This fact sounded off in my head like an air raid siren. Maybe it was for sport…but if it all came down to mindless fun, what would happen if an angel refused training? Someone like me?

All I cared about was getting back to God or bringing my friends to Heaven. Little else mattered.

"You're spacing out again," Raphael stated. I immediately turned my attention to the conversation at hand.

"Why do I have to fight? There is no one in all of existence who would defy God."

"God is omnipotent, and these are His orders. His motives may be unclear, but they will manifest if we are patient. But enough stalling – for now, you will accept your training."

The authoritative tone in his voice was unsettling, but I followed along. If these were God's orders, then I would obey - at the very least I might be able to get some answers out of Raphael.

"Lysander, you are an angel, of course, but of a specific type. Every angel in Heaven is classified based upon its abilities. Someday, you will have the complete list, but for now, I will explain your designation. You are what is called - a Messenger."

I didn't bother trying to hide my disappointment. My database was blank in the angel classification department, which meant I had to acquire the knowledge for myself. Surely there was a reason for this…but I didn't dwell on the matter. The moment Raphael mentioned the word "designation" I was intrigued. But upon hearing the title he gave me, I had to admit - that interest was now gone.

"Messenger" was the only classification I had heard of so far, but there was no doubt in my mind it was of bottom tier quality. For instance, after seeing Raphael's height, I knew he couldn't be a Messenger. Being eye-level to his chest told me that much.

The more the word "Messenger" overpowered me the gloomier I became. I unintentionally let my imagination wander, and soon it settled on the image of a "mailman". So this was to be my journey – that of a glorified, angelic mailman - delivering messages to angels about the great and wonderful things others were doing - and not me. I would be the storyteller, enunciating key words and telling tales with grand emphasis, until the real hero of the yarn I spun emerged triumphant, ready to add some spice to my bland exposition. I couldn't help but wonder...if I was a delivery boy, what was the point of fighting?

"I can see you're displeased," Raphael said, confirming the look of disgust plastered across my face.

"I'm a Messenger," I stated, my voice flat and dead.

"So what if you are? If it got you back into God's presence or ended up being favorable for your friends, what does it matter what your purpose is?"

I raised my head in surprise. Already I had begun to forget about my past. How long would it take before it was erased altogether? How long before I was too distracted with my job or overloaded with information to remember my family?

"Maybe it would be better if you had never been created," Raphael said coldly. His words were almost too much to bear. Was it possible I could be destroyed and replaced? Would I be aware of anything? I could hear the irritation in Raphael's words. He was trying to get a message across, and I wasn't getting it - my logic was taking too long to win out over my emotions.

"Listen to me, young one," he said quietly. "I know how agitating this can all be, especially since you've only been here a short time. But understand that God doesn't want a daycare. He wants a university. I can teach you how to be mature, but it's upon you to adhere to it – to grow into the angel He needs, to ensure His will comes to fruition."

An awkward silence hung in the air as he contemplated his next words.

"Now, as I was saying – you are a Messenger. Part of your job is to deliver important messages across Heaven, but that's not where it ends. Some angels like the Godhand are strong – they are the tanks or powerhouses of our world. Others, like the Glory, are able to call upon God at any time for His express help in a situation. Your ability is of a tactical nature. You may be of average size and strength, but the way your mind works, it can assess a problem and come to a resolution quicker than any other class of angel here."

Raphael waited for me to respond but I was still trying to interpret his description.

"So, I'm smart?"

"It has nothing to do with intelligence or having more knowledge. It involves being able to analyze data and use it efficiently. Trust me, your mental database is no bigger than anyone else's."

The notion was hard to fathom, and honestly, I couldn't imagine flying around telling people I had superior reasoning skills while a Godhand was toppling over buildings or whatever they do. What was I going to say? Hey guys! You think that's impressive? Watch me solve this puzzle in less than sixty seconds! I highly doubted I would be picked first to go on a secret mission.

"Don't underestimate yourself, Lysander. This is a valuable talent, given by God to better serve us all as a whole."

"So my reasoning isn't there just to figure out the best paper route in Heaven?"

Raphael laughed heartily, his colossal breastplate armor heaving like an exploding bagpipe, despite the fact I wasn't joking.

"If you're so unsure about the talent God gave you, why don't we test it?"

"What did you have in mind?"

"A little sparring session. Get the rust off those wings."

"But you're bigger than me. You'll win."

"What makes you so sure?"

"Because when I look at...you...I," my voice trailed off as I suddenly saw Raphael in a new light. My "Messenger mind" was tingling with life and now that my temper tantrums were over, I was able to think clearly. The world had been hazy since I had been blinded by God's light, but now my vision was adjusting, and an unusually sharp clairvoyance dominated my senses. I saw Raphael for who he was. Yes, he was far larger than I was, and a lot more experienced. No doubt he had participated in more sparring matches than I could count. But what I figured out very quickly and quite intuitively was that everyone had a weakness – you just had to find it. See, no one was God – no one had the foresight and omnipotence He did – and with that knowledge bursting forth like the arrival of a messenger with great news, I figured out how I could beat Raphael.

CHAPTER 4: Suffer Not

God wouldn't make an angel perfect – hence the reason for so many classifications – each angel could only be strong in one aspect, not all. Of course, this also meant that each class of angel had a fair share of strengths and weaknesses. Godhand angels may be the "powerhouses," but maybe they lacked in reasoning or intelligence. Maybe they were only able to tap into unfathomable power for a short time. Perhaps they were slow moving. As for the Glory and their ability to call upon God personally…it sounded like they could be the most powerful angels of them all - but just because they called, didn't mean that God always answered. I knew that personally. A conflict could arise that God wanted the Glory to learn from or figure out on their own. I also assumed the Glory couldn't be ridiculously strong, at least in foreseeable size – which meant Raphael was probably not a Glory.

He could be a Godhand, but all that supposition told me was to be careful, and this I knew regardless. My newfound tactical mind relayed to me that anyone who initiated a fight, friendly or otherwise, probably thought they could win. And Raphael, with all his expertise in dealing with new angels, was probably sure he could beat me, especially since I had never fought before.

But with experience also comes complacency. And that meant that he assumed he knew what I would probably do next. How I would fly at him or, as a Messenger, how much speed I had at my disposal because I was smaller. Basically, he was confident he knew everything about me and my tactics. But in the end, I believed it would be his downfall.

He probably had figured out a hundred different ways I would attack, so I was forced to go against my instinct and do the one thing no one expected – to be random. Yep, that was the master plan. Anything else, I'm sure Raphael had seen it all before and could counter accordingly. And it couldn't just be a little random – it had to be a ridiculous show so out of this world, Raphael wouldn't know what to do. Could I be random enough to beat him? We were about to find out.

"Are you ready?" Raphael asked me abruptly, separating my thoughts.

I tried to answer him – in my own way.

It was the first time I actually saw my slender arms reach forward, my closed hand the size of a pebble compared to the gong-like breastplate I aimed for on Raphael. Yes, I had armor as well, but I didn't want it. I didn't need it – I was sure one of the boulders he called fists had more than enough stopping power to render me useless with or without it.

Raphael saw my fist coming a galaxy away, already raising his right palm to meet it like a catcher's mitt. I dug deep within my database and pulled out a strange countermeasure. I stopped my assault abruptly and fell backwards, placing my right hand onto the floor and letting my wings maintain my balance – my left leg swinging into the air toward Raphael's cheek. His eyes widened in surprise as he dodged the kick, but I was still moving. My left leg came down, and though my back was turned towards him, I pivoted and swung my left leg back at him again, coming from the other side. I barely missed, but he was now slightly off balance. I let the momentum of my left foot carry me and I continued my attack after it landed, squatting low to the floor and trying to sweep him off his feet with my right wing, which was a ridiculous notion since wings were as dense as pillows. The wing could easily slam into his legs with no damage and little reaction. All he had to do was stand still.

Which is exactly what I needed him to do. Yes, wings were basically glorified rain clouds in formation, but they were as thick as silk in visibility. And I had my right leg swinging behind my wing to ensure Raphael would hit the floor. Incorporating a seemingly useless Earth fighting style – Capoeira – may just have been random enough to trick him into failure.

Raphael let an air current propel him upwards even though he knew of my wing's composition. I worried that maybe he suspected my plan, but it didn't matter for I had switched gears. My left wing followed his ascent with a fist to follow. This time, he let the wing connect to no effect, and though he felt confident for a second, he didn't in the next. My left fist forced his body rocketing upward as I hit him with every ounce of power I could muster. There was no guarantee I would get another chance at him again, so I put all I had into it, even to the point of hurting myself – my thoughts becoming faint and my body weighed down with a sense of lethargy and exhaustion. Raphael hit the floor like a drop of water, his crash making no audible sound, but his body flailing in all directions – all motor control lost. His head bounced up for a second under the blunt trauma, and then he laid there, eyes closed.

And this is when I grew afraid, fidgeting nervously over whether he would get up or not.

Because I could still sense he was nowhere near defeated.

I couldn't articulate it, even to myself, but there was something wrong about his fall. He hadn't been acting...but I couldn't shake the uneasy notion that he was still strong. Very strong. There was an aura emanating from him that screamed he had a lot of fight left. And the only hope I embraced was the verity that I knew little of what a defeated angel looked like. Especially since I knew inherently that angels are eternal.

What *did* happen to an angel when they were beaten in battle? Nothing? Did they just fall down for a second and then get back up as good as new? Or did they have to go to a shop and get their armor repaired? Was their armor an indication of their health? Or was it their hair? Their wings? Maybe they lost a bit of reputation - a mark against their record which is broadcast throughout Heaven...either way, Raphael was about to get up in a second, and I had nothing left.

"What do you sense?" Raphael asked me authoritatively, his eyes firmly shut.

"That nothing has changed," I answered obediently. "You fell, but that's it."

"Why do you think that is?"

"I don't know," I admitted. "I was wondering about that myself."

"What do you think happens to an angel when they fall?"

"It hurts?"

"Actually, no," he said, suddenly in a standing position and a few feet from my face. His speed was so scary I barely heard him speak. "We don't feel pain in a violent sense. To us, it's more of a discomfort rather than a crippling sensation. So tell me, if the angels of God had an enemy – hypothetically speaking – what would prevent an ongoing stalemate between the two? If you hit me, I fall, get back up and hit you and you correspond with the same – what's the point?"

"There must be some way to crown a winner."

"True. And there is. We are spiritual beings so we create the impression of having an endless supply of energy at our disposal, but that is not the case. Let me ask you this. Can an angel defeat God?"

"No," I said immediately. The idea was preposterous.

"Why not?"

The question disturbed me and I felt a quiver in my spirit. What was the point of dwelling on such things? Of course a creation couldn't be stronger than the creator...could they?

"God is all-powerful. We are not," I finally decided upon. Raphael nodded, apparently satisfied.

"Correct. We are made with eternal spiritual life, but not unlimited power. Even our abilities are divided amongst classes. No individual angel possesses all of the classes' abilities. On top of that, the spiritual capacity with which we are born with is our maximum limit. Unless God should allow it, we can never go beyond what we are given."

"I don't understand. Do you mean I can't become a Godhand if I want to?"

"No, you cannot, but what I am really discussing is angelic pressure, the energy that stabilizes you and keeps you in good health. For example, if I were to classify levels of spiritual energy and say I was a level 3, and you were a 1 - no matter how hard you try, how much you train – you will never be at a level 3. You will never be able to hurt me or cause me discomfort."

"But you still haven't explained how someone can lose a fight. Even if you are a 'level 3' and I was a 'level 1' what does it matter? I'll get back up again."

"Ah, but here's the truth of the matter. We cannot gain more than our current maximum of spiritual energy, ever...but we can lose it. If I were to hit you now, with all my might – your spirit, what we call your angelic pressure, loses some of its potency. The same thing happens when you exert yourself and put more energy into one attack than another. It's very similar to the concept of exercise. Exert more angelic pressure – and you get more tired. Receive 'damage' from another being, and you lose some as well, depending on how badly you were struck."

"So what happens when someone's angelic pressure goes to zero?"

Raphael cast his eyes downward and his right wing fidgeted momentarily. I couldn't help thinking of the new angel on the island, coiling his wings and contorting his body. It told me that Raphael had a past not worth asking about.

"Zero," he said in a stoic tone. "Well, it all depends on how hard you are hit when your angelic pressure is at a critical level, but...you lose consciousness. Your 'body' remains intact and present, but there's no animation. You cannot move, think, feel – you are completely oblivious to the world around you, like you were before you came into existence. From there, you are in stasis, a type of limbo until your angelic pressure steadily recovers, enough for you to gain consciousness. I don't even want to think about how long an angel would be unconscious if one continues to hurt them long after they have gone unconscious. One could be out of commission for centuries after enduring such trauma."

I was clueless to the severity of his message, and easily let it be forgotten. Like death, like gravity – it cast no weight upon me.

"Then how do we win? What if an enemy is stronger than us spiritually? What can we do that doesn't end in us being knocked unconscious?"

"Tell me – when you knocked me down with that crazy dance-style martial art –"

"-you know what it is?"

"Of course. Remember, we are born with the same knowledge."

"Some of it seems like a waste of space to me – like a land called Canaan, what is –"

"- that's irrelevant right now. What did you feel?"

"I was glad. Ecstatic…because you thought you could beat me."

"I never said anything insinuating that. What makes you think I was confident about the outcome of our sparring match?"

"It's like you told me – I'm a Messenger, a tactician. I assumed you had seen many 'new angels' like me before, and other Messengers too - so you already knew you'd win."

"And that upset you a bit, didn't it?" he sneered. I stretched out my neck to the side and stood up straight.

"A little," I said. "So I devised a plan on the spot. I figured that by trying random techniques, it might throw you off – and it worked."

"Did it?"

"What?"

"Did it work? Did you win?" he asked me casually.

"I didn't bring your angelic pressure down to zero. And if we continue our match, I'll have to factor in our conversation and try new tactics, but for now, yes, I'm winning."

"And how do you feel about that? Feel good?"

Raphael began pacing around me, his wings and arms held close to his sides as he studied me like a lab experiment. Whenever I managed to fight through my fear and look at his face, his body would seem to flicker and suddenly he would be behind me again. He was getting faster with each successive look and if I didn't get a handle on my nerves soon, I would end up on the floor in a ball, crying myself into absenteeism.

"It felt good, to prove you wrong," I said, clearing my throat. Now that I was alone, I had to start standing up for myself. Stop being afraid.

"A sense of pride, am I right?"

"Yes. Because I showed you that I'm not to be looked down upon."

"I guess you're ready to out-spar anyone, aren't you?"

"If they challenge me, then I will accept."

"You believe you are ready for anything?" he said with a half-chuckle. Where was he going with this?

"I'm ready," I said boldly. "For anything."

"Then I wonder how you will feel...when I show you this, young one."

He waved a hand into the air idly and the room was washed in a light so bright it was almost void of color. I couldn't even say it was white. It was simply so magnificent I was blinded into submission, dropping to my knees as Raphael was consumed in the light's radiance. I couldn't help thinking that it was God – but this light was borderline painful and I couldn't open my eyes. I could only wait for it to wane, whispering to myself unknowingly for comfort.

When I noticed the light had finally subsided, multiple individuals were in the room. There were four others besides myself and Raphael, standing around and looking at each other just as confused as I was. Each of them was different in size, stature, and colored armor – silhouetted under the excessive light inhabiting the room. Without anyone saying a word, I came to the conclusion that I was vaguely staring at four more classification types. I just needed to figure out which was which.

The biggest one stepped forward with great bravado but Raphael wasn't intimidated in the least, despite being smaller by a couple feet in both length and width.

"What is this?" the angel gruffed. Raphael, the only angel that wasn't bathing in light, smiled warmly toward him and calmly peeled the big man's fingers from his arm like a banana.

"I think you should have more respect for your mentor, Marcus."

Wait...*Marcus*? A different Marcus or the one I knew?

"Who they?" he growled. "I beat you fair – why call for help?"

I studied the silhouettes of my fellow angels, the way their bodies were shaped, the way each of them stood and twitched out of nervousness or boredom. I couldn't hold myself back. I flew at the tall lanky one with full force and tackled him backward. With a wounded cry, he caught me, and as the light Raphael summoned forth steadily declined, we recognized each other. Old friends, together again.

Cadence gave me a smirk and hugged me tight. As he let go, Farah, Alessa and Marcus all jumped in and we began hugging and patting each other on the back, congratulating and weeping, laughing and celebrating. No one could believe that we had all been given an appointment, that we had all made it to Heaven, at the same time.

It didn't matter that I would be pushed to the background. The group was reunited, and life felt right again.

"You have all been here the entire time," Raphael said, turning to look at us one by one. We settled down to listen to our guide. "Of course, you were blinded from each other's presence but that's because there is another lesson all new angels must grasp. One to be received immediately or you may never leave this room – pride will destroy you. There is nothing wrong with feeling a sense of accomplishment in one's actions, but once they cross the line into arrogance or a grand notion of self-importance, it becomes destructive and chaotic. Mark my words. It is a roaring flame, an unquenchable thirst that cannot be satisfied. You all believed that you had knocked me down, that by your own power I had succumbed to your might, when all five of you had actually been attacking me at once. None of you knocked me down alone. It was a...team effort."

"But, you spoke to me individually! I asked you specific questions!" Farah said. "Not that I'm complaining about working with my friends..."

"God allowed all of you to be present, but for time to stop in intervals so I could address you personally, as needed."

Was that why he was so fast?

"Are we to work together now?" Cadence asked, wasting no time. "Or do we get to take the next tests independently?"

"Drop the idea of individuality from here on out," Raphael stressed. "Someday there will be a place for it, but not now. Pride is counterproductive, and could even bring you to the point that you would deny or defy God's existence. Shun the very Master who made us, fashioned us, created us. Only by working together, unified, can we please Him and achieve our purpose. Alone, you do not have the power to succeed."

"A no would have sufficed," Alessa muttered. Cadence tried to console her with a back rub. Marcus clamored forward.

"I do not believe this," Marcus stated, storming toward Raphael. "I want to fight you alone - NOW!"

"Did you not hear a word I said?" Raphael seethed, his temper beginning to rise.

"I heard," Marcus growled. "Doesn't make it true."

Farah stretched upward from where she stood and placed a hand on Marcus' hip – as far as she could reach. "If we have to fall in line in order for us to stay here, then that's what we have to do. We're not going back to the island."

Marcus stared down at the little one and let his chest rise in intimidation.

"Why no fight?"

"Marcus, I know we like to have fun, but we should be serious for once. We're new here."

"Too many words," Marcus grunted and Farah laughed. Good old Marcus.

"God had Raphael train us," she continued, "so he must be legitimate. What reason would he have to lie? Besides, we've been a family since the beginning. Why are you so against our help all of a sudden?"

"Don't need help. I am Godhand," Marcus said proudly, "and Godhand are the strongest there is."

"Oh I beg to differ!" a sharp voice pierced through the air. Marcus and Farah ceased their conversation and followed our eyes to the entrance of the hall. Raphael noticeably squirmed, his eyes wavering as he began to lose his composure. His brow furrowed and his lips pursed.

"You are not to be here," he said weakly.

And whatever stood in the doorway, laughed.

CHAPTER 5: We Will Put Them to the Test

The voice, unaccompanied by a visible being, stopped its laughter short and spoke again.

"I wanted to see how the new recruits are faring. I hope you don't mind."

"You are not supposed to be here," Raphael stressed more boldly this time as the mysterious intruder stepped from the side of the entrance into view. He came in slowly, intentionally delaying his approach. Again, I felt this was someone worthy of respect, but it was a different feeling than the intuitive respect I had towards Raphael.

This being was so powerful, his angelic pressure alone began to weigh me down, increasing in burden with each step that brought him closer. I could barely make out his physical characteristics - his body boasting an impressive glow like he was a walking miniature star, building in intensity the closer he got. It was a brightness I instinctively knew that few had. And obviously, this angel was a bit different than the rest of us. His glow, angelic pressure and strength meant only one thing. This was a chief prince, a classification of angel we all knew, not from Raphael, but our database. We'd seen the name of this type of angel graffitied on walls in future cities on Earth and had come across the title in incomplete documents. This was an Archangel. An angel of the highest order.

"I have a test for them," he said slyly.

"No," Raphael said flatly, but the intruder's aura lit up as he almost smiled in amusement.

"I don't remember asking for your permission."

"Imagine if they get hurt. What then?"

"They can live forever. So what if they're out of commission for a spell?"

"I don't like your games," Raphael stressed through grit teeth. "I think you should leave."

"I think you should know your place, Raphael."

"You forget, I am an angel just like you."

The mysterious angel looked him up and down, as sunspots erupted simultaneously over his solar body. He chuckled again.

"Yes, we are – though even Heaven appears to have its princes...and paupers."

"Your charm is as appealing as ever, I see," Raphael quipped, unscathed by the intruder's scorn.

"Oh come now, Raphael. You have always been too sensitive. I was just joking around and you take it so seriously."

"It's hard to tell with you."

"Maybe that's why I was left in charge – because God needed an angel that is able to comprehend orders. He doesn't have time for someone who is unable to discern one's spirit and speech, taking guesses at what his master told him like an ill-trained dog."

"Contrary to what you might think, you aren't that hard to figure out."

"We will see if these young ones agree with that statement...Young ones!" he bellowed, the boom in his voice echoing like a cannon down the hall. "Welcome to Heaven! I am sure by now you are eager to spread your little wings and see the universe God has created. I do not blame you, for I too once stood nervously in your place. However, I quickly learned that there is more to this habitation than friendly races to the nearest dwarf star and irrelevant swims through the cosmos. We are created for a purpose, and that purpose is not play. We have been intricately designed to ensure that Heaven is tended to, and runs smoothly in God's absence-"

"But God is everywhere," I spoke abruptly. The kindling sun turned to me and nearly burst into flames.

"SILENCE!" he quaked as my colleagues gasped in reverence and fear, collapsing to the floor. I was immediately forced down to one knee and unwillingly bent my head low, quailing under his thunderous voice. I had never felt such trepidation. I cowered beneath him, shivering – begging him internally to never use that crippling tone again. The walking star's light had nearly come to the point of explosion, but now he dimmed it a little for my sake - so I would not be consumed by his might. He chuckled from within, a haunting song that burrowed deep into my mind.

"Of course God is everywhere, little one," he cooed as he placed a comforting...hand, I think, on my hair, "but you speak out of turn and out of ignorance. You need to be enlightened about current events."

"Lysander is correct in the context in which he spoke," Raphael said. "God is everywhere, even now. As we speak, He is watching us...watching you."

"My dear Raphael," the star spoke softly. "One shouldn't offer their opinion when plagued with a condition such as yours. If you are unable to interpret primitive body language and banter, it is best to keep your simple analysis of matters internally, before you embarrass yourself."

Raphael opened his mouth to respond with a comeback, but decided to keep his words to himself, letting the stranger continue his barrage of insults.

"Really, you should get that retardation of yours looked at," the glowing intruder stated coldly, but Raphael didn't budge as we slowly climbed to our feet, sensing that the danger had burned out for now. The star continued his conversation with us as he stared at Raphael's unmoving composure.

"Young ones, I have a proposition for you - one that you will find most appealing, though it comes with a prerequisite."

"What is it?" Marcus asked bravely as the star faced us in the blink of an eye. I cringed behind Cadence, shielding myself from any future flares.

"First I would like to know your names," he said in a haunting, wavering voice that could only have been intentional.

"Marcus," the Godhand said proudly, puffing out his chest in declaration.

"My name is Cadence. Classification, Guard." He said it like he was answering roll call in the military.

"Farah. I am a Faithful," she said, doing her best to sound formidable.

"I'm Alessa," the fourth of our group squeaked out, strangely quiet. Surely Raphael's words couldn't have humbled her that much. "I'm a Glory."

I stared at her in awe. A Glory...an angel that could talk to God directly. I had to admit I was jealous of her designation. Was this the cause of her silence and newfound meekness? Was she continuously in conversation with God, asking Him questions and receiving orders? As soon as I had the opportunity, I would ask her all about it.

"And you are Lysander," the star finished before I could claim my turn. Though it was impossible for me to be thirsty, I found myself gulping involuntarily.

"Yes," I replied meekly. "I'm a, um, a Messenger."

"An interesting mix of talent – I'm looking forward to your future performances. But first, I want all of you to know that should you pass a test of mine, you will each have the opportunity to join a special group of angels. This elite group is composed of angels that serve God the most, with all reverence. I lead this group exclusively into His presence and we praise...my Lord, we praise like no other. The fire under our feet, the dance in our flight, the bellowing of our souls – none can worship like we."

I was already intrigued, and based on the awe-struck, jaw-dropping faces around me, the rest of the group was too. On the island, being in God's presence was all we could think about, even when we weren't speaking about it. And our second encounter only whet the appetite. To have the opportunity to be in God's presence again – multiple times...and to praise Him with all we could muster? What an opportunity...but the star had said his group exclusively met with God, meaning – that if we didn't get in, there was no telling when we would be enveloped in His magnificence again. Maybe that was why Raphael, even now, stood frigid and unimpressed – it was possible he had attempted the test and failed, forced to now live out his time in Heaven telling others about an experience he would no longer enjoy.

That could not be me.

"Of course," he confirmed, "not everyone, like my good friend Raphael here, has the commitment and drive required, so like any true and faithful servant, you must be tested. How does that sound?"

"Whenever you're ready," I found myself saying, my cowardice dissipating with every syllable that poured out from my mouth.

"Good," he shone brighter in approval. "Then we will begin immediately. I am bringing in a specifically chosen angel to test your might. He will give me a report regardless of the outcome, that will either approve or deny your membership. Should you win, I will find you. If you fail, well...I hear Raphael is looking for employees in his daycare."

The star smiled wide for Raphael who refused to acknowledge his comments, and then vanished, his flight so fast that for a second an afterimage remained in his stead. Raphael unfolded his arms and addressed us urgently as we saw another mysterious angel appear – the star's proctor no doubt – enter the hall.

"Do not listen to his words," Raphael advised. "They are poison, smooth to go down but fatal to your being. Stay away from his 'club'."

"We are not you," Marcus said flatly, staring past Raphael toward the proctor striding toward us. Raphael cast his eyes to the side and hardened his jaw, but once more he chose to keep his mouth shut. Marcus didn't notice this at all.

"Are these the young ones?" the new stranger asked Raphael, who only nodded in answer. This stranger was not glowing like the other so we could see what he looked like. From what I devised, he was more than likely a Glory due to his average height, slender body, and silver armor with purple streaks. Alessa's armor may have been primarily purple, and a little different than the angel's who just walked in, but I thought it was safe to assume that specific colors were coordinated with the classifications - a knowledge which was essential to triumphing in our upcoming test.

The angel had a bored look on his face, his long hair flowing well past his shoulders and over sections of his face. He didn't even bother to move it when it got in the way. His blasé attitude said it all - he was not impressed with our ensemble.

"My name is Rufus, and I will be your proctor," he yawned. "This test will determine if you are worthy of my leader's inner circle. It is simple – I will give you exactly thirty minutes to strategize - after which, I will attack the five of you with everything I have. Bring my angelic pressure to a critical state, which I promise is no small feat, and you will have passed. If I bring all of you to a critical state individually, to the point in which you are indisposed, you fail. Are there any questions?"

The group remained silent as I tugged on Cadence's sleeve, signifying I might have a plan. He nodded in response and I waited for Rufus to sound the bell.

"You get thirty minutes – and in Heaven, a half hour will seem like seconds. Use it wisely. Your tactical planning starts…now."

The five of us flew into a huddled circle about seven yards away from Rufus to plan. Cadence spoke up for me before I could muster up any courage.

"Lysander here has a plan," he said approvingly, "and we should hear him out first."

"Why?" Marcus responded. Being designated a Godhand was getting to his head but Cadence defended me.

"Because we can't just go out swinging. If Rufus was sent to fight five angels, whether we're experienced or not, he must have some background in fighting groups by himself - not to mention we have no clue what his abilities are. Remember, all he has to do is place each of us in a critical state. That may sound like the odds are in our favor, but they will quickly diminish as we lose members one by one. We have to think about this."

"Why?" Marcus replied again, as if he hadn't heard a word Cadence had said. Cadence gave him a disgusted 'Are you serious?' look as Alessa spoke up.

"I'm with Marcus on this one. I don't see the point of planning when we can all attack him at once."

"If it was as simple as an all-out assault," Cadence commented, "we wouldn't have been given thirty minutes. It doesn't matter if we have a group, we can't let arrogance or pride get in the way. Recall Raphael's words."

"I'm not really too excited about Raphael's lessons right now," Alessa said disapprovingly. Cadence began to rub his forehead in frustration.

"Listen guys," I finally squeaked. "We can do this. The key is figuring out what his weakness is."

"And how are you the authority figure all of a sudden?"

"Because I'm a Messenger – it's part of my repertoire. I'm not that strong spiritually, but I have a tactical mind. If we devise a plan, we won't have to fight any harder than we have to."

"Let's hear him out," Farah chimed in, and the group shifted their full attention on me. I didn't dare betray their trust.

"Okay, first of all, I figured out he is a Glory based upon the nearly exact mirror image of Alessa's armor. The only difference is that the color purple is less accentuated. So Alessa, please tell us what your specialty is."

Alessa fidgeted nervously as she was now in the spotlight, but Marcus grunted and nodded and that seemed to calm her down. Maybe it was some kind of ooga booga way of encouragement.

"The Glory are the only angels with a direct line to God Himself," she said proudly, her voice overflowing with joy. "We are not skilled in either offense or defense, but we can still hold our own in battle. However, if we come up against a particularly hard opponent or situation, we can call on God and ask for His help in settling the matter. At that point, it doesn't matter who or what we are facing."

"So it's chance," I said flatly. Alessa scowled and poked a very threatening index finger at my breastplate.

"It is not chance," she said firmly. "We connect to God Himself every single time."

"But He's not a summon," I stated. "He's not a genie you just call on when you need Him. He's not a pet. He's almighty God, and your explanation of the Glory proves it. You specifically said that you 'ask for His help' meaning – He doesn't have to comply. Maybe you get to talk to Him every time, and He's more likely to help you – because of your class ability. Either way, He probably won't help you every single time – which gives us some valuable insight. It means that Rufus's strength will not be above Marcus's nor will his defense be above...uh, who has defense?"

"What makes you think someone specializes in defense?" Farah asked but Cadence raised a hand in the air.

"I'm a Guard," he said militaristically. "It's what I do. I take hits."

"That's hilarious," Alessa said. "You take hits? You?" Alessa made a point of looking up and down Cadence's lanky limbs.

"It's not a surprise," he said. "You've been abusing me ever since I met you. Maybe God sent you my way to prepare me for this."

"Then I guess a thank you is in order."

Cadence rolled his eyes as Farah placed a hand over Alessa's mouth.

"Lysander, can you please continue? I'm actually curious to hear more. I'm impressed!"

"Okay," I nodded, trying to downplay Farah's compliment. "If Cadence is a Guard, then that means Rufus will not have his level of defense. Isn't this better than blindly going in to face him?"

"Still no plan," Marcus grunted, rolling his eyes. Alessa nodded in agreement.

"Well," I started, hoping the words would just flow on their own, "I'm sure he'll expect Marcus to go out first because he's our powerhouse, so we have to save him for absolute last. We have to be sure Marcus will connect his strike before we send him in or we'll just lose our advantage. I'm thinking we do this…"

Even as I spoke, I couldn't believe what I was doing - planning strategy with my friends, teaming up with four other classifications of angels, ready to overcome a test to get the prize of being in God's presence forever. I had only been taken from the island, what, minutes ago? Hours? There was no telling what I would learn in the next few days, weeks, even years. God did not waste time training us for the future, and I hoped our future was connected to Him.

Invigorated by the prospects, I detailed my plan as carefully and simply as possible; knowing that it would be detrimental if the test began before I finished explaining it entirely. I had already relayed most of it to the group when Rufus raised a hand in the air and yelled out an unraveling "TIME'S UP! LET'S BEGIN!"

Rufus was serious about his time limit for as soon as the word "begin" left his lips, he was halfway across the room, swinging his right arm toward Cadence. Until Marcus, the only real threat to him stepped in; he would work on our Guard, chipping his "shield." But as I watched Cadence defend himself the best he could, I realized that I had no time to dwell on what the others were doing. I had to trust that they would carry out the plan I outlined while I continued to watch for any potential problems. I had to stay focused – stay alert. If I was ever to show the group that I contributed, it was now. I would not fail them.

I focused harder as I watched Rufus's fist hit Cadence's shield a couple times. It didn't matter that Cadence was the "armored tank." Rufus would eventually get a critical hit in.

So far, our Guard was carrying out his job adequately, dodging the little he could and taking the rest, but his angelic armor and pressure were also noticeably diminishing before our very eyes - his frame becoming more rag doll-like with each surpassing blow. As Marcus waited patiently next to me, and Farah flew around the room like an irritating housefly, Alessa prayed. I had saved her role for last because I knew there was no guarantee her contribution would help, but we had to cover all our bases.

So, following my advice, she prayed for the Lord to grant Farah more strength.

Because I had figured out something.

See, God was omnipotent, meaning He knew everything about the past, present and future. And He wouldn't grant a ridiculous request that would significantly alter His plans or the balance of His creations' lives. A prayer to simply knock out Rufus was unlikely to work, as we would probably rely on the same prayer in the future, and God wanted us to learn for ourselves, not rely on Him like a crutch to fight every battle for us. The fact that we were all pulled away from His magnificence, our first memory, was proof of that. The key word was "learn" – which, knocking out Rufus effortlessly, wouldn't help us do. So I would save the big prayers for a more pressing occasion.

This time, I would stick to something a little more economical – in short, give Farah great strength. Rufus was obviously keeping an eye on Marcus like a hawk, but Farah? He barely batted an eyelash. So Alessa prayed, and whether our request would be granted or not, our plan would work.

For not only did we have Alessa's prayer, but Farah also had a score to settle. Small, petite, squeaky in voice and cuddly in stature – she was a walking underestimation. For what she lacked in base strength, defense and strategy – she made up for in faith. Simple, illogical, old-fashioned faith. She had guts, and grit, and more resolve to rush into battle than the rest of us combined. She didn't care what the odds were – her God was greater than them, and surely, He would give her the tools she needed to win...

Cadence was swaying now, taking one hit too many, and Alessa had finished praying. I sent her in to help Cadence, knowing full well her combat skills were as average as his. It didn't matter, for the grand finale was upon us. I charged in.

And I saw Rufus smile, because he thought he had us figured out. His eyes locked on Marcus behind me – the hulking angel bumbling like a rhinoceros, picking up momentum and staggering like a train beyond its threshold. Rufus dug deep within his angelic pressure and swatted both Alessa and Cadence away with a casual fling of his arm and met me head on. We were meaningless to him now for he was confident that his victory would be secured in Marcus's defeat. I stopped and stepped to the side, letting the rhinoceros charge ahead, his muscles rippling with raw energy, his animalistic nature taking over, a war cry fueling him forward.

Rufus laughed heartily over the thrill of battle as he rushed ahead to reach Marcus, and Marcus, the powerhouse, did the one thing no one would expect a Godhand to do – he held back, and folded. Rufus's expression was priceless as his eyes swelled – Marcus now rolling into the shape of a ball and tumbling past his attack. But we couldn't give Rufus time to recover from the surprise now, could we?

With impeccable timing, Farah buzzed in front of Rufus's lunging fist, dodged it with a hummingbird shuffle, reared back with her tiny body, and delivered a fist full of angelic pressure, releasing every ounce she could muster from within, and hopefully an extra boost from Alessa's prayer and the Almighty Himself.

Rufus shrieked in pain as he clutched his face in blistering agony, and Farah puffed out a mini sigh - half flying, half collapsing backward from sheer exertion. I caught her and held her in my arms as I screamed out for someone with enough energy to put Rufus down.

And Marcus answered the call.

Still unharmed and crackling with power, he stomped over to Rufus, and pulled his hands away from his injured face. Seeing the end before me, I might have asked for Marcus to go easy on Rufus, but he had carried out his part in the plan so well, and he had been so patient – I let him do his thing the Marcus way.

With hands pulled away, and cries still escaping his lips, Rufus didn't see – and only barely felt Marcus's tree of an arm slam into his countenance, sending him flying across the hall and literally into the floor. Rufus's limp body twitched for a moment and then rested.

We were contemplative while we picked ourselves up, replaying the feat we had just accomplished. I let Farah back into the air, wondering how it had all gone so perfectly. Marcus was frowning because he had only gotten to swing one arm and Alessa and Cadence were laughing over their respective exhaustion. I did my very best not to cheer prematurely, waiting for confirmation that Rufus was indeed finished.

And then the clapping began, only one set of hands, but still ever so resounding and satisfying amidst the gigantic hall, and when we saw the source, we were invigorated, feeling alive and united as a family, forever bonded as a group that could never be broken. Raphael clapped fervently and only stopped when we heard Rufus groan. Raphael was vigilant as we clamored over to Rufus's limp body, inspecting his spiritual state. He only had one eye open, and the way his mouth moved, it was like his throat was parched, and his lips dry.

"How?" Rufus muttered, his head moving side to side deliriously.

"You didn't take us seriously, while we refused to underestimate you," Cadence replied. Rufus squinted in misunderstanding.

"I should have won. You're...so young."

"Maybe you should've," I said back to him, "but you forgot something. God is our Creator, and He doesn't fashion things haphazardly. We were all established for His will and none of us are to be belittled. We didn't prove our strength when we beat you. We simply showed that all of God's creations can reveal his. "

"Lysander," he coughed. "Yes, I see that now...I apologize...for being so aggressive. It should have been a test, and nothing more."

"So your group," I inquired, "the one that serves God beyond measure. Does this mean we're in?"

"Our leader...probably knows of your victory. He'll contact you soon, I'm sure...but if he doesn't show, inquire about him...all of Heaven's host knows who he is."

"Then in that case, I'll need to know his name."

"It's Lucifer," Rufus said as a disturbing, rejuvenating smile crept upon his lips. The very mention of this name was restoring his lost energy.

"Thank you," I replied. "We'll be waiting for him."

CHAPTER 6: In Heavenly Places

"I am proud of you," Raphael beamed as we walked away from the soon-to-be unconscious Rufus.

"We would say we are too," Alessa smiled slyly, "but then we might find ourselves on a path of destruction."

Raphael laughed despite himself.

"I didn't think you would take my words so gravely."

"Not all of them," I said as Alessa shot me a disapproving look. "We fought in that test like joining Lucifer's club was the only thing that mattered."

"We still plan on checking it out," Cadence confirmed for the rest of us as Raphael's sunny disposition began to wane. One of his wings twitched again.

"I would have fought no differently myself," he said. "You needed to win – if for no other reasons than to confirm your abilities, solidify your teamwork…I can understand that. But this group Lucifer has started – it doesn't sound appropriate. Heaven is not a place of secret societies and hidden truths. Everything is open. You will see what I mean when you step outside the hall."

"The two of you don't get along, do you?" Farah asked innocently and Raphael shook his head "no."

"Saying we are not fond of each other would be a gross understatement, but I don't want you to alter your perception of him based upon my opinions alone. Talk to him for yourself."

"Why don't you want to go into detail?" Farah asked again but Raphael folded his arms, adamant in his stance. I was curious myself. Wasn't Heaven a perfect world? Or was I just being naïve? I couldn't imagine a relationship getting to the point that dislike or even hate could fester.

Could it? Come to think of it, the Absent could have easily succumbed to these destructive emotions. It's not like I ever took the time to interview one of them. There was no way of knowing what went on inside their heads.

So did that mean Heaven was plagued with the same problems? Was our fight with Raphael and our test with Rufus a preview of what we would have to face, the true purpose behind God's commandment that we were to be taught how to fight? I'll admit, I was excited when we were huddled together, discussing our plan. Even the execution of it wasn't all that distasteful, but I was still resolved to live the life of a pacifist to the best of my ability. I liked how Raphael had kept silent when Lucifer had gone too far in their conversation. I was sure Raphael had wanted to strike him, and that this wasn't the first time they had exchanged harmful words, but he had kept his composure and left Lucifer's words to simply that: words. No fighting ensued, no violence, or name-calling on his end. I wanted to feel that peace and composure in every situation.

"There are times when we must learn for ourselves," Raphael said to us - his next words echoing with importance. "Only through tribulation does one truly grasp how strong their faith is in the Lord. Keep watch over Lucifer's group and no matter what – do not forget your first memory."

His last statement silenced us all as we had already begun to pile the dust upon our first memory. Marcus cleared his throat absent-mindedly, breaking the spell over us all, but I couldn't shake the thought of God now that it had taken hold upon me once more. Had God seen our battle? Was He proud of the way I had fared? It was true that I had fought with all that was within me, for Lucifer's group sounded like it was where I belonged. But there was no way to know for sure. I wanted to trust Raphael completely. He had quite a bit of knowledge. And surely he had been placed as a "mentor" over us for a reason.

But he hadn't made it into Lucifer's group, and I had to consider why. Was it that he was unworthy, or was the test too difficult for him? Why hadn't God allowed his passage? I didn't know if that meant his words weren't to be trusted, but it did give me pause.

Nevertheless, there was little time to dwell on trivial matters, for to us, there were more important things to consider: like our new home. Already we had spent too much time inside Raphael's hall, and now we were restless. Nothing short of exploration and good old-fashioned fun could cure it.

But of course, before we left, our surrogate father had one more thing to say.

"I'm sure you cannot wait to spread your wings and jump the nest, but I have one more surprise for you."

"Is it a shield?" Alessa asked, eyeing Cadence's. Cadence scowled at her and hugged his shield tight.

"No, but he will be a great asset to your team, which will now be six in number...Vergil? Can you come out here please?"

Down the hall, opposite from the entrance – a medium-sized, stocky angel peeked his head out from around the corner. His "hair" was alive, and each strand moved of its own free will. Some of the sunshine-golden threads played with one another, while others simply swayed in the breeze. His countenance was glowing, but nothing near Lucifer's level. It was a faint, tepid glow – as if he were constantly blushing. His "skin" was porcelain in composition, and his face was round and fat, with a bowl-like chin that jutted out like a frog's. The stature he possessed was chiseled but not intimidating because of his average height and less than imposing countenance. The fact that he wore no armor, but instead donned a white, silky, flowing robe, made me suspicious, although I couldn't quite put a finger on why.

At first, I didn't know what he was classification-wise – until he flew to meet us. One second he was down the hall, the next – he was shaking a very confused Cadence's hand. The rest of us dropped our mouths in unison and took a step back instinctively as the newcomer looked from one to the next, wondering why we were acting so strangely. We had all seen each other in battle only once, but you didn't need to be a Messenger to get a basic understanding of our strengths and speeds. This angel was on a level far beyond ours. And it was blatantly obvious. None of us could match his velocity. No one could imagine fighting without our armor to help protect us. What type of angel was this?

"If you didn't figure it out already, then I'll tell you," Raphael laughed. "He's an Archangel."

"Wow," Farah awed, star-struck. Unashamed, she began wiping her fingers along his luxurious butterfly wings, a gorgeous blue and purple bordered by green and black vines intertwined along the edges. Vergil giggled as if Farah's touch tickled him and he glanced down at her.

"Now I can't fly anymore," he said and her eyes widened in alarm.

"Really? I thought-"

"- I still can," he laughed, interrupting her justification. "I was just making a joke based on butterflies, how it's hard for them to fly if their wings tear."

"Oooookay," Farah said in a low tone, backing away from him. The rest of us weren't impressed either.

"So, he's like Lucifer?" Alessa wondered.

"No," Raphael said emotionlessly. "Not like him."

"Apparently," Alessa said. "I can actually see him."

"Needs wax," Marcus said. "Shine him up."

"I want you to take him with you and let him be a part of the team."

"Why he no fight?" Marcus asked. A very good question.

"I asked him to stay out of it so each of you could learn how to harness your abilities and use them adequately. It was a true test to see if you had put your pride aside and embraced the help of others."

"Hmm," Alessa said, and Marcus nodded to her. Cadence and Farah studied their faces carefully and smiled a little when they came to the same epiphany. Apparently I was out of the loop, and even my deductive reasoning refused to give me a clue. Meanwhile, Vergil was staring at me like I had eaten the last slice of cake and it had been labeled with his name on it. He was starting to creep me out with his bugged-out eyes and round face. He really did resemble a butterfly in a lot of ways.

"Vergil arrived just seconds before you did, so it's not like I'm giving you a babysitter," Raphael continued. "Actually, he has expressed to me a desire to join a group here in Heaven because he feels like he may be lacking in the social department. As soon as I saw how your group performed against Rufus, I knew he would be a great fit."

"We understand," Cadence said, extending a hand toward Vergil who greeted him properly this time. Vergil followed this gesture by shaking each of our hands eagerly as a goofy smile crossed his face. I began to tell him my name when he cut me off.

"I already know who you all are," he smiled. "I watched that fight intensely. The way you planned everything out was incredible. Especially you, Farah – I was sure you were going to knock him out in one hit."

"Thank you," she beamed as Alessa half-coughed, half-snickered.

"I know Raphael let me decide which team to join," Vergil continued, "but honestly, I couldn't bear being where I'm not wanted. I want each of you to decide whether I can join you or not."

"It's no big-" Cadence was beginning to say, but Vergil cut him off.

"No really, I'm serious – you all have such chemistry. I'm being honest when I say that I need all of you to help me grow as an angel, but I also don't want to interfere with the good things you already have in motion."

"You want honesty?" Marcus asked him but Cadence grabbed Vergil's shoulders and turned him back toward the rest of us.

"I'm sure I speak for everyone when I say, 'welcome to the group.' If any of us were in your shoes, we wouldn't want to be left out either. Isn't that right, team?"

No one said a word of opposition to Cadence's decision (not counting Marcus's attempt) because we all had experience in the loneliness department, but there was still a cloud of apprehension in the room and I couldn't help wondering why. Vergil didn't come off as an overbearing, variant, or unpleasant person. Actually, he was quite polite and, besides his incessant interruptions, he was a gentleman. It was obvious he wasn't to be our team leader or a dictator of some kind, so what was the problem? Where was the love in excluding others? I sensed Cadence wasn't fond of Vergil for some reason, but at least he had the fortitude to behave properly and treat him like one of us, even if he didn't outright say we wanted him on the team. Cadence had chosen his words precisely, explaining to Vergil that we only understood how we would feel if we were in his shoes. That was all.

But Vergil didn't seem to notice, or care, and thus our team of five became six.

"Thank you for accepting me," Vergil said meekly as he gave a standing bow. I couldn't help letting out a snicker at the funny gesture. Vergil snapped back up to attention, alarmed, while the rest of our team stared at me like I was insane.

"Did I offend you?" Vergil asked sheepishly but I just shoved him backward playfully with my right hand.

"Of course not, you're just funny," I said honestly and he didn't mind the explanation. Alessa muttered something about how they shouldn't have let me shove Vergil while Raphael cleared his throat for us to listen up.

"Enough small talk," he said happily. "It's time to check out your new home."

"You mean we can't stay here with you forever?" Farah asked playfully.

"Unfortunately, no," he smiled, "but you'll get over me soon enough. Go outside and enjoy your break. You earned it."

Raphael didn't offer up any more surprises or explanations but a plant of his hands on our backs and a shove out the door. In no time at all, we forgot about Vergil, and each other, taking in the breathtaking wonder before us. We had been so involved in Raphael and Lucifer's test that no one had thought of walking over to the entrance and taking a peek. Now, I didn't think I could ever look away. It was like I was back in God's ubiquity. I forgot all my worries in one sudden swoop.

From a purely cataloguing point of view, the moment I had landed in Raphael's hall, I had known of Heaven – my database downloading new information on where to go, what places we could visit, what buildings were ours – how magnificent it all was. But Raphael was right. Knowing about something, reading about it or seeing a picture - is nothing like experiencing it. Words could not do Heaven justice, and no prior knowledge prepared me for its majestic boldness.

We walked out of Raphael's hall to see a literal paradise. Angels darted through the air, so quick it was as if they were shooting stars. The sky was an ethereal masterpiece. Nebulae formed and faded instantly before our eyes. A black hole laid down its foundation only a few light years from our location, welcoming new worlds into our abode. Stars sped past us like schools of fish and yet, with a little bit of concentration, you could slow it all down. The chaos becoming order and dancing around us like an orchestra. A symphony of colors with no names, and unknown phenomenon exploded into being and then disappeared after we assessed its beauty. Music was being made visually and existence itself was the notes.

Heaven was a prototype, a blank canvas to be played with, an interactive preview of greater things to come. The world was fast, and almost crowded, but like the creatures of the ocean, each angel knew how to navigate it with ease. In one instant, I caught my eye on Cadence's mansion, planted on an acre of land, already fashioned and waiting for him. And in the next moment, it was gone, doing another lap around our sanctuary.

From Raphael's hall, one could surf through a small galaxy to Heaven's core, swimming with the stars or racing against asteroids. Or, if one desired, take a ride on the spacial/time current that took you directly there in a second.

My database told me that a royal city awaited at Heaven's core, circular in structure like a planet, but possessing no form or foundation on which its buildings rested. They just floated in space, maintaining perfect balance and symmetry to their neighboring architectures. There were four major sections to Heaven: the royal city and the three rings that encircled it. All together, they showcased an incredible display, turning in continuous motion at a slow but touristic pace.

Expansive plains and impressive mountains made up the outer ring, a sneak peek at the wonders of Earth God would create later on. Inside the outer ring, which was dubbed the 1st ring, was the 2nd ring, where the homes of the angels lay, all buildings of various sizes, shapes and creative styles. Each house started out crafted by God to reflect its owner, but if an angel chose, he could literally imagine into existence a new design, transforming the furniture, walls or house itself, and it would change entirely, shape-shifting before one's very eyes. These were never-ending possibilities that ensured one's house would never get boring or stale.

The third ring, past the angels' homes, were vacant buildings that anyone could play with, shaping them back and forth as they saw fit. Angels were able to manifest their visions artistically and temporarily, showcasing their creativity before they inevitably changed back into God's original blueprint.

There was no darkness here, and all of the surfaces glistened in warm light. The cozy, homely light inhabited every space and boasted God's fingerprints. Royal garments and colors pampered the streets, providing a soft material to walk on - though no angel would choose walking over flying. Food and drink were in abundance, though unnecessary for survival, and gold was commonly found – the substance being mixed in with krillic to define most of the architecture.

The center of the three rings boasted the royal city itself, and it had all of the amenities you could think of: possessing places to congregate, Symphony Halls to sing in, theaters, Fellowship Halls, and even archives to learn about God's past accomplishments and future endeavors – a place filled with information in and outside our mental database.

The city was understandably a bustling center in which angels spent most of their time, because somehow all the senses were enhanced a hundredfold there. All you had to do was breathe to be enraptured in joy, to open your eyes and let them dance in delight, to touch a wall and leave your signature, to smell a meal coming from the Fellowship Hall, to taste one of Gabriel's homemade cinnamon buns or make your own! Because every ingredient imaginable was available and in no finite supply. And yet even all of this, wasn't even the best part.

The best part of the city? Without question, it was God's Throne Room. Secured in the absolute center of Heaven itself, it stayed there as a reminder that God was omnipresent, and if it was anything like it sounded, I was determined to become a frequent visitor.

Before we could make a move, a nebula suddenly burst onto the scene and almost instantly, it expanded into a colossal white dwarf star, making all of Heaven's surfaces explode with a dazzling array of twinkling lights and majestic shine. Our very own fireworks display. Angels from all over shot up into the air like eagles and soared toward the star – a new toy to explore and enjoy. We were the only ones to remain, watching as the black hole near our invincible world began to tug on the white dwarf with its preliminary clutches.

With a panoramic view of everything around us: the spacial/time current in the front yard, the four rings of Heaven, the black hole in the back and the universe rounding out the sides, there was no question that this was God's handiwork.

"It's beautiful," Alessa mused. Even Marcus nodded in agreement.

"I wonder what they're all going to do in that star," Farah wondered.

"Probably race each other, or explore. Maybe they'll fight each other."

"I don't know about the rest of you," I said, "but I'm done fighting. I didn't really enjoy it."

"You fought?" Marcus asked me, raising an eyebrow.

"Don't you remember? I was running in front of you when we attacked Rufus."

"Oh…you mean…you ran away."

"I didn't run away. I was a decoy so you could get a hit in later."

"I understand. You ran away. I get it."

"It doesn't look like you're 'getting' anything at all."

"Marcus," Cadence began, always the peacemaker. "The bottom line is that without Lysander's contribution, we probably would have lost. Although he didn't contribute physically, he still gave us the strategy and played his role to perfection. He did his job. You did yours. Honestly, if we asked you to contribute tactically and provide psychological analysis…would you be able to do that?"

"Too many words," Marcus groaned again, and we all had to laugh at that. I forgave Marcus for his accusation. He was, after all, pure brute strength. His muscles and power were all he needed in most situations. What was the point of sitting down and playing mental chess? But I appreciated Cadence's words. I had never heard this kind of praise on the island, and I was enjoying this new sense of belonging.

"Does anyone want to check out the Fellowship Hall?" Farah piped up as Vergil leaned over her to see it in the distance.

"I think it's a great idea, but maybe we should see what the white dwarf is all about. All those angels must be going there for a reason."

Farah looked at Vergil with a disappointed look but he quickly chimed in.

"Of course, that can wait."

"Why do you want to go to the star?" I asked him curiously. To be honest, I wasn't in the mood to socialize with the other angels yet. We were the new kids on the block and that meant one of two things. Either we would be accepted with loving arms and given the special welcoming treatment, or we would be looked down upon for our lack of experience. God forbid someone should challenge us. By going to the Fellowship Hall now, with all of the angels distracted by the white dwarf, we could at least check out the buffet before they all came back. My mind got lost analyzing the possibilities.

"I'm sorry, I didn't hear you," I said, coming back to the present. "Why did you want to go to the star again?"

"Oh, no particular reason," Vergil replied. "It's just awesome."

"Can you see things differently than we can?" Cadence asked curiously. Vergil gave him a pained look.

"Why would I see anything differently?" he replied, irritated.

"Because you're an Archangel. You have more power than the rest of us."

"That doesn't matter. You know we're all created for specific purposes. Division isn't one of them."

"Okay," Cadence backed off. "Sorry for the interrogation."

"Your angelic pressure is strong," Alessa commented, keeping a noticeable distance from him.

"Uncomfortable," Marcus said flatly.

I chuckled again as Vergil tried to tone down his spirit. Anyone that could make Marcus squirm was okay in my book.

"Sorry. I can't help it sometimes."

"I'm sure Marcus is fine," Cadence said. "Alright everyone, how about we come to a compromise since we can't agree. It's obvious that no one is in the mood to socialize just yet, so how about we all meet at my place. It's about to come back around in a second anyways."

"He's going to fall asleep," Farah said to Alessa whose eyes widened in revelation.

"That's right! Why should we go to your mansion when you're never going to leave? Getting all comfortable..."

"Well I have you to wake me up now, don't I?" Cadence said in a condescending tone. "My little alarm clock."

"Are you trying to say I'm loud?"

"You're the one that said it!" he yelled at her as his house swung by us, well into its second rotation.

Farah released a sudden war cry that shook us all.

"RAAAAAAACE!!!!!"

She rocketed forward as we all followed in pursuit, but Cadence grabbed my leg midflight and held me back, stopping me completely. I watched as Vergil took the lead and arrived at the mansion doorstep before everyone else. He was laughing hysterically and jumping up and down excitedly. I shook my head in amusement and floated down to Cadence, who was obviously concerned about something. Standing on a passing asteroid, his head was low and his face sunken, his contemplation weighing down his very physique.

"Lysander, sorry I took you away from your fun but I have to talk to you."

"You sound so serious. What's on your mind?"

"It's Vergil — what do you think of him?"

"Why are you asking me?"

"You're a Messenger. You have that mind of yours. I just want to know what you think."

"I don't think my mind works like that. It's more of a situation type of thing. Puzzles."

I cringed at the word.

"Well, what's your opinion?"

What was my opinion indeed? Vergil felt like an outsider at times but I had no right to view him that way. We had only known him for a short time while the five of us had some history to fall back on. He had a knack for interrupting people, his behavior was eerie and his face was abnormal, but he made me laugh, and distracted me from myself. And the longer I didn't have to second guess my decisions, and fear the unknown, the happier I was. In retrospect, if I hadn't already known Cadence and the others, I might have been more of an outsider than he was.

"I like him." I finally decided on. "He's a little awkward to the rest of the them but he's fine to me. He has a good heart. He just wants to fit in so he tries too hard at times and it backfires. Why? Is there a problem?"

"It was some of the things Raphael implicated about him earlier."

"I only remember introductions."

"Raphael's very diplomatic, so he knows how to pick and choose his words. It wasn't necessarily what he said, but what he didn't say."

"You can be diplomatic yourself, I noticed. I can tell you're not fond of Vergil."

"If you've noticed it," he said sadly, "then I'm sure he has too…Lysander, it's not his personality. You know how I used to sit with the new angels on the island until they either joined us or went Absent. I'm not the type to judge and move on."

"Then why the apprehension? Did Raphael tell you a secret about Vergil?"

"It's not about Raphael…it's just – I don't know if I'm making this into a big deal…"

"What did Raphael say that made you so nervous?"

"Well, two things: the first was when he left Vergil out of the fight. How he purposely told Vergil to stay back. Now, I understand his explanation – teamwork, collaboration, how to harness our abilities. But if Vergil was to join us from the start, why leave him on the sidelines?"

"Maybe he wasn't paired up with us at that time. It's possible he was asked to watch several different groups of angels, but he liked the way we meshed so he chose us."

"But he came to Heaven seconds before us. That would mean we were the first group he saw."

"Maybe he liked us that much."

"No, I think the answer's simpler than that. I think Raphael left him out – because he would've ended it."

"I don't follow."

"Vergil would've stopped the fight as soon as he entered the fray. Think about it. Rufus wasn't an Archangel. He wouldn't have stood a chance."

"What are you trying to say? That Vergil is stronger than all of us combined?"

"In a sense – yes. Imagine how we would have felt. We've grown up a lot in a short amount of time, but that doesn't change the fact that we were unsure of our teamwork in battle, our collective strength. With the exception of Farah, we might have all lacked in faith – believing we were unfit for the task at hand. If Vergil had finished it from the start, we would feel even more useless. Obviously I can't just tell this to the others. I don't want to break their spirits."

"I don't think you give them enough credit. They probably already know. Looking back, I think I might have been the only one blind to what you're saying. The rest of you were giving each other glances like it was an inside joke."

"Maybe so. But I dare not admit it out loud, just in case."

"You said there were two things. What's the second?"

"When Vergil said Raphael let him join a group."

"How is that a problem?

"It's not, but think about what's implied. I wouldn't have it any other way but…we didn't choose to be paired with one another. But Vergil somehow got to."

I finally understood the weight of Cadence's words.

"Vergil doesn't need a team," I whispered in realization.

"Nope," Cadence's face looked stressed. "He'll try to fit in. Put on a good show. But it doesn't change the fact that he doesn't need us."

"He did say he needed help socially."

"Okay. But what would that matter in battle? I doubt there are other teams in Heaven with an unofficial lead at the helm. I know you see me as the leader, but I don't, and it's not like I was given such a title. We are supposed to be *equal members*, but Vergil is superior to us in almost every way. We could quickly become Vergil and his angels or whatever name you could think of. At any moment, he could take over as leader or a dictator and tell us what to do, and we would be powerless to stop him."

Cadence's voice was raised and his angelic pressure was fluctuating wildly. Even from a distance, I was sure the others could see the change and would start to wonder what had gotten him so riled up.

"We shouldn't worry about what angels might say," I said to him, turning him around to face away from the mansion. "This could be a test. Maybe God is seeing how we will react. We were tested on pride after all, and at the heart of it, this is what it sounds like the issue is. We're afraid that Vergil will steal our thunder. But it doesn't matter. Even if he did, our primary focus is to serve God and carry out His will. Get back into His presence and do our duty. I could care less what the journey is to get to that destination. We have a new life here, a wonderful life. And I'm not going to mess up. I don't want to find out that we can be thrown back onto the island because we didn't handle ourselves properly."

"It's not that simple, Lysander."

"Maybe it is. All we have to do is talk to Lucifer and follow his group back to God. Thinking about it and speculating on every little detail will get us nowhere. We just have to go with the flow. It's what we did on the island. It's what we do here."

"You went with the flow, Lysander," Cadence raised his voice an octave higher. "Not us. Sure, I didn't like sitting around and thinking, but we still took action in our own way. Alessa kept the group close. Marcus and Farah worked on the barrier and I sat with the newcomers. We weren't sitting idly by for God to return. We tried to solve the problem."

"And so did I!" I said, pushing his chest with a little force. "It may have looked like I just sat there all day, staving off Absenteeism, but I was researching. I grew weary at times, but ultimately, I was contributing to the group too! It's who I am. I think! And I'm telling you that I think we should let these suspicions of Vergil go. I'm here because you all kept me under your wings, but so far we're not giving Vergil the same treatment."

"It's different."

"Why? Because I'm weak and he's strong? It doesn't make a difference. You'll only be intimidated by him if you let yourself. It's the same lesson I came to terms with concerning Marcus. Let this go, Cadence. Just accept him."

"I respect your argument, but I still want to keep an eye on Vergil. To be blunt, I have a basic understanding of who each of you are, but not him. I have no clue what he's like. The best example I have so far of an Archangel is Lucifer, and to be honest, I'm not sure what I think about him."

"There's no reason not to trust someone in Heaven. We're family."

Cadence mulled over my words before deciding to let the discussion go.

"I'm sure you're right," he said solemnly. "I'm sure you're right."

CHAPTER 7: Fellowship

We walked into Cadence's mansion just in time to see Farah destroy Marcus in an arm wrestling competition. There was no way of knowing who initiated it, but it was apparent Farah was poised to finish it. Slamming down his arm with a powerful "HAH!" coming from her pint-sized lungs, Marcus growled in defeat and rubbed the back of his hand, glaring at her with a ferocity whose flames could only be doused with an outpouring of superiority. Without thinking, I tackled Marcus to the floor, but he retaliated with a palm straight into my chest, sending me toward the ceiling which was over a sun's height tall. This time, it was Farah who caught *me*.

"Don't fight! You no win!" Marcus called out to me. It was good to see he was back to his old self, and Farah could only giggle at the whole ordeal. While I was up high, I took in my surroundings. Cadence's mansion was tall, but not wide - a lanky structure that mirrored his frame. I tried to change the ceiling with my mind – a flat, boring, tiled thing with a chandelier hanging – but nothing happened. Since it was Cadence's house, it was up to him if he wanted others to be able to transform it.

There were jagged obtrusions coming out of the walls – little ledges every ten feet or so that looked as if there had been more floors in the house at some point. The room we entered in, which held the entrance, was the only one in the "mansion," furnished with long, circular, half-moon couches, and brightened by bay windows in the walls, letting the light of Heaven and its starry canopy engulf the room. A single table was fastened in the middle, with a velvety feather-like rug underneath – the softest object Cadence owned.

"Cadence – your house is a skyscraper," I commented from up above, my voice echoing up and down the structure.

"I know," he called up. "It's the way I like it."

"All bones. No substance," Alessa said to him from below. Farah and I sped down to be with the group.

"Doesn't it speak volumes on how resilient I am on the inside? Surely there's more to me than what you see on the outside."

"Okay," she laughed. "Then it says how you are a loner at heart, with great, big solid walls to keep your true thoughts hidden from others...which is manifest in this soft, purple-feathered rug. In other words, on the inside, you're a great big softy."

"I knew we should have went to the Fellowship Hall."

Everyone got a good chuckle out of that except for Farah, who was already setting her elbows up on the table for another round. I couldn't help but ask Alessa how she had such knowledge of Cadence, or if it was merely some form of intuition.

"I asked God about it, and He answered."

"Are you serious?"

"Of course."

I still wasn't sure if she was joking...but I decided to bounce a request off her anyways.

"Next time you communicate with Him, tell Him I said hello, and ask Him when we can be in His presence again."

"Wow, that's pretty bold."

"I'm taking tips from Farah."

"Then I'll be sure to ask Him," she laughed. I couldn't stop myself from popping the next question.

"Were you always in contact with God?" I said abruptly. She understood what I was implying. That as a Glory, she may have been able to get in touch with God at all times, even back on the island – but maybe she had been forbidden to speak of it.

"No," she said, "but it sure would've saved us a lot of heartache if I was. My ability was given to me while I was in God's presence the second time. He said that He would always be there to comfort me, and that this gift, was just a preview of things to come."

"What does that mean?"

"I don't know. But I got the impression it had something to do with Earth. To be honest, I was so infatuated with His light, I only half-paid attention."

"I wasn't even that aware," I chuckled. "It was like my first memory all over again. I didn't hear a word He said or notice at all when I was given my abilities."

"I'll be sure to ask Him about that too. No charge," she winked. Suddenly we heard a fist slam down on Cadence's table. Cadence yelled out a "HEY!" as Farah stood upon it.

"Who's next?" Farah called out to all of us in a challenge, sweeping an index finger around the room. "Don't be afraid of little old me. I'm a ladybug, an ant, a little butterfly, a-"

"How long did it take you to research all of those references to yourself?" I asked, but she stared at me with wide eyes. She had found her next victim.

"I like your sass, Lysander. How about you bring it to this table?"

"I saw how hard you hit Rufus. I'm fine right here."

"Don't be like that."

"I'll take his place," Vergil said, coming from a corner of the room. I hadn't noticed or thought of Vergil since I had entered Cadence's mansion, and now I was uncomfortable with his sudden acceptance of Farah's challenge. I hoped he didn't think he had something to prove.

I could already see Farah lose some of her faith. Her petite wings were no longer stout and teeming with boldness. Her face no longer smiling and overflowing with energy. Vergil leaned his elbow into the table, waiting for Farah to clutch his hand. She nervously took it and leaned in, more than half of her body over the table. She counted up to three slowly, and on three, she put her whole body into defeating Vergil. He didn't budge. He pretended to wince, to grunt as if Farah had some hope, but since he was the one needing help in the social department – we knew he was faking. Farah wasn't fooled either, and it only cast a shadow of doubt upon her face as her faith diminished with every passing second. Vergil finally saw it too, and thankfully, he didn't pity her and let her win, but simply ended it, to relieve her of any further discomfort. Farah played the good sport, congratulating him and even managing to pat him on the shoulder. But Vergil stood there expressionlessly, contemplating how he should have handled the situation better. I saw Cadence glance at me out of the corner of my eye, but I ignored it, changing the subject for all of us.

"So Cadence, I noticed those ledges jutting out of the walls, what are those?"

Cadence caught wind of my intentions and was happy to humor me.

"They're traps actually. The ledges shoot out at various speeds and strength to try to harm you or pin you to the wall. It's a great training exercise."

"Can they break?" Marcus asked, already flexing a forearm.

"Well, you can try. They're easily repaired. I just have to imagine it. When God made this house for me, He definitely knew what I liked because I can test my defenses whenever I want. I haven't tried the system out myself, but go ahead. Be my guest."

"I want to fight Vergil," Marcus huffed as his wings began to build momentum, carrying his massive body toward the ledges up above.

"Who said anything about fighting?" Cadence asked through a clenched jaw. "Just try out the system."

"I don't want to fight," Vergil said under his breath, but Marcus was already in the air, staring down at him like he was a piece of food that had gone rotten.

"Fight," he commanded.

"No."

"Marcus, he doesn't have to fight," Cadence tried to intervene, but Alessa began egging Vergil on.

"Why aren't you excited to meet this challenge? Should be a cinch, right? He's been wanting to fight you since we've met. I can tell."

"What's the point of this?" Vergil whined, facing away from us.

"Are you trying to say it's a foregone conclusion that you will win, so why bother?"

"No, but this is counterproductive."

"We all want to see this, besides, God said it's okay."

We all turned to her in shock. God said it was...okay?

Part of me did want to see a fight between our powerhouse versus...well, our more powerful powerhouse. It didn't matter if it ended up being more of a shoving match and less of a strategic game. That was irrelevant. What alarmed me was Alessa's message. Alessa said that God was allowing the fight to occur. Could He have really told her that? It was the first time I had thought about someone abusing an ability or a stance in an argument for their personal gain. I quickly shrugged it off because everyone was trustworthy in Heaven and she was my friend, but in the back of my mind, logic was asking me why God would allow such a match to occur...and if He really had at all. Vergil was right in his questioning. What was the point in it? If Marcus won, as unlikely as it was – nothing would change but an increase in his pride. But if Vergil won, and this was the most assured outcome, it would widen the gap between us. Vergil knew this. And so did we. Otherwise Cadence wouldn't have brought it up to me earlier. It was a time bomb – waiting for the day he would show us that we were meaningless and beneath him. Would that time be now? So soon? What if the fight got out of hand? Would we simply go between them and break it up? Or would some of us divide and pick sides? Would

Alessa go to Marcus's aid? Would I stand by and let it all happen? The situation was too unstable.

"Marcus!" Cadence called up, "this is not happening in my house! Come down here!"

"NO!" Marcus bellowed like an overgrown toddler on the verge of a full-blown tantrum. Cadence was ready to implode.

"Fine," Cadence said, clenching his jaw in worry, his eyes becoming listless. He let his wings fly out from his body and stretch, letting a current blow through them like a furnace. Marcus stared at Vergil, debating whether he should try to outmaneuver Cadence and engage his desired target in combat, but Cadence didn't give him the opportunity. He flew toward Marcus at full speed.

Marcus cocked back an arm to stop him, but a shield met him in the stomach. Cadence used his free right hand to punch Marcus in the face, just hard enough to send him off the shield and toward one of the ledges. Before Marcus could halt his ascent, two jagged ledges from each side of him shot out and pinned him around the middle. Cadence made his way past Marcus before it closed shut, placing him safely on the other side, where only Marcus's upper torso remained.

I couldn't hear the conversation that ensued, but from the shouting match that quickly lowered to whispers, I was sure Cadence had gotten his point across. Farah was humming to herself softly, sitting on one of the half-moon couches and waiting for them to return. Alessa was steaming in anger for missing out on a great show and Vergil was solemn, ready to speak only after he saw me look his way.

"You're going to the Fellowship Hall, right?" he asked meekly. "I think I'm going to meet you all there, if you don't mind."

"Don't," I said. "You're part of the group. Don't isolate yourself from us. I know we have some issues, but if we just talk about it, we can work them out."

"But that's the problem," he said. "Those issues are with me."

"Why do we need to talk about anything?" Alessa snapped. "We all know what you and Cadence were whispering about out there. You're not sure if Vergil belongs with us."

"He belongs here," I said firmly.

"Then tell him what you were talking about."

"Fine. Vergil, why didn't you fight with us when Rufus arrived?"

"I was told not to," he said sheepishly, "by Raphael."

"Why?"

"I don't know. I just obeyed."

"Okay, when you were born, how long were you on the island before you were taken to Heaven?"

"He wasn't there," Alessa began but I cut her off.

"There could have been more than one island," I said. "You saw the number of angels flying toward the dwarf star. We were right. There's a whole lot more of us in number than what we saw…so Vergil, how long were you on your island?"

"Not long. Maybe a day or two at most."

"You were able to leave because you got the lesson, right?"

"I guess so…I don't know."

"Let me ask you this then. When you were transported here, did you arrive with other angels or were you alone?"

"I was alone."

"You didn't receive a lesson in pride from Raphael?"

"He mentioned the gist of it."

"Why didn't you have to take the lesson?"

"Maybe I didn't have any issues with pride," he said, his words accusing and hurt.

"It's hard for me to understand why you were alone. Are you sure there weren't any others?"

"No. I was definitely alone."

"And why do you think that is?"

"Because God wanted me to be with all of you."

I didn't know what to say to these words. Even Alessa seemed to be taken off guard and ashamed about how she had acted, but there was no time for remorse. The hurt covered his face like a veil, and it was obvious he was done being questioned under our skeptical scrutiny.

"I don't want to do anything that would jeopardize this team. I just need to be alone, I guess. Think about choices I've made...I'll meet you at the Fellowship Hall, okay?"

"Vergil, you don't-"

But he was already gone, his Archangel speed carrying him away faster than my apologies. Simultaneously, the ledges above reset to their original position and Marcus and Cadence floated down. Marcus's angelic pressure had significantly decreased in that time.

"Where's Vergil?" Cadence asked. Alessa beat me to the answer.

"He went to the Fellowship Hall. He didn't like where this was going."

"I see..."

"Coward," Marcus spat out and Cadence smacked him upside the head.

"He did make a good point in your absence," Alessa replied, taking in recent events. "He said that the reason he was born alone was so he could be on our team."

"Then why wasn't he just on the island with us?" Cadence asked, and we had no response to that. "I have nothing against him personally, but...you know what, we're done discussing this."

"Cadence," Alessa began, "you can't just write this off like-"

"Can you please shut up for once!" Cadence yelled out with his eyes toward the floor, his hands shooting up into the air. The sudden vibrations from his words rang throughout the building and kept us all on edge.

"Look..." he said calmly, "I know that we are uncomfortable with how powerful he is. But the bottom line is that he wants to be a part of our team. That should be enough. More than enough. It's not like back on the island when we could barely find an angel to talk to us, let alone join our company. Vergil could have chosen any group in heaven. But he chose us, and he claims he needs us. We should never be an exclusive group where only those whose company we enjoy should be a part. Our whole purpose is to help one another, to better serve God and be what He wants us to be. Yes, there may be a time when Vergil outshines us all, and defeats an enemy far stronger than our combined strength, but so what? How is that any different than Marcus taking down someone with one hit? How is that any different than the power in Farah's faith? Just think. She just beat Marcus in an arm wrestling match. What about Lysander's tactical prowess? What about Alessa's connection with God, who is able to defeat even those whom Vergil cannot? There will always be a time when one outshines another, but we will all get our moment in the spotlight. Instead of focusing on the bigger picture, we're over here acting like a bunch of children. I say we put this aside and welcome Vergil into the group – no judgment, no strings attached. And Marcus? Next time you see Vergil, go ahead and fight him. I'll tell him to not hold back, and whether you win or lose, we will be closer as a group. Because we acknowledge our strengths, and our weaknesses. We embrace them all, because we aim to do better, and none of us can move forward alone."

His words moved us all to be better – to put our pride and fears aside for our fellow angel. I only wish Vergil had been there to hear it.

I also couldn't help but notice one key aspect of his speech...that we should have let Marcus and Vergil fight each other all along. We were afraid of the outcome, when in actuality, it would've ended in solidarity and alleviation. Now we still had a relationship to mend. Alessa had been right after all, and I should never have suspected her of abusing her power.

"Alessa, I'm sorry," I said, turning to face her. She raised an eyebrow but kept her mouth shut. Cadence's reprimand was still fresh with her. "I suspected you of abusing your Glory status back there, but what you said was exactly what needed to happen."

She gave a half-smile and nodded in acceptance.

"That's why I talk so much," she muttered. "No one listens to me."

"I do," Cadence replied, stepping forward. "I hear every word you say. And just because I get irritated easily, and I might say some hurtful things to you sometimes...I don't want you to think I would ever jeopardize our friendship, Alessa. It means too much to me. I apologize for yelling at you earlier."

"You were pretty rude."

"I was."

"You're usually pretty rude."

"I have to work on that."

"You hate work."

"Not as much as your voice," Cadence said, flashing a warm smile her way. Alessa stared at him from her downcast eyes and wrinkled her nose.

"Well, I guess if you're gonna work on your rudeness, I can try to put a leash on my words. But next time you yell at me like that, I'm going to petition the Lord for a special blessing to come your way."

"I accept that decision," he said. Marcus tapped him on the shoulder.

"Cadence," he said. "Not a blessing...she mean...not a blessing."

"Thank you, Marcus. I know," Cadence burst out in laughter and Alessa gave him a warm hug.

"Let's go to the Fellowship Hall and get our teammate back," she said. We nodded in agreement. Marcus was the only one who didn't make a notion to confirm our decision. But it didn't matter. He would come around eventually.

CHAPTER 8: Mend

As we flew from Cadence's mansion, I wondered if Vergil would really be at the Fellowship Hall. He could easily have had a change of heart and decided to go to his mansion instead. I wouldn't blame him under the circumstances.

The flight was short, as we navigated the shooting stars like an asteroid field, instinctively dodging them like we had a map of the universe memorized. And even when we happened to encounter an angel speeding directly at us, we never collided. Somehow, traffic control was wired into us, and we could only crash if one of us really tried. We saw a glimpse of twenty angels doing this, playing a crazy game of "building tag" in which you literally made a building stretch out to hit another player who wasn't "it". A second group was flying back and forth in a straight line while one sole angel tried to get through it unscathed. It was all fun and games, but even I knew it couldn't always be this way. Raphael had stressed the importance of holding on to our first memory, and Lucifer had expressed passionately how Heaven wasn't all play. Someday, our memories - of God, the island, the lesson in pride...they would all become pillars to lean on. Anchors to help us weather the coming fallout.

We were said to have been made for a purpose, to have a mission to carry out, yet no orders had been given. No directives had been relayed, no meetings called, and yet the time had to come at some point in which our assignments would manifest into reality. As great as everything was, as much fun as I anticipated in exploring in the city - I couldn't shake the feeling that it was the calm before the storm.

"Is this it?" Farah asked as we followed Cadence's lead to the 4th ring of Heaven, where the Fellowship Hall awaited. We descended to the lush floor that made up the street, right outside the place where Vergil was supposed to be. It looked like a gigantic stadium, the type basketball games were played in, but far more luxurious since this was not its function. The front portrayed the words "Fellowship Hall" in giant pop-up, golden letters that were accented underneath all of the light coming from Heaven's stars. Other than that, the entrance was quite plain. Angels darted in and out of the three revolving doors in the front - each kept in a constant spin that showed no signs of slowing down.

"The food must be excellent here," Cadence commented.

"God says that it was all made specifically for us," Alessa relayed. I was attentive immediately.

"What did God say about when we can be in His presence again?" I asked her. She shrugged her shoulders.

"He said 'be patient' and that was all."

"Well at least it's not a no. Did He say when I got my tactical mind?"

"He said you had it on the island, but you were such a crybaby, all you did was whine about how you felt instead of taking the time to realize what you had."

"Did He really say it like that?" I was devastated.

"I'm paraphrasing. Any other questions?"

"No. Thank you," I said half-heartedly. She gave me a chipper smile with her eyes tightly shut.

"Just let me know!"

"If you two are done talking," Farah said, flying between us, "I think we should make it a priority to try some of the delicious-smelling food inside...while looking for Vergil, of course."

We timed our entrance, concentrating our efforts and making sure we didn't run into any angels on the way in. When we sensed a split second reprieve in the revolving doors, we darted inside.

I didn't know how we were going to find Vergil. There were just...far too many angels. All types, including Archangels, flew around the room like a swarm of flies, indistinguishable at first glance, moving in such harmony and precision that I was instantly in awe. But I stayed back despite my desire to join the dance, if for no other reason but to admire the flow.

The main floor of the room was surrounded by areas where you could sit and converse. Although these sections declined down to the center floor, they weren't filled with stadium-style seats, but with rows upon rows of food and tables. Angles darted from the bottom floor to the ceiling, picking up a croissant here and a honeycomb there, before lopping down into a conversing group of their contemporaries and inserting their own thoughts into the discussion. The vibe was one of wholesome fellowship and fun, and I could tell by the way the angels spoke, that this was a spot Heaven's host visited frequently.

"This is soooooo much better than our patch of dying grass on the island," Farah said, clapping her hands and trying to contain her excitement. "Now this is a meeting area!"

"I don't see Vergil anywhere," Alessa said. Six angels whizzed past her before she could continue her sentence.

"We can inquire about him, introduce ourselves and see what's going on," Cadence suggested. Marcus grunted something and headed over to one of the booths near us, which was toppling over with raspberries. He reached out and grabbed one casually, popping it into his mouth as he lazily searched the room for our missing comrade. He chewed twice when his eyes promptly widened, in what I interpreted to be horror. He spun around like he was the wind and lifted the whole table up from its legs. He tilted the table, directing the entire pile of raspberries into his mouth. The raspberry pile was too big to make it flawlessly into Marcus's mouth - they burst onto his face and armor, leaving bright red marks. He didn't care as he swallowed and chewed as fast as he could, and when he "finished," he moved on to the next table with urgency.

"Gross," Farah said, and we hovered behind him, following.

"Should we intervene?" I asked Cadence, but he kept his eyes closed while he pinched the bridge between them.

"I don't know what to do anymore, Lysander," he sighed. "Marcus is...I just don't know what to do anymore."

I was about to ask him if he wanted to try the stimulating raspberries when the swarm stopped its rhythmical flow and formed a type of ball in the air. The movement was so slow and deliberate, I couldn't help but watch. Two angels were in the middle, engaged in a heated discussion.

"Yes, I remember Him. All of us do, but what about it? I was one of the first here and I haven't been in His presence since. Do you know how long ago that was?"

I knew instantly the angel was talking about God, but what surprised me the most was that, due to his miniature stature, he had to be a Faithful. What was a Faithful doing having doubts about God?

"You can feel His presence everywhere, Lionel," the angel addressing him said, a Glory, if I was not mistaken. "And besides, I was only two angels after you, so that excuse is meaningless. I mean really, we should be role models for the young and inexperienced ones, not bickering amongst ourselves. I thought you were supposed to be a Faithful!"

"Then you explain to me, Nathan, why isn't God here anymore?"

"The thing about God is that if you don't believe in Him, you won't feel Him."

"Ridiculous. Of course I believe in Him. That's not up for debate. The argument is, where has He been? I have a couple memories, but that's all I have left to fall back on. It's been so long since I've seen God face-to-face, it's like the memories were programmed into my database -along with a detailed account of what dishwashing liquid is made of and where I can eventually find some guy named Solomon. I'm telling you...there's something wrong going on here."

"What are you trying to say? That God is fabricated?"

"No, my friend. I can't even begin to fathom such a thing. No, I'm saying that we're thrown here with each other, forced to live together and make peace – left alone to figure out what to make of ourselves...and for what? What's the point of it all? We have no guidance, no direction. We just fly around Heaven all day playing, as if we're nothing more than a snow globe for God to place in His hand, and watch for His amusement. What the issue is...is why would He give us the opportunity to know Him, when He's never around afterwards?"

"It could be a test, a lesson in learning how to have faith in Him, without Him constantly looming over our shoulder like a parent."

"But even the concept of parents implies a presence that is periodically there. They're not supposed to just disappear."

"I think it's a test of faith," Nathan stated boldly and Lionel snickered.

"It's all speculation. At least we have Lucifer."

My attention perked up, and it was apparent by the murmuring in the crowd that Lucifer was a hot topic of conversation. Just by the looks on their faces, you could tell which angels had an undying allegiance to the powerful Archangel.

"What of Lucifer? What of him?" Nathan seethed, his voice increasing in volume and loathing.

"He is our day star. A light of lights. At least he is here for us. In spite of God's absence he labors tirelessly, keeping us in one accord and one focus. He is a great angel worthy of the highest respect. Have you heard his voice in the heavenly choir or felt the magnitude of his angelic pressure? It's simply beautiful."

Many in the crowd whispered in awe. Others murmured disapprovingly.

"Lucifer is just like the rest of us," Nathan stressed. "He's not to be praised. Yes, he is a hard worker and helps many of us throughout the day, but that doesn't mean he should be regarded as higher than us, higher than he is. We were all created equal, and I perceive that God is no respecter of angels."

"Why shouldn't he be held in high regard? Did not God create him that way? He could have easily made him the lowest of Heaven's host, but he was given great power by God Himself, to use for our good."

"Only God should get the glory and praise, Lionel."

"Why? Surely Lucifer could do a better job."

Cries rang throughout the Fellowship Hall. Angels that had been eating while listening on the sidelines stopped their gorging. Even Marcus gave an attentive ear. At least, I think it was Marcus. It looked more like a walking mound of mashed potatoes with a puree of diverse fruits strewn around his body for color.

"You speak heresy, Lionel," Nathan replied in a voice full of pity, "heresy, mutiny and lies. God would never allow another to take His throne."

"Why not? He isn't here. Wouldn't it be better to pass off the mantel to another?"

"Lucifer is not omnipotent. He doesn't have the abilities to perform God's job. Besides, no one in their right mind would want to take on such a daunting task. Even I must give Lucifer credit that he is not that foolish."

"Are you calling me foolish, Nathan?"

"To defy God in Heaven...yes, you are foolish and quite confused," Nathan seethed through grit teeth, getting ever closer to Lionel's tightened brow. "You call yourself a Faithful when I have seen nothing to boast such a designation. You should be dubbed 'the doubtful' from here on out, or maybe, 'the Lucifer lover'. That would suit you."

I only saw a twitch of Lionel's shoulder and they were gone, off to who knows where, settling their differences in the cosmos. The rest of the group murmured a bit but immediately went back to eating and talking as if nothing had happened. The ordeal had been too intense, and no one wanted to bring it back to the forefront. There was too much good food to enjoy. Anger didn't add much spice.

"So Lucifer is that popular around here?" I asked the group. "I don't understand why two angels would fight over him. No one can replace God. No one."

"It's like Lionel said, they haven't seen God in a long time," Cadence replied, "so maybe they have forgotten. Think about how easily our minds were distracted in such a short amount of time. I can't even imagine how frustrated they must be."

"It's like being Absent, but on the opposite end of the spectrum. They're willing to fight over their beliefs rather than shut down."

"All the more reason to find Lucifer," Cadence said. "We passed the test. So we're definitely in."

"He's definitely not here. We would have noticed."

"Not to mention that argument wouldn't have occurred."

We hovered in silence as we watched Farah, Alessa and even Marcus mingle in the crowd, introducing themselves and learning more about Heaven and what it had to offer. Farah was discussing the variety of shapes a building could be turned into and was invited to an outing with a few others. Alessa was with some other Glories, speaking with God and each other in a huddled circle, asking questions and relaying the answers they received. Marcus was the only one who was doing a back-and-forth between eating and talking, stuffing his face and then with a mouth full of berries, he would explain in a way only Marcus could - how great it tasted.

"Vergil isn't here," Cadence said flatly. "Any clue where he might be?"

"I have a couple guesses...but I think I might try talking to him alone first. After seeing that argument, I figure the less the better right now. Would that be okay?"

"Of course. If you think that's best. I'm probably going to stick around here and socialize. Maybe I can get more information on Lucifer's whereabouts."

"That's a good idea."

"GUYS!" Marcus appeared behind us suddenly, chipping into the conversation. "HAVE YOU HAD THESE?"

He was carrying a handful of grapes that were consistently failing at maintaining their integrity in his hand. Juices were flowing freely from his palm and Marcus started getting angrier with each grape that didn't make the journey from the table. But he was adamant about having us try one for he flew back to the stand where they were laying and brought more back, flying up and down awkwardly like he was carrying a dozen eggs.

"What's so great about these?" Cadence asked, taking a couple and popping them into his mouth.

"Amazing," Marcus said, a little too chipper. His eyes were wide with admiration and fondness. He petted a grape lovingly as I tried one myself.

"They're good," I admitted. They really were, but maybe Marcus didn't believe me because all he did was scowl.

"That all? Good?" he grunted. "Fine. I get more. Hungry."

Marcus flew back to the booth and continued to give the angel stocking the grapes a friendly challenge in replenishing them.

"I was going to ask him to mingle with me," Cadence said, "but it appears he's busy."

"How does he know what hunger is? It's not like we need to eat for survival...I don't even think we can get hungry."

"We know the definition, just not what it feels like."

We watched as Marcus ate with no shame.

"Okay, so...if he doesn't realize what hunger is, how will he know when he's full?" I asked.

Marcus grabbed another plate of apples, paused, then grabbed another, laughing heartily from the abdomen as he relished in his newfound love. He took both plates, and tried to shove their contents into his mouth at the same time. The angel stocking the apples threw up his hands in frustration as the plates shattered and nearly all of the apples flew behind Marcus and tumbled down to the stadium floor.

"We might be here a while," Cadence admitted solemnly.

"Correction. You will be here awhile. I will be with our dear friend, Vergil."

"Godspeed," Cadence laughed. "Tell Vergil that we're sorry for our attitude. We were out of line."

"I'll let you tell him personally," I said as I glanced back at Marcus. He was fighting the angel with the apples, as they both were trying to shape the broken plates in their own way. The angel was trying to restore them to their former glory while Marcus was trying to turn the platters into apples. The result ended up being a doughy, clay-like monstrosity that Marcus was happy to taste.

I missed the group already.

Leaving Cadence and the others to gain some notoriety, I took off to find our lost comrade, but someone tapped me on the shoulder mid-flight. I turned around and the angel – a Glory - placed an arm over my shoulder and pulled me to a table of oranges, where two other angels sat. It happened so fast I could barely express myself.

"Whoa! Hey! I – uh, hello?" I stammered as the two angels at the table stood up and grabbed my hand, shaking it like I was in an exhibition game of tug-of-war.

"This is Lysander!" my kidnapper exclaimed, patting me on the back. "His team defeated Rufus!"

"I recognized him the second he walked in," an angel beamed, a Guard I assumed.

"No you didn't," the second angel, a Faithful, replied, "Geez. Your short-term memory is worse than mine."

"I don't think we've been introduced," I said, eyeing the exit. My kidnapper guffawed and pushed me down into a seat.

"I'm Ananias. Big fan of your work."

"What work?"

"Why, knocking Rufus on his rump. His ego needed a beating or two. And it doesn't hurt that it was a test from Lucifer. I tell you, I am jeeeeaaalous."

"You didn't pass his test?"

"Heavens no. Can't say my team didn't make an attempt. Hey, Stasis, when was the last time an angel made it into Lucifer's company?"

"Too long...last one was Iron, I'd say."

"It looks like he has a ton of followers," I said, but Ananias chuckled and popped an orange into his mouth – yes, the whole orange.

"Followers, yes. Team members, not so much. Angels all over Heaven like to play his game but few make it into the inner circle. Angels had lost hope, but then all of a sudden, your troupe arrives on the scene and passes his test with flying colors. No kidding, there's a bright future ahead of you."

"Thank you, I guess."

"You're welcome, young one. Sorry to harass you. Just needed to say hi."

"No problem," I said, unsure of how I should react. "I'll see you later."

"Don't be a stranger!" he called as I hurried out of the Fellowship Hall, uncertain if I would be bombarded with potential fans. Taking to the skies with the grace of an arctic tern, I welcomed the universe with a revived interest.

There is really nothing like riding through the stars at full speed. The way the gases swirl around you like they want a touch, how the light of the stars hold onto your feet after you emerge from them and follow you even outside of their condensed ball, almost begging for you to come back, envying the next one that's greeting you with open arms. If I didn't know any better, I would dare say they were alive, and enjoyed angels' company as much as we enjoyed theirs. But I had no time to play with the stars, at least not the ones I flew past. Only one in particular caught my attention.

The white dwarf, already turning brown, reaching the end of its cycle and turning noticeably dimmer. This waning star, on its death bed – had already been abandoned by all of the angels, who had run off to play with its shiny, brand new brothers and sisters born into the world. All the angels, that is, but one.

How I figured out Vergil would be there, I wasn't sure, but if there was anything I learned from my battle with Rufus, it was that I had to trust my instincts. Over-thinking and complicating things tended to end badly, and I never was much of a fighter. I wanted situations solved quickly, the conflict and all of the emotions it brought with it to end expeditiously.

I screeched to a halt, a dusty trail of the last star I had emerged from glittering on my soles. I stared at the brown dwarf, steadily dying, glowing one second and dimming the next like it was on its last breaths, its final heartbeats. Vergil, who now had a little more light emanating from him than the star itself was staring at it in awe. Legs crossed and floating in the air, he levitated next to it, with a hand on its surface, like he was consoling an old friend. Without a word, I glided next to him, and sat down, reaching out to copy his movements. We sat there for a long time, just listening to the old-timer and thinking about nothing in particular. In the busy world of

Heaven, where everyone darted around like loons, it was nice for once to sit back and relax.

The bustle was a change from the lazy living on the island. A change I would have to get used to. But I still wouldn't give Heaven up for anything. Just being free to spend time with a friend, listening to the pulse of a brown dwarf, enjoying the calm and soothing hum of the galaxy as it placed celestial headphones over our ears and created a lovely song for us to close our eyes to – nothing was more peaceful.

And I refused to break this tranquility. No, I waited for Vergil to begin the conversation.

"I did go to the Fellowship Hall," he said eventually, "but no one wanted to talk to me."

"Why?"

"Some of them said I was a knock-off of Lucifer – my Archangel status and the way I glowed when I ate some bread. Others said they didn't converse with Archangels."

"That's strange. I saw Archangels there."

"And did you notice they only hung out with each other? Not to mention most of them thought I was too young to contribute to the conversation."

"I can get Marcus to punch one in the face."

"What I don't get," he said, ignoring me, "is how does being an Archangel mean anything? We're all angels. Why does my designation matter? I didn't ask for it."

"We can't help how we are made. The sooner we accept who or what we are and just strive to do good, things get simpler."

"Lysander, I'm finding out that I may never fit in."

"Is that so bad?"

"Who wouldn't want to be part of the crowd? Do you enjoy being an outcast? Separated from the group?"

"I'm here, aren't I?"

"Hmm...I think you're here to do damage control. Bring me back after some counseling."

"I'm here for a friend, Vergil. Nothing more. And despite what you might think, I can understand how you feel to a degree. When our group was back on the island, I didn't think I belonged at all. I even tried to leave them and go off on my own, but it never panned out. Because they care, about me...and you. I wasn't the only one looking for you. The whole group went to the Fellowship Hall because you're part of the team. Team Six." I made up the name off the top of my head.

"Team six, huh?" Vergil said, amused. He played along. "And why can't we be number one?"

"Because we don't have the cohesiveness one through five has," I pretended, "but we're working on it. That's what a team does."

"Working on it...you make me sound like a case number."

"Whatever you might think, we're with you. And we all have the same goals – to get back to God. From what I heard in the Fellowship Hall, He's been gone for a while. It's important we figure out why."

"A mystery to solve."

"So you'll come back with me to help?"

"I don't feel comfortable. I never know what to say to them."

"There is a reason you're socially awkward. The same goes with why some aren't. We all have our strengths and weaknesses. Sure, you might trip a lot verbally, but how many angels have your level of strength?"

"That's true," he said, staring into the brown dwarf star. "I am stronger."

"And what we discover is that when we unite together, my weakness is overridden by your strength and vice versa. We balance each other out. It's the only explanation to why God would design us individually."

Vergil contemplated my words for a few minutes, patting the star tenderly.

"Thank you for your words," he said eventually, and I felt a surge of joy - it must have been the same feeling Cadence experienced when he helped the angels on the island.

"Then let's get going. We don't have to meet up with the group right away. We'll search for God on our own."

"God could be anywhere," Vergil said skeptically. "We could search the whole universe and get no closer to His location."

"We're definitely not going to find Him with that negative attitude," I scoffed, pointing behind me toward space. "If Farah was here, we would both get a scolding for our lack of faith."

"She sure lost faith when I beat her in that arm wrestling competition," Vergil chuckled. Strangely enough, I couldn't laugh.

"Was that too weird?" he asked me. I shrugged my shoulders. I couldn't articulate it, but his words had touched a nerve, and I couldn't put together why without creating awkward silence.

"Not sure. But maybe we can get started on the search."

"I know the first place to try," Vergil said, his mood lighter. Apparently, he hadn't noticed my hesitation.

"Where to?"

"It's like this brown dwarf star. Everyone loves it when it's shining, when it's in the midst of its prime. It's so big and bright, it's very much like God – but as soon as its light begins to fade, like God's presence - they all scatter, waiting for Him to reveal Himself once more in a big way. No one denies His existence but few seek Him out. And when God does not show Himself, they forget about Him. They just want the feeling. Not the relationship. So…I think we should go to the one place no one has visited yet – the Throne Room."

I nodded and smiled slyly, turning slowly but letting my wings stretch out to capacity - letting him know what I was thinking. I didn't get to race him last time, and I didn't care if he would beat me. I had to try.

I took off at full throttle, a sonic boom cracking the stillness of space in my wake. Vergil was left behind, in shock, but he soon recovered from my outburst and he followed - quickly gaining momentum. I knew that racing was just as tactical of a sport as fighting was. Going faster than another wasn't always the best way to win. I decided to skip plowing through the stars, fully aware of their slight yet profound pull on our angelic bodies. It wasn't much to slow you down, but when we sped through a string of over a million stars getting from point A to B, it made a difference.

I swung around the stars, folding and diving, twisting and turning, letting my wings raise me over them. The stars reached out to me like children begging for candy, wanting me to play, but I refused wholeheartedly. Vergil was still forcing through them with his impressive speed, bursting through each star like it was a wall of water. But even I could see that he could improve his acceleration by skipping them altogether.

We eventually hit the final descent, and Vergil was only a light year behind, probably in straits over how I could possibly be in the lead. Unfortunately, the descent was starless, and this would give him a great opportunity to pull ahead. I gave it all I had, screeching forward, straining for extra millimeters. I could see Vergil gaining, his wings folded behind him. And right before I touched the Throne Room door, his fingers beat me to it.

I collapsed in exhaustion, laughing beyond the strain over how close I was. Vergil was perfectly fine, but sat down with me regardless.

"That was close," he said. "I was wondering what you were doing dodging the stars."

"I decided that I wasn't going to beat an Archangel with raw power, so I improvised."

"But you didn't beat me."

"Yeah, but I sure was close. And sometimes that's enough. It's all I need to secure my victory next time."

"Why's that?" he asked, scowling profusely.

"Because you'll have a little bit of anxiety next time. You'll realize that you should never underestimate –"

"THAT WAS INCREDIBLE!" an angel behind us yelled. It startled me to the point that I shot up into the sky and hovered there, shaking. Vergil chuckled at my reaction. I looked down to see a Godhand standing by the Throne Room door, wearing a blue and gold robe with streaks of red flying across it. He was a lot smaller than Marcus but there was no doubt who he was due to the size of his biceps, ripping out of the robe like he was sporting a tank-top. He was jumping up and down with excitement, clapping his hands, shaking a little of the ground beneath his feet.

"I watched the whole thing from where I was. That was amazing, young ones!"

"Surely you've seen a race before," I said, lowering myself, but he was still overflowing with enthusiasm.

"Obviously, I don't get out much."

"What is your name?" Vergil asked him, rising to greet him properly.

"My name is Arthur, and this is my post."

"God has you in front of the Throne Room? Is it to announce His return or give passing angels messages?"

"No, nothing like that. You should know by now that we have received no orders from the Lord yet. No, I am here because Lucifer asked me to be. He desired that I stand here in God's absence and carry out my duty of praise and worship."

"You're a lot smaller than the Godhands I've seen," Vergil commented, inspecting Arthur's robe. Arthur chuckled to the point his clothing shook.

"Yes, well, there are many ways to channel the massive quantities of energy we spout around. I choose to sing with it, not fight. My angelic pressure never drops as a result, but there is a slight adverse affect on the size of my muscles."

He raised an arm into the air, showing his lean forearm.

"Needless to say, I refrain from combat."

"Is God here?" Vergil inquired. The Godhand shook his head.

"I'm afraid not. You can enter if you like, but it's just an empty hall. And you'll need a few more angels to open the doors. The doors are krillic, but they're also 3 light years in height. You'll need a couple angels to take the top, some to brace against the middle and so forth."

I believed him. The door looked like it reached through space itself. The stone cathedral, where our Lord was supposed to be found, extended about twelve miles wide, with extravagant red and gold banners and blue tapestries. Angular structures and marble pillars protruded upward from the building's face, resembling the structure of a pipe organ covered in crystalline gold. I would have appreciated the artwork more if not for Arthur staring at me like a puppy craving attention.

"How long have you been standing here?" I wondered, attempting to end his glossy-eyed gaze.

"A week…give or take a few days. But it's not a bad gig. Lucifer was here yesterday to give me a little bread and cheese. He was in awe of my dedication and thanked me for my hard work."

"Where is he now?" I asked. "I need to find him."

"He has a concert starting within the hour at the Symphony Hall. If you hurry, you can make the opening ceremonies. Look into your database, you'll find the directions."

"Thank you."

"Before we go," Vergil began, "I was wondering if maybe we could hear one of your hymns. You said you sing."

"Oh, I'm not that good."

"But if it's all you do, you can't be that bad."

"Well," Arthur sighed, rocking his head back and forth, weighing both decisions, "I am tired of singing at the moment, but I can grace you with a poem if you like."

"Sure. We would enjoy that."

"Ahem…His splendor is uncanny, beyond each galaxy.

His grace is universal, extended to you and me.

The absence of His presence is not a hinder to my praise.

For my thoughts dwell on my Father who did not leave without a raise...

Of a great angel, that carries His order with glee.

A universal grace and love, offered to me and thee.

His vocals are everlasting, as well as his place in God's land.

His might is unyielding and sound, he crushes heresy in his hand.

For all that love him, will never truly know,

Of the Archangel named Lucifer, who in God's will helps us grow."

"The ending needs –" I started to say, but Vergil began clapping manically, throwing off my suggestions for improvement. Arthur bowed as Vergil couldn't help but gush in admiration.

"That was beautiful, Arthur. It speaks so highly of God's grace and it enhances Lucifer's character with such imagery."

Were we listening to the same poem?

"Didn't you enjoy it, Lysander?" he asked me. I couldn't lie.

"It did talk about God," I said, searching for the right words.

"And Lucifer. Hearing that poem – I can't wait to see him again."

"Again?" I asked him. Had Vergil run into Lucifer before I met him at the brown dwarf star? What could they have possibly talked about? Why wouldn't he have mentioned this earlier?

"It was when I observed your team for the first time. Don't you recall?"

"Right. You were in the back."

"I saw how powerful he was. How easily he subdued you all...I have to see him again."

"Is that the only reason you're excited to meet him?"

"No, of course not. What really excites me is the fact that we're going to be a part of his number! Don't you get it? It doesn't matter if we never get a mission from God. In the end, we made it into the group that praises God like no other! Isn't that exciting?"

I got it all right, and I was getting more suspicious by the second. Arthur's poem was eerie, and though I couldn't articulate all that was wrong about it, that strangeness was undeniably there. He had mentioned God, but that was basically all there was to it. A simple shout-out, as if he had injected God into the poem because he was obligated to. The rest of it, the heart of the poem, was all about Lucifer and how great he was in Heaven. And I wasn't sure if that was proper, regardless of God's absence.

But Vergil...it was the first time I had seen him really excited about anything, and just like when Alessa had spoken on God's behalf, saying it was okay for Vergil to fight Marcus – I was plagued by an unnerving thought. A thought that could turn Vergil's only real friend in the group against him. I had no idea whether I should tell Cadence about my suspicion, but whether I did or not, the assumption would always remain until I was able to clear my thoughts.

Did Vergil...join our group, simply to be with Lucifer?

Did he decide to join our group specifically because we passed Lucifer's test? Was that the only reason he had held his peace, avoided confrontation, and kept silent throughout his time with us? So he wouldn't be kicked out? So we wouldn't request a change? So we wouldn't get to the point that we shunned him or told Lucifer he was not to be included in our victory? The truth of the matter was that he hadn't contributed to our win. Sure, he could have beaten Rufus with minimal effort, but would Lucifer had accepted our group if Vergil had interfered? There was no way of knowing if all my suspicions were true, and I did not dare accuse Vergil for fear of what it would do to his psyche - but every angel in Heaven would probably agree...that he was in a wonderful position.

I hoped it was paranoia - that Vergil had truly wanted to be with us because of our teamwork, our unity and infallible bond. That none of his desires stemmed from a secret greed he had to keep hidden until the right opportunity. This was Heaven – surely such things didn't exist.

But yet I could not stop myself, reaching out to the Throne Room door and placing a hand onto its exterior. Bowing my head, I prayed that God's will be done. If Vergil had been deceiving us all along, I prayed that it would be revealed, and finally, that God would protect us from the conflict I felt in my very being was going to occur. Please Lord, let us brace the storm. Give us shelter. Please Lord, keep us safe...

CHAPTER 9: Solo Ballad

Arthur turned down Vergil's eager invitation to leave his post and join us for the concert. He wanted to go, but stressed that when Lucifer gave you a directive, you listened and obeyed. I wondered why Lucifer had so much authority. Maybe Lucifer was a Glory and received orders directly from God? No...he was an Archangel. Did Archangels also receive orders directly from God? No, that couldn't be it either. Vergil was an Archangel, and he definitely wasn't in touch with God - he wouldn't be so lonely if he were. Unless the loneliness was an act...

"Ugh," I groaned, rubbing my forehead. There was just no time to think anymore. It was like someone was uploading large quantities of data into my head without giving me time to filter it. My reasoning was starting to get cloudy and Vergil wasn't helping. As soon as Arthur declined Vergil's offer, Vergil grabbed my wrist tightly and whisked me away toward the Symphony Hall.

But I was not prepared for whatever lay for me at Lucifer's concert. I had to talk to Cadence, if for nothing else but to alleviate my doubts. He would have the answers.

"Vergil," I said sheepishly, as if I were afraid he would discover my suspicions, "I'll meet you at the hall. I'm going to get the rest of the group to come with us."

"Why?" he asked. "I don't think they'll want to come."

"They will. We all passed Lucifer's test."

"You did. I didn't," he stated matter-of-factly as we flew. I wrenched my wrist from his grip and halted my flight, concerned that I had let him hold it for so long. Vergil frowned and turned back to confront me.

"What does that matter?" I asked him. "Even if you became a member right now, you would get in."

"What if I go to the hall and Lucifer asks who I am?"

"Tell him you're a part of the team."

"He's not going to believe me if none of you are there. I'll be a nobody to him."

"Then come with me to the Fellowship Hall first and we'll get the others. No one said you have to go alone."

Vergil's wings were twitching impatiently, his jaw clenched as he tried to keep his irritation from manifesting.

"You're right, Lysander. We have to stick together."

He followed me to the Fellowship Hall, deliberately going at a slow pace behind me in case I changed my mind. I could see Vergil constantly looking over his shoulder, wondering if we were going to miss the concert - if we would be able to get in once it began.

"Did you enjoy Arthur's poem?" Vergil asked, catching up to me in front of the entrance.

"Why do you ask?"

"You never gave a straight answer earlier, and you've been acting weird ever since he recited it."

"How so?"

"You're not as warm. It's like you've gotten cold and calculating again."

"Cold and calculating?" I laughed. "Since when has that been my personality?"

"It hasn't. So when you changed, I noticed right away. Is there something on your mind? Accusations you want to get off your chest?"

Vergil's aura was emitting a strange warm glow. On the exterior he was stone-faced and calm, but on the inside he was struggling to hide his smoldering.

"I don't want to talk about it."

"But you can with Cadence, right?"

"Vergil, where is this coming from?"

"You want to talk to Cadence."

"I do, but we have to get everyone-"

"You don't think I belong in your group."

"Vergil, I-"

"You think I should be excluded when Lucifer invites you in."

"No, that's not-"

"I'll be at Symphony Hall, Lysander," he stated flatly, his last words colder than the rest. "See you there."

"I thought you needed us to-"

But he was gone before I could speak and my head was spinning. Was Vergil so unstable and socially awkward that he could flip-flop emotionally without notice, or was he just playing into my emotions, making me feel worse for not personally connecting with him earlier – a guilt trip to secure his place in our number, and in Lucifer's company. I could have chased after him, but I decided to go with my gut instinct and talk to Cadence about it first. If Vergil really was that emotional, then I would have plenty of opportunities to mend his feelings. And if he had been tricking us all along, well, there would be time for dealing with that too.

Entering the Fellowship Hall, I fluttered next to the first angel I spotted and tapped his shoulder. He seemed to recognize me instantly.

"Hey! You're Lysander," he said, rushing to face me. His wings did a weird shudder when he turned and stayed half-closed as he flew, but I didn't think much of it. I was taken aback by all the fame coming my way.

"Yes. It's me," I said in a stupor. I had no clue how to react to his greeting.

"You're friends with Marcus, aren't you?"

"Yes! Do you know where he is?"

"Not here, I'm afraid. Though I have to tell you I've never seen an angel clear out a table like he can. I've seen Godhands eat before, and obviously their appetites are huge, but this guy? He's a bottomless pit."

"So he's not eating anymore?"

"Not by choice. His feeding frenzy was getting out of hand, so they called in Michael, one of the Archangels, to apprehend him. Michael just swooped in and whisked him away."

"Is he in trouble?"

"No, but I heard a couple angels saying he was needed for faith training. God's orders. Before he was taken, Marcus said he was staying at the Fellowship Hall because he was waiting for you and another Archangel to get back. Asked us to tell you what happened to him."

"But you recognized me as soon I came through the door. Did he tell you who I was?"

"No, but everyone in Heaven knows about the ragtag team of young ones who managed to pass Lucifer's test. I tried it once, but I failed miserably. You're a strong team."

"Everyone knows?"

"Everyone. It's been a long time since anyone's made it, so news spread fast."

"Oh...well, what about my other friends then? Do you-"

"-HEY! It's Lysander!" an angel called from across the room. The general murmuring was beginning to subside and eyes were becoming fixated on me.

"Shhh!" the angel I was talking to whispered. "John, calm down. I'm talking to the celebrity here."

"Sorry, Boris!" he yelled back. "Let me know when you're done!"

"I apologize for that," Boris said. "So what were you saying?"

"Do you know where my friends are, besides Marcus?"

"Farah, the little Faithful, decided to go with him because she thought it was hilarious he needed training in faith. Cadence and Alessa were taken by a Messenger. Supposedly, they were selected to be part of a team overseeing Earth's construction."

"Earth? Planet Earth? It's happening?"

The second most important place in an angel's mental database. It was finally becoming a reality...would this be our next destination? Our next home?

"I know!" Boris exclaimed, his eyes lit up. "It was nothing more than a possibility before, but now it's happening for real! Isn't that exciting?"

I scanned my database for clues as to what the future held for Vergil and "Team Six", but nothing came up. My database had basic facts and concepts about pretty much everything, even names and places that did not yet exist, but nothing regarding the intricate details of a person's or angel's life – an encyclopedia with missing volumes. In the premonition department, we were as clueless as the next, and only God could boast such ability.

"If Earth is being created, then human beings will be there at some point," I said excitedly, "and that must mean we're going to be given duties to perform soon!"

"That's the general consensus. Seems God heard our prayers after all. There was no reason to doubt."

"God's creating Earth right now?"

"Yes, that's what we were told."

"Then I'll have to go to Lucifer's concert alone."

"That's where you're headed? The concert?"

"Why? Is something wrong?"

"It's just...um." Boris was at a loss for words and I couldn't stay long. Vergil was waiting for me. I noticed that a few angels who had been noticeably eavesdropping on our conversation were starting to look a little queasy.

"What is it?"

"I hear things about Lucifer...I don't know if they're true, but there's a rumor that Lucifer is making a move against God."

"What kind of move? Last I heard, his company praises God greater than any of us."

"The details are hazy, but the Glory are saying that his concert is actually a rally for all of his followers. They say God doesn't want this to happen."

"Can't God stop it whenever He wants?"

"He's trying to keep a balance, and He doesn't want to interfere with our free will."

"This can't be true. Did anyone check out the concert? Confirm the rumor's legitimacy?"

"I trust my friend," he said, pointing over to a purple-haired, skinny angel. "He's a Glory, and he's spoken with God on a consistent basis. Those in Lucifer's camp would have you believe that He's nowhere to be found, but that can't be true if we have a number of angels in communication with Him at all times. If He had deserted us, the line would have been severed."

"Even so, we should check out Lucifer – get enough evidence before we jump to a conclusion that could hurt us collectively."

"Lysander, we're already divided. Look around you. The Fellowship Hall lost a fair amount of its visitors due to the concert."

"That doesn't prove Lucifer is about to commit treason. I need facts. I'm sorry, but if we're lacking sufficient information, we should give him the benefit of the doubt."

"Are you going there now?" he asked, concerned with the direction our conversation was heading.

"Vergil's waiting for me," I said. "I have to go."

"I'm serious, young one. Be careful. If we've heard of you, then so has Lucifer. He'll demand your allegiance."

"That was originally part of the plan, but I'll check it out for myself."

I left the Fellowship Hall unsure of my next step. Vergil was sure to be waiting for me at Symphony Hall. What could I possibly tell him about what I had just heard? That he had to put his feelings aside and attend the concert with an objective eye, because supposedly it was a secret movement driven to hurt, not praise God? And the only evidence I had was a sinking sensation in my spirit and statements from a third party? Vergil had been so bewitched by Arthur's poem, I doubted he would forget the concert altogether if I asked him to. He would go in, no matter what I had to say. And I couldn't just let Vergil go in without me, in case Lucifer did have a secret agenda - Vergil was so enthusiastic he would be easily indoctrinated without even realizing it.

The only course of action was to attend the concert, but I wouldn't have any back-up. It didn't matter if I had the most influence over Vergil. If he decided to tune me out, I wouldn't have Marcus or one of the others there to drag him out...

I could hear the ear-pounding noise coming from the concert the moment I stepped out of the Fellowship Hall, and this was just the opening ceremonies. Cheers and worship were being lifted up and I could hear various instruments being elegantly played, from the bold trumpet to the lovely, delicate harp. In the midst of the harmony, was a voice – a soothing, liquid voice that somehow reached inside of you, grabbed your soul, and pulled you toward it like a siren. It was uncomfortably beautiful, each resonant note and mesmerizing trill echoing off the heavens and ricocheting back to the Symphony Hall's amphitheater, creating a vacuum of music and praise. I now understood why those wary of Lucifer's power stayed inside the Fellowship Hall. His singing was strangely inviting, and the music spoke to me in a way words never could. Logic nourished the mind and emotion caressed the heart, but music? It fed the soul.

When I arrived at Symphony Hall, there were seven angels on the stairs leading to its entrance. I didn't see the point, since there was no domed ceiling to keep angels inside the building...or out. Besides the ringed wall that stood before me, there was no foreseeable ceiling. I could see angels hovering top to bottom from where I floated, all of them fully attentive to Lucifer. On a high mountain above the stadium floor, he stood, singing to the best of his ability, giving off his natural light like a beacon for all to see. From outside the hall he was invisible, for the round silver exterior was miles above the mountain on which he stood. But his Archangel light had the intensity of a small star and even from the street, you could discern a breath-taking preview of what you were missing. I would be a liar if I said it wasn't appealing to behold.

I tried to go over the entrance and right into the hall but one of the angels guarding the stairs, a Godhand, noticed me immediately and shot up from his post to block me.

"No trespassing without an invitation," he stated in a gruff, deep baritone, staring past me as he relayed the memorized message.

"I'm here to talk to Lucifer, and see about my friend, Vergil."

"So you must be Lysander."

"You've heard of me?"

"From your friend Vergil. He's down below with my squad. He attempted to break into the service. He was denied. After due belligerence, we inquired Lucifer personally about his ties to him, but the prince claims he has never heard of your friend and instructed him to return with your group, if he truly is a part of it. No escort. No entry."

"So, now that I'm here, will we be able to get in?"

"Lucifer has granted you access, and he's already given permission to Vergil to accompany you if you are indeed members of the same team, so yes, if you are willing."

"Thank you, I'll talk to Vergil. Let your squad know we're going in."

"Will do."

I descended to the stairs where two Godhands were watching over my friend, sitting on a step with his head in his palms, staring off into space. As soon as I landed, he strode my way angrily.

"What took you so long?" he roared.

"And what gives you the right to talk to me like that?" I replied, the words streaming out of my mouth. He toned down his attitude. The outburst had caught me off guard. Was Vergil wearing on my patience?

"Sorry," he said solemnly. "I'm angry because I was here at the very beginning and I wasn't allowed to go in."

"That Godhand filled me in, but don't worry, we can enter now."

"You still want to go?"

"Not really," I shrugged my shoulders. "I can hear the music fine from here and honestly, based on a few things I heard about Lucifer, I would rather keep my distance and investigate a little further...but I know how much this means to you."

"That's really nice of you, Lysander," he beamed, his wings bouncing in excitement and his angelic pressure releasing a dim glow like a night light. "You really look out for me."

"It's what friends and teammates do."

"Then let's go."

The Godhands in our way parted to let us through the front door and when we walked in, I grit my teeth from the flames of light that engulfed me. Lucifer was indeed powerful, and he wasn't ashamed to let it be known. He shined it boldly, caring little if those in its path were consumed and destroyed. This was the presence the angels now craved and lived for - a palpable presence whose true physical nature had never been seen because its power was too great to behold.

As we navigated through the crowd, it was hard at times to determine whether the angels near me were cheering or screaming. Some cried unashamedly, though I was unsure if it was because they had found their savior or if they were being slowly burned alive.

Vergil, being an Archangel, was able to withstand Lucifer's might, though he too had to squint his eyes. He placed a hand over his brow to block some of the rays and smiled with glee.

"This is great, isn't it?" he nearly cackled. I gave an embarrassing yelp as I attempted to open my eyes a little further. It was a big mistake. I shut my eyes immediately, wincing at the pain and clutching the temples of my forehead. My angelic pressure was actually beginning to lose energy just by being near Lucifer's uninhibited presence.

"It's okay," I said weakly. Vergil stepped in front of me and spread his wings to shield me from most of the pain. The sharp flares, shooting through the iridescent mix of Vergil's blue and purple wings cast an impressive opalescent spotlight over me. The black and green vines on its borders were a perfect screen, and this small reprieve was all I needed to make it to the end of the song. Thankfully, Lucifer's song did not have an extended version and the fire exploding from him died out. Now, only a humming aura glowed from his body, even lower in consistency than when we had first met him.

The crowd was now able to breathe, and they cheered to deafening proportions. Lucifer smiled like a politician - his long hair flowing in the breeze with each shake of his head. His flawless skin and his angular yet smooth face scanned the crowd for more and more praise and admiration. Vergil screamed like he never had before, lost in the glory of this angel who was of the same class as he. I couldn't bring myself to join them as they lost themselves, but I did clap, just to make sure I didn't stand out.

Unfortunately, Lucifer seemed to notice, and he stared down at me with a predator's eyes. The crowd began to search my general area, wondering what had graced his attention. And thank God Lucifer let them wonder, as he began to wave a hand in the air, drawing their focus, thanking them for coming and simultaneously signaling to them that it was his time to speak.

"Godhands," he began. "Glories, Faithful, Archangels and Messengers, Cherubim, Seraphim and Guards, lend me your ears. For I have something heavy to lay upon your hearts."

The congregation hushed as they hungrily waited for his words.

"This…is the beginning of change…in Heaven. I want you all to ask yourselves when was the last time you felt God's presence, felt His embrace the way you were just enraptured in mine? If the truth is too grim for your hearts to admit, I will bravely answer the question for you. The truth is, you've only been in His glory twice: once, when you were born, and once, when you came to Heaven…never again. Like a parent that loathed you from the day you were conceived - this is how He has treated you. You've been aborted. Thrown into the universe to survive all on your own, cold and desolate, unable to discern your path, unsure of your purpose and direction. Your search for guidance has instinctively led you to me because you discovered that I serve God like no other. Do not lie to yourselves. When I took you under my wings, you hoped, just by being with me – that someday you would get a chance to be in His presence once more. After all, I had a greater relationship with the Lord than all of you combined. By attaching yourselves to my hip, you lived vicariously through me and hoped that one day; we would praise ourselves to the point of blessing. That He would come to relieve us of our worship and allow us just a second more with Him, to bathe in His glory."

The crowd clapped and murmured in agreement.

"But let me tell you another harsh truth. I feel His embrace no more than you do. In my time here, I've devoted all my strength and energy into serving Him, and for what? Why should I continue to serve a God that is so cruel and cold, stoic and distant?"

Gasps rang throughout the stadium yet there were no cries of dissension. No one made a notion to challenge his speech of heresy.

"Why should we serve Him? I ask you this not out of selfishness. I ask you out of love and with a heavy heart. I've thought about this for a long time, and many days have passed where I've gone back and forth over what I'm telling you now - afraid of your reaction, afraid of your judgment, because I know how it sounds. But based upon the fact that you still hunger for my words, I know...I know that deep down you agree with me...that we have been simply wasting our time. So you may ask, what do we do now? What can we do that transcends mere words? What actions can we take that will rectify this problem? My fellow angels, I will tell you. We will rise together as one, and overthrow God Himself. We will go to the Throne Room where He has not dwelled for centuries, and I will take His place. I will become like Him and ascend to His throne. If I take over as God, I will be able to give you the warmth and presence that we've all craved. Do not think of the past. Look to our future. Listen to what your mind tells you. You know this makes sense. You know that if you wait for God, it could be an eternity before He returns. So what will you do? Will you take up arms and join me? I know you will be forced to fight against some of your fellow angels, but remember, they cannot die, and when they awake from their slumber, a new world will await them. And they will see that you were strong – the ones that fought for them and introduced a new age. They will thank you for your strength and your foresight. So join me now. Let us gird ourselves up and prove once and for all, that we matter!"

The response was nearly unanimous. Only Vergil and myself were silent, taking in what we had just heard. It was a surreal feeling, and I was suddenly afraid. Was this the conflict I had sensed all along? I needed to talk to someone, but my team was scattered. Maybe that Boris at the Fellowship Hall would have some answers.

"Vergil, are you ready to go?" I whispered to him. He nodded timidly as we tried to inconspicuously escape. Lucifer was beginning to speak again, but I didn't care what he had to say. His words had left me terrified and I couldn't stand to hear any more. Some good had come out of his speech, at least. Vergil hadn't joined in, despite showing a great interest in Lucifer's "club". It was good to see that he had sensed the poison in the Archangel's words. There was no way that overthrowing God was the answer to our wistfulness. Couldn't we get all the Glories together and collectively ask for His return? Why did we have to divide and fight each other? Why did we have to rise up against God?

"Where are you two going?" an angel asked me as I bumped past him, but I ignored him.

"You're not staying?" a Godhand grunted as we ducked under one of his raised arms. I refused to answer, determined to distract Lucifer as little as possible. But we failed. Before we made it out through the massive steel doors, I glanced back and noticed that Lucifer's glare was fixed on us, following our horribly-planned getaway.

No one chased us but we strained ourselves to get to the Fellowship Hall as fast as we could. The same angels were still there, talking quietly and waiting for the "concert" to end – for someone to fly in and deliver the rundown on what had happened. Food was left untouched on the tables and not one of the congregating areas was occupied. All the angels stayed in the air, hovering, too nervous to sit down. They needed an update on current events desperately, and, with my entry, they looked to me to provide one. Well...I was a Messenger after all.

The angels waited patiently for my breaking news, parting out of my way and letting me get to Boris.

"We need to talk," I said to him. The crowd closed in to soak up my report.

"What happened over there?" Boris asked, his face sunken in worry. "I see you found your friend."

"Lucifer's lost his mind," I said, exasperated. "He wants to overthrow God and take the throne." All the angels in the room started clamoring over each other to hear more. They began whispering and arguing over the validity of my pronouncement, but I was just reporting the facts.

"He says that because we haven't felt God in so long, it's necessary that he takes over. He'll become God in a sense and provide everyone with the warmth we desire. But that's crazy. All he's doing is causing division, right?"

"I guess all that combat training and sparring wasn't for nothing," Boris said solemnly, rubbing his fingers through his short, prickly hair. "How did the crowd take the speech?"

"We were the only two that left. Everyone else seemed to agree with him. It's painful to consider, but I think Lucifer has formed an army."

"So what is he going to do? Declare war, or try to surprise attack those that are against him?"

"Not sure, but if we're going to have a fighting chance, we should organize before he gives out any orders. A lot of angels have no clue of what's going on."

"Like your friends," Boris stated.

"What?"

"Your friends, they're clueless, right? They won't know what hit them."

"I'll go tell them."

"No you won't," Boris declared. Without warning, he opened up his wings completely and reached behind him. Attached to a harness on his back was a sword. A sword...in Heaven. Where he had retrieved it or how it had come into his possession was beyond me, but what my mind wondered the most, was...if someone could punch an angel into unconsciousness for a long period of time, what could a sword do?

"Where did you get that?" an angel from the crowd asked, but Boris didn't bother answering him.

"It doesn't matter," he said. "There are exactly eight hundred and twenty-two angels in this room. Each of you are unarmed and the best you have is an inexperienced Archangel. If I can defeat you all, which is possible seeing as how I am a Guard, then I will earn great favor with Lucifer."

"You can't be—"

Boris swung the sword at my head but Vergil blocked it at the last second with one of his bare arms. I flew back in shock as Vergil braced himself for a follow-up strike, but Boris wasn't dumb enough to fight the Archangel first. He vanished into the crowd, swinging with all his might at every angel that tried to swarm him. Surprisingly, he was winning. No one had a weapon to counter his blows and, one-by-one, angels fell to the stadium floor, unconscious for an indeterminate amount of time.

I was frozen.

What if I was struck, blacked out, and woke up to Lucifer's victory? What if I couldn't get the message to my friends before they were ambushed? What if I wasn't there to help, to contribute?

"Lysander, stay back," Vergil said. "I have to stop him."

"Don't hold back," I said, my throat closing up. "Let yourself shine."

Vergil disappeared from my sight and re-appeared by Boris's side. Grabbing the sword's blade with his bare left hand, Vergil punched Boris in the abdomen with his right. Boris shot away like a bullet, slamming into the far wall and half-slumping/half-crashing into a table of bananas below. He didn't get back up.

"Thank God we had you here," John, Boris's purple haired friend said. He was nursing his left arm which was twitching strangely. "Don't worry," he said. "I got nicked by the sword but it will get better. I didn't think Boris was one of Lucifer's supporters."

"There's a lot of deception going on," I admitted, "but we have to act fast. I'm going to go talk to Raphael. He's the only senior angel I know that is against Lucifer. He can get us organized. In the meantime, we have to spread the word and be careful. I don't know what Lucifer's group will do to gain favor for his cause."

"Lysander, he's awake," Vergil announced, lifting one of Boris's limp hands. "Do you want me to hit him harder?"

"No, let me talk to him."

I glided over to his lifeless body, keeping a wary eye on the other angels behind me.

"Where are my friends?" I asked him calmly.

"Do...do you really think they were invited to Earth's construction?" Boris chuckled. "That's ridiculous. I think God has it handled...what are they going to do? Make stupid suggestions?"

"And what about the faith training?"

"That doesn't even make sense," Boris laughed, his strength regenerating at an alarming rate. "How do you train someone in faith?"

"THEN WHERE ARE THEY?" I screamed, frantically grabbing his armor. I had thrown caution to the side, giving him an opening to take me down by getting so close to him. Vergil crept closer.

"I follow my orders and I move on. I have no clue of what happened to your friends. They were escorted by my comrades to secret locations. I'm not privy to the details."

"How many others were captured?" I demanded. He attempted to shrug but didn't make it all the way.

"A lot of threats to Lucifer's campaign. Unsure of the exact number."

"When is Lucifer going to attack?"

"I was waiting for his decree during the concert, remember? All his future plans are unknown."

Boris was just jumping on the bandwagon. He was a foot soldier given a few meaningless orders that would hardly affect the overall war. His most dangerous attack – on the angels in the Fellowship Hall, was an act of his own. Nothing more. He was useless…

"My friend here is going to knock you out now," I said to him softly, sensing his angelic pressure rising faster and faster. "But this is not out of maliciousness, it's out of necessity."

"Spare me," he sneered.

Vergil waited no longer. He took Boris's sword and plunged it into his chest. Boris went limp gently, as if he were drifting into a nap. Vergil held on to the sword for a second, and then pulled it out of the fallen angel, clutching it with fervor. Sadly, I realized that this wouldn't be the last time great force would have to be used against my fellow angels.

I had no words for the rest of them in the Fellowship Hall. My optimism was very low and I saw no sign of the situation getting better. God's angelic host was divided. My friends, scattered. Lucifer's army was intimidating and many of his soldiers were dispersed among us, ready to strike at our most vulnerable moments. I myself was unsure how we were going to succeed. But one thing I did know - we all needed to pray. Unlike Lucifer, I needed God in my life.

CHAPTER 10: As For Me and My House

Raphael's hall was vacant, which was no surprise. Angels rarely went out of their way to visit the angel with the dragon attitude, not to mention that his humble abode was far beyond the normal living complexes. I can't say I was excited to speak with him, but he was needed now more than ever, especially considering his rocky relationship with Lucifer.

Raphael wasn't outside his home, nor was he answering our greetings, even when we called from the entrance. I began to suspect the worst. My string of disappointments kept coming. As we flew toward the far end of the hall, I heard Vergil gasp and turned to look. Raphael was crumpled in a corner. His angelic pressure was barely above critical, and his limbs were twisted like a pretzel. Someone had been here...and recently.

Raphael had been thrown to the side quickly - that was obvious by the position he was lying in. Probably the culprit had been working on him, and ran off when he had heard our voices. This was the only viable explanation because I could see Raphael was still conscious. We rushed to his side and he slowly lifted his eyelids, looking at us with regret. His eyes burned with rage, and he looked intently at us, trying to convey some message, but his body was ragged and beaten – his spirit shimmering, fading in and out. Vergil clutched his sword tightly, unsure if his power combined with the weapon would be enough for whoever had done this to Raphael. Watching an Archangel cower didn't exactly help my nerves.

I started searching the room for a sword of my own.

"Lysander, I'm sorry for getting you involved in this," Vergil said. Besides the stretch of hallway by the entrance, a small corner space, and a couple locked doors, there was nothing useful in Raphael's building. I slammed my shoulder into one of the locked doors, but nothing happened. Vergil gave it a try right after, but the door remained intact. Raphael's secrets would remain secure for now.

"I got you into the concert," I said, giving the door one last try. "And in case you forgot, it was actually a good thing we were there. We were able to warn the angels in the Fellowship Hall and stop Boris from causing too much damage. It was a blessing in disguise."

"You can't deny that I put us in danger. If you hadn't gone looking for me, the group would still be together."

"We'll manage."

"How cute," an unsettling, chocolate voice echoed from the entrance. We turned to see a nightmare manifest before our eyes. Lucifer was standing there, his massive, angular, sharp wings taking up the entire archway – its tips lined with silver and its borders...laced with wide open eyes.

It was the first time the flames weren't there to shield his body. His long, fine, blazing red hair flowed from the crown of his head like water, rippling gently in an unfelt breeze. His irises matched his hair in color and intensity, and the light that hummed from his spirit magnified the beauty of the gems placed around his armor: diamonds cut into half-moons, dotted across his face and gauntlets. The green emeralds and beryls on his shoulders. The red gem, carbuncle, mixed with krillic and sardius to form his powerful armor. The white onyx that was found in abundance over his abdomen and legs. Pure gold, yellow topaz, maroon jasper and blue sapphire were littered across his back and sides, boasting a balanced display of great beauty, and disheartening power.

"I've come here to talk," he said calmly, all of his eyes lowering into half-slits. I fought against the ache in my spirit and the weakness in my knees, boldly stepping forward to call down the hall.

"What did you do to Raphael?"

"Nothing. Why, is he hurt?" he asked with false concern. Even as he glided toward us, inch by inch, I knew we were no match for him.

Maybe Vergil could manage a good strike or two, but I was seeing the end before me, and it was coming with such finesse.

"This won't take long," Lucifer said coolly. "We will discuss it like equals."

"Maybe we should talk to him," Vergil suggested.

"And what? Join him? Wait to get beaten like Raphael?"

"Lysander, we have to do something."

Lucifer reached behind him, unsheathing a sword hidden beneath his wings. A specially tailored, jagged sword made of diamond and sapphire. Vergil planted his feet into the floor, ready for the first move, when I saw four angels appear in the entrance behind Lucifer. Lucifer saw the look of surprise on my face and started to spin around, but Marcus quickly grabbed one of his eerie wings.

Yanking on it with all his might, Marcus swung Lucifer in a circle for a few seconds and then let go, hurtling him toward the entrance. Alessa, Cadence and Farah moved forward and all got a quick hit in as Lucifer soared past. A second before Lucifer sailed outside the building, Alessa pointed a finger at the left wall. A block of raw krillic material fired out and slammed into Lucifer's face, sending him backward to us – his body crumpling to the ground. Cadence picked up Lucifer's sword without hesitation and held it tight. Together again, we would do our best to end the insurgence once and for all.

"How did you know we'd be here?" I asked Cadence, whose gaze never left Lucifer.

"An angel named John told us at the Fellowship Hall. I knew something was wrong when I arrived at the 'Earth construction site' and there was nothing but space. On the return home, we encountered a Faithful who had received the same orders. Apparently someone wanted us separated, so we searched for the rest of you and found Marcus and Farah tied up with about thirty other angels by the archive building. Something about 'faith training'."

"Hey!" Farah piped up. "We were told that we had to use our faith to break out of the ropes! How were we supposed to know that it was a trick?"

"What are you doing getting faith training anyways?" I giggled as she fluttered up and gave me a little kick in the ribs.

"I was there for Marcus," she huffed. Marcus placed a big hand on the top of her head.

"More like...make fun of Marcus," he said and we all laughed because she couldn't deny it was true. It felt good to be reunited, and I was suddenly revived with new vigor and strength. No matter what lay ahead, we would face it head-on and without fear. Even Vergil was shaking hands with everyone and receiving pats on the back.

"What an interesting circus troupe," Lucifer chuckled in a haunting, echoing voice, climbing to his feet. "Very entertaining and capable of such unparalleled teamwork. It's too bad that at the end of the day, all they are, is how they portray themselves – a joke. Laughable. Hilarious. Comical. Not to be taken seriously...Clowns."

"Then how did these clowns defeat Rufus?" Alessa asked him. Lucifer's eyes smiled and his body began glowing intermittently.

"Easy. You were part of the plan. See, I needed heroes. Heroes designed to be crushed whenever I saw fit - to lower morale in God's army. I couldn't use any of my followers because it would take too long for them to build trust among Heaven's host. I couldn't use one of God's followers either – their reputations had already been established. No, I needed someone young and naïve to pass my test. Someone new and unknown, to get the easily distracted minds of our fellow angels focused on the latest trend. And you came right when I needed you."

"You're underestimating us just like Rufus did," I said. "He failed because of his pride."

"Rufus," Lucifer chuckled. "I used him because no one had passed the test in a long time. Usually it's proctored by some of my strongest lieutenants but curiously enough, the exam was given by a worthless Glory this time. Why is that? It's because I needed you to win, to be popular and held in regard when I began my war - a pillar that I would crush at the beginning - to eliminate any hope of a champion coming to save the day. Now clowns, I can laugh, because it seems the joke was on you all along."

Lucifer howled in laughter, closing his eyes and clutching his sides as the six of us glared at him in fury. It couldn't be true. He had to be lying. How could our incredible fight with Rufus have been a hoax? It was like all of our accomplishments had been shortchanged. Was any of our teamwork real? Our unity? Were we as worthless as Lucifer claimed? A joke?

"Don't listen to him," Cadence growled through grit teeth, holding back his own doubt. "He's lying. He's trying to make us lose faith in each other and God. We will face him solidified. All six of us as one."

"Really?" Lucifer chuckled. "Do you think I would waste my time fighting a group of young ones if you weren't a part of my master plan? Honestly, you give yourselves too much credit. What did Raphael teach you about pride?"

"Silence!" I yelled at him, and he smiled at my attempt to be authoritative.

"I have a war to run, and my army is awaiting orders, so I must make this quick. You understand."

With his final words in the air, Lucifer's body began shuttering, going so fast side to side that it looked like there were four Lucifers instead of one. Four confident faces, with each of them smiling wide and creepy. Team six was unprepared.

We had no time to plan. And there wasn't a thirty minute strategy-planning session either. Lucifer was on the warpath. As we began to get into formation, offense and defense in the front, tactical in the back – Lucifer flew forward at a blinding speed and knocked Marcus out with an unbelievable uppercut to his jaw. We didn't need to inspect him to know that he was instantly down for the count. With his afterimages gone now, we were able to see him, but we didn't have time to counter. Lucifer turned his attention to Alessa immediately and grabbed her by the throat, punching her midsection ferociously so that she was unable to muster up any prayers. Cadence flew to my side as both him and Vergil raised their respective swords in fear. Farah went to Alessa's defense and managed to dodge a swat of Lucifer's hand, but there was no telling how long she would last that close to him.

"What's the plan, Lysander? Quick!" Cadence said, exhausted already. I could feel Vergil trembling beside me. I tried not to panic, to come up with a brilliant countermeasure to Lucifer's attacks, but Cadence could see it all over my face. We were doomed.

"What's the plan? Hurry! Anything!" Cadence raised his voice as Farah succeeded in wrestling Alessa from Lucifer's grip, while dodging another life-altering blow. I instantly saw the reason why Lucifer had given up Alessa - she was obviously out cold.

"Okay, it's all I got," I said. "But it's a horrible plan."

"Don't care. What is it?"

"Vergil's the only one that can probably hurt him at this point, so Cadence, you go over and grab Lucifer while you take his hits. Then Vergil will go over and stab his sword through you...into Lucifer."

"That's a horrible plan!"

"I told you that!"

"There has to be something else we can do."

"I can try to distract, but-"

I couldn't finish my sentence. While we were talking, Lucifer had grabbed a hold of Farah and knocked her unconscious by taking his bare hands and clutching the sides of her head, squeezing until she was drained of all her energy. None of us saw him coming toward us.

He hit me first in the chest, and it was like nothing I had ever felt. It was like I was being picked up and swung by my arms in every direction. The vertigo was nauseating and I couldn't make sense of my surroundings. The next time I could make out who was who, I was on my stomach. My body shivered as my angelic pressure tried to recover from the shock of taking major damage. I wasn't going to be of much use.

But I found some satisfaction in seeing Vergil and Cadence implementing my plan. Cadence rushed forward and tried to joust Lucifer but he sidestepped it easily, slapping Cadence with his left wing, which made Cadence stop and wince. Lucifer wrenched the sword from Cadence's hand, darted behind him, and thrust it into his back, twisting the blade liberally for extra measure. Cadence cried out and fell immediately. Vergil swung at Lucifer's head and barely missed, quickly recovering to engage Lucifer in a blinding sparring match. The two Archangels clashed their swords together with ever increasing speed, testing the limits of their power.

I couldn't keep my vision straight. My body violently shuddered one more time, and without even realizing it, I blacked out. My eyes were still open, but my essence was no longer there...

I was awake. I was alive. Testing my internal senses, I could feel no aches or pains, no shuddering or twitching. It was like I had simply awoken from a long slumber. I was whole, with a hundred percent of my angelic pressure intact.
I stood up from the position I had blacked out in and assessed the situation. Lucifer was nowhere to be found. Yet all six of us were still in Raphael's building, and all of us were conscious. The only one who needed assistance was Cadence, who was struggling to get to his feet after taking the most damage out of all of us. Being a Guard, I hoped he would be in full health soon.

"I don't think we won that, guys," Alessa said, rubbing her head as we picked ourselves up.

"Why aren't we unconscious?" I asked.

"We were."

"No, I mean, why are we awake right now? I thought Lucifer would have knocked us out for a longer period of time."

"Let's wait until we get outside and see if anything's changed before we start counting our blessings," Cadence said.

"It's because of me," Vergil lamented. He was sitting on the floor, slumped over, with his hands at his sides and his legs flopped to each side.

"What do you mean?" Alessa groaned. "Trust us, we all got beat."

"I was the only one that didn't go unconscious," he said. "After you all blacked out, Lucifer and I clashed and he said that he only came here to explain himself. He didn't mean what he said about us being clowns. He was just getting angry because we wouldn't listen to reason. He understands why though – thinking that he had knocked out Raphael and all."

"Wow," Marcus said as he walked away from Vergil. I could understand why Marcus was furious. Having a warrior spirit, he couldn't fathom the idea of talking it out with the enemy after watching his teammates fall, but we couldn't lose Vergil now. We had to hear the rest.

"Then what happened?" I asked him, letting him continue.

"He told me that we could still be in his group, even if our side of the war loses. Isn't that good news?"

"Vergil," Cadence said calmly, stooping down and placing a hand on his shoulder, "I'm sorry, but you were fooled. Lucifer tricked you into letting him go because you're also an Archangel. It may sound unlikely, but you probably had a chance of defeating him – here and now. As for us 'thinking' Lucifer knocked out Raphael, it doesn't matter. Lucifer is turning against God - that's enough to engage him in combat."

"What do you mean we're still in his group if our side loses?" Alessa said in disgust. "That's what I want to hear more about."

"He said that we are young," Vergil recited carefully, "and that we don't always see the right path. We are easily confused and stick to what we're familiar with rather than use our logic. He said that if our side lost, we could still join him without consequence."

"It sounds like he said a lot," Alessa said, "and you listened. What makes you think we want to be on his side, period? Why would we plan for a future in which we lose?"

"I saved you," he said sheepishly. That did nothing to alleviate Alessa's anger.

"You saved me? No, you mean you saved us, right? Or are you so powerful, you would've been fine no matter the outcome?"

"Alessa, that's enough," Cadence ordered. "This is what Lucifer wants, for us to be divided."

"Because being united did us a lot of good," she sulked, and walked off to fume alone near the far wall.

"We're furious, I get it," Cadence said in his best deep voice, "but this doesn't solve anything. There are angels out there that need our help right now. We need to get out there and work together, if not for ourselves, then for them."

"Let's go," I said, walking toward the entrance, ready for a distraction. I couldn't face the fact that I had accomplished nothing in the battle against Lucifer.

"How are we going to fight against Lucifer when Vergil over here might make a deal with him again?" Alessa demanded.

"We trust him," Cadence said. I heard the trembling in his voice. It said - what other choice do we have? But I still trusted Vergil. The others hadn't been there when he had saved my life from Boris in the

Fellowship Hall. In my opinion, Vergil might need more guidance in the "whom to trust department," but he was still part of the team.

"I can vouch for him," I said. "He saved my life earlier when he didn't have to. And another thing – it doesn't matter if he let Lucifer go. If Vergil hadn't been here, we would have been left entirely at Lucifer's mercy."

My words seemed to register with the group and even Alessa quieted down.

"So where to now?" Cadence asked.

"The Throne Room," I said. "If Lucifer's won the war already, he'll be there. Either way, we should stop by to check it out, and if he's not there yet, we follow the noise."

Cadence nodded and waved a "move out" gesture into the air as the group took flight, leaving Vergil behind to sulk on the floor. I stayed back to help him to his feet.

"Vergil, don't dwell on your decision too much. It's done."

"But I could have ended the war right then and there. Wouldn't that have been better?"

"If we only concentrate on the past we will never live in the present."

Vergil grabbed my hand and I lifted him up. Together we caught up with the others and headed to Heaven's core. The trip was quiet, but at least no one had any harsh words to say to Vergil.

I was debating whether we should change course. War was being waged in the distance – the sound of swords clashing rang between the buildings and flashes of light twinkled amongst the stars, showing where pockets of angels met and fought for dominance. We stayed low to the ground, went past the angels' homes and the city where no battles were being waged and moved as fast as we could until the Throne Room was in sight.

The place was deserted. Not even Arthur was there to sing us a ballad of the day's events, though I'm sure it would have been pro-Lucifer. Still, it was strange to desert God's throne altogether, not leaving even one angel to hold down the fort for either side.

"Let's try opening it," Farah suggested. "Maybe God's in there."

"If He were inside, He would have come out," Cadence replied, putting both hands on the doors, feeling how sturdy and heavy they were.

"Have a little faith."

"Do you want to open it?"

"I think I will."

"You're wasting your time," a Guard offered from a couple feet away. He had been sitting on the front stairs, so stoic that we had written him off as a statue. Now he sprang to life, lurching forward with an imposing emanation. I thanked God he had no sword in hand.

"We mean no trouble," Cadence said, but the Guard maintained his course.

"Peace is in short order today, friend," the Guard said, relaxed, drawing out his words. "My name is Iron. A fit name for a classification such as mine."

"It is a pity I can't say the same," Cadence said, amused. "Anyways, we were just leaving. Could one hope for a friendly pass to the battlefield, or will we have to fight you before you let us go?"

"I'm afraid that would be a negligence of my duty if I turned a blind eye. Lucifer's given me specific orders to apprehend all those who come to the Throne Room, whether their stay is permanent or temporary."

"You must be strong, for you to be the only one here."

"I'm not that strong, but my defense is second to none. I'll have you know that Lucifer and I spar for hours every day. Well, except for today of course."

"We're going to leave. It will be difficult to stop us without a weapon."

"I promise you, friend, that I need none. Now, there's no reason to be dramatic," he said, walking back to sit on the steps. "Why don't we sit down and have a nice long chat here on these steps, wait out the war and see how it all ends."

"We can't do that," Cadence said firmly. Iron stopped himself before he sat down. He sighed and placed both hands on his hips.

"...or we can choose the hard option. It's up to you."

"It's sad that you're such friends with Lucifer. I actually like you," Cadence laughed. "You have my kind of style." Iron slightly bowed as Cadence lunged forward without warning, hitting Iron square in the nose. Iron smirked behind the knuckle and chuckled from deep within his belly.

"You know, Cadence. I know you and your friends quite well," he said as Cadence lowered his arms. "I heard of you before you even stepped out of Raphael's hall from Lucifer himself. Wonder why?"

Cadence stepped back as Marcus cracked his knuckles. He was getting ready for his turn to bat.

"I was supposed to be your proctor that day," Iron replied.

We suddenly understood why only one of Lucifer's angels guarded the Throne Room.

"You're one of his lieutenants," Cadence said as Iron bowed again.

"One and the same. I'm not the violent type. Don't really care for this war as it is, but it's the only way we can give the family what they want. If it means anything, I'd rather not fight you, but...orders come before preference."

"Let me," Marcus growled, but Cadence stopped him with a hand on his chest.

"Don't bother, Marcus," he said. "We need your raw power for when we join the rest. No point in wasting it on a defense of his caliber. Alessa, get over here."

"Yes?" Alessa asked, surprised we had willingly made her the center of attention.

"All we want is to be able to move on, but as long as this Guard is here, he won't let us. So, can you do me a favor and ask God to take out Iron for us?"

"Why can't I do it?" Vergil asked, but Cadence gave him a sly smirk.

"You save your energy too. Let's see what God can do."

"I'm liking where Cadence is going with this," Farah remarked, bobbing her head up and down like she was grooving to some music.

I chuckled as I played the odds mentally. God was definitely somewhere. There was no debate about it - we had already established this on the island. Which meant He would hear Alessa's prayer. If God decided that we were needed on the battlefield in any capacity, Iron would be taken out, especially if we needed to conserve our energy. I had little doubt that we could defeat Iron, but it would take more energy than we were willing to put out. Alessa's prayers were a great option, especially since this wasn't a test. We didn't want to fight Iron. Not because we were afraid, but because we still felt that brotherly bond with him. So many angels on Lucifer's side had gotten cold and reckless, but Iron, had a heart, and he wore it right on his sleeve. Why he followed Lucifer and stuck to his orders so rigidly, I couldn't figure out.

"It would be my pleasure," Alessa said as she closed her eyes and began praying silently. Iron scoffed but stayed where he was.

"I don't think that's going to work, if you don't mind my saying so. I've fought many a Glory in my day. Haven't been beaten by one yet.

Not saying God don't answer prayers – He just been a little picky lately."

"Yes, I'm sure that's true," Cadence smiled, "but it's still not up to either of us what happens here. You and your friend Lucifer forget that God is still in control of the show, no matter how much He stays behind the scenes."

"So what happens now? We wait until God shows up?"

"No, it seems like He already has."

"Thank you, God," Alessa said out loud, eyes wide open, smiling Iron's way.

"I don't follow, frien-"

Iron was cut off as a literal house came out of the sky and smashed into him with the force of a comet. The debris and rubble whizzed past us with the force of a hurricane, but not one piece touched us. As the residue of Iron's demise subsided, we looked above and saw about seven hundred angels flying toward the distant battle. One of them came down and greeted us, making sure we hadn't been hurt.

He was a big, burly angel with no hair on the top of his head, but growing in abundance on the bottom half of his face. His colossal red armor signified he could only be one thing.

"Sorry about that," the angel said. "Thought you could use some help. I recognized that Iron guy from Lucifer's troop."

"Thank you. We did need a hand," Farah replied.

"How about God's?" he guffawed, placing a hand on his large paunch. "WHEW! Sorry about that, it gets me every time. You know, cuz I'm a Godhand and all. God's...hand. Ha ha! So, ya'll headed to the battle?"

"On our way. Mind if we join you?" Cadence asked, extending a hand. The Godhand shook it in excitement.

"No problem. Name's Amos."

"Cadence. We'll fight anywhere you need us."

"Cadence, huh? Well, Mr. Celebrity, just make yourself useful. I haven't gotten there yet, but I hear our side isn't doing so well. Not worried though. I'm sure God will make an appearance soon."

"Thank you for taking us in."

"Sure! It's just good to find some more folk who are determined to hold till the end."

We quickly joined the squad of angels, silently waiting for our flight to be over so we could join the others in war. It was a scary notion, and even we were unsure of the outcome. So far, we had gotten by, but there was no telling what would happen if we were forced to face an angel like Iron on our own. What if God had not answered our prayer?

"I'm not saying I didn't have faith or thought I wouldn't be answered," Alessa said, breaking my concentration. "I was just wondering...what's the plan for when we get to Lucifer next time? I don't think he'll be as forgiving the second time around."

"We have an agreement," Vergil said. "No harm will come to us."

How could I to respond to that statement? Sure, maybe Lucifer had said that, but he had lied before and I couldn't bank my future upon a what-if. It was a miracle in and of itself that he had only knocked us unconscious for a short time.

"Well, I for one am glad God helped us out with Iron," I said. "He was just a Guard but he had the potential to take out our whole team! I mean, just think, what if we have to face a Godhand next time?"

"Hey!" Cadence interjected.

"He speaks truth," Marcus replied swiftly. "Godhand scarier. Truth hurts."

"So what's been happening so far? I hear we're losing," Cadence yelled to one of the Faithfuls nearby, changing the subject. The angel winced at the question.

"From what I heard, we're down nine hundred angels," the angel yelled back over the speed of our wings, "with three hundred at critical levels. We outnumber them, but we were really scattered when Lucifer took us by surprise. It's hurt us pretty bad. We're trying to launch a counterattack but Lucifer's been elusive. We believe he's camped out somewhere in the plains to the north. All we have to do is get there."

"Is it an all-out battle? Or are there pockets where this is occurring?"

"One big battle royale for the most part. It started in the field in front of Symphony Hall but it's spilled over into the city. Of course, the city can't be harmed due to its metamorphic composition, but it's still been laid in chunks all over the place. No one's bothering to fix it yet but that's alright. We need all the energy we can muster for the war. I tell you, it's worse than we could have ever imagined."

"Any sign of God in all this?"

"Besides Glories making contact, there's no sign of Him being here or even planning on coming. He's remaining mum on some of the more intrusive questions."

"Thanks for the update."

"I just hope we can make a difference at some point."

"We will. We will."

As soon as Cadence said the last "will," something rocketed past our formation and slammed into Farah. Whatever it was took her with it and she screamed in more rage than fear as it carried her down to the rubbled city below…

CHAPTER 11: Battle Stations

The last thing we could make out of Farah's departure was her gaze of determination. Whether we helped her or not, she was ready for battle. I looked back at Cadence, his face scrunched up in worry. My eyes asked the question for me, and he nodded in reply. We both knew that I had been the closest in proximity to her when she had been attacked, and we didn't have time for all of us to go down and save every angel that was separated from the group. I knew what Cadence was thinking. The only way we were going to overwhelm Lucifer now was to beat him with our numbers. Vergil's power, Marcus's strength, Cadence's endurance, and even Alessa's prayers...they were needed. I would go to save Farah - the rest would continue ahead.

I broke from the group as Alessa cried out for me to save Farah. I felt my throat tighten, but I pursued. I didn't know what had hit Farah, and I was tired of the little fighting I had already done. The most I'd ever done was in that spar against Raphael, but ultimately, that wasn't even legitimate. And in the fight against Lucifer I had only gotten sucker-punched. Hardly a "W" in my stat card.

"Farah? Farah?!" I called out to her. I stood on the once soft and velvety flooring that adorned Heaven's streets - it was tangled and ripped now. Chunks from broken buildings littered the streets. Craters were everywhere like they were common potholes in a major Earth city and I could barely make out what section I was in. I thought I was near the second Fellowship Hall - but I wasn't sure.

Finally I saw Farah nearby in one of the craters, lying on her back and groaning unashamedly. I ran over to her and tried to pick her up but she pushed me away with one of her tiny hands and darted upward until she was face-level with me.

"What are you doing?" she snapped. "Why did you break from the group?"

"I came to help you."

"I don't need it. No offense, Lysander. But I have God. That's all I need."

"I'm still your teammate, and besides, I'm already here."

"Okay, but stay back and let me handle it for now. If you see me getting too hurt, then I'll let you know when you can jump in. Just be ready."

"That's not a very economical plan. I would suggest-"

"Just be ready!!!" she squeaked.

"Geez, you're starting to sound like Alessa."

"Sorry," she said quietly. "I'm just mad I got hit. I saw her coming toward me but...I just didn't move."

"Don't get reckless because your pride is hurt. Let me help."

"Lysander, just trust me, okay?"

"Fine...so you saw what it was? It looked to me like a small meteor hit you."

"It was a Guard - using the same tactic Cadence implemented on Marcus back at his house. She used her shield for extra strength to weigh me down."

"Where is he now?"

"She is right there, up ahead, coming our way now."

Indeed she was, and she was huge, especially for a Guard. Bigger than Cadence. She had a mean countenance with dark, almond eyes that stared directly into us. She clutched her shield, which was half the size of her body, wound it back and hurled it at us. Or more like at me. And I was too paralyzed by the object screeching toward my forehead to move. I screamed in shock as Farah reacted on my behalf, breaking through the shield and shattering it into pieces - her whole body behind one pint-sized, but very dangerous, punch. I heaved in relief and Farah grabbed the collar of my breastplate armor.

"Stay alert, Lysander. We're in the war now. From here on out, our enemy will try to end us."

"Right. Right," I said, still shaken by the attempted decapitation. "Thank you."

Farah shot up into the air with her hummingbird shuffle and hesitated before she charged at the Guard. The Guard picked up a large boulder from the ground, a former piece of a building, and manifested it into a shield. She was able to block Farah's next punch with it, and this time, the shield didn't break. Farah didn't let that phase her though, as she did a backflip in the air and went for the Guard's legs. The Guard blocked that with the shield too and then slammed it into the back of Farah's neck. Farah plopped onto her belly and shuffled back just in time for the Guard's shield to miss a fatal blow to the head. Farah backflipped to her feet and went back into the air, stretching out her neck as she searched for a boulder of her own.

She eventually saw one she liked and picked it up from the soft floor, hurling it at the Guard, manifesting it into a javelin at the last second. The javelin went through the shield but didn't harm the Guard at all, who kept the shield at bay during the impact. She hurled the shield, javelin and all, back at Farah who easily dodged it. The Guard sprinted to a fallen building and started hurling boulder after boulder at Farah, shape-shifting them into shields one after the other. Farah dodged them without even trying, but she eventually lost focus, and failed to see the Guard fly behind one of the larger shields. Just as Farah dodged the first of the last three shields thrown, the Guard appeared behind her and grabbed her tiny body, stretching Farah's arms behind her, making her painfully open for the last two shields. They slammed into her abdomen with full momentum, and she screamed horribly in reaction.

Watching from below, I could tell that Farah's angelic pressure was decreasing rapidly. And it didn't help when the Guard grabbed Farah by the head and chucked her into the krillic rubble below like she was a baseball. The Guard returned to the ground, but she still had a lot of energy left - she was laughing now, throwing boulders onto the pile Farah was under, just for fun.

That was too much for me. I flew forward as fast as I could to stop the Guard but she saw me coming. As soon as I was within striking distance, she hurled another shield my way, which caught me straight in the chest. I fell over into an embarrassing tumble and the Guard cackled at my attempt.

But her bullying was not rewarded as Farah burst from the pile. I thought she was going to attempt a tiny barrage with her miniature fists, but she refrained. She didn't even bother flying. Striding on the ground toward the Guard, she walked forward like she was going to win it all in one punch, but when she got to the Guard's feet, she collapsed and went down to one knee.

The Guard didn't show any mercy, hitting her over and over again in the head as Farah remained motionless. It went on for too long, but I couldn't move. It was like something was pinning me down, not allowing me to help her.

The Guard was growing impatient now, finding it impossible for Farah to be taking so many hits without going down. She got so fed up, she gathered up most of her angelic pressure, grabbed Farah's throat, lifted her up, and slammed her charged-up fist into Farah's baby face. Farah didn't make a sound. Instead, she reached forward with both hands and grabbed the Guard's wrist like she was picking up a sandwich. She squeezed lightly but the Guard shrieked in agony, letting Farah go free. Farah casually went over to the Guard, who was now on both knees and clutching her wrist like she was holding her last drop of life. Farah wiped the hair from her face, put her right wing and fist back, and then delivered both to the Guard. I didn't even have to look to know that the Guard was unquestionably out. Farah dusted herself off and walked over to me, offering me a hand.

I chuckled and took it. She had to fly and use her whole body to pull me to a standing position.

"What happened?" I asked her. She smiled warmly at me.

"God intervened, Lysander. I was losing but I knew He would give me the victory. Eventually it got to the point that when I was in the rubble, I asked God to take away the force of her blows and I had faith that my prayers would be heard. Which it did! Now, I have a question for you. When I was under the rubble, were you too scared to help me out or did God hold you back?"

"God held me back," I said, thinking of the force that had held me down. Her eyes smiled.

"Of course He did, because you wouldn't let little defenseless me handle it alone, would you?"

"I wouldn't be a very good friend if I did."

"True. Now, let's get back to the others. I'm sure they're in battle by now."

"Do you ever waver in faith?" I asked her as we flew as fast we could. Farah cast her eyes down for a second and then stared straight ahead.

"I'm not strong like Marcus. I don't have defense like Cadence. Even with your abilities, you still have basic fighting skills. Without faith, I can barely change a building with my thoughts. My faith literally keeps me breathing, Lysander. I start doubting? I begin going unconscious. I find my vision fading and my body growing weaker. And yet, I wouldn't trade my classification for anyone else's, because though God may never talk to me directly, He's right here with me, lifting me up, pushing me forward. I can feel His presence constantly – like a heartbeat. It's faint, but it never fades. And that, keeps me resolute."

"Do you think we'll win this war?"

"Yes," she said confidently.

"How do you know?"

"Because," she turned toward me, smiling with her eyes, "if we could lose, He wouldn't be God."

We didn't see the others at first, and for this I was glad. There was a massacre before us. We were too late to be at the frontline so we were forced to see the aftermath. Angels were lying dormant all over as we got closer to Lucifer's main army. The condition of the boroughs were increasingly worse, and the sounds of agony kept getting louder. Lucifer had made sure to recruit as many Godhands, Archangels and Glories as he could, focusing on strength, power, and a strategy of limiting God's involvement in helping the other side. Based upon the decreasing numbers on our side, it could have been said that he planned his war tactics wisely, but not so. His pride would be his undoing.

God had created each of us to be parts of a whole, complementing one another, and Lucifer had neglected this part of the equation. The Messengers were tactical, but Lucifer thought he had the war all figured out, so he determined that he didn't need them. The Faithful could bring distinctive, game-changing elements to the table, and the Guards could protect themselves and their comrades. In his thirst for chaos, Lucifer had forgotten the importance of order and balance. He couldn't win. Not while the rest of us were still able to move.

And it didn't matter if the situation looked abysmal. Who cared if there were millions of angels strewn around Heaven's floor, indisposed for an interminable amount of time? God would come through in the end. My conversation with Farah had given me new courage and I was eager to test it in my next encounter. Farah may have been a Faithful, meaning that her faith ensured her battles were constantly guided by God's hand, but that didn't mean that He loved me any less. Surely what He did for her, He could do for me.

We finally saw the group, but Vergil was nowhere to be found. I couldn't bring myself to dwell on why - I had to help them. Even from a distance I could tell that Alessa was badly hurt, stooped over on one knee and clutching the back of her head with her right hand. Apparently the team had been facing two Godhands. One of them had been taken care of but Cadence and Marcus were busy focusing on the second. It was obvious that they were weary from their first fight and it was debatable whether they would win their second. Cadence's shield was gone, and he was currently taking hits from the Godhand, covering his face and abdomen to the best of his ability, giving Marcus precious time to recover some of his energy. He would need it. The second Godhand's angelic pressure was still very strong - they had not done much damage. It was a losing battle.

"What should we do, Lysander?" Farah asked me. I was taken aback by her words. Why was she asking me for help?

"Why don't you do the same thing you did with the Guard?"

"Faith doesn't work like that. It doesn't rely on past experiences and things you can see. It's pure belief. Doing the exact same thing, just because it helped once, doesn't necessarily mean it will work again."

"Or are you just losing faith?" I asked her. She laughed lightly and grew silent for a moment.

"Well, I've never faced a Godhand before."

"Neither of us have, but it looks like they have one under their belt already. We should get down there and help with the second."

We hurled toward them just as Cadence fell to the side in a slump, having finally taken too many blows. Marcus's eyes lit up in a blaze and with every ounce of power he could muster, he slammed a fist into the Godhand's chest. The Godhand stumbled back a little bit, but Marcus, despite having only minimal power, kept coming. He wailed on his opponent like he was turning grapes into juice, and with one last, weak heave and a push, the Godhand toppled over and didn't get back up. Cadence began laughing hysterically as Marcus lifted him up. They gave each other high-fives and hugged Alessa, almost a little too tightly. Together, they had taken down not one, but two Godhands. Not a feat to sniffle at. With Cadence letting the second Godhand waste energy, Marcus was able to finish him for good.

But even I knew they probably couldn't survive another encounter. Alessa couldn't even speak, she was so weak, and Marcus and Cadence were barely able to stand, smiling through their significantly depleted energies.

"That was intense," I said to Farah as we slowed our speed. The battle was over, so there was no need to hurry.

"I wish I had gotten the chance to fight a Godhand," she said, envying the others' victory.

"You've never fought with Marcus, even for fun?"

"No, he loves me too much to spar with me. He refuses whenever I ask."

"He sure didn't care about that when you beat him in the arm wrestling competition."

"That's because he thinks I cheated."

"Oh, I get it," I said. Cadence waved us over. Farah and I landed and stared in awe at the two defeated Godhands, lying in an Olympic pool-sized crater.

"You guys okay?" Farah asked. Cadence nodded weakly.

"Glad to see you survived," Cadence said. "In case you're wondering, Vergil went on ahead. We figured he was needed more on the frontline."

"So you don't care if he gets more credit?" I asked him slyly.

"Don't care," Marcus said, and Cadence nodded in agreement.

"After what we just accomplished, he can have the glory. I'm just happy we contributed. I knew Lucifer was wrong about us."

Right at the end of Cadence's speech, something the size of a boulder crashed into him, sinking him deep into Heaven's floor. We all flew back in shock as we realized that it was not a piece of rubble from one of the buildings, but another Godhand, and he was bigger than either of the previous two. Cadence was finished.

Marcus stepped back, eyes wide in both anger and fear. No matter how much bravado he might try to show, we all knew, including the Godhand himself, that he had no energy left. He needed time to replenish his angelic pressure - and that was where we would come in.

Farah didn't play around. Zipping past us like a dragonfly, she immediately punched the Godhand in the face. He fell over like a falling tree and timbered to the ground, simultaneously giving Farah her first Godhand victory. Our jaws all dropped in unison. Farah rubbed her fist vigorously and we went over to help Cadence - but we had no time to assist him. This was war, and Lucifer's angels were taking advantage of any weak angel they saw.

Farah was a victim of this, as yet another Godhand decided to drop in, seeing her weakened angelic pressure and small frame. Farah wasn't afraid and met the intruder head-on, but like she had stated earlier, faith didn't mean a situation would always play out the same way.

The Godhand caught Farah in mid-flight and threw her into the ground, proceeding to stomp her into a crater, kicking up rubble all around her. I flew to stop him, but Marcus beat me to it. Giving it his last, he hit the unaware Godhand in the throat and followed with an uppercut to the jaw. The Godhand was knocked unconscious instantly but Marcus fainted on impact and I barely managed to catch him. He glanced at me, smiling for the first time, and then went unconscious. Using a substantial amount of energy, I half-dragged, half-carried him with me to inspect Farah who I found curled up in a fetal position, still in the crater. She had given her very heart and soul in the fight.

As I thought about Cadence and Alessa, who were awake, but paralyzed - I felt a rushing wind go past me. When I looked up to follow the breeze's trail, I saw Vergil, standing on the other side of the crater. He still held a sword in his hand, and his armor and angelic pressure were unscathed. I could only imagine how many of Lucifer's angels he had "slain."

"Vergil," I whispered and he looked at me, a concerned look on his face. "What's going on at the frontline? Are we winning?"

"No, not yet," he said, inspecting Farah, running a finger down a crack in her weak armor. His demeanor was noticeably serious, and his stance was rigid. He had seen more war than we had and it was beginning to take its toll. He was turning from an uncertain Archangel into a formidable, battle-hardened warrior. His face was stoic and void of emotion.

"Vergil, are you okay?"

"I'm sorry I wasn't here for the group. I sensed Cadence and Marcus losing against the Godhand so I rushed back as fast as I could, but there were too many of Lucifer's army in the way and I got sidetracked. This war…it's too brutal, Lysander. Any time one of Lucifer's angels takes one of us down, any time we decide to show a bit of mercy - they take full advantage, hurting us long after we've blacked out. There are some angels who will be out of commission for millennia…But I did meet up with Michael, the leader of our army. He's also an Archangel. And he says that once we stop Lucifer, it will all be over, so we've slowly been making a path to him. All we need to do is break through."

"How long will it take?"

"No telling, but I haven't lost an ounce of angelic pressure. I intend to exhaust myself completely, trying to end this once and for all. I'm going to drill through the last of Lucifer's protection and strike him down."

"I'll go with you," I said. "I'm still fresh. I can help."

"Lysander, I don't know what we will face up there. There could be a line of Archangels guarding Lucifer."

"Then I can distract them," I said firmly. "I'm not useless. All I'm asking is that you show me the same trust I showed you."

Vergil smiled from a corner of his mouth.

"Okay, Lysander, I'll be honored to have you by my side."

"I'll come too," Cadence groaned, coming alive. I rushed to his side and saw his armor flicker disturbingly.

"You're hurt," I said. "It's best if you stay back."

"I know you're not going to force me to stay here after that speech you just gave. I can also be a distraction."

"It's dangerous."

"If we don't give every ounce of energy we have now, we may never get another chance. This is it, Lysander. There are no second chances."

"He comes too," Vergil decided and I didn't bother arguing. I helped Cadence to his feet.

"Can you fly?" I asked him.

"Can you stop worrying?" he asked me, chuckling as he pushed me away lightly.

"Not to sound offensive," Vergil began, "but I'm going to be flying at full speed, plowing through angels as I go. I don't plan on stopping, no matter what happens."

"We wouldn't have it any other way," Cadence said.

"Alessa, are you okay watching Marcus and Farah?" Vergil asked her. "I can see you're hurt but they definitely can't defend themselves."

"I will pray to God for their protection," she said weakly, "and for yours."

Vergil gave one last grin and took off, light years away before we even realized he had left. Cadence and I lifted off like rockets to follow him. We couldn't catch up to him, but we stayed true to the path he laid before us – fallen angels dropping out of the air like a jet stream, some still awake but stuck in a gyrating spin from the level of force Vergil had exerted upon them.

Somehow, one of them managed to grab Cadence's leg as we sped along, pulling him far behind. I slowed my speed to help but Cadence already knew what I was doing.

"GO ON!" he screamed as the Glory dragged him down below. "BE A VOICE OF REASON!"

I swallowed my instinct and went after Vergil, determined to catch up. Past the city and the broken homes was the first ring of Heaven – the mountains and the plains. I had never been to this side of the ring so some of the landscape looked foreign. Somehow I found it fitting that Lucifer would set up his camp on the side closest to the black hole. Maybe if things got sticky, Lucifer would have an easy escape route.

I couldn't see Lucifer's army, and the area past the angels' homes was eerily quiet. With a trail no longer left for me, I had to figure out Vergil's path on my own. After a minute, I took a chance on the gargantuan mountain towering a few miles to the north. My database told me there was a massive expanse beyond it, large enough for an army. That was as good a guess as any.

I flew up the mountain that I assumed Vergil had ascended, keeping my wings tucked behind me for optimal climb. I made it to the top, where a platform stood, with half-broken pillars encircling it. It wasn't a very big platform, only about a mile wide in diameter. But in the middle, radiating brightly, was Lucifer himself, extending his arms wide in a welcoming gesture. I hid behind one of the pillars to watch, carefully watching my step and staying silent. Vergil was glaring at him, both hands on his sword, ready to strike. Lucifer didn't show any sign of fear, for in the midst of peril he was performing his most dangerous technique: talking.

CHAPTER 12: More Like Thunder

"Are you going to strike down someone this defenseless?" Lucifer asked pretentiously.

"You need to be stopped," Vergil responded flatly. "We need to stop this war."

"You're afraid, because of what you see around you," Lucifer said, "but when the war is over, there will be no more need for fighting. Why do you think God had everyone learn about combat when they were born? It's because He knew this day would come. He was preparing you for His absence, preparing you to fight for yourselves and stop the blind angels that follow God without cause. He wanted you to take up arms with me."

"HE PREPARED US TO FIGHT YOU!" I screamed from behind one of the three pillars at the platform "entrance." Lucifer extended his neck to see who had given the retort.

"Lysander? Is that you? Still yelling out things from behind a cover I see...tell me, where are your comrades? Weren't there more of you?"

"They're out fighting your army," I said, my voice straining as I stepped from behind the pillar, "but we managed to find the time to come stop you."

"Stop me? You mean like last time?" he chuckled.

"We will win," I muttered. My words were shaky. I wasn't sure why, but he was a lot scarier this time. It wasn't his stature, but the foreign aura he was emitting. It was...cold and frightening. I felt a lethal danger seeping out from his spirit, and it let me know that if I engaged him in battle, he intended to wound me deeply. He was still glowing like he always did, but it was a false warmth, like the sun shining high in the sky on a bitter, cold day. Something was off about him.

"I could end you both right now," he said with assuredness. Almost as if to prove his point, a Faithful flew down from the sky and tried to stab him in the back. Lucifer easily struck him down. In the same breath, he continued speaking. "But where is the profit in that? There's a reason why our paths keep crossing."

"I thought you said we were clowns," I spat at him. An injured look appeared on his face.

"Anger was necessary to put a fire under you all. Insults guaranteed that you would come after me. And I needed this. I needed you...and your unity on my side. Everyone is so divided, and this conflict has been going on since long before you came. I had to make it seem like I was the enemy, so you would fight on Heaven's behalf, and solidify your teamwork."

"That doesn't make sense..."

"Do you know that I wasn't always what I am now, that in the past-"

"What are you talking about?" I interrupted, throwing up my hands. Lucifer didn't budge.

"How many teams do you see in Heaven? You might have heard of a few, but I bet you haven't actually met one yet - because they're rare. You see, everyone is such an individual, but your group is united, so much so that you could accept an Archangel, a far superior being as an equal, and make him feel as such. We need that kind of unity in Heaven, so I used you. I had angels announce the defeat of Rufus in the streets. I had you lose by my hand so you would seek revenge, but I did not put you out of commission. I needed you to show Heaven that no matter what, one could bounce back, that somehow you had survived a fight against Lucifer himself! The other angels would love you even more and applaud your tenacity! They would line up to be a part of your group and take in your words like hungry baby birds. All of this elaborate planning - so that when we talked here and you finally came to my side, all of Heaven would rejoice and put down their weapons - seeing their champions choosing the better way. Don't you see? With you as our poster child, they will realize that we are not to serve God who is cold and distant - an individual...but me, who will usher everyone into my presence and unite all of Heaven as one!"

"No...you're confusing me," I said. Something was wrong. I could feel it. I could feel it.

Suddenly, a rumble sounded off in the distance, like a thunderstorm on the horizon. Lucifer's aura lit up, and his incredibly long wings began to quiver.

"There He goes," he seethed. "I was wondering when He'd show Himself."

"Who?" Vergil asked.

"God, that's who. It's His way of announcing to me that He's coming, and there's no telling when He'll arrive...don't you see? This is the moment. It all comes down to your group. If He gets here and ends me, without your consenting to join and unite us all, He will win. How does that make you feel? Knowing that you all would have fought for nothing? That you could have turned Heaven into the sanctuary of joy and content that it is supposed to be, but instead you chose to uphold its cruel neglect? How will you survive, when God throws us back onto the islands as punishment? Join me, and we will make Heaven a better place."

"I don't understand," Vergil stated. "You said that you served God more than anyone. How can you be against Him?"

"I did, Vergil," Lucifer lamented, "but if you had served God for as long as I have, and saw how nothing ever changed, you would be frustrated too. Now we see the light. If I serve God the most, and He never shows His presence, even to me, then what hope is there for all of you?"

"But that's wrong!" I screamed as Lucifer cautiously put a hand on the hilt of a new sword, lying in its sheath.

"Wrong? Don't be naïve. It's only wrong because God decides what's right and what's wrong. And if God is wrong, then His decisions are wrong. Don't you see?"

"No…" I was getting confused again. "You're wrong."

"What will you do if you become God?" Vergil asked - his tone low and submissive.

"Share warmth and goodness with everyone, of course. I will let my presence be in constant supply. But first, I will end this war, and ensure that even the angels who sided with God are nursed back to health. They are not to be hated. They are just confused like our good friend, Lysander."

"Then that's all I needed to hear," Vergil said. "I will join your cause."

I couldn't believe what I was hearing. Was this what my database called a dream? An illusion? This couldn't be real…Vergil could not have just switched sides.

"VERGIL!" I shrieked, grabbing his shoulder and pulling him close to me. "What are you doing?"

"Joining him, Lysander. He's right. Didn't you listen to his words? We are to be the voice of reason for the rest of Heaven's host. We are to convince them of how right Lucifer is and end the war, not because of who we are, but because of the way we connect with one another. Our unity needs to spread throughout all of Heaven."

"Voice of reason…" I trailed off. Those were Cadence's last words. He had known that our greatest battle with Lucifer would not be physical, but of a psychological kind. He had wanted me to be the guiding cry heard in the wilderness, to show…Vergil the path? Lucifer? I was so confused, I could barely see. I tried to hold on to my conviction and to what I felt in my heart had to be right, but my mind still tingled over Lucifer's words. Lucifer had made sense, but what was it about his message that kept me from being fully persuaded?

And how could I be a voice of reason to either of them when I didn't know what was the right path myself?

"Lysander," Lucifer said softly. "We need you too. We can't do this alone. Search your tactical mind. You know that what I'm saying makes sense. If you don't join us, then we will have accomplished nothing. We will all just go back to being divided again. And all of us will go back to the island, just like when you were born."

Born...yes. When I was born. That was the key. That was what had held me back all this time, what had preserved me from Lucifer's words. Because I still remembered. I remembered all too well what I had felt at my birth.

I lifted my head to face not Lucifer, but Vergil, my friend.

"Vergil," I said, touching his shoulder, "don't let his words confuse you. This isn't right. I know we're young, but I know one thing...God is not confusing."

"Lysander, we have to join Lucifer. We're running out of time," he said, disgusted, brushing off my hand and taking a step back. I felt my emotions swell. I was losing him.

"God is simple, Vergil," I cried out suddenly, unashamed of how I looked. "He loves us, and He's warm and caring, and if He's not revealing His presence, it's for a reason!! Remember His embrace! What it was like. Recall Raphael's words – to never forget our first memory! Don't you remember how warm and powerful He was? He's nothing like Lucifer. Can't you feel it? Lucifer's light is cold and heartless. How could anyone like that give off the love and warmth you desire - the love and warmth you remember? He never will, Vergil. You can't trust him. You can't. Think of how so many of us were willing to fight for God because of just two experiences. Two voiceless, loving experiences. Every moment, every thing we've seen and heard with Lucifer, can't even begin to compare to those experiences with God. Lucifer has to use words and lies and deceptions because the love of God is not in him. He plays off our fears and makes us choose out of confusion. You can't side with him!"

"I hear what you're saying, my friend," Vergil said, "but I've made my decision. Though I want to stay with you, I don't want to be with the rest of the group. Marcus, Alessa, Cadence, Farah – they put up with me. They care for me out of duty, not this love you speak of."

"That's not true! I know we had some growing pains, but they see you as part of the team now! You're one of us!"

"And for what, Lysander? So we can continue this war blindly? I would rather put an end to this now. I've taken down hundreds of angels since this began, and I don't want to take down any more. Lucifer wants to end the division, not promote it. Can't you see that? God had us divided the moment we were born. What about that logic? He could have put us all together, but I was separated from you – because I think He knew what I would become. What I would do. So He cast me away. The others sensed that disconnect in me. Only Lucifer saw my potential."

"Do you hear yourself?! No, Vergil. We love you. We accepted you when you asked to join us. We didn't require you to take a test. We took you in. You're our teammate and friend."

"You're right, you are, but I have to do the hard thing now and go beyond our friendship. I know you care about me, but by sticking with you, the war will not end. Or worse, nothing will change. And maybe Lucifer and all the angels on his side will end up unconscious forever, but where will we be? Still craving a God we do not see. Still bickering, debating, and arguing amongst ourselves as God watches us from the sidelines. Until someone rises up and starts this all over again. No, we need to end this now."

"Vergil…"

"I won't fight you, but my mind is made up. This is where I belong. I knew the moment I was born that I was different. I knew there was no cohesiveness in our group when I was present. I know why now."

"Yes," Lucifer said. "You were destined for greater things, Vergil. That is why you are an Archangel. You are superior to them and you can see how matters should be resolved - for the greater good. This is, after all, one of an Archangel's many abilities. Maybe I was wrong about the group as a whole. Perhaps I just needed you. I'm sure you sensed how much stronger you were than them."

"I did," Vergil said boldly, his eyes looking down upon me, "but I wanted to belong so badly."

"And you do," Lucifer soothed. "You are part of my family. Now, let's leave and figure out how to end this war. We still need to convince the other angels of our cause."

"What about me?!" I screamed as they began walking away, their backs facing me. Lucifer turned around like he had forgotten I was there.

"You won't listen to reason, so we will leave you be. Don't pursue us."

"If you can't even persuade me, how are you going to persuade Heaven's host? Is this what you do? After all your talk of unity, you cast away those that need to understand 'reason' the most? It's 'obey or perish?' Is that it, Lucifer?!"

"We will use force if we must," he said, walking away with Vergil again, "but we would prefer if you just stay out of our way. I won't let you corrupt Vergil any further. You are no longer needed. He alone took down more angels than your group could ever hope to. This war is won now, thanks to him."

"NO!" I screamed, flying forward to attack. I didn't know what damage I could cause to two Archangels by myself, but I didn't care. This was my chance to put an end to things, and if there was ever a time for me to fight with all my strength and succeed, it was now. But I didn't get the chance. Right as Lucifer and Vergil floated down the other side of the mountain, a Godhand and a Glory with a sword got in my way. The Godhand put a hand on my chest and pushed me back to the center of the platform. I tried to stand solid, hoping that God would hold me up like He did with Farah, but I fell backwards and banged my head. Both of them stood there idly, waiting for me to try again. They were sure I wasn't going anywhere.

"Get out of my way!" I roared. They continued watching me listlessly and didn't budge an inch. There was no way I was going to win by using brute force, so I had to try tactics. And it had to be done quickly. Vergil and Lucifer were no longer in sight and I didn't know how fast they were flying. I already knew from my race with Vergil that they were faster than me. Every second counted. So I created the best plan I could in the short amount of time I had.

"COME ON!" I screamed as I flew forward and hit the Godhand in the face. His lack of a reaction showed that he didn't feel a thing, and I didn't expect him to, but I was ready to annoy him into a fury. I punched his cheeks and nose over and over, flicking it, slapping it, doing everything I could to make him angry. He remained stoic, but I noticed his jaw was tensing up. My antics alone weren't enough to send him over the edge, and it wasn't until the Glory next to him started laughing that he gave a cry of rage and attempted to swing at me. He missed, for I had been waiting the whole time for him to try it.

Godhands were strong, but on average not very fast. With Marcus, we had to continually set him up to deliver his crushing blows. Alone, he would've kept striking out. Just like this guy. The Godhand swung at me over and over, missing me barely each time - which was all part of the plan. If I was too fast, he might realize that there was no point in swinging. I couldn't let him figure that out – that if he just stood there and kept me from Lucifer, he would accomplish his mission. No, I needed him to keep swinging, thinking that he was close, hoping that the next hit would be the one to connect. It was a dangerous game, for one well-placed punch could easily put me down, and I had to keep my eyes on the Glory as well, making sure he didn't step in.

After a while, I saw that this Godhand had too much strength and it was taking too long to tire him out, so I switched up my strategy. I let him hit me. Not full on, simply a graze against my skin each time. His fist would slide off my cheek and I would purposely stagger or spiral away in the air, only to come back for more. This made him even angrier, putting more force into each blow, enraged that I was enduring the hits of a Godhand. And somehow, I was.

Eventually, he had enough. His patience long gone, he placed all his angelic pressure into one blow like I had seen Marcus do to the Godhand he had faced earlier. I waited for it to almost connect, and then I dodged it completely, not even risking a graze. The Godhand stumbled forward and I let my wings carry me up for a moment. Wasting no time, I flew downward, my feet planted together and extended like a torpedo. Both feet hit him on the right side of his face, and he went flying off the platform. Down the mountain he went, to where the battle raged on.

The Glory realized how serious the situation had suddenly gotten, but before he could react, I unsheathed his sword and slashed a clean diagonal swipe across his body, from shoulder to hip. With a look of shock, the Glory blacked out, and I clutched the sword with fervor.

I sped down the mountain as fast as my wings allowed and I could see Lucifer not too far away, due to his ever-glowing aura. Thankfully, he and Vergil had continued to float, not fly, down the mountain. Even now they were steadily making their way across the field below, talking about what to do next.

Despite my anxiety, I pressed forward. I could see that in the field before me there would be no support. Lucifer's army was waiting straight ahead. They militaristically parted for Lucifer and Vergil, but otherwise stood vigilant in the field. Their lines extended hundreds of light years away, arranged by classifications, staring straight ahead and waiting for God's army to make it over the mountain. I didn't know if they would attack me, seeing as how I was obviously no threat, but I didn't care. I had to save Vergil.

"VERGIL!!!" I screamed as I swung the sword with all my might, the blade cutting through the first line of angels that stood in my way. Seeing their comrades fall, the army took it upon themselves to apprehend me. They had been patiently waiting for the battle to come to them, but a single defiant angel would have to do for now. I lasted for a good minute, dodging and swinging. I even managed to clash against a couple of angels and push them from me like I was a mighty Archangel, but Lucifer's army was too vast and powerful. A Guard eventually stood in my way and took a couple of hits from my sword, just enough for him to get closer and closer and eventually grab the hilt. I tried to wrestle it from him, but a Godhand grabbed my puny arms and held them behind me like I was being arrested. A Glory hit me in the abdomen and another Guard was about to slice at my neck with his own blade when a shout came from ahead. Lucifer had taken notice of the commotion and had ordered Vergil to follow him - to where I was imprisoned.

"I'm impressed you made it this far," Lucifer mused, cupping my chin in his hand. "But we cannot continue to give God's army hope. Like the rest of your friends, you need to be put down."

"Even without us, they will have hope," I said to him courageously. He slapped me across the face.

"Have you stopped to listen to the battle going on atop the other side of the mountain? There is simply yelling and cries of pain. You can't sense much, not being an Archangel, but your side is losing, and fast. They will make it over the mountain, but their spirits will be crushed when they see what's waiting for them on this side."

"Vergil," I called out, ignoring him. "Stop this!"

"He will," Lucifer said, waving him forward. "Vergil, I know you have been apprehensive about leaving your friend. I tell you now - this is the last link to be severed. Take your sword and cut through him with all your angelic might. He will be unconscious for over a millennia. Do this, and you will be free of your guilt and your confusion."

"I don't want to cut him. He is weak. I don't need to prove myself with him."

"Stop making excuses. You know that despite your power, your emotions hold you back. Let go of them, and you will be on the same level as I."

Vergil glanced at Lucifer with a gaze that begged for his power.

"Then we could end the war?"

"Yes. But I need you by my side. With your emotions in check, you will be able to fight against anyone. Together, we will strike down God. We will have that amount of power, I promise you. But you must strike this Messenger down. I know this is hard, but you already made it over the first hurdle by joining me. Remember, God will not take you back at this point. We are too far into our rebellion. Therefore, we must continue our mission or be destroyed. You must overcome this mountain, Vergil. You must subdue your emotions."

"Vergil…you are my friend," I pleaded. "Don't do this."

"I am sorry, Lysander," he said, his voice choking and growing weak, his breathing erratic. "But I must. I am too far gone."

He lunged into me with his sword and it felt like it was going to break my body in two. My angelic pressure plummeted as he twisted the blade. His face was in mine now, and his eyes were wide with internal pain as he saw me open and close my mouth, trying to talk as I began to go blind. My body went numb and in my last moments, I reached out with my right hand, the hand not struggling to remove Vergil's sword from my chest, and I grazed his cheek - caressing his face affectionately. I couldn't speak, but I hoped I got the message across.

I forgave him.

I don't know why, but I forgave him. He would never cease being my friend. In fact, none of my love for any of my brothers and sisters in Lucifer's army had gone away.

And as I closed my eyes to rest, the pain suddenly dissipated. It completely went away, and I gained my full angelic pressure back in an instant, like I had just woken up from a nightmare.

And I felt it.

My first memory relived. That warm soothing presence that calmed my fears, placed a comforting hand on my back. My pain subsided instantly and suddenly there was nothing but blinding light all around me, washing me and going through my spirit like it was blood coursing through my veins.

It didn't last long.

And I had barely turned to look at the light, when it was over just as suddenly as it had begun.

My surroundings came into focus. I was alone in the field. The sword had disappeared from my chest. Lucifer's words were no longer whispering in my ears. His army had vanished. And Vergil…was nowhere to be found.

At first I thought that I had woken up a millennia into the future, but that couldn't have been true, for in the next instant, millions of angels flew over the mountain and cheered. They flew through the air in circles. They hugged one another and threw down their weapons to the grassy plain below them. I stood there dazed as one floated down to me and lifted me up, giving me a great big hug.

"What happened?" I asked him, and a whistle sounded off near us, directing our attention to an angel I instinctively knew was Gabriel. He was smiling and practically shaking with joy.

"Everyone, there is no need to worry! In our darkest hour, victory was laid in our hands, and Lucifer's army has been defeated! I can say little else but this: God – has ended the war!!"

The cries of worship and praise were deafening as the angels flew around each other, the colors of their armor and hair blending together like confetti as they hovered in the skies. I stood in the midst, dazed and unsure, looking at my hands as Farah came out of nowhere and put me in a friendly half-headlock. Revived by God Himself, she laughed and hugged my neck tightly, patting my back and talking excitedly. Alessa flew down from the mountain and soon joined her, jumping up and down and greeting others as they flew past. Marcus, not far behind her, was bouncing off the ground like a rabbit, failing at trying to imitate Alessa. He stretched his arms out wide as he leaped, hitting passing angels by mistake and causing minor vibrations in the ground itself.

Saving us all, Cadence soon appeared in front of him and calmed him down. After some coaxing, Marcus eventually settled for clapping and, with the threat neutralized, everyone started giggling uncontrollably at how funny Marcus had looked. The sight of my family rejoicing in the field made me smile, and it reminded me that I had a reason to be happy too. I had never seen them so excited, and they deserved to celebrate. I wouldn't burden them with my troubles. Not now. The war was over, and the enemy had been removed. Why would anyone be in a sour mood? ...Why was I?

I wanted to ask Cadence for his advice, but he and the others had already taken to the air, bidding for me to join them. I waved them on. At first, they stared down at me, unsure of my sullen demeanor. I waved them on again, insinuating that I was okay, and they flew off, seeking to participate in the heavenly song that the angels had begun to sing. They moved with such harmony and grace that my spirit pulled at me, begging for me to put my feelings aside and jump in the chorus.

Only...I stood still.

I wanted to join in the praise, relish in the joy and victory. Worship God for saving us all and bringing every single angel that had fallen back to full health. But I couldn't move, and I lost myself in my thoughts. By the time I came to, I found myself floating in the air by the Throne Room.

Supposedly, something had transported all of us there, and it could only have been our Father. Upon our collective arrival, the whole host of Heaven was talking so loudly and energetically, I knew my assumption had been correct. God had brought us home, to the Throne Room, to celebrate together, as a family.

And that is why, upon gazing at the Throne Room, I was not surprised to find the massive doors opening. They creaked slowly, moving all on their own, a brilliant light shining from beyond like a magnificent star. I could feel the love baking me from where I hovered, and all of Heaven immediately flew down to the newly repaired city floor, restored to its former glory. They bowed as the doors spread wide open and waited for the beckoning of our Lord. I copied their actions. Though my heart was elsewhere, it didn't mean God deserved my disrespect...

You could not see through the light to perceive what was inside the Throne Room, but you could feel it. God was there, and He was not demanding for us to show Him love and respect, He was offering us His unconditional love - it was up to us if we wanted to feel His presence once again. The same presence we had fought for...that so many had argued for, bickered for, vanished for...

Our first memory, which we were told to never forget, could now be reinforced and solidified. Our minds now able to make new memories to supersede the old. A refreshing. A revival.

And there was a mass flooding into the chamber doors as God's divine presence welcomed us in. In the blink of an eye, every single angel remaining in Heaven was inside.

Save one.

I stood there for a moment, staring at the light through the open doors. And I wanted to go inside. I wanted to bathe in God's glory like I was a child playing amongst his toys in a bathtub, but something didn't feel right, and I was starting to learn to trust my instincts.

Not that anything was wrong with God, or my teammates, or Heaven, but I had never felt the pain of loss, and somehow, I knew that God would always be in the Throne Room from here on out - an ever-present Father for all of eternity.

And I would see Him soon, but I needed time to heal, for I may have been the only one who had lost a true friend that day. Not a comrade, an acquaintance, or a teammate. A friend. What was worse was that I had no clue where he was, or how he was doing or what he was thinking. I only knew he wasn't here, and I had to find him. I hadn't given up on him yet, even if everyone else had. I wished I didn't feel that way, but maybe I still had a lot to learn about growing up.

"Lord," I said to Him through the chamber doors, hoping He still accepted me, despite my hesitation to join Him. "I love you, and I thank you for saving me, but I cannot feel your embrace, while Vergil is lost. It wouldn't be fair to you, for my heart wouldn't be in the praise."

The chamber doors began to close quickly, but right before they shut tight, a single ray of light shot out, slowed down as it neared my face, and splashed over my cheek. It warmed my entire body with love and grace and I nodded, knowing that God had understood, and accepted.

And so I flew away, leaving all of Heaven to rejoice without me, my mind still warring over a battle that had now become nothing, but history...

CHAPTER 13: Sharpeneth

"Raphael," I said endearingly as I entered his hall unannounced. "It's good to see you're not sleeping on the job."

"Yes, I have been slacking lately," he laughed. We both knew that his being knocked unconscious by Lucifer had had nothing to do with sleeping on the job. "But on a more serious note, why aren't you at the celebration?"

"I could ask the same of you."

"Well, I received a message from a Glory that you were headed this way and that God asked that I meet you here. I didn't mind leaving the festivities early to have a conversation with you. So you see, I have quite the excuse."

"I can't believe you made it here before me."

"It being my house, I am fully knowledgeable about the shortcuts you have yet to learn."

"I see," I said, surprised. "Then I guess I'm in the right place."

"Yes, you are...sorry for not being of much help during the war. I hear that your team fought Lucifer himself in my hall."

"We didn't win," I stated flatly, "but we made sure to give your place some redecoration while we were at it...to be honest, I really wish it had ended then and there."

Raphael shook his head.

"That's not the right attitude, Lysander," Raphael said, using his best empathetic tone. "At least you weren't completely knocked out - you were able to fight again. That's the most important thing. Imagine if you had been in my state...all the fun you would've missed out on. At least you contributed."

"You were there with us too," I admitted. "When it was just Vergil and myself left, your words were the only thing that helped me remember that Lucifer was wrong...but I was too late to save Vergil. Lucifer's poison had gotten to him."

"Yes...Vergil had a very troubled soul, and I was actually surprised he didn't join Lucifer sooner. One of the reasons I thought he should work on a team was because of his personality. He was the type Lucifer attracted, those that are easily manipulated and want to belong to a group more than anything. And, as I hoped, you were able to keep him out of harm's way."

"Not in the end," I replied. "It wasn't enough. We didn't have the time to strengthen our bond before the war happened. Maybe I didn't talk to him enough. I don't know. But it doesn't matter now. I was too late. And now I don't know where he is."

"You want to find him."

"Yes. Do you know where he is, Raphael?"

"Come here, young one."

Raphael started walking down the hall and made a left behind the corner from where Vergil had once watched us, where the two locked doors were. Now, one of them was open and Raphael placed a hand on my back and pushed me forward, giving me access to his secrets. Inside was a large room with a low ceiling, turquoise drapes over bay windows and paperbacks on a bookshelf. I made a mental note to check those out later, and to ask Raphael why there were books in Heaven when we had an internal database.

In the middle of the room, there was a gigantic crystal-clear dome, hovering in the air above a circular bronze table. The table was about the size of a small lake and some kind of dim light was shining from the middle of the crystal dome. Upon closer inspection, I noticed the dim light was actually a small, round, holographic sphere, showing off the colors blue, brown and green. The blue, my database told me, was called water. And the brown and green were land. It took me only a second to come to a conclusion.

"It's Earth," I whispered to myself. "It's really there."

"Our mental database told us Earth would exist at some point," Raphael said, coming by my side. "That time has arrived."

"So it was being constructed."

"Yes...though God is everywhere, and He could have stopped the war in Heaven at any time, He let it play out so that all those in Lucifer's camp would reveal themselves. God did not want anyone singled out, so He waited until the last angel made his own calling and election sure, from within. At the moment God came and ended the war, there was no longer any gray. Each individual had decided in their own heart whether they belonged to God or Lucifer. In the meantime, God spent His full concentration and wisdom on constructing this world and the galaxies around it."

"Is this where Vergil is?" I asked, afraid of the answer.

"Lysander, listen carefully. What I'm about to tell you is not easy to hear, but it's the truth. Lucifer, and all those associated with him...are banished. They will no longer be angels in Heaven and this will never again be their home." I was silent for a moment, coming to terms with what Raphael said.

"Earth is their home now?"

"For a time, but it gets worse. As of now, they are able to roam the Earth, and Lucifer will rule that world for a time, but afterwards, he and his followers will be thrown into a place called Hell."

"What is Hell?"

"The very opposite of Heaven, designed specifically for them. When their time on Earth is finished, they will be cast there for eternity, and words cannot describe the torture and suffering they will endure. The presence of God that we've all felt, that soothes our longing? They will have the opposite. They will feel cold and alone at all times. The warmth, comfort, and pleasure that we've experienced? They will only feel burning and pain. Just as we are in the midst of ecstasy in God's presence, they will constantly be on the verge of insanity."

Pain. Torture. I knew these words, but I would never feel them. Never truly understand how horrible they were...and this Hell that would become the home of my fallen brethren, would be of the worst kind.

Vergil...what have you done? If only you had held out a little bit longer, you would be okay...

My love for God had not changed or diminished. On some level, I understood why He had created Hell...to not only punish Lucifer and his followers for the chaos they had caused, but to also ensure that such an uprising would never happen again. But still...to be eternally damned...the thought was overwhelming. Eternity? Was this right?

But one thing was certain.

Vergil wouldn't have to go to Hell yet. Maybe there was still a chance I could save him and bring him back. I just had to find him and be that voice of reason once again. After being kicked out of Heaven, surely he'd see my side of things.

The thought gave me new hope and I eagerly looked at the globe, spinning in its glass shell. Raphael studied me, and I was sure that he knew what I was thinking. He probably pitied me, assuming that what I imagined was impossible, but it didn't faze me. I was determined to save Vergil.

"There's more to Earth than just Lucifer and his fallen angels," Raphael said abruptly, breaking my thoughts.

"There's more?"

"I can't talk too much about it...but God has made new creations. And they're not angels."

I knew what they were before he could tell me. After all, they took up a considerable amount of my database.

"Human beings," I said, and Raphael affirmed it with a nod.

"Yes. They are more fragile than us, but made in the likeness of God Himself. They live on Earth, and already God has had a lot of interaction with them. Fascinating creatures. Very intelligent, but I worry about them, even now."

"Why is that?"

"Because, Lucifer is down there as well, along with his entire army. You saw what he did in Heaven. What will stop him from figuring out how to ruin peace on Earth too? I fear he will try to bring the human beings to his side, and do everything in his power to prevent his fate of going to Hell."

I heard his words loud and clear. In only a short amount of time, Heaven had gone from a majestic wonderland to a raging battlefield. Within days, we had been at each other's throats, trying to destroy one another like we were bitter enemies.

Lucifer was crafty...and he was there on Earth, seductive words and all.

If he could persuade a third of Heaven to join his cause, what could stop him from persuading the young humans that now inhabited the planet below? How could they fight against such manipulation? What would stop them from making the same mistakes Vergil did?

God could protect them at all times, but that was not His way. He had kept everyone in Heaven that had wanted to be with Him. No one had been forced to choose Him, and I was sure the same type of care would be given to the humans. How long would it take before they grew weary of His distance? How long before they rose up with Lucifer to try to destroy us entirely? No. This could not happen again.

"There are only two of them right now. Adam and Eve," Raphael said. "But there will be more."

I felt my wings surge with energy, my body swell with excitement. I had found a new purpose. Another reason to live...and I would not fail this time. I would do everything in my power to save them all – each and every one.

"They need to be protected," Raphael mused, seeing my spirit ignite with determination.

"And protect them, I shall," I said boldly, my body rigid with fervor and dedication. Lucifer would undoubtedly try his tricks again, but I would be there this time, stronger than ever, ready to thwart any plan he had the audacity to form...

The war in Heaven had ended, only for the war on Earth to begin...

Angels of Eden

Book II

Prologue:

In the beginning…

God created the islands.

Small testing grounds that new angels were taken to after birth.

Some would pass the test and be transported to Heaven.

Others…became the Absent: angels who couldn't handle the pressure and therefore found solace only in their mental databases – the internal encyclopedia given to all angels when they are created.

Not many…would escape this condition…

However, one notable group managed to pass the tests, resulting in the formation of a powerful team of six:

Lysander – the Messenger, well versed in tactics,

Cadence – the Guard, their leader,

Alessa – the Glory, with an inseparable connection to God,

Marcus, the Godhand, the muscle,

Vergil, the Archangel,

And Farah, the Faithful.

Together, they quickly became known throughout Heaven for their teamwork and commendable bravery.

Yet even these attributes would soon be pushed to their limits.

Lucifer, a powerful Archangel, decided to wage war against God in Heaven, arguing that he would be a more fitting ruler than their Creator.

And in the process, he managed to persuade many to his cause.

Including a member of Team Six: Vergil.

After an exhausting battle, God ended the war.

Lucifer and his followers were banished.

And Vergil...was lost with them.

No one is certain of their condition...

And there is no time to investigate.

With the advent of the human beings on Earth, all focus is averted to their sole well-being, leaving the status of the fallen angels to an afterthought...

Still...there is a feeling that the planet and its new inhabitants are more than just another of God's creations...

That if one could see beyond its beauty and majestic aura

They would realize...it is a battleground.

And a raging thirst for blood and spirit is in the air...

"Open rebuke is better than secret love. Faithful are the wounds of a friend; but the kisses of an enemy are deceitful."

— Proverbs 27: 5-6

"...for Satan himself is transformed into an angel of light. Therefore it is no great thing if his ministers also be transformed as the ministers of righteousness; whose end shall be according to their works."

— II Corinthians 11:14-15

CHAPTER 1: Think on These Things

"I am too far gone."

His words echoed through my mind as I stared at the clear, transparent dome again, rotating silently in its bronze holder – nothing more than a circular table composed of polished wood. I barely noticed anything else, the rest of the room eclipsed by my curiosity. Only my hands realized the design of the table, for it was all they had to rest on. And I needed this support, so I could lean in, and examine the contents beyond the crystal shell.

It was a globe.

A full representation of Earth itself - displaying all of its weather patterns in an animated fashion.

Spinning ever so slightly, it tilted at an impressive angle, allowing seasons to occur intermittently across its surface. The way its core, mantle and crusts were assembled, it reminded me of Heaven at first glance. After all, we had our own circular structure. Four rings to be exact, making up our city, neighborhoods, fields, and spatial background, respectively. One could argue that what differentiated Earth's structure from Heaven's was the latter's interactive dynamic. While Earth's composition was static, Heaven's was ever-changing.

And yet, the funny thing was that, no matter how much time I spent at home with the rest of my angelic brethren, I found myself captivated by the blue and green Earth rotating below. I kept returning again and again to stare at the model in Raphael's esoteric room. Some called it an obsession. Others brushed it off as a hobby. But for me? It was reconnaissance, for a special mission I had placed upon myself.

I just hadn't mustered the courage to execute it yet.

And besides, I had little information to go off of, and I was never much of a risk-taker. Recent events in my life were proof enough of that. Despite my friends visiting the planet like it was their vacation home, I refused to go there entirely. Not that they didn't try to make me. But I habitually declined their invitations (much to their annoyance) and stayed home to hold down the fort, so to speak. They just didn't understand. I had to prepare my mind first, and determine a course of action in case I saw him. They had nothing to worry about. He had never really cared for them. But I had been involved in his life up until the end, so that made me the only one he would bother striking up a conversation with, and listening to. The amount of pressure was rapping on my nerves like a ruler, but I couldn't acknowledge the pessimism. It was of the utmost importance that I made our first talk after the war worth his while – ensure that each word counted...was flawless...was perfect. Going down to save him, unprepared, would just end poorly for all of us.

I stuck my nose down further toward the holographic Earth, unable to reach past the glass shield and give it a poke. I asked Raphael once why it was forbidden touch it, but all he said was that if I did, the world might explode. For two Earth days I believed him, until he outright laughed at my refusal to go back into the room and finally revealed that he had been joking. It wasn't funny. Sure, I laughed at sarcasm as much as the next angel, but with the creation of Earth and the human beings, we were in a whole different domain. There were too many concepts we didn't know. Not even our mental database gave us answers to all the questions.

Questions like: what was our mission concerning the humans' well-being? Who would introduce them to the angels if God decided to leave them alone and not take a personal stake in their lives? Would they trust us if they found out about our existence? These were troubling notions that kept many an angel quiet, even at the Fellowship Hall. And it wasn't uncommon to find several angels stooped over a table, silently munching on apples or honeycombs, contemplating these mysteries. Sure, some went over to the Throne Room and asked God Himself these questions, but not one came back with an answer. Of course, we waited patiently, knowing that God would reveal all in time, but that didn't mean we weren't a little bit anxious. Since the Earth had been created, the two humans and their botanical sanctuary had been kept off limits, leaving us wondering when the grand opening would occur. Everyone was excited to see the new creations, but until the day we were given permission, He offers only His presence and the Earth's landscape - to revel in, and enjoy.

"Geez," a voice squeaked behind me. "There's enough gloom in this room to knock an angel unconscious."

"Hello, Farah," I said flatly, not budging from my position. I heard her pipsqueak shoes tapping, getting louder as she walked closer. Soon she was right beside me, leaning on the table harder than I ever would. "Farah, what are you…" I began to say, but she had already reached beyond the glass dome, that impenetrable armor, and poked a stubby end of a finger into the Earth. Being a holographic projection, it didn't stop or skid, and thankfully it maintained its spinning as if nothing had happened at all and I heaved a sigh in relief. After a quick recovery, I decided to follow suit, ready to pounce on the wonderful opportunity Farah had just presented, but my finger, despite being of the same spiritual composition as hers, bounced against the shield, nearly causing my hand to whip back and hit me in the forehead. Farah giggled and rubbed my back in consolation.

"How did you do that?" I marveled, but we both knew the answer. It was her specialty.

"Faith," she declared proudly, a grin cracking from ear to ear and ridiculously overshadowing the rest of her facial features. "You can do it too, Lysander. Just believe that your hand can go past the glass."

"I'm not supposed to touch it…and neither are you," I added. "Raphael's orders."

"Yes, I was there when he claimed the world would explode, but c'mon, he was joking! God wouldn't destroy the world because you touched a model of it."

"Says you…"

"And yet you tried it right after I did," she mused, shaking her head. "Double standards…"

"Well, why did you do it in the first place?"

"I had to see what it felt like…just once," she whispered mischievously. "You've never considered it?"

She stared at me with big puppy eyes, waiting patiently for a response, and knowing full well I'd thought about it since the first time I saw it spinning in its case.

"So what was it like?" I asked casually, like I didn't care that Farah had just done the impossible. "I mean, if you want to talk about that sort of thing."

"You're so funny," she giggled and inspected the glass once more. She reached out, and tried poking through the shimmering globe again, but her finger didn't faze through the dome this time. She stepped back and stretched the same finger out in front of her, searching for flaws.

"You lost faith on purpose," I accused her childishly. "You could do it if you wanted."

"Losing faith on purpose," she snickered. "I've never heard of such."

"Okay. Fine," I sighed. "I'll stop pretending. I really want to know what it felt like."

"Break the glass with your sword - that should do the job," she said assuredly. "Then you're free to do as you please and touch the globe to your heart's content. I can't believe you didn't consider it earlier."

"I'm not trying to break it, it's not mine. And besides…I forgot I had a sword altogether."

"It sits right on you," she whined in disbelief, pointing directly at the scabbard dangling by my thigh. I had barely noticed it since the war in Heaven. It didn't matter if it wasn't the same sword I had used to slash my way through a horde of Lucifer's angels, desperately reaching for my friend to come to his senses. It didn't matter that it was a completely different blade than the one that had plunged through my chest when I was ultimately betrayed by my brother. It was of no consequence. Whether it was this one or the next - a sword to me was a symbol of destruction and violent suffering. A trinket that drudged up too many bad memories: the island, the Absent, God's disappearance, the bickering in Heaven over whether Lucifer should take His place, the war, the division, Vergil's betrayal and banishment from Heaven...as long as I was able, I was determined to keep that sword chained and locked until all was restored to its rightful place, no matter how long that took. After all, I was immortal...

"I don't want to use it," I said. "Not unless I have to."

"You might as well. We weren't given these after the war for decoration."

"It stays sheathed," I said adamantly and Farah puffed in disappointment, her dragonfly wings twitching slightly.

"Well, anyways, your time is up. We're supposed to be meeting at the Café."

"That wasn't even close to five minutes."

"You're right. It was actually ten. We know how much you like to sulk so we gave you some extra time."

"You can go without me. Seriously."

"Lysander, don't make me get Alessa..."

"Why can't you just let me stay?"

"Because we're concerned," she said. Her eyes remained fixed on the globe, but her fingers were manifesting her emotions through a rhythmical tapping on the table.

"I'm fine."

"Are you? We hardly see you anymore. And I'm not talking about our trips to Earth. You haven't been to any of our houses except Cadence's, and sometimes you go out of your way to avoid us."

"It's not you," I muttered, cringing over how corny it sounded. "It's me?"

"You're the saddest angel I've ever seen!" she exclaimed. "Do you realize what I'm saying? You're in Heaven…and you're depressed! That shouldn't be!"

"But I am, Farah…you weren't there."

"Yes I was! I fought in the war and had to put aside my fears like everyone else. I had to watch angels get stabbed! I saw our troops getting slaughtered, our morale defeated. And I worried about going unconscious too! Waking up to a Lucifer-dictated world…but it's over now. It's over. And nothing's changing. We're not going back in time. We're not able to reinstate the angels that fell, so why dwell on it anymore?"

"We could talk to them - make them see that their decision to side with Lucifer was a mistake."

"It's done, Lysander. Let it go," she said frantically. "If there was a way Lucifer and the members of his army could be saved, they would have been. God is omnipotent, remember?"

"What I can't understand is how you can act so normal. As if none of it ever happened."

Farah began walking out of the room, motioning for me to leave with her and sit down on the carpeted floor in the main hall. I followed reluctantly and sat down beside her, surprised by how plush the rug was. Raphael had definitely upgraded the tapestry in the past year, though the walls were still pretty bare. The same metallic purple drapes extended down the hall, culminating into the arched entrance, although a couple new banners did hang across the ceiling. But that was basically it. The layout of his home hadn't changed, merely the décor. Besides the stretch of hallway, there was an alcove at the opposite end of the entrance to the left, making Raphael's entire building the shape of an "L" that was lying on its side. The alcove housed two rooms: the first being the Earth room, and the other - its contents were still a mystery. I'd tried to open the second door on occasion but it never budged. Once, Raphael caught me and goaded me on, telling me that if I wanted to know what was in there so badly,

I should break the door down, use all of my strength. This, of course, was impossible as some kind of force field outlined its edges, but I still tried with all of my might and Raphael laughed heartily at my efforts. Lately, I've left it alone.

"Hey, what is that?" Farah asked me, now that we were relaxed on the carpet. The second locked door was well within view.

"The second room, right?" I said excitedly. "Raphael's keeping secrets in there and I would love to find out what they are."

"No one's seen what's inside?" she asked and I struggled to suppress a grin.

"No one but Raphael," I said slyly, "but you can investigate."

"Sneaky sneaky," she mused, wagging a finger at me. "Trying to get me to do your dirty work?"

"Maybe," I said, looking away like I had seen a gnat zip past.

"I should let you suffer and not even bother."

"Aren't you curious?"

"Not as much as you. Really, you think too much."

"Only about what's important."

"Nooooo...you dwell on memories that won't change anything. Just let God be in control."

"I'm trying, but it's not that easy."

"At least talk to Raphael about what you're feeling. You two seem to have a good rapport with each other."

"I would, but he's been busy."

It was true. One would think Raphael's home belonged to me with how often I visited. And I had to admit that my afternoons there only increased once I saw how seldom angels came for advice. The hall was never closed to outsiders but many were determined to keep their distance from Raphael's less-than-sunny disposition. He had the tendency to say what was on his mind, and his established tone of speech didn't exactly welcome you to his advice. I found, however, that if you could get past his cold exterior, you couldn't ask for a better mentor and guide, and this instilled in me great respect for him. As a result, I visited his hall more than anyone, whether he was there or not, constantly watching the Earth spin or waiting for him to return so I could ask another question. He was always happy to oblige.

But recently, God had called on him to oversee many of the duties in Heaven, such as ensuring that all of the angels were satisfied and happy after the war, giving speeches in the Fellowship Hall, or asking Gabriel to create new and exciting foods. Ironically, I was one of the sole angels who found it hard to move on after the war, and yet I saw Raphael the least out of Heaven's host, constantly missing him in transition. I could barely remember the last time we had spoken.

"Our paths don't seem to cross anymore," I admitted and Farah shook her head.

"Well, you need to speak to someone."

"Raphael will be here eventu-"

"-I guess that someone will be me!" she exclaimed cheerfully. I groaned. Farah gave me a scowl but then she quickly reverted back to her excitement, motioning to me with her right hand to lean in closer - to catch her words of wisdom.

"Listen, I wasn't conscious in the end," Farah said to me softly. "I didn't hear what Lucifer said, or what persuaded Vergil to join him, but we can't harp on it. If angels still feel pain caused by the war, then Lucifer's clutches have not yet been broken. Why do you think God's top priority in Heaven is to make sure we're all happy? Why do you think His Throne Room is always open and you can be engulfed in His presence at any given moment? Because we need to move on."

"How?" I cried out desperately. "How can we forget what happened?"

"If there's sadness and unrest, we could start having unhealthy thoughts again. What if a sect of angels, unhappy with the way Heaven is progressing, decided amongst themselves to take up Lucifer's doctrine? Think of the division it would cause...and there's no guarantee it couldn't happen again. Imagine the fallout of a second war...you sure would have a reason to be depressed then. At that point, you may as well become an Absent just to deal with the pain."

"Might as well be Absent?" I said solemnly. "What are you saying...that I'm a threat?"

Farah slapped me upside the head and I winced at the sudden drop in my angelic pressure.

"Lysander, if you were a threat, would God have kept you here? He knew what angels were going to turn from the beginning. He just waited until all of them were accounted for, then He made his move."

"But Vergil wasn't like that."

"It's hard to tell what is going on inside an angel's mind...but all I know is that Vergil sided with Lucifer, and that was wrong."

I rubbed the back of my head absent-mindedly, and I was reminded of how terrifying it was when we had fought Lucifer and his army – the fear of going unconscious and being unable to move scaring us far more than his endgame.

When we fight, we lose "angelic pressure" from exerting ourselves, and the same thing also happens if we are "hurt" in battle. Take enough damage or expend enough energy, and your spiritual body shuts down, forcing you to go unconscious for an unspecified amount of time. Part of Lucifer's plan had been to knock out all of God's followers for millennia, thus making an opportunity for himself to shape Heaven after his image. All in all, being unconscious sounded better than death, which I knew little about, but it was still nothing an angel was willing to experience.

"I don't see how Vergil had evil within him," I said, refusing to budge from my stance. Farah relinquished her side of the argument, bowing her head in secession.

"Maybe if you find him someday, we'll have the answer."

"Maybe…" I said, satisfied the discussion was over.

"So!" Farah piped up cheerfully, shooting up to her feet in excitement. "Are we going to leave now?"

After recovering from her sudden burst of joy, I chuckled to myself. From where I sat, I was still noticeably taller than her.

"What's so funny?" she eyed me accusingly, placing her hands on her hips.

"Nothing we can fix," I laughed. I eyed the top of her head and she joined in my laughter.

"Yes, yes. I'm small. I get it, but don't change the subject!"

"I don't remember what we were talking about."

"I was going to say that we should go look at the Earth soon."

"I'm absolutely fine with that," I said in a chipper tone. Farah closed her eyes and sighed.

"I meant we should go there and see it…in its actual physical form."

I had realized what she had meant from the start, but I wasn't ready to go yet. I didn't feel like my research had been exhausted yet and a couple more ideas were at the forefront of my mental database, nagging at me to realize their full potential. Perhaps I could still get out of this…

"Well, it wouldn't be right for just the two of us to go," I related to her quickly. "We should wait for the others."

"I never said we were going alone."

I let her words sink in as anxiety crept up my back. It was going to be harder to wiggle my way out of her clutches than I had thought.

"Cadence asked you to check on me, didn't he?"

"Yep," she confirmed, "but if it makes you feel better, I did want to see you too."

"Where are the others?"

"They're at the East Café, enjoying the new food."

"And you didn't mind babysitting? I hear Gabriel's new raisin bread is the talk of Heaven."

"It's not babysitting when you're checking on a friend," she said, running a hand through her lightning green hair.

"I'm not losing my mind," I said matter-of-factly, "so you don't have to worry about me. But with that said, I'm not ready to see the group yet either. I figure I'll get some fresh air first – stroll around a bit. Give me a solid hour and I'll join you at Café when I'm ready. Then, we'll discuss this trip to Earth."

"You're sure? I don't have to follow you?"

"No," I said, giving my best cheesy smile. "And to put your mind at ease, I'll say this. If you have to search for me after an hour, I promise I'll go to Earth. No discussion, no dragging involved."

"That makes me feel better," she said. "You do have to keep your word."

I said nothing else as we walked out of Raphael's hall, and admired the galaxy from the front steps. Nothing, as far as space was concerned, had changed since the war and the view was as breathtaking as always. The stars and nebulae firing past like bullets, our houses gliding around us on their own small islands, the bustling city core where the Fellowship Hall, the Throne Room and the infamous Symphony Hall lay. I didn't get out much but I had heard there was talk of future remodeling, which would include some new architecture. I wondered what an angel had to do to get on that planning committee.

Farah, hands on her hips, shook her head in awe and threw a hand out toward the landscape.

"Depressed with all this beauty around," she said in a low tone. "You know, you should visit the Throne Room. That will cure your ailment."

"Perhaps I will," I said, beginning my preliminary take-off, slowly floating upwards and keeping my face toward her. "Are you sure you'll be at the Café? When I'm done sight-seeing?"

"Definitely. Before I came here, I heard rumors that another Godhand had challenged Marcus in who could eat the most."

"That doesn't sound too good," I laughed, backing further away. "Well, I'll see you there."

"Yes," she said suspiciously. "Yes you will...or I'm sure Alessa will come looking for you."

"Bye," I said as my voice wavered, doing my absolute best not to dwell on Alessa's matriarch complex.

I headed toward the city, preferring to maintain a healthy distance from uncomfortable conversation. Occasionally I would glance out from the corner of my eye to see if she was following me, but I was sure she wouldn't be - after all, if she needed to find me, she could do so with little effort. Her uncanny ability to defy impossible situations and do the unthinkable were well known, even among those of her class. She had more faith than any other angel I'd met, and this granted her some kind of unknown power that made me uneasy at times. Her classification was that of a Faithful, a generally small type of angel that had extraordinary faith in God, and Farah lived up to her namesake with horrifying excitement. During the war, I'd seen her take down Godhands and Guards like it was second nature. So, I was sure a game of hide-and-seek wouldn't end in my favor.

And, to make matters worse, I was undeniably a creature of habit. Therefore, it didn't take a detective to figure out where I was going - which right now was my second favorite spot in Heaven: the Fellowship Hall. A gigantic athletic stadium that boasted a buffet-style dining commons, lavished with diverse foods cooked and tailored for our consumption. Being angels, we didn't need it for survival, but the tastes were enjoyable and many of Heaven's host were not shy about it. Because we had no indicator in our anatomy to tell us when we were "full," many fell to borderline gluttony. Marcus, my fellow teammate, was a habitual offender, and we often had to drag him out of the cafeteria kicking and screaming.

But I wouldn't have to worry about that today. One of the reasons I loved the Fellowship Hall so much more than the brand new Café was because it was now deserted. Before the war, there had been an obvious division between those who embraced Lucifer's doctrine, and those who followed God. The violence hadn't started yet, but there was still separation. Those in Lucifer's camp had resided in what was now the Café, and as a result, many who sided with God kept their distance. It was just a simple cafeteria at the time, but that didn't mean it didn't peak anyone's interest. Every so often, an angel from one camp would visit the other, but from what I'd heard, the awkwardness had been profound, not to mention the fear of a fight - verbal or otherwise - breaking out. Rumors had only intensified the anxiety and eventually, each angel had stayed exclusively with the faction they had sided with.

After the war, with Lucifer and his fallen angels banished from Heaven, the Café was open to everyone, and in a great migration, the angels had stampeded there with abundant joy, thrilled over the all-new hot spot for them to enjoy. Not to mention the prospect of new food and new surroundings.

Naturally, I stayed behind.

It wasn't that I didn't want to see the Café, it was just that I needed more time to think, to mull over my next move. But the longer I took, the harder it was to concentrate. My friends, the unofficially designated Team Six, wanted me around. And in lieu of recent events, an angel in isolation looked suspicious at best, prompting their increasing number of visits to be laced with more and more concern. But I had to come up with some kind of plan to save Vergil, and ideas were coming up short no matter how hard I tried. Spending my hours staring at the representation of Earth was becoming synonymous with hoping a magic 8-ball could provide the right answer, and despite my immortality, I knew I couldn't be in this pondering limbo forever. Sooner or later, I would have a job to do. Sure, no duties had been assigned, and the humans had yet to be revealed to us, but the end of our leisure was near. As soon as we were to report for duty, I would have no more time to plan, and I would be no closer to a solution than when I had first started...

So what was the answer? Maybe...maybe a trip to the Earth, unprepared or not, would give me some insight into my next move. As long as I was cautious and didn't get too heavily involved...

And who knows?

Maybe it would be fun.

CHAPTER 2: Infiltration

Floating above the Fellowship Hall, I wondered if I should even bother going inside, when I heard an irritating guffaw behind me. I turned slowly, because, like facing any big animal, it was best to not make any sudden movements. This particular beast was a large, husky angel named Amos – a Godhand, sporting the only beard and bald head seen in Heaven. He stood out like a dead plant in paradise, which was only exacerbated by his indifference to his appearance.

"LYSIE! WHAT YOU DOING UP YONDER?!" he called from the steps below. I was currently about a mile up in the air but his voice was so loud, it was like he was right in front of me.

"DON'T CALL ME LYSIE!" I yelled back.

"WHAT?"

"DON'T CALL ME LY-"

"HUH? YOUR VOICE IS TOO SOFT! SPEAK UP!"

"God help me," I muttered as I made my descent. The burly angel was chuckling to himself like he had just told himself a good joke.

"Hi, Amos," I said, waiting for him to come back to his senses. If he were anyone else, I might have taken off to the sky, avoiding the conversation altogether, but Amos deserved all of Team Six's respect. After all, he did help save us during the war by throwing a house on top of one of Lucifer's generals.

"Why are you at this place? The Café's better," he said, his accent thick like he had a swarm of bees in his mouth and it was his mission to not let one sting him.

"I need to be alone," I said, hoping he would get the hint. "Sort out a few things."

"But why be alone outside then? You got food and thinking on the inside." Amos gestured toward the Fellowship Hall.

"Well put...so why are you here?"

"Marcus," the big angel said, rubbing the top of his bald head. "He asked if I could come here where the honeycombs are and pick up some to go with the onions he got. The honeycombs aren't over there at the Café."

"Onions and honeycombs...it doesn't sound like a great combination. "

"Naw. But Marcus was all determined and serious, saying he's doing it for research."

I had to laugh at that. Whenever I had a project I was researching, Marcus was usually the last one to assist.

"Marcus doing research, huh? When it comes to food, he's full of surprises."

"Speaking a surprises, how do you feel about my company?" His wide grin was beginning to creep me out, and somehow I suspected there were ulterior motives behind his question.

"Why don't you tell me why you're asking and I'll consider answering."

"I might be joining Team Six!"

I felt an alarming drop in my angelic pressure. Was it possible for an angel to faint? Could I go unconscious from a feeling? Amos didn't take much seriously, even in battle, and he had the reputation of being a klutz.

"Who told you that?" I asked, maintaining my composure.

"Cadence offered me the job when we were discussing...uh...you know, what happened....to uh, why Team Six only has five members right now."

"I'm not a baby. You can say it – when Vergil left. And now it's strange that we're a five angel team with a name like Team Six."

"Yeah," he said, rubbing his paunch idly. "But, I wouldn't join if it weren't, you know, unanimous." He said the word like a bee had finally hit its mark.

It took me all of two seconds to find my answer. Team Six had fought many angels in the war, including Lucifer himself, and had somehow survived to battle on, but we had been unsuccessful in averting Vergil's betrayal. And that wasn't because he was evil from the beginning, or had a hidden agenda. It was because we had chased him into Lucifer's arms. We had made him feel unwelcome. He was an Archangel, and we had been so afraid of his power, and worried that he would outshine us, that we treated him like an outcast. By the time we realized our folly, it was too late. The damage had left serious scars and Lucifer had been able to persuade him to join his cause. At that crucial moment, I was the only one there to see his transformation take place. I was the only one able to stop it, and I didn't. Such division couldn't happen again. Regardless of my opinion or anyone else's, if someone wanted to join the team, they were on the team.

"You have my vote," I said strongly, grabbing his hand and shaking it. "Never too many Godhands right?"

"Thanks, Lys-"

"But on one condition," I said, interrupting him. "Don't ever call me Lysie again. It's Lysander. That's the name God gave me. I want to keep it that way."

"Sure thing," he chuckled. "That name sure gets you heated, don't it?"

"I've discovered I can get quite serious when I'm emotional," I laughed, the anger dissipating.

"I see that. Hey, while we're talking – Cadence wanted to see you when you're free. He left the Café to head over to his place. Says he misses his friend and wants to talk to you about something urgent."

"Thanks for the message. I'll go see him now."

"Welcome. And uh, you think it's okay for honeycombs and onions to be combined like that?"

"No," I chuckled. "But Marcus would declare war on the whole building if you came back empty. Let him have it."

"Thank you for the advice," he said and I gave him a half-salute, gliding upwards to catch an adequate current. I couldn't help but notice the black hole in the distance, so close to Heaven, sucking in everything around it like a chained-down tornado - everything except Heaven itself. Heaven was so animated and alive, yet unaffected by the powerful phenomenon in its backyard. There was no doubt in my mind. God was still in control. If He wasn't, Heaven would have been sucked into that hole a long time ago. There would be nothing but chaos and disorder. I mean, why put a black hole there at all? Why not another expanse of land, or more space? Why not another painting of colors, blues and reds, oranges and greens, swirling around endlessly like pollen in a light meadow breeze? Why a monster, that destroyed all in its path, yet unable to devour the one thing sitting beside it? Why would God have put that black hole right next to the paradise He built?

Perhaps Heaven had a future in God's plans that extended far beyond the black hole's pull. Perhaps it was needed and therefore protected in sight of a greater plan…or maybe I was just overthinking again. Maybe God just liked black holes…

I considered asking Cadence about his opinion on the subject when I arrived at his home. As I descended to his front steps, I saw that I wouldn't have to knock because he was already closing his door, rushing out like he was late for an appointment, his thin wings outstretched and ready to fly. I met him in the air.

"Where are you off to so fast?" I asked him. He chuckled to himself, half startled by my intrusion.

"Looks like I'll have a partner in this."

"Where are you going?" I asked, feeling that old sense of brotherhood at his use of the word 'partner.'

"I'm about to check out Alessa's house."

"Okay," I said flatly, furrowing my brow. What was the hurry?

"I see that look on your face," he laughed, his lanky arms pointing at me. "You're wondering what's going on."

"I would say that's a fair assessment."

"You know how Alessa comes over to my place all the time? Unannounced?"

"Yes. I remember watching the two of you argue about how it was becoming a staple in our get-togethers."

"Well, she makes fun of my furniture arrangement every time she's here, constantly trying to change it around."

"I'm sure she gets frustrated when nothing happens," I laughed.

"Furious," Cadence confirmed amusingly.

"I take it you've never budged on this."

"Of course not. I just ignore her ranting, but she has been getting more aggressive lately."

"It's because she's bored," I said. Cadence nodded in agreement.

"True. She's been to the Earth a couple times, but she doesn't want to go anymore until we all can, like a family. She says we should have another war if it will mean we can all sit down and have a simple dinner together."

"She's insane," I snickered, "but at least her heart's in the right place."

"Or she wants more attention..." he trailed off. "Lysander, I've missed your company."

"I've been busy," I said shyly. "You understand."

"I do, but just remember that we're all here to help. Being divided never ends well, and unfortunately we learned that the hard way."

"That's the issue, Cadence. We are still divided. Our team is incomplete."

"Lysander, you understand what I'm saying."

"But you refuse to acknowledge what I'm saying," I stressed, slowing down my flight. Cadence matched my speed but still kept an eye out for Alessa, in case she intercepted us.

"I get it." He said, his voice rising an octave. "We're an angel short, but there's nothing we can do about that right now."

"You can help me with my mission."

"It's..." Cadence sighed, closing his eyes. "It's..."

"Pointless?"

"You said it, not me."

"It's only pointless if you believe it is. Whatever happened to God being in control of all things? There may be a way to save him!"

"He made his choice."

"So now he's not family anymore?"

"If you really want to go down this road, then why don't we get to the heart of it?" he said, gritting his teeth, waiting for my permission to say some harsh truth.

"Fine. Go ahead."

"You're scared," Cadence replied. "You're so afraid to fail that you hide away at Raphael's when you should be scouring the Earth, searching for him. If you truly put his well-being above your feelings, you'd be down there. Tell me I'm wrong."

"No," I said, picking up speed, more to avoid the conversation than to reach our goal. Cadence was my confidant, my brother and my friend, but sometimes I hated it when he spoke the truth in such a cold, matter-of-fact tone. Saying I shouldn't be afraid didn't make me any less apprehensive.

"I guess you're right," I muttered finally. I saw him relax at my response.

"I don't want to be," he said. "But it needed to be heard. Tell you what. If you go to Earth with us and be a part of the team, then I'll make sure we do things your way if we see Vergil. We'll stand behind you and support your lead."

Now this was different...my team willing to join in my Vergil project?

"You'll help me?"

"We were never against your research, or what you've set out to do. It's a noble thing to save a friend. It's just...we think his decision finalized matters, while you think it hasn't. I'm not sure how to put it. But maybe I'm wrong about this...and my doubt...is enough to convince me to give you a shot."

"Well, thank you," I said, beaming with joy. It would be a lot easier to face Vergil with the others by my side, especially since I wasn't sure if I could accomplish anything on my own. I was beginning to believe that all I did was think too much for my own good and spend all my time analyzing, rather than actually doing something.

"There's one more thing we need to discuss," Cadence said, growing serious again.

"You better hurry," I said. "We're almost at Alessa's."

"We're still an angel short," he said solemnly. "And until we find Vergil and get him back, we could use some extra firepower."

"I already talked to Amos," I admitted, to Cadence's surprise. "He told me about your conversation. I shook his hand and congratulated him, giving him my vote for his membership."

"That was pretty nice of you."

"Is it that hard to fathom considering recent events?"

"True," Cadence laughed. "Then I guess that's taken care of. You were the last vote to usher him in. I figured -"

"Shhhh," I whispered, cutting him off. "We're here."

Alessa's building was quite anticlimactic. To be honest, I had half expected a bronze, moon-sized statue of a lion as her house, claws outstretched in mid-pounce - a wide, gaping mouth boasting the entrance to her home. But the structure before us was quaint and cozy, taking on the appearance of a colonial house in the midst of a suburban neighborhood. The exterior was covered in bay windows framed with tiled shutters, coated with fresh white paint and an out-of-place purple door in the front. A small door knocker hung in the middle of the door. Funny enough, it was a perfect likeness of the lion I had in my imagination. I couldn't help snickering at the thought but Cadence put a finger to his lips. I stopped my laugh short and fluttered down to one of the windows. Cadence headed to the entrance.

"Is she here?" I asked. Cadence shrugged his shoulders, brushing a hand against the front door.

"I barely pay attention to her when she's right next to me."

"I can't really see inside," I said, pressing my face and hands against the window. "It's very fuzzy."

"Is there purple?"

"I can't see any colors at all. Maybe gray."

"That doesn't sound right," he sighed. "And this is definitely her house, so what's the plan?"

"The plan?"

"Yeah, I was hoping I'd run into you because I needed your help."

"This is what was so urgent? I thought you wanted to talk to me about Amos."

"No. No. I needed your expertise."

"On breaking and entering?"

"You break into Raphael's every day."

"I have express permission!"

"To what, vacuum his floor? C'mon, let's get to the heart of the matter."

"If that's going to become a phrase of yours..."

"You'll what?" he asked, bored. "What will you do?"

"Are you getting confrontational?" I said, scowling his way. He threw up his hands in surrender.

"I could never embody a word that long," he chuckled. "I just want to get into Alessa's house, and I need your help to do it. You're the master coordinator."

"Why does that make me sound like I plan birthday parties and weddings?"

"What are those?" he asked, very confused. I forgot that I was one of the few angels that searched the mental database for fun. I was sure Cadence had only just scratched the surface of it - for whatever knowledge he had actually needed in Heaven. Sure, he was intelligent and wise enough on his own, but he was also very, very, very lazy sometimes.

"Fine. Let me think of a way in," I said, examining the house. "Wait here."

I hovered around the house, taking in its unimposing features, the friendly vibe it gave off, and how cozy and inviting it appeared. It was so unlike Alessa that the answer popped in my head almost immediately. I circled the house once more for confirmation and then went back to Cadence who was nervously shifting his eyes back and forth, crouching in a corner by the front door.

"What's wrong?" I asked, gently floating next to him.

"She's here," he whispered. "I'm sure of it."

"What makes you so sure?"

"Trust me," he said, his eyes widening to its limits. "When you're around her as much as I am, you get a sixth sense."

"A sixth sense?" I snickered, but he slapped a hand on my shoulder.

"This is not a game!" he exclaimed. "Who knows what she'll do if she finds out we're here!"

"So is she or is she not here?" I asked.

"Not sure. Not sure. What do we do?"

"Let's go inside. Maybe she's just flying past. C'mon. Let me show you."

I reached out, grabbed the door knocker, and beat it against the door twice. Cadence was unimpressed. I waited patiently for the echo to cease. After a second, I grabbed the doorknob and turned it, granting us entrance into the house, and an exit from Alessa's potential wrath.

The interior blew away all of my expectations, for I had envisioned about ten different possible layouts of Alessa's home before we entered...

...And none of them matched.

There was nothing inside. Nothing. No furniture, or fixed structures like a fireplace. No lamps or pictures. Not even multiple rooms. It was one, bare-walled room with an unknown color so dull and invisible, my eyes had to constantly search for a point of origin, a place to fix my eyes upon or else I would be lost in the monotony. It wasn't scary or intimidating, just boring and vague. Cadence was obviously feeling the same way I did because his face was scrunched up in disgust, unable to interpret this strange ensemble. Had she even been in the house yet?

"What is this?" Cadence said, immediately thrown off by the sound of his own voice. It was so strange - it echoed, but it didn't.

Almost as if, while it was just starting to gain some speed, someone stomped it out.

"This is Alessa," I said, not entirely sure what I meant. Cadence started giggling to himself.

"Well, maybe this only confirms my greatest suspicion. That Alessa's head is full of nothing but air."

We started chuckling to ourselves, examining the room to the best of our ability, when a whisper was heard between us.

"I heard that."

CHAPTER 3: One Accord

Cadence screamed, or I screamed. Either way, we were both terrified. We jumped forward and turned, looking more for a way to escape than to find our aggressor. To our horror, there she stood, before us, arms by her side with clenched fists shaking in rage, her wings outstretched to block our exit. Purple-streaked, silver hair hid her face like a veil, and her body heaved up and down beneath the thin purple armor. Her eyes, barely visible beyond the hair, were thirsty for vengeance. Cadence instinctively reached behind him, unsnapped a harness beneath his wings and produced a flimsy shield. He held it in front of him, blocking most of his body from potential harm while increasing his defensive stance.

Cadence, the Guard, was ready for action. A classification of angel with unparalleled defense, he could be hit over and over without worry of going unconscious. I'm sure this only caused further frustration for the angel in front of us – the rightful owner of the home we had broken into.

Alessa.

"Stand back from the door," Cadence demanded, shuffling forward with his shield pressed close. "This is an order from your leader."

"You never wanted to be our leader," she said, her mouth hidden behind the curtain of hair. "Besides, no one appointed you as our captain. As far as I'm concerned, Team Six is composed of equal members."

"I don't want to hurt you," he said, his voice muffled and beginning to lose authority.

"Cadence," she nodded to him, then me. "Lysander...what are you doing in my house?"

"It was his idea," I said too quickly. I got a shield to the chin for that.

"Traitor," Cadence muttered, resetting his shield back to a defensive position.

"Tell you what," Alessa said in a menacing tone, wiping the curtain from her eyes so we could see her glare in its totality. "Lysander, if you confirm to me that this was all Cadence's doing, then I will let you go…WITH the condition that you go to Earth with us within the next couple of hours."

"No need for the threats," I said. "It was all…"

Another shield to the face. My nose got this one.

"Alessa, what will it take for us to get out of here alive?" Cadence asked, his eyes peering over the shield just enough to scope out the room.

"Tell me the truth. Why are you here?"

"Because you make fun of my house. I don't like it so I wanted to get some leverage against you."

"I thought my comments didn't bother you. You just sit there on your couch and shrug your shoulders and say 'whatever' like you're cooler than the ocean."

"Your comments have weight. They affect me more than you think."

"Oh really? Then why don't you tell me next time rather than invading my privacy?"

"You're hard to talk to."

"I guess so," she huffed, and turned to me. "And I take it Lysander thinks the same!"

"Why would…"

"You never hang out with us! That's how I know!" she screamed, her hands becoming whips, snapping at the air like they were striking rattlesnakes.

"We just want to leave," Cadence half-whined, "or…or…I'll throw this shield at you."

Alessa glared at him in fury, clenching her jaws and squeezing her fists like she was destroying a stress ball in each of her hands.

"Okay. I know how to end this," she said. I didn't mean to gasp in horror.

"This won't take long," she said, glaring at me now. "You think I'm an airhead because my house is empty…but there's a purpose for this, like there is for all things with God. You forget, I'm a Glory – an angel with constant communication with the Almighty Himself. And that plays out here. You broke into my house, so you might as well stay for this, and in the end, I'll have gotten you back."

"Get behind me, Lysander," Cadence ordered and Alessa put her hands together like she was praying. I began to say something, but before the words left my lips, my mouth disappeared. My eyes. My hands. My legs. My entire body disintegrated, and became one with the air of the room. In the next moment, a light poured into the house like a flood, filling it to the brink like water.

God had entered the room.

His presence massaged every atom of my being, and warmed them like they were each sitting in their own individual toaster, baking with love and care. I was put back together again just so I could be stretched out – the knots of stress and the negativity of my mind soothed, the worries of the future taken from the fabric of my mind, cleaned, folded, pressed, and handed back to me brand new and soft, radiant with new life and hope.

I opened my eyes and was allowed to see, however briefly, God's face. I'm sure it was just a manifestation, a picture for my benefit and not actually His express image - our angelic compositions couldn't handle seeing God in all His glory - but I saw it nonetheless. It was vague, and I could only see the outlines of two eyes, the faint border of a head, traces of hair. He seemed to smile, or at least what I felt inside me told me He smiled. I couldn't interpret Him with any senses known to me as of yet, but I tried hard, and I felt a beam of light, like a small hand, press gently past my lightning blue armor and onto my chest. It remained still and warm and told me to relax. But it wasn't a command, it was a suggestion lined with such warmth, it would have been insane not to obey. The hand moved deeper still, to my spiritual heart, and maintained its press, reminding me of when the war had first been over. When I had denied myself entry into His Throne Room, concluding that, as long as Vergil couldn't be there, I wouldn't be either.

But it had been such a mistake.

Such a foolish mistake.

I had refused His presence when it was what I had needed all along to invigorate me, to cleanse the darkness and enrich my capacity to bring Vergil back to God. My friends were a welcome help in my quest, but ultimately, it was God I needed the most. This I now understood, and for my folly I was sorry.

Before the light began to wane, I apologized over and over, repenting of my neglect. And He forgave me, because I genuinely needed it.

And then the light, and God, were gone.

And we were outside Alessa's house, shaking with delight, energized by His personal visit. Cadence dropped his shield to the ground and rubbed his hands through his hair while I laughed to myself. Alessa stood by us, smirking, shaking herself over the outpouring of bliss.

"Told you I'd get you," Alessa chuckled. "Now you'll always want to come over to my place…AND YOU CAN'T!"

"That is so mean," Cadence whispered, shaking his head in amusement. The overflow of emotion was beginning to subside, but I still couldn't get over the experience.

"You're telling me your house is designed for God to enter and exit as He pleases?" I exclaimed, pointing back at her place.

"That's right. No need to go to the Throne Room when I can fellowship with God right here."

"And you never invited us over?"

"Obviously you never asked!" she yelled. "Why you seem to think I'm so heartless is beyond me, but I do actually care!"

"Did God tell on us?" Cadence asked, holstering his shield behind him. "That we were over here, I mean."

"Yep," Alessa said. "I was in the Café with Marcus, watching him stuff his face, when God told me to leave urgently. He said that you, Lysander, needed some help. Imagine my surprise when He gave me the directions to my own house and I found you two breaking in!"

"Are you ever going to let this go?" Cadence winced over her excessive display. "That was so ten minutes ago. It's in the past."

Alessa rushed forward, taking Cadence off guard. Before he could react, she quickly ducked under him, spun behind him, and somehow unsnapped his shield. In the same breath, she threw the shield as hard as she could into space. Cadence just stood there in disbelief.

"Why would you do that?" he asked her calmly. His right eye twitched.

"That was so ten seconds ago," she mocked. "It's in the past…now fetch."

"You're so mean," Cadence huffed under his breath. Without waiting for a reply, he flew out to retrieve his shield. Alessa giggled at his departure but I was still nervous about any future vengeance that could come my way.

"So you're coming with us to Earth, right?" she said, more like an implied command than a question.

"I was going to go regardless. Cadence had already asked me."

"Oh, we all just listen to Cadence," she grunted. "How did he convince you to hang up your sulky pants?"

"He said the team would support me in how I want to handle Vergil when we see him."

"There's no guarantee he'll listen."

"I think he might. I haven't given up on him."

"Don't see why. Last I recall, he took a sword and stabbed you in the chest. I mean, if that's what you call love…"

"You weren't there," I whispered. "And how do you know about that? I didn't tell anyone. Did God mention it to you?"

"He didn't have to. I took a trip to the Archive Building, plain and simple. Lots of information and videos there."

"There's a video of me getting stabbed?" I exclaimed, suddenly very anxious. How many people had seen it?

"Don't worry, there's more interesting footage to look at, if you can call it that. But yes, unfortunately it's there."

"Can I delete it?"

"Haven't you done enough breaking and entering for one day?"

"It's just embarrassing."

"No, what's embarrassing is hiding out at Raphael's when the rest of the angels are spending precious time together. This is a stage in our lives allotted for peace, harmony, and unity. That might not be true forever so we should enjoy it while we can."

"It's still embarrassing."

"Do you want to go see it?"

"No…no, not right now."

"Then shut up about it."

Cadence flew back, shield rescued and secured in place. He landed roughly, skidding on the ground under his feet. Alessa snickered at the descent and hugged him abruptly, almost sending him flying back off the small island again.

"I went too far," she said remorsefully. "With the whole throwing the shield thing."

"You're unstable," he laughed, staring down at her. "And crazy. Why the sudden change in attitude?"

"Who says I have an attitude?"

"We're all crazy," I said, thinking about our group in general. I heard a chuckle up above as three more angels joined our ensemble.

"Welcome to Team Six," Farah said, waving a hand toward us. Amos was the recipient of this gesture, gliding down behind her with Marcus under his arm. By the way Marcus's face was pained, I could tell he had eaten so much his angelic pressure had begun to drop. I made a mental note to see if Alessa could ask God sometime about how that worked.

"It feels soooooooooooo good to be together again," Farah mused as she stood in the middle of us all, laughing and patting us on the knees. Marcus tried to laugh but groaned instead. Amos guffawed and Cadence shook his head while Alessa sighed.

My family.

Insane.

Strange.

Maniacal at times.

But the greatest group of angels one could ask for in a bind. I was grateful that God had placed me in their care, and I promised myself that I wouldn't betray their trust. This was where I belonged. This was our team. Six angels all waiting for direction and purpose, but relying, in the meantime, on one another to weather the trials that came our way. Or more like trial...there had been only one so far.

"He better?" Marcus grunted, pointing straight at me as the laughing subsided.

"I have a name," I said. Marcus shuffled over and picked me up by the wings. I stared at him with listless eyes as he bounced me up and down lightly.

"Your name is sad face."

"Don't hurt yourself coming up with adjectives, Marcus," I said flatly. "You might have an aneurysm."

"Cadence!' Marcus whined in his deep voice, finally dropping me. "He's using big words again."

"Marcus, you know all of them. Just access the vocabulary section of your mental database," he sighed in a bored tone. "Just stay away from the food anthology this time."

I didn't have the formula perfected, but I devised that the more people there were near Cadence, the greater his propensity to lethargy and boredom.

"Oh," Marcus replied, searching his mind for the definition. "Okay. Got it."

"What are you doing?" Cadence asked, irritated.

"Comeback," Marcus grunted, rubbing his hair like it was full of dandruff.

He faced me and lifted his chin like I wasn't worth his breath. He pointed a meaty index finger my way and declared for all to hear -

"Stupid Lysander!"

"You're in the vocabulary section and that's the best you came up with?" I snapped back at him. Cadence caught Marcus's fist before it hit my face.

"You two get worse whenever you're together," he sighed. "It's why I don't let you visit my house anymore. It gets trashed and none of you bother helping with the clean up!"

"We go to Alessa house?" Marcus asked, pointing at it.

"Uh, no!" Alessa replied fervently. "No one's breaking my stuff!"

"What stuff?" Cadence huffed. "You have no stuff. Not even a couch to sit on!"

"Really?" Amos spoke up. "That's weird. Maybe we should take a looksee."

"No one's taking a looksee!!!" Alessa began to scream. "And what is a looksee?!"

"What does it matter?" Farah said to Cadence, miffed that she had only gotten to see his mansion once. "You can easily use your imagination and fix any damage we cause."

"That's not the point," he muttered, rubbing his forehead. I had to laugh.

"Giving up already?" I asked, patting him on the back.

"That's bad if Lysander's giving you encouragement," Alessa said. "You know what? I actually like the fact that he's speaking up for himself now. He used to be so reserved before."

"He still is," Farah chipped in. "It's just that he gets irritated and then throws a tantrum as if someone just stole his favorite shirt."

"I'm right here," I said.

"Speaking of stealing," Alessa spoke over me, "if it weren't for the fact that I have nothing inside, I'm sure these two hoodlums would have taken my furniture."

"What? Why?"

"We're right here," I said, a little louder.

"They broke into my house!" Alessa exclaimed. "If it weren't for God giving me fair warning, who knows what other crimes they would have committed! Lysander says it was Cadence's idea, but of course, he was the mastermind, figuring out how to get past my locks —"

"Seriously, I'm right here," I stressed. "And it's not my fault you can get in by banging on the door a couple of times with the door knocker."

"Gee, thanks!" Alessa shouted, throwing her hands up in the air. "Why don't you announce it to all of Heaven! Go to the center of the city and pass out brochures on how to get inside my house like it's a raging tourist attraction!"

"It might as well be! You can bask in God's presence whenever you want!"

"What does he mean?" Farah asked innocently, turning to Alessa.

"Lysander needs to go down to Earth," Cadence said calmly, changing the subject for the greater good. "That will lift our spirits."

"I've been saying that forever," Amos chimed into the conversation heartily. I could only imagine what he must think of us – our bickering and friendly teasing.

"You...no talk that much," Marcus muttered low. "Forever is long." Amos put a gigantic arm around him, pulling him close while he laughed from his belly.

"Marcus, you just like making comments like that cuz you know it will get my attention. You like my attention, Marcus?" he guffawed. Alessa sucked her teeth and walked away in disgust. I couldn't help but crack a smile.

"I guess Lysander likes the idea of going to Earth," Farah misinterpreted. "We should leave as soon as possible then. We'll be able to travel there in less than five minutes, if we go quickly."

"Do we have to go right away?" I offered. Now that the trip was so close to actually happening, I could feel the anxiety seeping back into my spirit. "Couldn't we go to the Fellowship Hall and get some food first?"

"YES," Marcus stressed slowly, sticking out his chest. I knew I would get his vote.

"It's better if we go to Earth now," Alessa said. "Before it's announced that the humans can be seen. Pretty much everyone has seen the landscape already so it's not too crowded."

"This might not be a good excuse..." I hesitated, wondering how they would take my stalling, "...but I promised myself that if any problems arose on Earth, I'd help...as needed...but since there's only two humans right now, and they're in God's protection, I'm not needed. He is the one that ended the war, after all...so, um, maybe you should call me when there are more humans around, when I can actually make a difference. Like when some of them start to go away from God..."

From the looks on their face, I could tell my excuse was way past the point of being rejected.

"Wow," Amos said, cringing at my words. "That was dark. You need a trip more than I thought, buddy!"

"Before you start assuming they'll turn away from God," Farah said, "shouldn't you at least see what they're like first? I mean, no one but God has a clue of what happened to Lucifer and his angels. For all we know, they're chained up forever. Not even the Glory are getting a straight answer when they inquire about the fallen angels' status."

"It's true," Alessa confirmed. "No clue of what happened."

"So the humans may never turn away," Farah continued. "And even if they do, shouldn't you get to know how they operate so you'll realize the best way to handle them?"

"And you are the tactician," Cadence said flatly. "If we ever have to go to war with or against the humans, it's best if we have our strategist well-informed."

"Fine. Fine!" I said, realizing they weren't going to let me slide on this. "It seems you're all in one accord on this. Way to gang up on me."

"What are friends for?" Amos chuckled.

"This is exciting," Cadence yawned. "It's been a while since I went on a vacation there myself." Marcus scratched his head and looked up at the sky, lost in his own thoughts.

"Vacation," he repeated. "Let me find meaning of word."

"God help you," Cadence said wearily. Farah and I couldn't stop giggling. Only Marcus would have to access his mental database for the definition of a word like "vacation."

"I don't want to leave just yet," I said, encountering a few sudden, disapproving looks. "I want to visit the Throne Room first, if that's okay."

"Of course," Cadence said. "We won't deny you that. But afterwards, you're going, even if it means we have to drag you down to Earth."

I nodded and we silently made our way to the Throne Room, my five escorts following me closely to make sure I didn't try to escape.

We made it with little effort, letting our wings take us there autonomously like we were flying back home. It was still strange to me, seeing Heaven restored to all its glory, still majestic, still a land of wonder - especially with its canopy of stars traveling around it like a kaleidoscope. It was quite beautiful. Yet when I closed my eyes, I could only see Heaven as it once was – a war zone. A land in which buildings crumbled and angels darted through the skies clashing swords and fists. The dazzling portrait that was now displayed before me seemed like an illusion, or some kind of trickery, hiding its real form behind a cloak. As if all the angels who darted around were really in a state of amnesia, participating in the masquerade. I knew it wasn't true, that they were probably trying to block out the memories just as much as I did...but what could alleviate my thoughts? My friends had been a wonderful distraction, but already I was losing strength to carry on. A trip to the Throne Room would surely grant me an extra boost of energy. Of course, I had already experienced God's presence in Alessa's house, but it was so much more personal if I went to Him directly.

The doors were open, which was a blessing in and of itself. The building was so enormous, its frame stretched miles and miles into space, and the doors matched its height. It took an impressive group of angels just to budge them an inch so many often got frustrated and sat on the front steps, waiting for God to open them Himself. Thankfully, God had been waiting for me.

I was barely inside when I felt His welcome, greeting me like I had arrived from a long journey. My first step into the Throne Room was like walking on lava, a liquid yet firm path manifested itself for me to stand on as I strolled deeper into His presence. My friends waited for me by the door, letting me take my time and causing no distraction. My body tingled in joy as I was engulfed in light. All my negative thoughts were lifted and once again destroyed instantaneously. What thoughts were left in my head brought me to my knees in worship, when suddenly a massive group of angels, different from any type I'd ever seen, shot across the massive hall, crying, "HOLY, HOLY, HOLY, is the Lord of hosts: the whole Earth is full of His glory!" I had never seen them before, and despite the warmth filling my spirit, I couldn't help but watch in awe at how they praised God. Their cries alone shook the door posts, and they were so fast and relentless in their worship that I could barely see what they looked like. All I could make out was that they had six wings: a pair to shield their face, a pair to cover their feet, and a final pair for flying. I tried to search my mental database for what they were, but I was cut off by a flood of emotion as God's presence increased in intensity. I gave up. Honestly, I really did think too much.

This - the feeling that Lucifer had claimed we'd never experience again, was right here. Ironic that he had fought for it, or so he had claimed, but in so doing, he had ensured that he would never feel it again…

The unknown angels that flew throughout the Throne Room, using every ounce of their angelic pressure to praise the Lord – this was the group that Lucifer had claimed he belonged to, yet he was nothing like them at all. He was a liar, and his current status alone was proof of that…

When I came to, I was back outside, energized and facing my friends who were all chuckling to themselves. To be blunt, I just felt good, so I didn't care that they laughed at my expense. If I had gone to the Throne Room from the start, I probably would've been cured from my depression long ago. But like a drug addict, I had kept returning to the source of the problem in my search for answers, instead of giving the real solution a chance.

Turning back to the doors, I silently thanked God for His help and promised Him that next time I was in the Throne Room I would try to pay more attention to Him, get a better understanding of who He was, and not just take in His light selfishly. For now though, I was sure God was happy I had come at all.

"Well look who's found some joy," Cadence chuckled. I playfully slapped him on the cheek.

"Sorry about that everyone," I said. "But I needed it."

"Don't have to tell me twice," Cadence replied.

"Did you get a look at the Seraphim inside?" Alessa asked me, arms folded across her armor.

"That's what they're called?"

"God told me what they were on my third visit to the Throne Room. I tried to research them but the mental database has no entries on them."

"And they're not mingling with us at all," Farah added. "Isn't that strange?"

"What were they created for?"

"If I had to guess," Cadence chipped in, "I would say constant praise."

"If only I could have been a Seraphim," I sighed. "Praising God all the time, being with Him every moment - it's what I wanted from the beginning."

"I didn't see any Seraphim fighting alongside us," Farah replied, "so God must have other plans for them. Being in the war clearly wasn't one of them."

I refused to let my good mood be ruined by talk of the past. I was finally excited to see Earth and nothing was going to sour my mood.

"It's irrelevant now," I said. "Let's go visit Earth and see what all the fuss is about."

As those last words escaped my lips, a whooshing sound was heard and an impressive wind flew between our group. Alessa cried out a "HEY!" as I realized just as she did that it was an angel on the move, almost colliding with us unnecessarily.

"Sorry. Sorry about that," the angel said. A Glory.

"Where are you off to in such a hurry?" Alessa asked him. "You almost hit us."

"I'm surprised you're just standing there, talking like you didn't hear the news."

"What news?"

His eyes widened in amazement as he pointed directly at me.

"What you do now?" Marcus asked me as I shrugged my shoulders.

"Isn't that a Messenger with you?" the angel asked and the whole group looked at me for answers. I gave them a dumbfounded look as the angel slapped a palm to his forehead.

"Okay, well, I have to go so I'll make this quick. The word is that we can observe the humans now. The Garden of Eden, where they live, is open and it seems like all of Heaven is headed down there to see them."

"NO WAY!!!" Farah screamed out as the rest of the group started trembling with excitement.

The angel left before I could ask a question, leaving us all to wonder what the humans would be like. For some reason, I was more excited than I had been in a long time.

A mischievous smile suddenly graced Farah's lips.

"RACE!!!!" Farah screamed, but Cadence grabbed her shoulder, giving her a silent message. Interpreting the gesture, I lifted Cadence's hand from Farah's shoulder and nodded that I was okay.

"Don't worry, Cadence," I said. "I understand that you're scared I'll break down again because racing reminds me of Vergil, but you know what? He never held back whenever he was challenged to one, and neither will I. So...the first one to Earth wins!"

I leaned back, letting my wings catch me from falling and, with an influx of air puffing them up like a hot air balloon, I was catapulted to the skies. Quickly turning around, I felt a surge of energy course through me and I willingly summoned all the angelic pressure I could muster. With a laugh escaping my throat, I took off, leaving them all to follow my lead. Marcus bellowed in excitement from the challenge and was second to lift off. Another second later, we were all powering forward, leaving nothing behind, and focusing every ounce of angelic pressure within us on our speed. We raced not out of sport, or competition. We did it because we needed it, to cleanse our minds and our emotions. To put all of our negative thoughts aside and just perform an act, as childish as it may be...together.

CHAPTER 4: The Other Thing Created on the First Day

I tightened my fist and pushed forward, fighting for millimeters as we rocketed toward the Earth. Through the black hole by Heaven's door we flew, spiraling past all of the special debris it had picked up since its birth, dodging planets and stars, meteors and psychedelically-colored gases that had once made up a galaxy. Farah even let the black hole absorb her for a second, separating her angelic body into microscopic pieces and casting them in all directions like she was sand being thrown in the wind. She came back together almost instantly at will and laughed like I had never heard before.

We eventually emerged from the void, its gravitational pull still begging to shackle our legs as we abandoned its clutches. We made our way to Earth riding a wave of excitement: spinning on the small black holes that traveled through space like a flock of geese, skating on the icy rivers that flowed throughout the Milky Way, and bursting through the many planets that made up Earth's solar system. We all cackled hysterically as Marcus tried to fit through one of them, which was a horrible idea since he was obviously too big, and as a result, the miniature black hole failed to suck him in entirely. In frustration, he climbed from its grip and joined the pursuit in beating me to the Earth.

Somewhere around Jupiter, I let go of all I had left, trying not to let the planet's hydrogen composition hold back my spiritual body. I let my wings grasp every ounce of spiritual air I could manage from the cold space, drinking from the light within the darkness, the life within the inanimate blackness, and I let it propel me beyond my angelic limits, my body becoming a beacon of light within itself, a miniature star moving like a comet toward Earth's atmosphere.

I hit the atmosphere with the force of a tsunami but it didn't hurt. Nevertheless, I free-fell towards the ground as if it had, caring little for who would win the race. I just let the darkness disappear and transform into a beautiful sky, slowly closing my eyes and dropping to my destination, opening my wings and spinning wildly like a top that was unable to wobble. My friends were thrilled at my new playful attitude and followed suit. Except Marcus - who was still trying to win. He sped past me for first place, looking back periodically to make sure I didn't start accelerating again. But within a mile from the finish line, Farah came out of nowhere, attached herself to the back of Marcus and used him as a launching pad. Ejecting herself at the last second, she sped forward just enough to win the race entirely. Marcus kept silent, but I could see him fuming even from a distance – his shoulders raised and tense as he huffed angrily. One day, camaraderie wasn't going to be enough anymore. Couldn't Farah let him win once in a while?

I hit the grass on one knee, breathing in the mixture of oxygen and nitrogen, though I didn't need it to survive. I just wanted to feel it crawl through my body and know how it felt for myself. It tasted kind of like water actually, just not as heavy. I had once, on a dare in Heaven, tried some grass from a plain near Raphael's and it had tasted horrible, so I had rinsed the feeling away with water from a nearby river. This oxygen was quite similar.

The rest of the group dropped to the ground as I surveyed my surroundings. We were in a meadow, similar to the ones in Heaven actually, yet there were some significant differences. One of them was the rows of trees outlining the meadow's borders, standing like sentinels against an impending army. Behind those rows were small streams that eventually led into larger rivers, giving off the impression of further protection.

I brushed my hand leisurely through the grass, thinking of how strange it felt. It was soft but prickly, very distinct from the fluffy turf back home. This grass couldn't have been made for purely sitting. So I decided to dig deeper and eventually I found dirt. Scooping some into my hand, I was ready to play with it, but as I stood up, the soil didn't come with me. It stayed exactly where it was. Confused, I stuck my hand in the dirt again and lifted my hand up a second time, but nothing happened, as if I were made of air. Thankfully, Amos attempted to relieve me from my encroaching madness.

"I did the exact same thing the first time," he said. "Grass, dirt, trees, plants...they're all alive and breathing but they can't talk to us the way we do to each other."

"Then what's their language?" I asked. Cadence stepped in.

"What Amos is trying to say," he replied, "is that our interaction with the surroundings down here will be very unique. In Heaven, nothing is truly off limits and we can touch or play with everything to our heart's content. But unfortunately, it's not that simple on Earth."

"On my first visit," Farah giggled, "I tried to turn a tree into a shield, alter the structure the same way we can in Heaven. When nothing happened, I was just as surprised as you are."

"You couldn't do something?" I mused in astonishment. "You?"

"Looks like there are set rules here," she said solemnly.

"It's so different," I said, more to myself than anyone in particular. "It's like every single organism is an entity unto itself, even the plants, the grass..."

"Take that tree, for instance," Alessa said, pointing out a maple tree. A rush of excitement shot through me. A maple tree! I knew what that was! At some point I had come across it while carousing the mental database.

"Uh, Lysander?" Alessa said, raising an eyebrow. Apparently when I was excited, my face betrayed a rosy confession of my thoughts.

"Sorry," I said sheepishly, "I'm listening."

"As I was trying to explain," she continued, "you can see its internal makeup changing before you, constantly reacting to its environment. It has its own cellular structure that –"

"Interesting, huh?" Amos interrupted, causing a grunt to emerge from Alessa. He put his hand on a sapling next to him and leaned into its bark while he talked. "They're not like us. As angels, we all have the same spiritual composition, just different classifications. At the same time, we can't get any stronger like these organisms can. We're bred of the same genetic makeup while they have their own individual blueprints to follow, which gives them unlimited potential."

"Look up there," Amos instructed. I obeyed. "You see that star up there? Shining in the sky? That's their sun. It literally lights up the whole planet."

"It gives every living thing sustenance and warmth," Alessa said. "And the Earth itself rotates regularly so each side of the planet is able to receive the sun's light. And then there's the moon - it reflects the sun's rays and acts as a dimmer light for the side that's facing away from the sun, so that no part of the Earth is ever completely cloaked in darkness." Alessa looked up at the sun above us and paused before continuing. "When I first saw it, it reminded me of our first memory."

"Our first memory..." I trailed off, caught up in the sweet scent of nostalgia. I could already see the purpose of God's handiwork. In Heaven, there was a time in which God had seemed non-existent, and what had followed was much debate and eventually the war in Heaven. Lucifer had claimed he could take God's place and be the light for us, but the battle didn't end in his favor. Now God's presence in Heaven was felt constantly so there was no cause for division. But here on Earth, there was a sun and a moon to be ever present, two colossal lights to comfort and fascinate, to remind the humans that they were never alone, never abandoned, for even when the great light of day went down, there was still a remnant of it in its place. And with a cycle of night and day established, there would always be a sunrise. The Earth's star would return – assuring the humans that God might not always be manifest, but He is forever present.

"It's clever, right?" Alessa asked. "I believe He made those on the first day of Earth's creation."

"No," Marcus said with glazed-over eyes, revealing to us that he was in the database again. "First day – blueprint of Earth, light, and darkness from light. Second – water, both in sky and ocean. Third – land and plants. Fourth – sun, moon, stars. Fifth – water animals, birds. Sixth – land animals, Man, Woman."

Marcus suddenly fell forward and hit the grass face-first, producing a loud thud and shaking a nearby tree. Farah rushed to him and started tapping his back but all he could do was groan.

"That has to be the most Marcus has ever said at one time." Alessa commented. "I'm impressed."

"I think his brain died," Farah said flatly, tapping Marcus on the crown of his head. Amos came over and picked him up.

"C'mon," he said. "You know us Godhands can't be reciting all those words. Our bodies are made for hitting, not studying and sitting."

Marcus grunted and I turned my attention back to the world around me.

"Is this where the humans live?" I asked.

"No, they live just beyond the Pison River there," Alessa said. "We'll show you."

"I thought no angel has seen them yet."

"We haven't, but that doesn't mean we didn't get a good look at the Garden's exterior. Many of us have even tried breaking in."

"Hmph," Cadence replied, pursing his lips at Alessa. Apparently, we weren't the only ones who had tried breaking into something recently. Alessa refused to acknowledge him.

"Just keep walking that way," she said, pointing toward the river.

I started walking toward it, entering the tree border and rummaging through a row of bushes that lined a nearby stream. I figured I would take the scenic route based on how low the water was and, besides, it would be more fun to splash through the brook than fly over it, so I headed down the bank.

But something stopped me short.

It felt like my face had unexpectedly slammed against something hard and unyielding. It didn't hurt, but it threw me off guard enough to cause some alarm and I rubbed my face in irritation, waiting for an explanation. Alessa giggled and came to my side.

"I thought you could analyze any situation."

"What was that? What happened to me?"

"It's an invisible barrier. A wall of sorts."

"You knew that was there?"

"Of course, but I wanted to see your analytical skills in action. I'm disappointed."

"My mind doesn't work like that."

"Apparently."

"Well, thanks for telling me," I said sarcastically, poking the invisible shield with a finger. "What is this made of?"

"How should I know? I can't see it."

I walked a little bit to the left and decided to take an alternate route to the north, seeing a tree that had branches that extended over one of the rivulets. I decided to climb it and use the branches to try to get over the invisible barrier. I reached out to get a grip on the trunk but my hand went through the tree like I was a ghost. The lack of definition threw me off balance and I fell over. I was about to tumble down and splash into the river, but the invisible field was there to catch me, and somehow I ended up in a 45 degree angle between the shield's side and the ground, crumpled into a contorted mess. Alessa and Cadence moved to help me get up, but by this time I was furious.

"No! No! I don't need your help!" I cried out. "WHAT IS GOING ON?"

Alessa giggled again and I grabbed her by the collar of her armor. "IT'S LIKE WE'RE BACK ON THE ISLAND!"

"Calm down," she said. "You haven't even let me finish explaining this place to you yet."

"Are we trapped here?" I yelled out frantically, having a horrific flashback. Back on the island, a similar invisible barrier had surrounded our penitentiary, keeping us from flying out into space where our freedom laid. However, in Heaven there were no barriers, so why were they here on Earth?

"You were folded up like a pretzel," Farah commented, still giggling. Even Marcus chuckled gruffly in amusement.

"Fine." I snapped at Alessa. "What is it? What's wrong with this place?"

"God placed safeguards between our world and theirs, mostly for their protection, ensuring there's as little interaction between us as possible. It's not like Heaven where we can talk and commune with everyone we see."

"Except the Seraphim," I muttered.

"Are you paying attention?"

"Why the separation?" I complained. "We can learn so much from each other."

"Well," she said in a low tone. "They do get to talk with God so I think their education about the universe is covered. With Him teaching the humans, there's no need for us to intervene."

"But what about us? Surely we could learn something from them."

"All of this might change in the future, but for now, He's making sure they have space to live on their own."

"Then why bother letting us come to the Earth at all?"

"There are certain sections we can go into. And there are objects we can interact with, but just not anything that would reveal our existence to the humans. For example, this side of the river is pretty much unvisited by them since they're kept solely in the Garden, so we were able to touch the grass, but the dirt must hold some kind of future significance - that's why we couldn't interact with it. The tree there you tried to climb is in direct sight of the Garden of Eden. What if one of them happened to be walking by and saw the branches moving on their own?"

"He would assume it was the wind," Cadence whispered, lying on his back in the grass.

"Basically, there are rules here," Alessa continued, giving Cadence a death stare. "We can't just do whatever we want. This isn't a playground. Sure, it's disconcerting at first, but you'll get the hang of it. I was confused too on my first few trips here."

"Few? Ugh..." I said. Her explanation did make sense, but tactical situations were already playing out in my mind. What role would these barriers play in the future? Would they hinder the success of any future missions?

"Anyways," Cadence piped in, sitting up to face us, "we can get to the Garden of Eden by flying over this part and landing directly in the center. Yes, everyone. I actually used my database to look something up."

I was ready to get to the main event, so I decided to follow Cadence's lead. The flight was a stone's throw away, only a few yards from the Pison River. We all took to the air. As soon as I caught a glimpse of the actual Garden, I was in complete awe.

Heaven was majestic and undoubtedly God's home, but Earth was His garden - a place for strolling, relaxing, and tending to His marvelous creations. The sunlight delicately pierced through the trees' canopy, giving the space underneath a glimmering aura that was both warm and cool at the same time. The leaves created a spectacle of light on the ground as they gently danced in and out of the sun's rays. Flowers and vegetation were flourishing in abundance, gracefully overspreading the terrain, bowing down in carefully orchestrated patterns to form pathways for animals to traverse, two-by-two, like young lovers. The air was fresh and soft like a cloud, and the sky was a bright baby blue. Crimson, indigo, and violet-colored petals drifted in the wind and a crystal (yes, a crystal) flower reflected the sunlight, insinuating the hues of its colored counterparts, yellow and pink and purple dancing along the borders of this masterpiece. This perfect painting…was a breathtaking example of what God and His brushes could do. And I could only marvel, for there was no doubt that God had left His signature upon this place. With this vision now ingrained in my memory, I was even more excited to see the most talked-about creations in all of Heaven: the human beings.

"Where are the humans?" I asked as we floated above the entry point. "What are their names again?"

"Adam and Eve, I think," Farah said. I nodded. I had heard those names before.

"Yes," Cadence said. "At first, it was just Adam, but God saw it wasn't good for man to be alone, so he created Eve out of Adam."

"Must've hurt."

"Sixth day – land animals, Man, Woman," Marcus muttered, nearly fainting again. Amos had been helping him walk and fly, so fortunately he was there to keep him from falling into one of the barriers below. Amos gave us a warm smile to reassure us that he was okay.

"Are we close to them?" I turned my head and asked Cadence. Alessa quickly butted her head between us.

"They have to be," Alessa responded. "Can't you hear that? Can't you feel that?"

I don't know how I missed it earlier. The collective voice of my angelic brothers and sisters waiting for the human beings to appear. Based upon the noise, I could tell not everyone had yet arrived, but still there had to be over ten million angels in attendance. They flew or sat, just a few miles ahead.

"Do you think the humans are there already?" I asked Cadence.

"It would be louder than that if they were," Alessa said and I scowled her way.

"I believe I asked Cadence where they were," I remarked.

"And I believe you are being rude and that if you're going to get an attitude, I should ask God to take you home immediately."

"You can't do that."

"I'm a Glory, remember?"

"I remember that your calls get disconnected sometimes. He didn't tell you what happened to our fallen brothers and sisters."

"Would you care to test that?"

I glared at her as she scrunched up her face, mocking me. I sniffed and rolled my eyes.

"Proceed," I sighed.

"That's what I thought."

"Attention hog," I muttered.

"What was that?!" she shrieked, swiveling her body around like a salsa dancer.

"Is Marcus okay?" I asked Amos behind us, ignoring her completely.

"He'll be fine," Alessa replied for him. "He's just overstimulated because it's his first trip here."

"Really?" I exclaimed, turning to him. "I thought every angel had been on Earth."

"Let's just say you weren't the only one in danger of getting dragged down here. We figured you definitely wouldn't come if Marcus had been allowed to stay behind."

"Why didn't you want to come?" I asked him. Marcus lifted his head and grunted before plopping it back down.

"That was him complaining about the long trip here," Alessa translated. "But he also said he was reluctant to come because he thinks there isn't enough to eat here."

"He didn't say all that," I retorted as the Godhand threw his head into the air.

"FOOD!" Marcus bellowed, flinging himself out of Amos's arms. Farah erupted into a giggling fit as Marcus descended below to a tree full of oranges. "You promise!"

"Where's he going?" I asked.

"I told him there was food down here," Alessa said. "It was the only way he'd come with us."

"A little deceptive, isn't it?"

"Last time I checked, all the bad angels were banished, and I'm not one of them, so I would watch the tone."

I left that comment alone as we collectively floated down to the grass clearing, getting front row seats to the Marcus show. It was identical to the meadow we had just come from, except for a number of fruit trees that were spread about in a semi-circle. Marcus grunted in annoyance as he strolled over to the tree in the middle and swung his hand through a ripe and tantalizing orange, hanging right in front of him. Delicious, but apparently forbidden, its elusiveness only served to agitate him more. Marcus swiped at it again but his hand fazed through the fruit unhindered.

"Of course," Farah chortled, "we didn't disclose that he'd never be able to eat it."

Marcus spun around and glared at Farah, his shoulders coming alive with energy.

"Hey!" Farah said, backing up, her hands in front of her. "I never said you could eat it!"

"TRICKERY!" Marcus bellowed.

Farah put her fists up in a fighting stance as Marcus jutted his jaw out and began striding forward. Amos positioned himself, ready to stop Marcus if need be.

"You never could stop eating," someone said in a raspy voice, and we all stopped in our tracks. Marcus ceased his assault and tapped the side of his head. I understood what he was feeling. The voice had been so tiny, we all instinctively looked to Farah who stomped a foot to the ground in rage.

"Oh c'mon, just because I'm small!"

"Where did that come from?" Cadence wondered. We all searched the orange tree fervently but found nothing.

"Who are you?! Show yourself!" I called out, very confused. The voice barely squeaked out a response. Some bushes nearby rustled, and out stepped the ugliest little thing I had ever seen. Not to call one of God's creations ugly...but it really was hideous, and I made a mental note to ask God about it the next time I visited the Throne Room. As if hearing my thoughts, the impish creature snarled at me and turned to Cadence.

"How do you like me now, friend?" it asked. Cadence took a step back in disgust. It was apparent he had no clue what this Farah-sized, hunched-over, purple and black monstrosity was. It had sharp claws for nails on its hands and feet, its teeth were jagged, and its eye sockets empty. A banana-yellow tongue whipped past the creature's lips as if it had a mind of its own.

"Friend of yours, Cadence?" Alessa whispered. Cadence looked like he was going to throw up.

"No. Not at all," he said.

"I thought you said you liked me," the thing squeaked weakly. "You said that we could have been friends. Well, it's not too late, pal."

I started putting the clues together. The syntax of his sentences and the way he dragged his words. The realization hit me so hard that Amos had to catch me. Cadence became alarmed and stared at the creature in accusation. I tried to gain my composure, to tell him convincingly what I had discovered, but the words only came out in terror.

"Cadence…that's Iron!" I yelled. "He was one of Lucifer's generals!"

Cadence's eyes widened in horror and the thing, formerly known as Iron, smiled…

CHAPTER 5: Paradise

Cadence reached forward and easily caught the creature by its throat, lifting it up and away from himself, watching as it wriggled and squirmed.

"What happened to you?" Cadence asked. Iron reluctantly calmed down and sulked under his captor's crushing hand. "You don't look like an angel anymore."

"We lost, remember?" he snapped, awkwardly squirming again. Cadence carefully loosened his grip.

"Why are you here then? Is Lucifer starting another war?"

"Not at all, friend," he rasped. "I'm just an usher."

"An usher?" Cadence said, bewildered. "Usher for what?"

"The performance. The event...the humans finally being able to live their lives without being under God's shield."

"You would be here for that!" Cadence said as he pulled him closer. "Trying to take advantage of them already?"

"No. No. Let me down and I'll explain."

Cadence threw him to the ground where he scurried back, keeping a safe distance from Cadence's reach. He cleared his throat and addressed us all formally.

"Those who lost the war in Heaven were banished to Earth, and we've learned the error of our ways. I can't even explain how hard it is to not be in Heaven with the rest of you...but while we're here, we figured we might as well make the best of a bad situation. So, until we get back into God's good graces, we're doing all we can to ensure the humans don't turn on each other like we did."

"I almost believed that," Farah said as she stepped forward. "So if you want to convince me, you'll have to explain a little more."

"We knew this event would be huge for the angels, so acting on faith, we decided to show you all that we are not enemy by ushering you to where the humans will be."

"And where's that?"

"There's a nice plot of land in the middle of the Garden. It was put there so Adam and Eve would have a blank canvas to build off of. Create anything they like with the tools God gives them. They are headed there right now."

"Is that where all the angels are?"

"Of course, and the festivities already started. We have a whole performance going on over there. If you head over right now, I'm sure you can catch the tail end of it."

"Fine," Cadence replied. "Take us there. We'll trust you for the moment."

As Iron scurried along and we walked down paths of tropical foliage and diverse flowers, I couldn't help but think that if Iron was here, then surely Vergil had to be as well. Perhaps he too was an usher, escorting angels to the optimal positions while scanning the crowd, looking for familiar faces. I was anxious to see him. Was I ready to speak with him? Not that it would matter if anything Iron said was true. It seemed like these "fallen angels" had simply made a mistake in defying God, and now they were ready to make amends.

"Ah, here we go," Iron remarked as he waved a hand through a set of trees. Through the branches, I could see angels hovering in the air, sitting with legs crossed, waiting for the humans to arrive. Other fallen angels like Iron ran across the ground, giving directions to others as we walked forward. I couldn't help but notice how alike they all looked and I struggled to find a familiar face amongst their scarred visages.

Applause interrupted my thoughts as Marcus pushed me forward. I hadn't noticed that I had stopped moving. I kept walking, striding through the final spotlight of sunshine at the entrance to the plain and I suddenly felt a surge of commonality.

The angels of Heaven on one side. The fallen angels on the other, miles from each other but still reunited for this wondrous occasion. Many of them looked no different than when they were in Heaven, and their angelic aura shone no dimmer or brighter than ours. They waited patiently as we did, while also acknowledging each other's presence, waving and calling out names like we were all at a football game. I couldn't wait until later, when we would all surely get together and have some fun. Maybe they were confined to this planet. Maybe they wouldn't be able to go back to Heaven, but at least we were still a family. And I prayed that nothing would change that.

"Hello, everyone!" an angel called out from the middle of the field. Her name was Skyler, if I recalled correctly. A Godhand who used her power in her voice and singing abilities rather than her fists. She now projected this power, silencing both sides as the program continued. I saw the fallen angel known as Arthur approach her and stand by her side. He was another Godhand - a singer and poet who had defected to Lucifer's side in the war.

"Adam and Eve are almost here!" she cried out and we responded with thunderous applause. I continued to scan the crowd for Vergil, but I couldn't find him amongst so many faces.

"Arthur here has asked to speak to you and I see no reason to deny his request, seeing as we have been treated with such hospitality!"

Our side of the crowd cheered in approval as Arthur's torso swelled, channeling his angelic pressure so that he could project his voice to us all.

"Welcome to the Garden of Eden!" he cried out as the applause continued. "I am here to speak on behalf of Lucifer and all of the angels of Earth. I know that many, including myself were persuaded by his words, and so, he has deemed it inappropriate to address you at this time. But he has asked me to express his apology and that he is greatly sorry that we were separated in the first place."

"What a change in character," Cadence muttered next to me.

"We are all here to witness a new era for all of us, and I ask that we all put our differences and the past aside to embrace this age. The human beings will multiply as we did, and they will have problems as we did. But let us learn from our mistakes and do what's best for them. Though you are in Heaven, and we are confined to Earth, this does not change the fact that we are still angels."

"Then what happened to Iron?" I heard Alessa whisper to Cadence. Cadence shrugged and whispered something back.

"At this juncture, I would like to ask one of our own to sing a song for you. At the end of this song, the couple will have arrived, and then my friends, we can celebrate!"

Both sides cheered and cried out in joy as Arthur and Skyler left the middle of the field, allowing another to come forward. This angel, I did not recognize. She was tall, skinny and pale as if her skin was made of ivory, but it was behind a veil of some type of gel. Her hair was streaked with fiery red and coats of tar black, and it extended down her face and back and all the way to the backs of her calves. Her demeanor was meek and timid but in order to speak to us all, she had to have been a Godhand.

She reached the middle of the plain and the crowd hushed, waiting to hear her words. She lifted her head and brushed back her hair and many in the crowd gasped unexpectedly, including myself. Her eyes were like voids, mini-black holes in which no light entered, and to some degree, it terrified me. But she left us no time to contemplate what we saw. She simply began singing. And her voice was nothing short of legendary.

It echoed throughout the valley and bounced off of each of us as if we were the acoustics. It was an eerie yet seductive voice that grabbed our attention violently and refused to let go. And for the next seven minutes, we were at her mercy, as she sang a hymn that she had pulled from the recesses of our mental databases:

Amazing Grace, how sweet the sound

That saved a wretch like me.

I once was lost but now am found

Was blind, but now I see.

T'was Grace that taught my heart to fear

And Grace, my fears relieved

How precious did that Grace appear

The hour I first believed

So when we've been here ten thousand years

Bright shining as the sun

We've no less days to sing God's praise

Than when we've first begun.

Amazing Grace, how sweet the sound

That saved a wretch like me.

I once was lost but now am found

Was blind, but now I see.

Upon her last words, they appeared.

"There they are," Farah whispered, pointing toward the end of the plain, located between our two factions.

Eve came into view. Although she was still a good distance away, I was able to see her clearly. Symmetrical in form and stride, Eve's hair flew behind her like a bride's veil and glittered in the sun's light, garnishing all the attention to it and not the fact that she was naked.

Her eyes were playful and innocent, wide like a baby doe's, and her arms and legs swung from her delicately and freely, as if they rode the wind. A glowing aura clothed her like a dress and her body moved without shackle or chain. She danced and hummed as she walked and held Adam's hand tightly and he grinned from ear to ear, strolling leisurely behind her. Nearly an exact image of his wife, the most noticeable difference was that his hair was made up of little curls though it was cropped short. He walked with confidence yet his face was graced with humility. I noticed he constantly looked to the sky, probably waiting to hear another word from the Lord. I couldn't explain it precisely, but it was like he was boasting a suit of invisible armor, like a noble knight accompanying his lady to a fair.

The crowd was speechless, and I was just in much awe as they. Immediately, without rhyme or reason, I loved them. No romance was in my heart, merely an undying need to protect them at all cost. They were more than God's creations. They were God's children, like me, and a part of my family now. I would do my absolute best to ensure that the divisions that occurred between us all in Heaven, wouldn't happen again.

No one moved as the couple surveyed the plain, saying nothing but admiring the view. Eventually, Eve tugged on Adam's arm that she had seen enough and they turned around, and went back from where they came from.

Both sides of the crowd rushed the field, embracing each other and exchanging stories. I lost my friends in seconds, as the mass became a blurry cohesion, spread across the grass. But somehow, through it all, I caught a glimpse of someone trying to get my attention. Through a small break in the mob, I saw someone pointing at me and waving me towards them. I made my way to them and followed the fallen angel through the trees, just a few hundred yards from where the celebration took place. As dusk appeared from over the horizon, the Garden of Eden lit up naturally, the setting sun and the rising moon ricocheting off the crystal flowers and creating a world of illumination. The fallen angel I followed, who displayed the physical attributes of a Faithful, turned around to address me.

"Sorry to take you out here, Lysander. I just had to speak with you privately. My name is Elsie." She extended a hand for me to shake and I accepted her greeting.

"What is all of this about?"

"Vergil."

Her words cut off my cautiousness and before I realized what I was doing, I had stepped into her striking range.

"Where is he?"

"He can't be here right now. Lucifer won't let him."

"Why? What's wrong?"

"A lot is wrong, Lysander. Nothing is what it appears to be."

"Then tell me everything."

"Lucifer has the power to control us. Don't be fooled by this display. He's still pulling the strings and he wants nothing more than every angel in Heaven to fall."

"Then how can I trust what you're saying?"

"Did you see Arthur use his voice in the field today? That's because he's a Godhand. Though we are fallen, we still retain some of our old abilities. I'm a Faithful, and I was able to temporarily break Lucifer's hold over me. He doesn't know what I'm up to."

"So what do you want me to do? How can I help?"

"Vergil wants to meet you tomorrow, but he has to break Lucifer's hold first. Is there any way that you can be exactly in this spot at dawn?"

"I'm sure I can. But tell me, is it just me he wants to talk to, or can my friends come as well?"

"Only you. He doesn't want to risk Lucifer catching wind of what's going on and punishing us all for it. You understand."

"Of course, I'll be careful."

"Thank you," she said. "Good-bye."

She headed toward the celebration in the plain as I contemplated her words. Lucifer was in control? Of course he was. Cadence had been right to say that an apology would be against his character. He was far too proud and arrogant for that. This was all a ploy to get back at God. The only problem was figuring out when he would strike. And how much influence he had over the others...

"Do not go tomorrow," someone said behind me. I turned and almost fell over in shock.

"Do not go," Adam said again, standing before me amongst the bushes. His face was serious and he was looking directly at me when he spoke.

"You can see me?"

"I can see all of you," he said.

"How is that possible?"

"I do not know...but I believe God allows it to be so."

"Wow," I replied, calming down and stepping toward him. "I don't intimidate you?"

"I have no reason to fear you."

"What do you know about fear?"

"What God tells me about it...I haven't been afraid yet, but I understand the concept."

I was shocked to hear him speak so fluently. For some reason I expected him to be very primitive, almost dumb. But apparently, that wasn't so.

"You shouldn't go tomorrow," he repeated.

"Why?"

"Because they are different. Their voice is not like God's."

"Is mine?"

"Yes. But they are not."

"Does anyone else know you are here?"

"Your people are still in the plain laughing and talking. No one knows I'm here. It's not like when we stepped onto the field."

"So you saw us all, huh?"

"Yes," he chuckled a little. "I didn't expect that. But...I have to go. I wasn't supposed to talk this long."

"Well, it was nice talking to you, Adam. I hope we get to do it again."

"Yes," he replied, looking around. "But more importantly, remember what I told you."

"I will, but one last question before you go...how is it that you aren't afraid of anything?"

"Easy," he said. "Because God said nothing bad will happen to us as long as we do not eat of the Tree of Knowledge of Good and Evil. My wife and I both know this."

"Where is this tree?" I asked but he simply smiled.

"Not sure anymore since I kind of forgot. But, I do know what it looks like if I happen to come across it. It's easy to follow God's commands when you do not dwell on the opposite."

"Well spoken," I said and he turned around and walked back from where he came, accompanying a lion that met him from behind some bushes. Together they walked down a grass trodden path as he brushed the lion's mane, praying to God as he went. It was an interesting sight to behold, yet all I could see in the end, as those two innocent creatures continued on into the Garden, was how the lion had claws. And just like when Raphael had first told me I needed to learn combat training in Heaven, I wondered what exactly, those claws were for…

CHAPTER 6: We All Fall Down

I found it quite by accident.

After my conversation with Adam, I had much to think about - whether to see Vergil in the morning or listen to Adam's advice. Contemplating both decisions, I started walking and found myself at an intersection, all made of dirt paths. Three of them led to inner gardens, complete with vine benches, fruit trees, and bushes. Animals slept or lay lazily on the floor, yawning and flinging their tails back and forth. Lions and lambs, elephants, aardvarks, zebras, giraffes and wolves all spent their days in a diverse community filled with harmony and peace. Eagles soared the air currents with a grace any angel would respect, and a variety of fish swam in the tiny ponds littered throughout the meadow. Toward the east, however, was the tree Adam spoke of, standing tall and majestic, thriving and full of life, with an inviting aura emanating from it. It was hard to explain, but there was something appealing about that tree, as if it blatantly called out for all near it to partake in its forbidden delights.

I wasn't about to test it, even if I was sure my hand would faze through. However, that didn't stop some of my old comrades from trying. The celebration was apparently over because angels both of Heaven and Earth were all over the place. If Adam could truly see them all, then he probably wasn't going to get much sleep that night. They were literally in every tree, across each path and trying to eat of all of the trees in the Garden. Thankfully, God had made it so we couldn't, but the angels of Earth were especially relentless, swinging the palm of their hand through the forbidden fruit with alarming fervor.

I dwelled on Adam's warning. Deep down, I wanted to believe that they all had the best of intentions, but I had to remember, Elsie had said they were still under Lucifer's control. Maybe Lucifer was trying to see if he could have the fruit for himself, or maybe it was all a lie and my old friends were acting of their own free will, and this was all a devious plan to weaken us.

But that would also mean Vergil was in on the plan...and I couldn't accept that possibility just yet. For the good of my well-being, but most of all, my sanity – I would skip out on the meeting. I would just have to meet up with him another time and hope for the best.

"There you are," Farah said, as she was followed by the rest of Team Six. "Where have you been?"

"It's a lot to explain, but I don't want to talk here, if that's okay with you."

"I second that," Alessa said. "I can't explain it, but something isn't right here, and I'm not talking about the Garden."

"Suspicious," Marcus replied. I stared at him in awe.

"What?" he asked. I chuckled to myself.

"I take it the celebration didn't go well?" I asked as Cadence shook his head.

"It went too well. They were acting like nothing had ever happened."

"Maybe they don't want to dwell on the past," Amos said but Cadence dismissed it.

"No, Amos. I'm telling you that there's more going on here than we think. That celebration felt fabricated."

"And I tried talking to some," Farah said, "about how we're going to get them back into Heaven. They just said it's impossible and they didn't want to talk about it. What kind of faith is that?"

"I have some news of my own, honestly," I said. "But again, we can't speak here."

"Why not?" a fallen angel said from behind us.

"Aren't we family?" another said to our right.

"I thought we were putting the past behind us," a third one said to our left. Before we could rebuttal, we were surrounded by fifty fallen angels, and the numbers were increasing with each passing second. They all spoke excitedly, questioning us, and the general tone of their speech was getting more hostile with each word. Finally, Marcus had enough and promptly punched one in the face. The victim went flying and phasing through a forest of trees as the rest pounced on us in response.

"STOP IT!!!" Farah screamed, and they stopped their assault in mid-air. As if being jolted back to normal, they all began apologizing and sulking off into the Garden, as if nothing had happened at all. Alessa was furious.

"Oh no, you don't!" she screamed at one of them. "You started it, we're finishing it!"

"Calm down, Alessa," Cadence said. She glared at him.

"We're not just going to let them go, are we?!"

"Technically, we started it, remember?"

"Show division," Marcus grunted and I nodded in agreement.

"Marcus is right," I said. "The way they attacked us shows that that they either have some unresolved issues with us beneath the surface, or they're being controlled."

"Controlled by who?" Farah asked.

"Lucifer," I said. "The only one it could be."

"Doubt it," Marcus replied.

"Yeah," Alessa said. "Why would God give someone that much power? Especially when he's very much about free will and letting us decide our own fates."

"Then it's option number 1 – they still resent us."

"Which means they'll attack us," Cadence said. "Or the humans. Maybe both."

"With an outburst of that magnitude, it won't take too long."

"Then let's find them," Cadence said, "make sure Adam and Eve are okay."

"Is there any way we can get some reinforcements?" Amos suggested. "I mean, we almost got jumped by a horde of 'em."

"Since it's night and the humans are going to bed, most of the angels of Heaven have already gone home. We won't have much."

"Better than none," Alessa said. "Let's split up and gather some help before we go searching."

"Agreed," Cadence said. "Marcus and Alessa will come with me back to the plain. The rest of you start a basic search for Adam and Eve, but stay back. Don't alert anyone, and whatever you do, don't engage in a fight."

"We won't, boss man," Farah chimed in, punching his arm. The three of them took flight as Amos, Farah and I stayed by the tree.

"So where do we begin?" Farah asked me. I took a moment to consider.

"Well, if God doesn't want them to eat from this tree, then we should head away from it. I doubt they'll be coming over here to sleep."

"Why can't they eat of the tree?"

"It prevents something bad from happening. Adam told me himself."

"You spoke to Adam?" she asked in awe. "What's he like?"

"He's concerned for our health. He suspects our fallen friends are not who they claim to be."

"Well if he can see a difference then there must be one."

"I wouldn't go that far..."

"Can we get started?" Amos interjected. "Like Lysie said, if they're not supposed to be here, it's best we get a move on."

"Lysie," Farah giggled under her breath. I groaned inwardly. Farah zipped up into the air and started flying, leading the way as Amos and I followed suit.

Instinctively, I accessed my mental database for any helpful information I could find for our mission, and it didn't disappoint. A full layout of the Garden of Eden was now available and ready for use when only a day before, it had been nowhere to be found.

An idea suddenly came to me - maybe one of the reasons why we as angels weren't allowed to freely interact with the humans was because we had knowledge about things that didn't exist yet - knowledge that, if shared with Adam or Eve, could change their minds when making a decision - or could even change the very future itself.

Yet at the same time, I also realized the importance of the mental database when it came to Earth. It enabled us angels to help out instantly in any situation, for we already understood a great deal about the planet. Countless hours that would have been spent learning about Earth and all of its intricacies and inhabitants could be spent instead on just carrying out God's orders. This made our mental database an invaluable tool. However, we still were not omnipotent...

What Iron had become...this was not in my mental database.

I imagined that if it had, there wouldn't have been a war in Heaven. Real opinions about God's absence would have been kept hidden because no one would have wanted to be kicked out of Heaven and given such a disgusting, vile body. A light bulb went off in my head. It was almost as if...not knowing certain things...served a purpose - it made us reveal our true thoughts, our true desires...our true selves. Even Lucifer would've remained in God's good graces if he had had such prior knowledge. But without it? Our inner selves were as clear to behold as water.

Again, I felt that uneasy quivering in my spirit. We had found Iron in a completely different form than he had been in Heaven, and I could only imagine that it had been a painful process. So - had that painful transformation happened to Vergil too? And Lucifer? Were they like most of the angels that seemed to have kept their former glory, or were they small and deformed like Iron? I hoped so. Maybe if I found Vergil in such a state, he would be so small that he would have no choice but to listen to me.

"I think I heard one of the humans speaking," Farah said as we traversed. My attention came back to reality.

The path we had followed was taking us to a second intersection, with each respective path carpeted in grass but otherwise bare. In the middle of the crossroads was a decent-sized patch of grass with a small pool in the middle, filled with reflective, crystal blue water that rippled lightly in the breeze. But there was no Adam to be seen.

"Could have been anyone," Amos replied, and we were ready to move ahead when I felt my body shudder. Just a shudder – like I had gotten bitterly cold. Alarmed, I turned to Farah and Amos who were looking at me like they had just felt the same thing – their eyes wide and brows scowled.

"What was -" I started to say, but before I could finish, the three of us dropped to the ground, as if a giant hand had pressed down on us. Our faces were in the grass, creating an imprint in the dirt as we struggled to fight against the force that ailed us. The hand increased its pressure and we sunk even further, our angelic pressure creaking under the weight. Even in our predicament, my mind was racing, wondering why our bodies were able to impact the dirt beneath us. It wasn't like we were in the meadow, away from where the humans lived. We were in the middle of their home - why would we be able to interact with the grass and dirt here? Did it mean that this spot would no longer matter in the grand scheme of things? What was happening?

The one thing I could decipher, was that this was not the hand of God.

It pulsed with hate, and it strained and struggled with itself to keep from crushing us entirely.

"What is this?" Amos cried, the only one still able to speak.

"My angelic pressure," a voice whispered ominously from behind us. "If it can still be called that."

My eyes widened as I heard someone step behind me, stopping just next to my right side, barely out of my sight.

"Who?" I managed to say weakly as the mysterious intruder suddenly reached down and grabbed the back of my neck. In the same quick movement, he lifted me up and roughly turned me around to face him. I tried to cry out but he was squeezing too tight. My vision blurred as I fought to properly examine him. My entire body was choking, straining to stay conscious. It wasn't his clutches that hurt, but his proximity. The closer he was - the harder it was to see, to move, to think. His pressure was not angelic in nature, not even close, yet it affected me all the same, but in a suffocating, crushing way. I felt enslaved, weighed down – as if massive chains had been attached to each of my limbs and the anchor was sealed miles underground and continuously pulling. The intruder was stretching my angelic body to its limits, contorting and abusing it, making it scream, making me feel like it was going to split apart at any moment.

"You have nothing to say now?" the intruder growled. His voice was seductive and flowed like honey, yet it had a bite that cried out murderous intent. I took a crack at his identity, for few angels I knew possessed such a tone.

"Lucifer," I gasped as his pressure increased, and suddenly I realized that I could no longer speak. I could only concentrate on staying conscious.

"That is no longer my name, Lysander," he said. "It is Satan now. I claim nothing God has bestowed upon me." He leaned into my eyes and I cringed at the sight of his face.

Jagged shark teeth and wide, blazing red eyes. Crocodile skin that cracked like magma rock. Every word that seethed out of his mouth was followed by smoke, so that it looked like he spoke death into the air. You could feel hopelessness and rage cling to him like a robe. Fury was held in his fists, and he had the aura and embodiment of a dragon, with scaly skin rippling down his back like it was a bike chain in motion. God is in control, my thoughts told me, but I still couldn't stop myself from being utterly terrified. I prayed these feelings wouldn't reveal themselves on my face.

"You won't get in my way this time," Satan said, a hint of amusement in his tone. "You have no choice in the matter. No power to stop me...but don't worry, I did not come for you. You are safe for now. But I will make you suffer for as long as I am able. And I will start...with them. You know who I speak of."

"The humans," I managed to cough out.

"Exactly. Imagine my surprise when I learned that not only could Adam see angels, but he could speak with them as well. I can't have angels and humans joining forces against me, so I must strike now, before it's too late."

"But you are an angel too."

"No," he chuckled as he squeezed tighter. "Not at all. Not anymore."

I started praying for Cadence and the others to arrive, desperately longing for someone to come and save the day, but Lucifer noticed what I was attempting and violently shook me.

"Asking for God to fight your battles?" he seethed. "Why? Can't break free from my grip on your own? I can't control the others. Why can I subdue you so easily?"

My eyes widened at his words and he grinned.

"That's right, Lysander. The 'fallen angels,' your old friends, your family, the angels of Earth...they all act through their own free will. I don't control a single one. You know what that means, don't you?"

I opened my mouth to speak but no words came forth, and he chuckled at my attempt. Gripping me tighter, he leaned in to make me suffer even more under his pressure. I couldn't even dwell on his words. Just when I thought I had hit my limit, my spiritual body flickering and wavering under his might, he stopped suddenly, and glanced to the right.

"It looks like my appointment has arrived, Lysander," he smiled, his mouth gaping wide as if he were going to take a bite out of me. Out of the corner of my eye, I saw Eve stop to inspect a flower bush, only a few yards away. Could she not see us? Couldn't she feel the massive energy Satan was putting out?

Satan let his pressure decrease to almost nothing once he saw her but it didn't matter. Amos, Farah, and I had been far too damaged by his vicinity for the cessation in pressure to do anything. My body crashed limply against the Earth as Satan threw me back to the ground. I tried to keep my eyes fixed on him as I mumbled, searching for the words I needed.

"Stay away from her," I managed to gasp determinedly. "You...won't succeed anyway. We can't touch them unless God says so...there are barriers."

"No," he breathed heavily. "You can't touch them without God's permission, but you will soon find, my old colleague - that this is my kingdom. Not His. Mine. So be a good boy now and stay put."

"She...can't see you. She's no threat," I gasped in my last attempt to plead with him. Apparently, Eve did not have the same awareness Adam did.

"No, she can't. I already tested that out...but, she can understand something else. I will show you."

His spiritual pressure sky-rocketed and my body locked up, frozen in agony. I couldn't even move my eyes from the direction I was looking. I was powerless, and based on the positions we were all in, I was the sole witness to what would happen next. I could only pray that someone would come and rescue Eve as I saw Satan approach one of the nearby animals. Then, he did something I had never imagined he would do - he inhabited its body, inserting himself into it by the microscopic pores that covered its body, his spirit turning into a type of steam. The animal didn't seem to notice, and made its way to Eve through the tree tops, until it was just above her head.

She wasn't startled by its sudden appearance for there was nothing to fear in the Garden, but even I could see that she thought it was a little unusual for the serpent to be following her, trying to make small talk as she continued her leisurely stroll. Eventually they got into earshot and I gobbled up every word.

"We may eat of the fruit of the trees of the Garden," Eve said to the serpent, unaware of who was inside. "But of the fruit of the tree which is in the midst of the Garden, God hath said 'ye shall not eat of it, neither shall ye touch it, lest ye die.'"

"Ye shall not surely die," Satan said, "for God doth know that in the day ye eat thereof, then your eyes shall be opened, and ye shall be as gods, knowing good and evil."

So this was what Lucifer meant. Maybe she wasn't as spiritually aware, but somehow, she could understand what this animal was saying.

"Ye shall be as gods," Satan repeated again.

And Eve contemplated this. I tried to fight Satan's pressure as best as I could, feeling my own pressure beginning to gain strength through my increasing rage. He hadn't learned anything. Satan was once again up to his old tricks, convincing God's creations that the only way to be happy, complete – was to either undermine God's authority or become like Him entirely. I knew it had to appeal to her to some degree. After all, she and Adam had spent countless hours with Him and were no doubt in awe over His presence. I knew I had been, and I still was.

Eve said nothing after their exchange, but walked to the Tree of the Knowledge of Good and Evil, staring at it for a long time. The serpent followed innocently, and traveled through the branches slowly, making sure Eve got a good look at each of the delicious fruits upon them. Her eyes glistened in desire.

"Is there nothing we can do?" I cried out, my voice returning to me while Satan's attention was on Eve and not us. I felt my abdomen crunch, and with enough angelic pressure pouring out of me, I was able to slowly get myself up to a seated position. Farah was on her feet, but still unable to walk. Amos was on his knees as if he were doing a half push-up, trying to tell his body to use the Godhand power that was surging within him.

And we were still as helpless as ever.

"Why doesn't God intervene?" I cried out and Farah cast her eyes down into a corner, reluctant to tell me the answer.

"Tell me!" I cried to her. "What do you know?"

"It's like with us," she said solemnly, squinting at me through Satan's pressure. "He wants the humans to make their own decisions. No matter how much Lucifer talks, they need to be convicted in their hearts and come to their own conclusions. It's purely up to Eve to decide what happens next."

"But we can't just let this happen! He can't win!" I screamed as I fought against the last of Satan's pressure holding me down. "I won't let it! I promised I would be there when they needed me!"

With a cry of rage, I broke the chains that bound me, and shattered the residue left on my angelic body. I didn't waste a second, leaping into the air and flying toward Satan and Eve, watching as she grabbed one of the fruit and examined its exterior, tossing it between her hands...playing with it.

Satan said nothing, but looked up at me through the serpent's eyes, glaring as I flew down with my last ounce of power. I reached for the fruit, my hand outstretched to snatch it from Eve's hand and throw it far away.

But I didn't make it.

An invisible barrier, planted an inch over the tree's top, slammed into my hand. I couldn't even find the strength to speak as I felt the helplessness wash over me. I watched with dooming acceptance as she paused, glanced in my direction, decided nothing was there, and turned back to the catalyst in her hand. With a simple bite, a mere nibble, she began eating the fruit… and it changed her life forever.

Immediately, I saw a difference.

The innocence.

That illuminating aura that beamed from her skin naturally - it faded like it was on a dimmer switch, decreasing in intensity until her skin was dull and plain. She fell to the grass below the tree in horror, clawing her head desperately as I literally saw her eyes glaze over and narrow, losing the innocence that once brightened them. Her countenance sank, and her smile disappeared. She reached a half-hearted hand to the sky, as if to reach for what was lost, but it was nothing more than a vapor now.

It was gone.

Satan backed away into the branches and leaves of the tree, slinking quietly and disappearing entirely. I heard a rustle nearby, and my heart broke at what I saw.

It was Adam. A vibrant reflection of what Eve had just lost. His skin shone brilliantly and his eyes were powerfully vibrant and alive, even as he saw his wife on the Garden floor. I couldn't help but feel a sense of nostalgia. Of Vergil…and myself. Watching him resolve to join Lucifer and changing his destiny in Heaven. Watching him change into a being unworthy of the goodness I knew to be in him, even to the point that he was able to personally plunge a sword through my chest. I understood the aching pain Adam was going through…and I could not blame him for what he decided to do next.

It was a decision I had mulled over far too often…

Adam gazed upon his wife, lying there in distress, and he gasped in shock. I could see the hurt in his eyes as he surveyed her pain and suffering, but was unable to fathom its intensity. And when Eve saw him, in all his shining glory, she realized the consequence of her crime. The acceptance began to manifest on her face as her imagination erupted into a slideshow of life without the Garden, without Adam, without God. And feelings began to fester. Unfamiliar emotions...of envy and bitterness...

I cried out for him to stop.

And he heard me. He lifted his head and looked at me directly in the eyes. But with a pained look upon his face, he cast his gaze back down to his wife. I cried out again, but he ignored my words. The only sign that he heard me being the shudder of his body with each of my cries. I couldn't bear to see him in such suffering as he thought hard about what to do next.

And for a moment...he considered...

Just for a moment...what the repercussions would be if he left her there – so that she contended with God on her own...

But it was only a moment.

He couldn't bear to watch his wife's pleading eyes, her guilt flowing down her face in never before seen tears. Her hand reaching out for help. Her begging. And so, with a clenched jaw and watery eyes, he snatched the fruit from her hand quickly and took a bite in disgust, performing the deed before he could change his mind. A low rumble was heard in the distance and I already knew it was God, coming to talk with his creations.

I called out to him as loud as I could.

But he could no longer hear my words.

He was no longer in tune with my world.

And I couldn't bear to see what would happen next.

I was not strong enough to witness it.

"We can't help them now," I said lowly. "But we can get the one who tricked them."

"Satan's long gone," Farah said from my side. I had barely noticed my friends flying in right beside me, landing on the invisible barrier above Adam and Eve. "There's nothing we can do."

"I have to try," I said. "I don't care how fast or strong he is. I'm taking him down right here and now."

"Do you really think we can?" Amos spoke up. "You all felt that back there, right?" I began to protest but Farah patted his back in consolation, as she liked to do.

"Have some faith," she said. "I was a little worried too, but Lysander changed my mind. We should go after him while we have the chance. And we'll lose him if we wait for the others."

"Far be it from me to hold Team Six back when they're fired up," Amos said reluctantly, rubbing his bald head.

"Then let's head out," I said, looking down at the human couple one more time. They were both on the ground, leaning up against the forbidden tree. Adam embraced Eve who angrily cried into his chest. And he simply stared upwards, directly at the fruit in which he had taken part of, silently cursing it into the ground. Finally coming to, he began taking some leaves from the bushes nearby and gave a half-hearted attempt to cover them both. His face was now identical to Eve's, and the sky had somehow darkened even more in hue. But I couldn't study them now. I had a job to carry out.

I don't know how long we flew across the Earth, across plains and mountains, oceans and valleys, searching for Satan or his trail, but we couldn't even pick up the slightest trace. Soon we crossed a familiar looking valley, decorated heavily with a myriad of colorful flowers for the third time. Upon this rotation I began to notice that even the fallen angels had seemed to disappear altogether from the surface of the Earth.

Yet we continued the search.

But after the sun had been down for hours prior, and the landscape was beginning to blur, I shouted in frustration and suddenly shot upwards into Earth's atmosphere, back toward Heaven to get some answers. Farah and Amos followed without a word...which was good, because I needed to think, harder than ever. If there was to be a war on Earth like in Heaven, then I needed to plan – to stop and think about how I was going to destroy Satan once and for all.

CHAPTER 7: Now What Did We Learn?

"You can't blame yourself," Raphael said as he paced around the hall. "Any one of us except the Archangels would have been defeated."

"We didn't have a chance to fight him," Farah retorted. "We were beaten by his angelic pressure alone."

"I wouldn't say angelic," I commented. Cadence stepped forward. He and the others never did meet up with us on Earth. By the time they had come back from their mission, we had been long gone. Seeing Adam and Eve crying and wondering what happened, they had rushed back to Heaven for an update before we had finished searching for Satan. Raphael had been there to fill them in on the situation when we had returned, exhausted and upset.

"We should have been there," Cadence lamented. "I'm sorry for our absence."

"I don't think it would've made a difference," Raphael said as coyly as possible. "In any case, you made the right decision going for help. It was the smartest move to make by far, especially when you had no idea what you were up against. Also, having three of you go to protect each other was ideal. It's not inconceivable to think that the only reason Cadence wasn't ambushed is because Alessa and Marcus were there to guard him. These...demons, as we have come to classify them, are sneaky. They wait for a moment of weakness."

"Not Lucifer," Amos said. "He wanted to make sure we felt how powerful he was."

"Yes, that has been Lucifer's way since the beginning. But don't let your hearts be heavy. Your experiences have helped to confirm our suspicions. You couldn't have known this, but on Earth, the rules are quite different."

"We've noticed," I said assuredly. "We couldn't interact with most of the Garden."

"It's true," Raphael nodded. "What is flesh is flesh and what is spirit is spirit. There are ordinances in place we must abide by."

"But why?" Farah interjected. "We almost got through to Eve. I saw her pause when Lysander was above her, like she sensed him. If he yelled a little more, maybe she would have felt the danger and refused Lucifer's advances."

"Even now they are not completely unaware to spiritual beings or oblivious to what goes on in our realm," Raphael said. "But therein lies the only way an angel can help a human...if they want it. Their praying to God is very similar to how the Glory interact with Him. It fosters a powerful relationship between creation and Creator. And with a genuine connection intact, nothing is impossible. They will be able to ask God for help in problematic situations and even invoke your express help in fighting the demons."

"But only if they pray?"

"Their relationship with God will be quite onerous with Adam and Eve's disobedience. They will constantly be persuaded to side with Lucifer's beliefs and give in to the demons rather than follow God's commandments. Praying is absolutely essential for them for it's the only way they can truly be in God's presence."

"And we all know what a lack of God's presence can do," I replied.

"This can get dangerous really quick," Alessa said and we all nodded at her remark. Who knew better than the angels of Heaven? Those who had survived the island and the war?

"So they pray for assistance..." Cadence said. "And that's where we come in."

"But that might not work in every case," I retorted. "It's not so simple. For example, Eve wasn't aware she was being deceived. No help was asked for because Satan used an animal she had seen in the Garden already. A threat wasn't perceived so I doubt danger crossed her mind. With that being said, how are they going to pray if they are unaware of when they are being attacked?"

"It would best if they prayed all the time," Alessa spoke up. "Seek a conversation with God the way I do. That way, they'll be able to discern when they are being attacked spiritually."

"But what occurs if they don't know about prayer or abandon it entirely?"

"Then nothing will happen," Raphael interjected. "The demons will be able to influence them however they please. Naturally, they will still have a choice in the decisions they make, but it's hard to choose good if all that influences you is evil. Living in darkness, the light will seem foreign and strange. It will understandably become the enemy, the stranger. Without a balance being put into place and God's presence also in their lives, they will automatically follow Satan's commands and find it hard to break any undesirable cycle. Think of how easily Eve gave in."

"So what happens now?" Cadence asked. The question we all dreaded to ask and no one wanted to hear answered. We had all kept silent, waiting for Cadence to inevitably come forth, for we knew that he would sacrifice his fear to give us the truth, to ease our troubled minds. He was an angel of sacrifice, and sadly, we took advantage.

"You want to know where the humans will go from here," Raphael stated, delaying the dreaded answer.

"Yes," Cadence said boldly. "Lysander told us that they weren't supposed to eat from the Tree of Knowledge of Good and Evil...so what now? Are they banished from the Earth? Will they become demons?"

"They will be cast from the Garden of Eden," Raphael declared in an informative tone. "You may not have seen it, but the Tree of Life was in the midst. It can give the humans eternal life like we have – making their bodies unable to decompose and die. Now, they will lose their immortality on Earth. Sooner or later, all of them – Adam, Eve, and any future humans born into their world – will experience death."

"Death?" Marcus repeated, his eyes disclosing to us that he was reading the definition in his mental database. I didn't blame him. I needed just as much clarification. Being eternal, never having to fear an end...I was aware of the concept, but not the execution. I had been unconscious before so I understood what it felt like to close your eyes and suddenly open them, finding out that time had passed without your knowledge...but there was no finality to it. No matter how long I would be unconscious in battle, I was still assured that my eyes would open someday and I would continue about my life with no less precious seconds than when I slept. But for the humans, the consequences would be far greater. What fear would take hold upon me if I discovered that a close of my eyes might be my last?

"It's hard to explain, being immortal ourselves," Raphael said, his wings expanding and retracting in irritation. "I guess it is best to put it like this – do you remember the angels that were kicked out of Heaven?"

"Yes," I said, as the room got noticeably more awkward - the others' eyes struggling not to glance my way. "How could I forget?"

"I don't mean to bring up sensitive topics, but how do you feel about them, knowing they will never return?"

I pondered his question carefully, trying to find the precise words. But since I could come to no concrete conclusion, I went with my emotions.

"There is an emptiness, a missing part of my life. They should be here, but they're not and it's strange. When I fly around Heaven, or I gaze at the stars, I forget that they're gone. Sometimes when I fly to the Fellowship Hall, I turn to make a joke to Vergil...but of course I end up speaking to no one...and not that I miss it, but, it's still eerie when I don't hear Lucifer's singing blaring from Symphony Hall. And I feel a little uncomfortable visiting Cadence's house because it was where we last hung out. Basically, I have all these memories...but it feels like they were all fabricated. Like it was a life I never lived."

"This is what the Absent of your island experienced," Raphael said matter-of-factly. "No longer convicted of God's existence, they turned inward and searched for catharsis – answers in the endless flow of their mental database. They browsed endlessly, until they were unsure of who they were anymore, their consciousness being mixed in and integrated with the infinite supply of knowledge. Thankfully, you did not succumb like they did, but you can empathize with their plight. You feel the shallow lingering of their lives…"

"Is this what I will feel when the humans die?" I cast my eyes to the floor, unsure if I could carry any more bad news, but I quickly gathered myself and lifted my head. I had to stay strong. I had to keep my promise.

"Death," Raphael stated, "will be their emptiness. When a human being 'dies,' their time on Earth will be over. In a sense, it's like they'll be banished from the Earth. Afterwards, there is only one place their soul, their version of our spiritual body, can go."

"Where?"

"Hell. The world reserved for Heaven's fallen angels – the demons. They will all go there. Not because they want to, but because of the sin that now covers them. You saw it cover Adam and Eve - the darkness that overshadowed their light and tainted their essence. It's like filthy water poured into their clean, washed vessels. That disobedience and unrighteousness against God is all over them, and until the sin is removed from their nature, Hell will be their only destination. Of course, God will not leave those who love him to suffer there, but they still won't be welcomed into Heaven. Not yet. They'll still have to watch their family and friends who forsook God suffer, as they are separated yet present, hearing a constant torture put upon them while they are unable to help. They will be in their own solitary confinement. An island, if you will, of their very own."

The very mention of the island still continued to send shudders down my back.

"Why can't those who follow God be able to go to Heaven when they die, regardless of the act Adam and Eve committed?"

"If they were of an angelic composition, then perhaps. But their bodies were designed differently. They are able to produce more human beings amongst themselves, and traits they possess are passed along to their offspring. With Adam and Eve being the first human beings, all children they will have from here on out will inherit the sin that is in them. Maybe if they had had children before their disobedience, and passed on their genetic sin-free nature to their sons and daughters, their offspring could get into Heaven, or at least stay in Eden...but unfortunately, it didn't happen that way. "

"So they will never get to Heaven? Ever?" I asked in disbelief, but Raphael shook his head.

"God is developing a plan to put an end to it once and for all...but it will take some time. Until then, we have to do our best to make sure they end up in the protected side of Hell, and not the eternal torture. The only way we can do that is to help them keep a relationship with God, even in their sin."

"That sounds difficult," Cadence muttered, which surprised me, because I never before had heard him mention that anything could be beyond his abilities. Sure, he was reluctant to jump into action, but not because he thought he couldn't succeed.

"The demons are hiding in the background," Alessa said, "so you're telling us we have to constantly fight against them until this plan is in place?"

"Yes," Raphael said, not holding back. "And meanwhile it appears that Satan and his demons will try their absolute best to corrupt them. They hate the humans, simply because God loves and cares for them. Not to mention the humans have a chance at redemption, which is contrary to their fate. Since there's a chance they can escape the suffering that Hell will bring, it drives them insane."

"They have to be protected," I said, "but Raphael...how did Lucifer get that much stronger? When we fought him before, at least we held our own for a little while. Now, he can beat us with his presence alone."

"Our power on Earth is directly linked to the humans' resolve and conviction," Raphael said, "while the demons have no such boundaries. I suspect Iron lost his power because he was occasionally on the fence about whether to follow God or Lucifer and therefore, he gained his small, unimposing stature as a result. But that's just my opinion."

"Then Vergil should be just as small," I said adamantly. "Good. It will be easier to speak with him." No one in the room said a word as Raphael cleared his throat awkwardly.

"In general, the demons are stronger than us, and this could be a problem considering we're unable to increase our maximum angelic pressure…but if the humans side with God and solicit His help, you will always be victorious."

"I want to help," I said. "We want to help. But what good are we if we're defeated by pressure alone? What's the point if we can't even get to a human's side to influence their decisions? To me, it sounds like all the humans need is a good relationship with God, not us."

"Lysander makes a good point," Cadence agreed. "Shouldn't we be up here in Heaven devising a counterstrike against the demons? Take more initiative?"

"Look at Cadence," Farah mused, "taking initiative."

"Don't let him fool you," Alessa mumbled under her breath, "he just wants to hang out in the fields all day. Copping out of protecting the humans means he can chill up here."

"Copping? Chill?" Marcus inquired. Alessa tapped her forehead.

"New slang," she said proudly, bobbing her head like an idiot.

"It doesn't matter!" Cadence turned and said to her sharply. "And this isn't a cop out or whatever. If we're useless on Earth, what can we do about it? Shouldn't our service be taken elsewhere?"

Alessa wasn't fazed by his outburst.

"We don't leave anyone behind," Alessa said firmly, crossing her arms. "Not an angel. Not a human. We're together in this."

"You drive me insane," Cadence huffed as Alessa flashed a smile. I gathered up the courage to speak.

"This still doesn't change the fact that Cadence and I are right. If they can stave off a demon without our help, we have no function there."

"It's true," Raphael suddenly said ominously, nodding his head. His wings were stretched out wide, his arms becoming taut, his fists clenched. "How could you help? Why exist at all? You might as well do the proper thing and commit an angelic suicide."

"Raphael?" I asked, startled by the sudden change in his voice. "Are you okay?"

"Allow yourselves to be knocked unconscious for eternity. Or better yet, become an Absent. Isn't that more productive? Because what good is your presence in Heaven or Earth? What good are you to any of us?"

His word flowed forth vehemently as he menacingly took a step in my direction. We were all so shocked by his advance that no one moved, watching our mentor spout out disdain with so much natural emotion and intensity that we had to believe his words. Cadence listened to a few more words before his hand, shaking in fear, reached behind him to unbuckle his shield. Raphael noticed immediately and glared at him, spitting his hateful words straight at him.

"You never should have left the island," he seethed, his eyes ablaze. "Since you've arrived, all you've done is become a thorn in God's side. A thorn I will rip out immediately."

"Raphael..." I started, emerging from my paralysis and putting a quivering hand on his shoulder. "Why are you -"

He didn't answer as he spun to face me, picking me up by my armor in the same motion. With his eyebrows scowling and his teeth trying to refrain from gnashing at my face, I couldn't help but think of Lucifer…Satan, grabbing my throat and telling me coldly about my inadequacies. I tried to see through the image, to dwell on my mentor behind it, so I could somehow wake him from his confusion. But before I could speak again, he threw me across the hall. I let my wings catch me in a drift and I floated to the floor in shock, trying to make sense of things.

"What are you doing?" I cried out, but he had left my sight. A second passed and he reappeared from the back room, where the holographic Earth lay, clutching a sword in each hand. I made a mental note to check the room more thoroughly next time…provided there was a next time…

Cadence put up his hands, stepping forward to reason with him, but Raphael didn't flinch or hesitate to slice through the Guard's upper torso with both swords, sending him sprawling to the floor in a lifeless crumple. Marcus rushed behind Raphael and tried to hold his arms at his side, but Raphael casually turned around and delivered a roundhouse kick to the Godhand's head, using his wings for added momentum. Marcus stumbled to the side and groaned as his head collided with a wall. The giant was dazed just long enough for Raphael to take the advantage, as he began hacking away at Marcus's exposed back. Marcus bellowed in rage but Raphael was relentless, making each swing of his sword faster and more powerful than the next. All Marcus could do was put his hands to his face and try to block the onslaught as best he could.

By this time, I was confident something had to be wrong with Raphael for he wasn't listening to a single word we said. And his anger was teeming with such ferocity; it was totally unlike anything I had ever seen. I immediately called for Alessa and she rushed to my side without question.

"Ask God what's wrong with him!" I commanded and she obeyed, closing her eyes and whispering to God for answers. It was interesting how I could be a doormat for everyone in the group, even Farah, but as soon as a conflict arose, my words miraculously had great value. As if a switch went off and told them to give me my place in the group – the reason I belonged. It was a short-lived invigorating feeling that only fueled my desire to win, to prove that I was indeed worthy of their respect in these hours of need. I had to be a stronger Lysander. A better and more mature me.

"AMOS!" I called to him authoritatively. "Raphael is quick, but he lacks in direct hand-to-hand combat. Get Marcus free so the two of you can rush Raphael together. Don't try to hit him, just use your bodies to trap him to a wall or a corner. Remove his mobility!"

Amos nodded and headed toward Marcus. Raphael had obviously heard our plan but I didn't care. The whole point of saying it out loud was to get his attention away from our favorite powerhouse. With only a second's reprieve in the barrage, Marcus lifted a cupped hand from his face to survey the situation, saw Raphael distracted, and proceeded to reciprocate the beating. Caught off guard, Raphael used his swords as a shield, putting them into an X and systematically deflecting each of Marcus's punches. That's when Amos arrived.

Plowing into Raphael's unguarded side, my mentor's body twisted awkwardly under Amos's lowered shoulder. Following his lead, Marcus aimed for the other half of Raphael's torso and with both in agreement; they slammed into him like charging bulls on the stampede. As Raphael flailed his arms for control, Farah, who was waiting for an opportunity to participate, swooped down. Raphael saw her coming out the corner of his eye and extended a blade her way. She managed to weather through the sword swipe, the sharp edge phasing through her body like it was made of air, her faith coming to the rescue and saving her life. In a bold move, Farah grabbed the sword by the hilt - while it was swinging downward - and yanked it out of Raphael's hand, making him significantly less dangerous with one less weapon.

Figuring that the Godhands had him pinned, I shuffled over to Cadence who was climbing steadily to his feet. Farah zipped over and dropped the sword she had retrieved down at our feet. With her cargo free from her hands, she plopped down to the floor and sighed, placing a hand on her bubble-sized stomach. The blade had been so heavy, she had been dragging it across the hall floor. Cadence gripped the fallen sword and unsheathed his own, dual wielding and preparing himself for retribution. I pulled out mine, just in case.

I glanced over at Alessa who was still praying when we heard a startling cry of pain. Raphael had somehow gotten his second sword through Marcus's chest and, consequently, the Godhand wasn't doing so well. Having taken so many hits already, the impalement was beginning to make his body shake uncontrollably, even after he pulled it out. Amos was engaging Raphael in a fist fight now and Raphael was winning, using a street form of Muy Thai, elbowing and kneeing the big angel over and over so fast, Amos was stumbling more out of dizziness than pain. I made a second mental note to study more fighting styles in the database. They were obviously an asset for Raphael, enabling him to take on a Godhand single-handedly.

Cadence and I joined in, swinging our swords wildly. Raphael had no choice but to back up and dodge our crippling blows, right into a recovered Marcus. Amos quickly regrouped and joined Marcus, crushing Raphael against the wall, pinning him and using the last of their Godhand strength to keep him immobilized. My mentor groaned and struggled against the pressure but Cadence let his hand whip forward, placing his sword at Raphael's throat. Raphael breathed heavily but let his muscles finally go limp, letting my friends keep him at bay. A little more comfortable, I eventually heard Alessa calling for me.

"What's wrong with him?" I asked her, glancing back. She flung her hands up in confusion.

"God says 'nothing.'"

"God isn't speaking?"

"No. He said 'nothing is wrong with Raphael.'"

"That can't be right."

"No…it's the truth," Raphael chuckled, his face relaxed, eerily smiling as he turned to the Godhands. "Can you two let me go?"

The request was so friendly and unthreatening that Marcus and Amos easily backed off. Cadence moved slowly and relinquished control cautiously as Raphael stretched his wings and back.

"Sorry for testing you, but I knew you were all strong enough."

"That was a test?" Farah snapped. "We thought you were losing your mind!"

"You must have faith not only in yourself, but more so in God," Raphael relayed to us, wiping off his breastplate armor. "When you came to Heaven you fought against Lucifer and a third of Heaven's angels. You remained convicted and survived the war. These are not things to be taken lightly and you must never forget this. You can make a difference – as long as you never give up. The moment you quit, the demons will win each and every time. Staying up in Heaven and lying in the grass won't make Adam and Eve any safer. As a matter of fact, your very presence keeps most demons at bay, and those bold enough to test you won't be able to leave unscathed. Now do you see your importance?"

Once again, I considered Raphael's words. The last time he gave me advice, it had been an anchor for my mind, one of the few fortresses that had kept me unharmed from Lucifer's poison. I wouldn't forget his words this time either.

"Thank you, Raphael," Cadence said approvingly. "We'll do our best."

"Or at the least, we'll make sure Cadence does," Alessa said. "We already give it our full strength." Cadence rolled his eyes.

"Before you leave, can I make a suggestion?" Raphael asked.

"Of course," I said.

"Go back down to Earth, and spend some quality time there. Get to understand what the humans are like and who they are. They may not be in their former glory, but what's done is done. They have been punished and now they seek forgiveness. Naturally, they're having a hard time adjusting, so it might be good for them to feel some heavenly presence."

"What if we face Satan again?" I asked him, but Farah patted me on the back, reminding me of her faith.

"God is in control," Raphael smiled. "Don't make your decisions based on fear. Don't stay away from the Earth because you are afraid to face what's ahead."

I nodded in appreciation. We would show what we could do.

We left the hall energized, excitedly talking and highlighting our favorite part in the battle against Raphael. I was about to ask if anyone knew where his weapons were hidden when Cadence motioned for me to stay back and talk with him. The others seemed unaware, but I knew they were watching from a distance. Despite our journey back to Earth, the group understood that when Cadence had a lot on his mind, he usually turned to me for questions. And I had no clue why.

"I'm sorry we left you, Lysander," he said, but I laughed it off.

"Don't tell me you're still dwelling on that."

"You had to face Lucifer alone…again. I don't want to miss another battle against him."

"Ready to blow us away with your shield throwing expertise?"

"No, but you saw how cohesive we were back there. It was no fluke. When our teamwork kicked in, we were able to subdue Raphael easily. Just imagine how powerful we'll be when the six of us are in one accord. We'll be able to accomplish great things. I'm sure of it."

"I wouldn't worry about it now," I said. "In each instance you were doing the best you could. When we were heading toward Lucifer in Heaven, you were already in a weakened state. And as far as the Garden goes, you made the right decision in going to get help. Even Raphael said so."

"I just wonder if I truly am making the right decisions or if you all are just trying to make me feel better."

"Cadence, this doesn't sound like you at all. You're doing fine."

"I don't want to lose another teammate...not like we did with Vergil...he was confident of how we felt about him. I think that if we had accepted him sooner, he wouldn't have been drawn to Lucifer."

"Like Raphael said, what's done is done. We can't change what happened."

Cadence gave me a raised eye and turned his face toward me in inspection.

"You're sure not as shook up about this as you once were."

"Are you kidding? I'm scared out of my mind," I laughed. "But there's hope now. Don't you see? We saw Iron and Arthur and Lucifer and the rest of the fallen angels! And although they have been changed into these demons, they still retained their memory and recognized us. Iron and Lucifer have always been our enemies to some degree, but Vergil was a friend that simply got confused in the end. If we saw those three and the rest of the fallen, then we will eventually run into Vergil."

"Lysander...I wouldn't get your hopes up too much."

"I'll take my faith," I said in retort. "We won't know until we see him."

"I hope for all our sakes that you're right. Lucifer's gotten more spiritually powerful since he became a demon, and don't forget – Vergil was an Archangel too."

"All the more reason to keep our guard up."

"And what if it doesn't work out the way you intended? Say you talk to him for weeks but he stays convicted in his decision. What then?"

"It will work."

"But what if theoretically it doesn't? Can you accept him as a demon? As an enemy?"

"He's not an enemy," I said. I refused to accept anything less. Now that I knew he wasn't being controlled, there was hope.

Cadence shook his head profusely and chuckled under his breath.

"Well, regardless, you'll get your chance to talk to him. We all agreed to it."

"Thank you, Cadence. For sticking to your word. This means a lot to me, and I do realize you're compromising on this."

"I just hope this compromise doesn't turn into a slaughter."

I glanced over at him and saw the anxiety rippling throughout his body…I had been wrong. Since Vergil's departure, I had assumed the group didn't give more than a passing thought about him, but this wasn't true. From the worry surrounding Cadence's face, and the fear vibrating along the border of his wings, I could see that this had been a recently visited topic. Being the unofficial leader of Team Six, he had taken on the burden of assuming the worst. That someday we could encounter Lucifer and his army again and be forced to fight. Now it was a certainty, and this brought on a whole new wave of nervousness.

"I didn't think he would be in the Garden," Cadence lamented, "trying to destroy God's creations so soon. I assumed he would be off on the other side of the Earth, gaining strength to attack Heaven again, or maybe sulking in a corner, having learned his lesson."

"I won't sacrifice us," I said to him, and he glanced at me, pained. "I'm serious. If it comes between Vergil and Team Six, you already know who I'll choose."

"I know, Lysander," he said weakly. "You'll be strong, and fight valiantly."

Valiantly was not a word Cadence would use, and this only worried me more. No matter how much he smiled, deep down, I don't think he believed his words.

And the scary thing was, I wasn't sure I did either.

CHAPTER 8: Protection

We hit Earth's atmosphere right as our conversation ended, with our sole target being the Garden of Eden. We had heard that Adam and Eve had been banished from it, but we had to see for ourselves. Farah confirmed it the second Cadence and I caught up to the rest of the group - they had arrived at ground zero long before us.

"The invisible barriers are gone," she said, fluttering all over the place, ducking trees and zipping through bushes and flowers. "Some of the shrubbery is still untouchable though."

"No humans," Marcus grunted. Cadence peered down a long path, squinting ahead.

"The Cherubims must be driving them further away then they like," he said.

"What's a Cherubim?" I asked. Everyone shook their heads and groaned in agony. No one looked my way. "Isn't anyone going to tell me?" I asked.

"Why am I not surprised you don't have a clue?" Alessa sighed. "We don't even react

anymore."

"Then what was all that groaning about?"

"Don't worry about that."

"You could just give me the information I need."

"It gets annoying explaining stuff wherever we go."

"We," Marcus declared firmly, "not your parents."

Farah laughed and gave Marcus a high-five. Amos guffawed loudly after a second and clutched his belly, which disgustingly bounced up and down like someone was shaking a carton of orange juice. If Marcus was making fun of me and getting away with it, I was in real trouble. I had to really start doing my own studying and take it upon myself to improve my craft.

"Okay okay," I said. "This one last time. Tell me what a Cherubim is."

"Why don't we see for ourselves?" Alessa asked. Cadence didn't seem too sure about that.

"Do we really want to disturb them? They're said to be guarding a flaming sword, and even from here I can tell it's quite powerful. It's making my angelic pressure ripple like wind on the ocean."

"So poetic," Alessa laughed. Cadence remained stone-faced.

"It's probably best we leave them to their job," I said. "I can access the database later to find out what they are."

"A flaming sword...I wonder if we can pick it up," Alessa whispered to herself and we all looked at her like she was crazy. Except Farah, whose spirit had suddenly been lifted.

"We should definitely try!" she said excitedly, clapping her hands together. "I mean, if we can, there's no reason God can't put another one there! We can use it on Satan next time. Swoosh. Swoosh."

She started flying around the air, swinging an imaginary sword and laughing hysterically.

Marcus began nodding and gave his chest a pound of his left hand.

"I try first," he said, and took off to the entrance. Cadence rolled his eyes but let the group have their fun. It was needed and long overdue.

As we got closer to our destination, we came across a few rows of invisible barriers, so we were forced to fly up and outside the Garden, meeting the Cherubims and the sword from the outside. Far above the Earth, it was hard to make out the details of the celestial beings, but with a squint of my eyes their physical features became clearer, and I almost gasped at how strange they looked.

There were two of them, and both of them were short, slightly taller than Farah. They had small limbs but a large square head with four faces; one face on each side. They never turned their heads because of this and when they flew, they went in one of four directions: either up, down, forward, backward, left or right. No diagonals, as if they were set in place on an invisible track. Their torsos were made of a wheel, intersecting and melding into its being, and this was apparently the core of their being. The middle of their abdomen shimmered in the sunlight and each of the wheels turned slow or fast depending on how quickly they flapped their four wings. Strangely, the wheels lagged behind them when they took flight, as if their spirits were trying to catch up with their solidified bodies. They were definitely spiritual in composition, but I wasn't sure if they were actually angels.

Still, they were interesting to behold, and I continued to stare as we slowed our descent, watching the two of them darting through the air in their own way, engaged in some kind of heated debate. Their wheels spun so fast, they were as bright as lava and outshone the Cherubim's other features with the aesthetic intensity of a sun. Their strange six-way flying made me snicker on the inside and the spectacle was so distracting, I barely noticed how much the landscape had changed.

The Garden stayed where it had always been, unmoved, but the rolling plains and plush meadows were gone. In their place was a rocky, dirt terrain that stretched for miles. Pebbles littered the ground and the little grass that showed stood out because it was choked by the soil. It reached up like thinning patches of hair, dying slowly in the sunlight that slapped its hand down upon the Earth without mercy. The world had changed...

Was all of this a result of Adam and Eve's choice?

"HEY! HEY HEY!" one of the Cherubim said, appearing suddenly in front of me. I yelped in surprise and flew down to the ground instinctively, my wings straight behind me like I was a wounded animal. It followed me like a bee and gnashed all four sets of its teeth like it wanted to sting.

"HEY HEY HEY!" it cried again. "Go somewhere else! We're protecting this spot!"

"Not doing a good job, partner," Amos replied, floating right beside me. "Especially with us floating a mile above it. Besides, you two were pecking at each other like a bunch of seagulls fighting over bread."

"WHAT?"

"What my friend is trying to say," I said, "is that it doesn't seem like you're guarding the sword too well."

"Oh! Oh! Okay, well if you think the sword is so unsafe, why don't you walk on over and take it?"

"Well, well, well," the other Cherubim said cheerfully, coming down to join the commotion, "looks like we have another customer!"

"We don't mean any trouble," I said but the two of them started hovering in my face and flying side to side, screaming so incoherently, I just cupped my ears. The first one was enraged and displaying the proper emotions while strangely, the more upbeat Cherubim was smiling and screaming happily as if this were all a game. The confusion didn't improve my nerves as I closed my eyes and waited for the barrage to pass.

"Thinking that they can just pick up the sword God placed here and walk off with it." I finally understood the first Cherubim's words, but he didn't let me process it completely as he let out a loud "HA!" at the end.

"Good morning, gentlemen," Cadence said, coming down to join us and offering a hand to shake. The first Cherubim stared at it like it was a serpent and declined, but the second shook it fervently.

"This isn't an exhibit," the first one said firmly, the wheel at his center slowing down in momentum. "My name is Anton, and I say that we aren't having any gathering here."

Farah giggled and Anton glared at her.

"Are you laughing at my name?"

"It's as funny as your accent," she snickered playfully as he wrinkled three of his upper lips in disapproval.

"Well! That was rude..."

"She was just being truthful," the second angel said excitedly, "and they're only here because they're curious. It's not every day you see a flaming sword the size of a streetlight standing between two vine walls leading into the most beautiful garden on Earth."

"Do you ever stop talking, Synon?"

"I do talk a lot, don't I?" he said quickly. "I really should mind my tongue."

"You don't have to agree with everything I say. I'm just saying you tend to ramble."

"I do. I do...and I really must develop my own thoughts. You know what? You're right Anton. From this point on, I will absolutely agree with everything you say."

"No. No. You're supposed to disagree."

"With what?"

"With everything I say. You are to not agree with me anymore."

"Oh all right. I agree to do as you ask."

"Synon," Anton said, exasperated. "You're still agreeing with me!"

"Yes, I suppose I am! I like being your friend."

"It has nothing to do with friendship. It has to do with individuality."

"Do I have individuality?"

"Yes. Or I hope you do."

"Then I do," Synon beamed, looking quite pleased with himself. Anton shook his head in disbelief and sighed heavily.

"For all of eternity...with this guy," he muttered. We all burst out laughing.

"Both of you are very confusing," I informed. Synon smiled.

"You're right about that."

Farah giggled again.

"We don't mean to disturb you," Cadence said, "but my friends wanted a try at unearthing the sword. Is that allowed?"

"Don't see why not," Synon said. Anton elbowed him.

"Have you forgotten already? We're supposed to be guarding the place! You don't just let anyone walk over and steal the very treasure you're supposed to be protecting! We'll be accomplices!"

"Yeah!" Synon cried out, pumping a fist into the air like he had been in agreement with that statement the whole time.

"How long have you been here?" Alessa suddenly asked. "I was just talking to God and He said that we spent more than a few years in Heaven after Adam and Eve were banished. How is that possible?"

"What makes you think a few years have passed?" Anton asked.

"For one, the land is dying. The fields are gone, and the air is different. Stale...dry. And even with the sun shining just as bright as ever, the sky's gotten darker, by a few degrees. What happened?"

"A few Earth years?!" I exclaimed. "We were talking to Raphael for a few years?!"

"Year," Marcus stated. "Hmmm..."

"What's wrong with your friend?" Anton asked, pointing to Marcus.

"Never mind him," Alessa said. "You can answer my question, if you will."

"You're a pushy angel for a Glory," he stated.

"Thank you!" Cadence said, laughing freely. "Someone's said it. Now let's wait for the threats."

"If you know I'm a Glory," she said menacingly, "then it's important you stay on my good side or I'll relay a message to God you won't like."

"He placed us here," Anton said coolly. "We're not going anywhere. Go ahead. Try it."

"What is it about the small ones that makes them bark so loud?" Alessa shouted to the sky in frustration while Farah commenced with a giggling fit.

"She can be ridiculous," Cadence said. "But now I'm curious too. How could time have passed so quickly?"

"At least you have manners," Anton huffed, keeping his eyes fixed on Alessa's silent tantrum. "The truth is that time is different down here. It might be a few minutes to you in Heaven, but down here it could be decades."

"But I've been here before," Alessa said. "I don't understand."

"Maybe when time didn't matter you were unaware. Now that the humans are no longer immortal, it matters a lot. There's cause for concern."

"Hence the sword," Cadence replied. "It guarantees the humans never get back to the Tree of Life."

"Yes, I know," Anton confirmed in a bored tone. "We're not idiots."

"Since you've been here, has anyone tried to take the sword?

"No human," Synon stressed. "Plenty of angels have though. It's the latest attraction. And it's…"

"Quite irritating," Anton continued where Synon left off. "We just want to do our job. But no need to worry now. Not a single angel's been able to get near it, let alone pick it up. Why do you think we're standing a mile away from the entrance?"

"Hmph," Alessa commented, staring back at the enflamed blade from where we stood. "I thought you were on break."

"NEVER!" Anton and Synon yelled, pumping fists in the air. Marcus broke the conversation by taking a massive step between us.

Rubbing his palms together, he started marching toward the flaming sword. He was on a mission...but this would be no easy feat to accomplish. Boasting eight feet in width and standing over eight yards high, this was not an ordinary sword. It had been crafted by the Master Blacksmith Himself with a polished, clean finish for the edge and a hilt made of diamond. The tip was fastened securely into the dirt, and the ground around it was packed in immaculately as if the sword had been there since the beginning of creation. The fire itself gave off mini-explosions, crackling and bursting like clockwork, producing more flames the moment others began to die down.

Marcus made it about halfway to the sword when his steps became sluggish, his body only able to move forward in slow motion. It was as if hurricane winds were pushing him back and he was trying his best to fight the torrential force. Almost as if the sword were alive, the flames around it began glowing brighter, and its power increased, pushing Marcus back abruptly with impressive strength.

Eventually, the Godhand hit an unseen wall, but not because an invisible barrier had been installed. It was simply because the power being emitted from the sword was too great. Even from where I stood, I could see Marcus's body flicker, his angelic pressure losing its density. Marcus stood there, trying to push his hand forward but he could barely raise a finger. After a few seconds of bracing against the sword's might, he took a couple steps back. He tried to hunker down and force his way forward, but by now he had lost too much energy. He ended up being sent backwards, rolling like a tumbleweed, spinning back to us head-over-heels. He ended up landing on his stomach, crashing into Synon who was happy to assist in stopping him. I noticed that Synon only used one hand to do it. This confirmed my suspicions - that despite their size, the Cherubims were very strong. Marcus groaned and stood up, dusting his wings off, and taking inventory on our facial expressions. He stopped at Farah's, and looked down at her with a bit of disdain, unashamed to admit that she was his outspoken rival.

"Impossible," he grunted and walked to the back of our group. Farah started stretching.

"For you," she said when he was a couple of feet away. His growl echoed across the barren valley and followed her trail as she suddenly shot forward with all her might, leaving a ripple in the air. Unafraid of the sword's power, she picked up speed as the sword answered in its own way. But it appeared her faith wouldn't grant her complete victory this time. She made it only a couple of inches further than Marcus had when she was propelled back like she had just been launched from a catapult. Alessa caught her instinctively and let her back into the air like a baby bird. Marcus let out a chortle at her attempt but it didn't bother Farah, who was still breathing hard from all the exertion.

"That was fun," she laughed. "I could do this all day. How long do you think it'll take before I touch it?"

She looked around for approval, for some kind of confirmation that we were willing to stay there for as long as it took, but the honest answer was that we just weren't, and it was all over our faces.

"Oh c'mon!" she cried. "I was so close!"

"We'll visit later," Cadence muttered, turning back to Anton. "Where are the humans now?"

"Go about ten miles west," Anton said. "They should be there."

"Thank you for your help."

"No, thank you," Synon said proudly and Anton shook his head in disapproval.

"See, that's what I'm talking about," Anton replied. "What you said doesn't even make sense. They did nothing, and you're over here thanking him. We're the ones who gave the information."

"I guess you're right. Silly me."

"You don't have to feel sorry. Just follow along."

"Didn't think about that. It's true. I should just follow the conversation…"

Cadence decided not to say another word, in case the two Cherubims struck up another conversation. We all backed off slowly, tiptoeing as if they were dynamite ready to ignite at the slightest disruption. By the time we took to the skies, they had faced each other and started their initial dance all over again, arguing about who knows what. Farah was the only one to mention how fun they were.

Flying west was easy, but finding the humans was hard. About as hard as finding the demons now that they had decided to go into hiding. Back in Heaven, I had had no desire to see the humans, but at least I could still sense them on Earth, their souls radiating like small light bulbs, a sort of kindred spirit. But now their spiritual signatures – their very souls - were faint, like we were lost at sea and only a couple of flashlights on the shore were our beacons in the fog. We spread out instinctively, surveying the land. Soon the dead terrain transformed into a hint of its former glory, and I figured we were going the right way. It made sense. If I had been banished from Heaven, I would be searching the whole universe for a parallel to my former home. I wondered why the demons didn't do the same. Were they so angry that they were focused more on getting back at God than relocating? Or had they tried and bitterly failed? The more I thought about it, the more it made sense that Earth would be a prison of sorts. After all, if they could easily travel through space, who was to say they wouldn't run into us having fun in the cosmos? What would stop them from going back to Heaven? Perhaps a few of God's invisible barriers could provide some protection but it was hard to say where the line would be drawn. Someday I would discover the answers.

More mental notes.

Just what I needed.

"Question," Marcus spoke up. "Land not dead?" He was pointing down at the increasingly luscious valley below, comparing it to the section we had just come from.

"The land is able to be watered from the ground," Alessa said informatively. Now I was intrigued.

"Uh, I don't think that's a good enough explanation for Marcus," I said, feigning understanding. "What do you mean it's watered here?"

"The earth is watered from the ground."

"Okay, saying the same thing doesn't instantly make me knowledgeable of the subject."

"Can't you check your database?"

"You get frustrated when you explain things. I'd rather you teach me. It's an entertaining study."

"FIIINE," she whined, shaking her head. "What I mean is that the entire Earth is watered via a complex system under the ground called an artesian aquifer. There were plenty in the Garden of Eden. Do you recall the fountain in the middle of one of the intersections along the path?"

"Vaguely," I sighed. I was already taking the jargon spewing out of her mouth and making a list, a queue of unknown words that I had to find the definitions to.

"The fountains were part of the system, except in that case, it was an extreme example. A lot of water came from that aquifer."

"Okay."

 "Most produce a mist that gives grass and shrubbery just enough water to live on. Apparently, the artesian aquifer outside of Eden was disrupted or it wasn't there to begin with, hence the dead valley."

"Mm-hmm," I affirmed unconvincingly. "So what is an artesian aquifer?"

"Think of a bowl. Now at the bottom of the bowl there is water, filling up the bowl from underneath. This water comes in from the ocean and underground rivers. Now think of a covering over this water, halfway up the bowl, like icing on a cake. This is deep ground and shifting plates that produce low hydraulic activity – there are small holes, like pores in this ground as well. After that, there's more water and finally the last covering, which is the ground and land that we see - the soil."

"Got it," Marcus replied at the end.

"Seriously?" I asked, dumb-founded. He just stared down at me.

"Yes."

"Then explain it to me."

"Thought you were smart."

"Don't stop on his account," Cadence said to Alessa. "We'll explain it to him in better detail when you're done. This is just a crude example."

"Crude? Oh, so you would do a better job?"

"I didn't say that. Just keep going. Geez."

"Okay, so these aquifers aren't everywhere but they are placed strategically all over the Earth."

"But how do they work?"

"When too much water comes in from the oceans, it shakes and shifts the plates above it. Some water breaks through the plates and goes into the second chamber. When the second chamber starts filling up, it shoots up water to make more room, and this water hits the surface, creating a cooling mist! Ta-da! Lesson completed!"

"So it gets pushed up by water pressure? And the first layer is more like a screen than a vault door?"

"Yes, it's designed to not let the water on the bottom get out of control, but it still lets some up to maintain equilibrium and water the surface."

"Hmm, yes." Marcus nodded. "Equilibrium."

"Oh, c'mon!" I exclaimed at him. He just laughed.

"Explain further," Cadence sighed.

"How do you see these things?" I interjected. "And is there another aquifer nearby?"

"To answer your first question: I ask God about their locations when I'm curious. And as for your second: yes, there is one – one that is especially big and very similar to a well. And that's where we'll find our humans."

"Why didn't you say that earlier?" Cadence whined. "Don't tell me we've passed them."

"A long time ago actually. Remember those few hills in the beginning? Near the Garden? The humans were pretty much a couple miles beyond that."

Cadence sighed aggressively and Alessa flew over to pat him on the head. Cadence swatted at her hand and she dodged, turning around and flying back to where we came from. We followed suit, ready to put our minds at ease and relax on the ride there, but as we got closer to our new destination, an angel flew past us with lightning speed, disrupting our comfortable flight.

"Sorry!" he cried out, slowing down to apologize. She was obviously a Guard based on the spiral silver and gold shield on her back. Unlike Cadence, her wings didn't cover it.

"Are you coming from where Adam and Eve are?" Cadence asked.

"I know. I was late to the celebration. But at least I got to see them."

"Celebration? Late?"

"Yeah, and I have to say they are absolutely adorable, and so alike at the same time!"

"We actually have no clue what you're talking about," Farah said.

"Oh...oh, you've never seen them? The kids?"

"They have goats?"

"No," she chuckled. "The children. I'm usually late to events so this is my first time seeing them. Sounds like it's yours too."

"We were busy talking to Raphael," I said and her eyes widened in awe.

"I knew I recognized you! You're the ones who faced Lucifer in the Garden! Wow. That must have been intense."

"Unfortunately, it's becoming a tradition of sorts," I said. "We fought him in Heaven too."

"I'm impressed. Hey, don't beat yourselves up over the outcome. I think the only one who could've made a difference was Michael."

"Hopefully we won't have to find out," I said and she began floating backwards.

"Well, nice talking to you! I'm Jacqueline by the way. Hope we meet again!"

"She was nice!" Farah exclaimed as Jacqueline sped away.

"You love everyone," Alessa laughed. "But it was nice of her to relay that information. Children...what could that mean?"

"I think it means the beginning of the human race," I responded excitedly. "Do you remember the first time we came to Heaven, and we went into the Fellowship Hall and saw all those angels congregating? We were awe-struck."

"So there will be more of them," she said. "Hmmm..."

"What's wrong?"

"I already know what she's thinking," Cadence said. "I'm surprised you haven't thought of the same."

"I don't understand," I said, contemplating Alessa's words. This was a good thing, wasn't it? More human beings to populate the Earth. But if there were more humans…that also meant more demons would show their face…and if it didn't take long for Satan to personally pay Adam and Eve a visit - with the Earth being populated, it was only a matter of time before each individual would be targeted and quarantined for a demon's personal use.

"This could get bad," I said.

"There he goes," Alessa replied. "Welcome back."

"Don't worry about it yet," Cadence said, glaring at me hard. "We'll just keep an eye out for any demon scouts."

"And no matter what, we'll stay together," Farah winked at Cadence who shook his head.

"No matter what."

We continued to follow Alessa's lead. Eventually we were able to hone in on two signatures, but when we arrived, there was something apparently wrong.

"What's that?" Marcus asked in shock. We shared his sentiment. The two humans that stood before us were like Adam and Eve, but significantly smaller, and they were…I'm not sure how to describe it - newer and smoother. They were only a shadow of what their adult counterparts were and their eyes were so wide and playful, they were reminiscent of Adam and Eve's innocence in the Garden of Eden.

"So these are children," Cadence said to himself. "Why are they so small? Adam and Eve didn't start out that way."

"Not sure," I said. "But if I had to guess, I'd say their physiology and mental capacity haven't matured yet."

"That's a lot of words to say they're different."

We were in a meadow on a massive hill. The grass around us was short due to the elevation not giving it the proper amount of sunlight. Dandelions were in abundance and butterflies fluttered aimlessly over the nearby rolling hills The sun was warm and inviting and the two small humans laughed and played, running around in circles. One of them would hit the other on the back, and then run off as he was chased in turn. Both resembled Adam more than Eve in structure, yet they inexplicably had doe-like almond-shaped eyes that smiled like hers. In the distance, I could make out a tall figure coming over the hill, his stride filled with urgency.

"Cain! Abel! It's time for work!" Adam yelled from where he stood. "The ground won't till itself!"

The boys ceased their assault on one another and stood at attention, composing themselves and dusting off their clothes from the snippets of grass that had gotten in their hair and the stains that now hugged their shirts. Adam came over and grabbed each of their arms as they sulked, and led them back to where he came from. He was muttering about how high he had to climb in order to reach them, and I couldn't help but laugh despite his struggle. The Garden of Eden had been as flat as ice on a lake. No way could they strain themselves traveling to and fro. But now, a retrieval mission easily turned into a high impact workout.

"Did you notice one was bigger than the other?" Alessa asked as we stood there and watched them disappear into the distance. We were still in awe over the new human beings, so none of us followed Adam yet – which was fine. We'd catch up.

"Maybe he has God's favor due to his height," I said. Farah kicked me in the shin.

"Favor has nothing to do with height!" she sulked and I winced at the remark. "We're all created differently, so there must be an explanation!"

"It's simple," a voice echoed behind us, swooping past our group and floating down in front of us. The angel was undeniably a

Messenger. Not because of the blue armor or anything. Simply because he was unimposing and flew to us with a sense of urgency, like he had a message to deliver…

"Do you mind explaining it to us?" Cadence asked and the angel bowed.

"My name is Dan," he said. Marcus snorted.

"Angel…named Dan," he muttered slowly and Dan frowned in reply.

"I don't have to explain anything, you know. I could fly right back to Heaven."

"Wouldn't that be a breach of your orders?" Alessa asked. Dan glared at her in rage.

"I have feelings too, you know. You think that because I go around delivering messages that I don't matter. Well I do! How would you get any news without us? Huh? Anyone? Are you going to fly back to Heaven and retrieve the information yourself? No. I didn't think so! I'm the one that has to travel back and forth while the rest of you frolic in the fields and pat bunnies and stuff! I'm sick of it!"

Dan ripped a gauntlet from his hand and threw it to the Earth, frantically huffing like he had been flying at full speed since creation.

"Whoa. Calm down," Cadence half-chuckled, putting his hands forward. "We didn't mean to be rude. And we don't look down on Messengers. If you look to our friend here, you'll see he's a Messenger too."

"Really?" Dan exclaimed and began pointing a finger at me. "Why aren't you running errands? Huh? What's your route?"

"Uh…uh," I stammered. "I have no clue. I guess I have a mission to carry out with my team."

"Oh yeah? What's your mission then?"

"Um…well…Raphael said we should analyze the humans. Learn about them."

"And why do you get to go on this top secret adventure while I'm stuck passing out mail?"

"I don't know…"

"I'm going to talk to God about this."

"Hey!" Alessa said, speaking up sharply. "No need for that. We need Lysander here with us. He's a valuable part of the team."

"And I'm meaningless? I don't matter?"

"Geez," Alessa sighed, turning to me. "Are all Messengers whiny?"

"Do you actually want me to answer that?"

"No," she laughed. "It's rhetorical. Of course we already know the answer."

"HEY!" Dan and I cried out in unison. Farah began giggling in the background. Amos stepped forward to save us from our ongoing prattle.

"Ignore them," he said. "So what's going on? How are the children made like that?"

"Don't try to change the subject," Dan huffed in Amos's face. Alessa stepped between them.

"Listen, Dan, was it? I'm a Glory. I can contact God at any given moment. Just give us the message you were sent here with so you don't get in trouble. I'll tell God about your complaint."

"You would do that?" Dan said with wide, hopeful eyes.

"You would?!" I cried out, spinning toward her and glaring at her cheek.

"If it means getting this over with," Cadence muttered, mindlessly poking a finger through one of his wings.

"Fine. I'll tell you how they're designed," Dan said. "But I want that complaint issued."

"No problem," Alessa said in the softest tone I'd ever heard her use. "Please give us your message."

"The children were born from their mother's womb," he said informatively. "This isn't like when God made Eve and took a rib from Adam to form her. These children were conceived between their parents and born individually. Cain, the taller one, was born first, and Abel came second not too long after. It's not a matter of favor or ability, but chronological order."

"Well, we're excited to see more humans despite what their presence implies," Cadence said solemnly.

"Of course," Dan piped up, introducing a smile. "It's the reason why I'm here. Raphael sent me to take you all back to Heaven. The fact is, because there will be more children and generations to come, we're finally receiving our assignments! Heaven has added a new building to expedite the process smoothly and it's filling up quickly. So if you don't want to be on the 'study giant squid' mission located in the ocean's deep, you should get moving."

"What of the new family? Who's watching them?"

"God has it covered, but you can choose a member to stay behind if you like. Since you are deemed as a team, I'm sure an assignment won't separate you unless it's extremely important."

"We don't have to vote," Amos said, stepping forward proudly. "I volunteer."

"Why do you want to stay behind so badly?" Farah asked him.

"I like the playful nature of those kids," he said. "Reminds me of myself before the war."

"Oh brother," Cadence chuckled. "Sounds like a story is coming."

"Oh no. No story. Not yet anyway," he winked. "But I do want to study the situation more. Figure out what Adam meant by work. Besides, it don't hurt to have a Godhand to, you know, lend a hand. Get it? Lend-"

"Yes. Yes," Cadence interrupted, waving him away, "we've heard it already. Alright, team, let's move out. Amos, I'll try to make sure you don't get a job like scrubbing the streets."

"Thanks boss," he replied, and took off down the hill to where Earth's first family lay.

As we began ascending from the atmosphere I looked back, and a couple of miles away, I saw a figure, standing tall in the middle of the meadow.

And it wasn't Amos...or a human.

The shadows of the hills seemed to block its identity from the sunlight, so I had little time to study it before Cadence brought me back to attention. I couldn't make out any distinct features, but as we were hitting the stillness of space, I noticed that it was no longer standing like a statue amongst the grass. It was looking directly at me...and it was waving...

CHAPTER 9: Guardian Angels

"Did anyone see that?" I asked the group as we boomed out of the black hole like an asteroid, landing just beyond Heaven's vibrant world. I had wanted to ask about the mysterious shadow figure earlier, but I had wanted to be certain of what I saw. There was no use worrying the others unnecessarily, and with my recent obsession of finding Vergil, I didn't want them looking at me suspiciously.

"See what? Amos's bumbling flight to the humans?" Alessa asked me.

"What? No..."

"Because I saw it. I was wondering what was wrong with him."

"No, I meant the figure standing in the meadow. I couldn't see who it was."

"What? Sun was in your eye?"

"That's impossible," Cadence said. "If you did see someone, you should've been able to make out their features. Doesn't matter if it was angel or human."

"What if it was a demon?" I suggested, knowing I better have a good explanation at the ready.

"So you're saying that there could be a demon near Adam and his children, and we just left Amos there - alone?" Cadence turned to face me as his voice raised an octave. "And on top of that, you didn't say anything until now?"

"You're blowing this out of proportion. I didn't say it was a demon. I was just wondering if anyone else saw it."

"So what was it, Lysander? You tell me," Cadence was getting frantic. By his count he had already been absent from two cataclysmic battles – both in which he had lost someone important to us and God. To think that Amos could be in danger was all over his conscience.

"I'm not sure," I replied, knowing that my response wasn't what he needed. Cadence leaned in closer and loudly whispered.

"Or did you see what you wanted to see?"

"What's that supposed to mean?" I yelled at him, backing away. Farah got between us immediately.

"This is counterproductive," she said in a low voice, looking back and forth into both of our faces. "If it was a demon we would've felt its presence, right? Remember Satan?"

"Then what about Iron?" Cadence replied. "He was a demon and we didn't sense a thing...Alessa, ask God if there's a demon near Amos right now."

"Sure thing," she replied as she closed her eyes and carried out the request. Cadence glared at me angrily, but for some reason, all I could think about was whether Alessa had honored Dan's complaint or not.

"I hope you did see a demon," Cadence said through grit teeth, bringing me back to reality, "and it wasn't just wishful thinking over you-know-who."

"Listen Cadence, just because you weren't there when..." I stopped myself. I didn't want to hurt him just because he was attacking me verbally. I knew why he was upset and he was beating himself up more than enough without my input. Snapping back at him wouldn't change the past and besides, he wasn't angry with me per se. He was just upset that he could be leaving another one of our teammates in a horrible situation...all alone. Calling out his fears openly, when he had confided in me so candidly, would only damage the team's morale and possibly our friendship...not help it. I had to tread carefully.

"I'm sorry, Cadence." I said honestly. "The truth is, I don't know what I saw. It could have been an animal for all I know."

"We'll wait for Alessa's report," he said solemnly, his thoughts dwelling on the incomplete sentence I had muttered. Alessa cleared her throat for us to listen.

"No demons nearby," she said in relief. "Amos is fine."

"Good," Cadence snapped and took off toward the city core. Alessa came to my side and shook her head.

"It's not getting easier for him, is it?"

"He has a lot on his mind," I nodded. "He puts too much on his shoulders."

"Should clear mind," Marcus offered, jumping into the conversation. "Does good."

"As long as he knows we're behind him," Farah said. "That's all that matters. It's not his fault he wasn't there to fight Satan. He might have helped in the end, but we'll never know."

"We seriously have a score to settle with that demon," I laughed. "It's funny how he's the one banished from Heaven and fated to an eternal hellfire, yet we're more worried about his actions than he is. This is ridiculous. Technically, we already won."

"One day at a time," Farah said in a chipper tone. "That's the best we can do."

"Cadence is getting ahead," Alessa interrupted us. "Let's get to the city."

We turned to face the city and follow our leader when Farah let out a gasp. At first I didn't notice the alteration but with some focusing, it came into my line of sight.

The Symphony Hall had been replaced.

Not that I minded. It had, after all, been used as more of a recruitment center than a place to praise and worship God. Still, it was strange not seeing it there. In its place was a tall skyscraper with a humongous back side that extended out into a courtyard – a place where angels could still fly around and mingle if they chose. However, the rigid and brick-like structure, the steel doors and beams which created the window sills and struts, gave this place a completely different feel than the other buildings in Heaven. It wasn't about food, play or existential bliss and it made sure we realized this from a visual perspective. It was all about business, and every hardened, scowling face that littered the courtyard and the various offices inside confirmed it. It was like they were ordered to make this impression, and many of the angels, so used to going from one event to the next with bouncing playfulness, found themselves straightening up and waiting their turn with a militaristic attitude.

This was the Mission Center - the place where angels would receive their orders for Heaven and Earth.

The flow was orderly and fast-paced, with angels receiving their assignments in a matter of seconds. But unfortunately, we must have missed some kind of briefing or family meeting because the procedure wasn't so easy to understand to us. We awkwardly stumbled from one office to the next asking for directions and getting "I'm too busy" frowns in reply. Stacks of papers and large groups of the Faithful flew everywhere, further complicating our stay until, finally, someone got fed up and pointed us down a long corridor, out into the courtyard. We exited the main building onto a grassy expanse, filled with benches, marble paths and bright green trees. The surrounding brick layout of the Mission Center loomed high above, surrounding us in reminder that we still had work to do. Marcus was about to plop down on a bench when Farah practically shrieked in excitement. The noise put Marcus off guard and in surprise he mistakenly smashed the bench in two with an oversized fist. A few angels stared our way.

"Sorry!" I yelled out. "Our friend got startled!"

"Don't worry about it!" a Glory replied. "With all the commotion going on, the Godhands have been doing that all day out of frustration. Gary will clean it up."

"Gary," Marcus snickered. We saw a Faithful appear from behind and begin using his mind to manifest a new bench. He did it monotonously, like this was the millionth bench he'd fixed and he was an expert by now. Sure enough, a new bench replaced the old in three seconds.

"Thank you, Gary," Farah said warmly. Gary flashed a smile in her direction, then sped off to another job.

"What was all that noise about, anyway?" Alessa asked her. Farah pointed toward a corner of the courtyard, and there, we saw an old friend, standing very much out of place.

"Raphael!" I shouted, practically skipping over to him. "What are you doing here?!"

"Um," he said, obviously unhappy with having to mingle, "I'm an angel. Angels are to be here."

"Raphael, you're too funny," I laughed, slapping him on the shoulder. He immediately punched me in the face.

I cried out in agony and sprawled to the ground, clutching my face. My teammates hurried to pick me up as the other angels in the courtyard snickered or murmured at the display. I was furious.

"What was that for?!" I cried out, rubbing my poor nose. "You put a lot of angelic pressure into that!"

"Someone's obviously forgotten who they're talking to," he said rigidly, his body as still as a board. "We're not buddies. I'm not a part of Team Six."

"Geez, sorry," I whined, as I felt my angelic pressure get worse. How hard had he hit me?

"Well played," Marcus stated. I gave him a glare. Marcus stared back at me as if to say 'go ahead - see what happens' and I backed down, deciding to have a private sulking party for myself.

"Did you get your assignments yet?" Raphael asked us. We shook our heads. "Why not? It's not hard. You go in, give your name and ask what you're doing. Easy."

"It was confusing," Farah interjected and Raphael sighed heavily.

"And of course, you had to come crawling to me for answers."

"I wouldn't put it like that," Farah muttered. "Now I'm not so excited to see you anymore."

"Well, I don't care."

"Who can help us?" Cadence asked him. "Can't you give us our assignment?"

"I'm here to help," he sighed in a dead tone. "That's why I'm here. To make the process go smoothly. Hand out assignments and watch the assembly line go forward."

"Someone's bitter," Alessa laughed and immediately covered her hands over her face.

"No, not bitter. Bored," he replied, deciding whether to hit her or not. "But this is my job for the time being. Even though I'm used to more exciting adventures and exploits…"

"Do tell," I piped up and he glared at me. "I mean…you know, if you want to."

"Since I'm here…I can help you with what you ask. Okay. Let's see…you are Team Six, correct?"

"You know who we are," Cadence said.

"OF COURSE I DO!!!" Raphael snapped at him. "BUT I HAVE TO SAY IT! I HAVE TO CONFIRM YOUR IDENTITY BEFORE I LOOK UP YOUR NAME TO GIVE YOU YOUR ASSIGNMENT! IS THAT OKAY WITH YOU?!"

"Quite," Cadence cringed.

"Thank you for adhering to protocol and ensuring this process goes smoothly," he said in a disgustingly chipper tone. "Now, you are Team Six, correct?"

"Yes," we all half-muttered in unison.

"Okay, let me check for your names…" he pulled a clipboard from behind his wings and surveyed the contents. "Hmmm….well, it looks like your team isn't on the list. Let me check individually. I'll start with Cadence, since I know him so well."

Cadence gulped as Raphael poured through an endless supply of names. Although there could only be about ten sheets of paper on the clipboard, he went back and forth through those ten pages as if they renewed constantly with a whole new list of names.

"It looks like your names aren't on the list."

"What does that mean?" I asked worriedly.

"It means you are banished from Heaven," he said flatly and we all gasped in horror.

"I'm just kidding," he said, smiling. "Little joke."

"That's not funny!" Farah cried out. "I almost…I almost cried! You know what that would do to my angelic pressure?"

"Ah yes, I forgot Faithful go unconscious if they start losing faith."

"We do."

"Maybe that's why you're not on the list."

"So we're seriously not on the list?" I asked, trying to end the nightmare. Raphael turned his attention over to me.

"No. But this is a good thing. It means you get to volunteer for a position."

"What's available?"

"There are espionage missions to infiltrate Satan's army and figure out his plans. Missions to fight against the most powerful demons. Council board meetings with top-ranked angels. Training regiments under Michael. Surveying missions of the Earth. But I think you are best suited for a guardianship."

We all started laughing on the spot at his ludicrous idea.

"Babysit," Marcus guffawed as Farah tried wiping tears from her eyes.

"I told you guys I can't cry!"

"So you list all of those fantastic things," Alessa mused, "and then...and then you have the nerve to end if off by suggesting a babysitting position? Why would we do that?!"

She fell over in laughter as Raphael closed a fist tightly.

"You're not ready for the heavy duty assignments. It's true, you can volunteer for them, but there's a lot at stake. You won't just be fighting for Heaven, but to ensure that generations of human beings make it into God's graces. Imagine if you failed an espionage mission and they tortured you, demanding information. And you reveal some of God's plans for the humans in the process. Imagine that."

"How could they torture us?"

"There are ways. Trust me, young ones. I have seen things that you can't even fathom. Your team almost fell apart because Satan intervened on your little vacation. Big deal. Remember the lesson. It's not how many times we fail. It's how many times we keep trying."

"Then why couldn't we try one of the espionage or war missions?"

"Because there's too much at stake. I won't allow it."

"It's not up for you to decide," Cadence said authoritatively and Raphael snickered at his façade.

"It's not about being scared, Cadence. Sometimes it's not even about faith. Sure, Farah over here can do things no other classification of angel can, but that doesn't mean it's always the smartest idea to rush into battle. That's where Lysander comes in. Or maybe your leadership is needed in a situation. Alessa's connection. Marcus's brute strength. Collectively, you are a force to be reckoned with, but only when you are united. As you speak, I see the cracks, small and microscopic, but there all the same, gaining strength and potency upon each set of the Earth's sun."

"There are no cracks here."

"Who are you trying to fool, Cadence? Remember that it's me your team comes to for advice. I see your strengths and weaknesses before you do and I'm telling you right now, there are issues to be resolved. Say what you will. There are cracks."

"If you say so."

"Then take the guardianship. For Cain and Abel."

"The children?!" I exclaimed. What harm could they do? What damage could a demon influence them to cause? If we were to volunteer for a guardianship, shouldn't we go for Adam and Eve? I was determined to gain some much needed redemption.

"What about Adam and Eve?" Cadence asked, catching my wavelength.

"They already have guardians. But Cain and Abel need some."

"I'm surprised they haven't been picked up yet."

"Perhaps no one wants them because they see no importance in the children. But you forget that they are the future of the human race. No generation is unimportant. And the demons will target them with no less animosity than their parents. Sure, there will be some babysitting, but during the lull, you will have time to work out your differences. And when the demons attack, as they inevitably will, you will be ready to face them."

I could see Cadence debating the decision. Raphael's argument was sound about the children's importance, but what kinks could he see in our group's armor? We were solid and working cohesively as always. It wasn't like back when Vergil was involved and we had to decide whether to accept him or not. This was different. We could never leave one another.

"This job was held for us, wasn't it?" Cadence asked after some thought. Raphael nodded.

"Very good. You've figured it out. Of course, you're not forced to take it. I'm sure if you still wanted a tactical mission, you could ask one of the other angels inside and they'd give it to you. I'm confident God would allow it since He is God, and no matter what mess you might create, it could be fixed. But ultimately it won't help your journey and your understanding of matters, and you won't grow the way you should. So again, the choice is yours."

"Vote," Cadence said firmly and we glanced at one another. Without Amos, it was a five-way vote. Three to two, if we were divided, but was it fair to vote without him?

"Amos vote for children," Marcus said, and we understood what he was communicating. If Amos were here, he would undeniably vote in favor of guarding Cain and Abel. He had rushed to their side without a shred of hesitation when we needed a volunteer.

"I say yes to Cain and Abel," Farah said. "We still have a lot to learn."

"I say no," I said quickly. "It's not that the prospect doesn't sound interesting. It's just that I think Team Six is ready for greater things."

"I agree with Lysander," Cadence affirmed. "We find another mission. But don't let me sway you." It was now tied, and it was all down to Alessa and Marcus.

"Cain and Abel," Alessa said solemnly. "If God wanted us to take this mission, then that's what we should do. Besides, with the fervor Satan showed in attacking Eve, there's no telling what the demons will attempt to do to their sons."

Now it was left to Marcus. The brute. The powerhouse. The warmonger. I already knew his vote because he would want the greatest chance for battle available. There was no way he would choose-

"Cain. Abel," he said, pounding his left fist into his chest. Cadence and I stared at him in shock, dropping our jaws. We were beaten in a four-to-two vote. Majority win. No matter what we said, we were now the guardian angels of Cain and Abel.

"But why?" I whined. Raphael patted me on the shoulder.

"Excellent. Now, the term for guardianship is for twenty years. At that time you can decide whether you want to extend it. Until then, you know what to do. Get down to Earth and protect Cain and Abel from all harm. Watch them and treat them like they were part of the team. Clear?"

"Crystal," Cadence murmured. "I guess I have to look at the bright side. I can take breaks again."

"Oh, no you don't!" Alessa exclaimed, pointing at him. "You'll put in your share like the rest of us. The only break you'll get is me breaking your face!"

"Where did we find this girl?" Cadence asked Marcus sarcastically. "I just love her."

"Am I the only one who heard twenty years?" I whined, but everyone ignored me.

"Farewell, young ones," Raphael said to us, standing still and waving at us as we remained flat-footed on the courtyard ground. "I will see you in twenty years and then we'll talk about all the glorious adventures you overcame… Seriously. Go. You have your job. Let me finish mine."

"I hope you're doing this for the next twenty years," Farah said and he raised a fist at her. Farah chuckled and took to the sky.

"Have fun!" I shouted in smothering cheerfulness to my mentor, shooting up into the air before he could say a word. Alessa and the others chuckled and followed, anxious over our new assignment. It had happened so fast. Were we really up for the challenge?

"Hey, Marcus," I heard Cadence call to him from the back. "Can I talk to you a minute?"

Marcus murmured something inaudible and went back to Cadence. He hovered next to him as they began talking in whispers. Was this what the others felt like when we did the same? I'll admit it was a little uncomfortable, and for no particular reason I felt like they were talking about me. But I had little time to think about this during our flight to Earth for Marcus was back up in front in a heartbeat, his face stoic and firm as if nothing had happened at all. I slowed my flying and waited for Cadence to catch up. When he appeared next to me, he was staring straight ahead.

"What happened?" I asked him. He huffed humorously under his breath.

"I asked him why he voted for Cain and Abel - why he didn't enjoy battle."

"What'd he say?"

"Nothing."

"And then he just left the conversation?"

"No. Then I asked him if he knew why you and I wanted the other missions. Do you know what he said? Pride. Can you believe that? Pride? I tried asking him what he meant but he just left and moved forward."

"Pride...but we're past that. It was one of our first lessons."

"According to him, we're not past it."

"Well, it's irrelevant anyway. We're with Cain and Abel for the next twenty Earth years. Nothing we can do to change that."

"Two decades is a long time, my friend."

`"What does it matter to us?"

"Point taken."

"So…why did you want to go on the missions?"

"Because we could easily get lazy," Cadence replied, "and since this is coming from me, you think I would know what I'm talking about. Ever since the war in Heaven, I've slowly come out of my shell, really accepting this leadership position. I didn't ask for it, but I guess the group had some reason for me to assume the mantle. Now that I'm starting to accept it, I'm finding myself loathing the old, lazy me. And with this new assignment, he could come back. No battle, no war, just waiting."

"The demons are still around. They'll attack. You heard Raphael."

"Yeah, but remember that Satan is their leader, and he's all about being sneaky. When they attack, it won't be in our faces, it'll be behind us, and only when they can truly have an advantage. With the six of us there, I highly doubt they'll make a move."

"I hope you're right. A demon with half the strength of Satan is still more powerful than all of us combined."

"You were there. I wasn't. So forgive me if I still want a shot at them."

"Will you be okay? Waiting twenty years for that shot?"

"I'll be fine. We have each other, and that's all we need. As long as Team Six is strong, I won't regret a second of this."

The trip to Earth was far quicker than the last one. I barely noticed our journey, coming to attention only when we flew past some familiar plains. As we passed the Garden of Eden, the two Cherubims waved excitedly and I reciprocated, assured nothing had happened in our absence. The hills where the humans had settled were as luscious as ever, and when we flew over the final one, we saw Amos, sitting on a large boulder before and between an impressive display of work. On one side, there was a twelve mile stretch of grass, where sheep lazily ate and bleated, walking mindlessly back and forth. Abel was there, a little older than when we had last seen him, clothed in a long maroon-colored robe. He held a cane in his hand, designed for function more than fashion as it wasn't carved out very well, and a small container of some kind hung from his waist, filled with water. I got the impression that Abel might have made both the canteen and the cane himself. In the middle of the grassy knoll was a makeshift shelter, complete with a wooden ceiling but no walls, held up by a structure of bound planks and logs. Abel often sat in the middle of it, watching panoramically with his cane by his side, chewing on some grass himself and whistling a whimsical tune.

To the right of the field was tilled ground, the soil separated purposefully for seed to be planted. Cain toiled away here with no shirt over him, although a type of scarf did cover his neck. In his dirt-matted pants, he hammered at the ground with a makeshift hoe: a wooden pole with a sharpened rock at the end. From the sweat that beaded his brow, I could tell that he was tired, but he kept working vigorously anyway. Periodically, he would glance over at Abel sitting idly in the shelter and shake his head, but otherwise, he kept to his labor.

I didn't see Adam or Eve, but I surmised that they were in the house which was a mile or so off in the distance. Unlike Abel's shed, this house was far larger and quite complete, with all of its walls intact and a garden surrounding it for further nourishment. As we flew down to Amos, we saw Abel laugh at Cain, who had just been hit by a bout of mist, naturally spraying up to water the earth. Being in his small hideaway, Abel was protected from getting wet but Cain didn't seem to notice or care. He accepted the mist with open arms, appreciating God's reprieve.

"What took you guys so long?" Amos asked, looking over his massive shoulder.

"How'd you know we were coming?" I asked him. It wasn't like we had announced ourselves.

"Well, it's usually quiet around these parts, being that there's only a few humans. I could hear you all talking from miles away."

"Anything to report?" Cadence asked.

"No, not really. I saw a couple o' demon imps like that fella Iron, but they were just sniffing around like a couple of dogs. Left as soon as they saw me…no violence to speak of."

"So they know we're here standing guard?" Cadence said.

"Of course. Who wouldn't know? These are the only humans on the whole planet. I doubt Satan would be off talking to the tigers. Heh. Can you imagine? Big bad Lucifer trying to persuade a cat to join his brigade. Never seen such."

"No one has," Cadence sighed.

"Well, we have some exciting news for you," Farah said, sitting next to him on the boulder. "We got an assignment."

"Oh yeah, we leaving?"

"Nope. We're Cain and Abel's guardian angels. Twenty year tour."

"No kidding?" Amos perked up. It was the first moment since we came back that he gave us his full attention.

"No joke about it. We're here to stay."

"That's swell thinking on your part," he said, slapping Cadence on the arm. "I like where your head's at. Them boys need us."

"I was actually…"

"It doesn't matter," I said abruptly, my eyes drawn to Cadence. "This is what we're going to do."

Cadence looked out at the boys, performing their chores respectively. Whether he liked it or not, this was now our mission, and so he decided to sit down on the other side of Amos and enjoy the view.

"Anything we should know about them? Their personality? Dislikes?"

"Not much," Amos replied. "Cain, the big brother, is a farmer like his daddy. Makes sense with him being the older one and all. Family has to eat. But Abel, he's a shepherd. 'Course he knows tilling as well, but he would rather spend his afternoons herding or shearing. They tend to stay separated mostly, only get together for dinner."

"Where's Adam and Eve?"

"Parents are inside, preparing for supper. Onions, figs, some nuts. Nothing too exciting."

"But adequate," Farah replied, looking back at Marcus. "What's wrong with him?"

Marcus was staring off into space, but his eyes were a little more listless than usual. Glazed over. It was probably the mention of food that had sent his consciousness spiraling.

"Marcus, are you okay?" Farah asked him and he blinked suddenly, ending it with a frown.

"Okay," he replied, but it sounded more like he was trying to convince himself rather than us.

"Are you sure?"

"Okay," he said firmly and we left it alone. No one could break Marcus when he had his mind made up.

"Hey," Amos spoke up, "dinner's about to begin. Maybe we should go have a peek, huh?"

"Definitely," I replied, eager to see more of our new protégés.

The sun had now set and the moon had started its shift, bringing an eerie and enchanting glow to the Earth, illuminating it in some spots and casting shadows amongst the rest. Being of a spiritual composition, it didn't bother us, as we were able to see in the darkness just as clearly as in the light. Sure, the landscape didn't appear the same, and the brightness wasn't as high as when the sun was out, but there was no advantage over us for those of the nocturnal kind. We could still assess every detail, each intricate design of the world around us, and the path to the house that the humans had built was no less visible.

We trailed Cain as he rushed home, dropping his hoe in the field. Abel stayed back to herd the sheep into an enclosed, gated area behind the house. Amos nodded to us that he would stay behind and keep watch over him as we glided through the door.

There wasn't much, and it didn't compete with the Garden of Eden, but it was the humans' home nonetheless. There were painted pictures hanging on the walls, made with strips of bark and dye derived from mashing various grapes and fruits. Adam had created crude depictions of his stay in the Garden, showing off its features for nostalgia and rudimentary storytelling. Pots made out of rock and hollowed out clay-like material were placed on a wooden shelf, and there was a wooden table in the middle of the room complete with six chairs. I looked over to the left-hand corner of the house and saw a basket with another baby inside – a little girl. I was shocked by how quickly another child had come into existence, but Farah didn't give me any time to think about it, as she touched my shoulder fervently and pointed to the right-hand corner of the room. In it, sleeping soundly, were two more children, smaller than Cain and Abel, but obviously beyond infancy. Too young to truly work the ground, they had already gotten fed and put to bed before their older brothers came in. I just couldn't believe what I was seeing. So much had happened already…perhaps this twenty-year tour would pass much more quickly than I had expected.

"There's more of them," I breathed out, in awe over how large the family was getting already.

"Why are you whispering?" Farah whispered, giggling like it was all a game.

"How is this possible?"

"Don't worry about it," Amos grunted, coming in behind us. Abel ran through the doorway, creating quite a commotion on the floor boards. Adam was busy tinkering with something in his hand – an attempt at a new invention – when he saw Abel bust in. He strode over from where he stood and grabbed him by the sleeve, whispering sternly that his sisters were sleeping. Abel nodded and proceeded quietly to another compartment in the house, stripping down and washing himself with a bucket of water. Adam sat down at the table in the middle of the main room and went back to his tinkering, as Cain came in from the right, his mother, Eve, hanging onto his arm.

She had changed so much in such a short amount of time. She was a little taller, and her skin grittier - she also boasted a huge belly that stuck out noticeably underneath her maroon-colored smock. Cain helped her to the table and allowed her to choose the chair she wanted - her selection was no surprise. She sat next to Adam and smiled warmly his way as he put down his invention on a shelf behind him. The room was getting darker by the second, but not to us. Only when Adam got up and started adding wood to a fireplace did I realize how dim it really was. The fire crackled and lit up the room as best it could, the snoring of the younger children accenting the noise like someone had jumped in on the other side of a piano to turn a solo into a duet. As the flames lapped at the darkness, I noticed that the whole house had a cozy feel to it. Besides two rooms on the left, and two on the right, there was the large one in the middle possessing the fireplace, table and sleeping area for the younger children. There was also a loft upstairs. The loft was apparently Adam and Eve's bedroom, and upon a quick inspection, a sleeping area for one more infant daughter. It was obvious they would have to expand the house before the new little one arrived, and the worry was all over Adam.

"I'll have to travel further," he said, watching Cain serve the food from the same shelf Adam had placed his future invention on. Eve listened intently, gently poking her belly subconsciously with her right hand.

"We've already cleared out so much," she said, switching from poking to rubbing her stomach. She sighed and turned to Cain. "Did you wash up?"

"No," he said flatly and she grabbed his wrist, still holding a clay plate full of nourishment.

"Go wash up."

"Yes," he said respectfully and headed off to where Abel was.

"He never wants to," she sighed. "But it's so important."

"All he knows is dirt," Adam replied, eyeing the food. "I don't blame him."

"But it feels good to be clean."

"Not when you're used to the filth. He didn't feel what we felt in the Garden."

"I don't want to talk about the Garden."

"Eve, I thought you were over what happened."

"I am, but you know the boys will ask. They always do at dinner. You might as well save the conversation until then."

"I will. For you. But that doesn't mean I'm going to stop speaking on the subject altogether. It's important. Not just for the boys, but for us as well."

Eve let her eyes fall to the table as she went deep in thought and silence ensued as they waited for the boys to finish. At one point, Eve got up to inspect the sleeping children, rubbing the back of her hand over their faces and giving them kisses on their foreheads. Adam sat at the table in contemplation, until he had something to say.

"Cain has done such a good job with the field lately. I think I'll take him with me tomorrow to cut more firewood. We'll get started on the house expansion right away."

"What part of the house are you going to knock out?" she whispered.

"The east wall. There's nothing over there. West side leads to the sheep and I don't want to disturb them any more than I have to. You remember what happened last year."

Eve chuckled at the memory.

"My goodness, when you and Cain tried building that fence. It was so funny."

"Those sheep stayed out in the rain no matter what we tried. Abel started barking at them like a pup to lure them to shelter and they were so terrified it only made the situation worse!"

"But those sheep sure have listened to him ever since," Eve giggled and went over to place her hands on Adam's shoulders. She rubbed them endearingly and Adam sighed.

"Our job is never done."

"It's hard work, Adam. But it's worth it. And you get to spend so much time with the boys. I hardly see them anymore. I'm always in labor."

"Our daughters are getting older every day," he said to her, rubbing her belly.

"Well, of course they are," she said wittingly. Adam kissed her stomach twice.

"Speaking of never getting to see them…where are those boys?"

"Over here!" Abel squeaked as he and Cain came from the west room. They quickly grabbed their plates and sat down at the table, ready to eat. They were in different clothing than before, sporting adult onesies from the look of it.

"All clean," Eve asked. "Pajamas on?"

"Yes!" they said in unison, one more enthusiastic than the other.

"Good. Then let's eat. Adam, the prayer please." They all bowed their heads as Adam cleared his throat to speak.

"Lord, God of Heaven and Creator of the Universe, thank you for the sustenance that you have provided for us this day. You have been gracious to supply our every need and we do not take it lightly. We thank you for shelter, food and clothing. Water to drink and air to breathe. We thank you for knowledge and family. For your never-ending mercy and grace that keeps us throughout the day. Lord, please bless this food that is set before us. Help it to nourish our bodies and keep us in good health, until that blessed day that we may be reunited with you again in glory. Amen."

"Amen," they all said and began to eat silently, famished over their long day.

"That was beautiful," Farah said and I thought I heard a snort, but when I glanced over, it was Alessa, getting all choked up.

"I know! I know!" she cried out. "I need to go back home soon."

"Oh, brother," Cadence sighed, rolling his eyes. "Keep it together. There's going to be a lot more nights like this in the future."

"Prayer good," Marcus grunted and I turned my attention back to the dinner. Cain was speaking up about something.

"But we do all the work," Cain said quietly. Adam was clenching his jaw, struggling to restrain himself.

"We are the tools, but He is the increase," Adam said firmly.

"But if we didn't till the ground, nothing would come forth."

"That's not true. When your mother and I were created, the Garden of Eden was already complete. We simply tended the grounds to stay busy. There is a balance to all, Cain. A time to rest and a time to work. We are not created to sit down and watch as God feeds us."

"I don't know anything about the Garden."

"I've told you about it."

"But I've never seen it. It's all just stories to me. Why can't I go over and see it for myself?"

"I've already told you. It's dangerous. Since we were banished, God is keeping it off limits so that no one can get to the Tree of Life. Cain, you know this."

"But why can't I see it from a distance?"

"No, you cannot - I won't allow it. We are to trust in God and His judgment alone. If you prayed more, you would know this."

"When God talks to us, it's formal. Like we don't matter to Him. I hear it in His voice."

"That's not true. When we were in the Garden, we would casually talk with Him about all the aspects of the universe. He is very caring and compassionate."

"Then why doesn't He talk that way now?"

"He does with me."

"Not with me."

"I talk to Him," Abel chipped in, popping a grape into his mouth, "and sometimes He responds. I like God's stories. He makes me laugh."

"You're lying," Cain accused his brother. Abel glared at him angrily.

"No, I'm not! You too can talk with Him like I do! You just have to talk to Him!"

"I do, and I don't get an answer."

"Because all you do is ask for stuff like a forest already being cut down, or a bigger house. You have to talk to Him!"

"That's ridiculous," Cain huffed and Adam got up to slam his hands on the table. But at the last second, he caught himself, remembering that the children were still sleeping. Adam calmed down but Cain still got the message.

"Be patient, son," Adam said to his oldest son, who was playing with his food. "You will have a wonderful relationship with God. And you will know for yourself that the Garden of Eden is real. But you must be patient."

"Yes," Cain said, and the conversation was over. Eve sighed and fidgeted in her seat. Adam looked over to her in concern.

"Is it the baby?"

"Yes," she said meekly, staring at Adam with soft, tear-filled eyes.

"I'm so sorry, Eve. I'm sorry you have to go through this pain again."

"It's not your fault," she said, straining to smile, "it's mine, remember?"

"I ate the fruit too," he lamented lovingly.

And that's when I felt it…

Something was wrong…very wrong.

"Do you feel that?" I asked, turning to the group. Amos was gritting his teeth, his face pained as if they ached.

"Yeah, I got a funny feeling," Amos said. "Whatever it is, it's in the house."

The family's conversation was suddenly unimportant as we searched, observing each corner and shadow for the culprit of our bad vibe. As we hunted fervently, Cadence suddenly jerked his head around and looked behind him toward the fields.

"Out there! It left!"

We fazed through the walls of the house and stepped outside to face the rapscallion. Cadence wasted no time in telling Alessa to stay with the family and pray for God's assistance in shielding them. She agreed and went back inside. With the humans now protected, we turned to face our intruder.

And it was assuredly a demon. But unlike Iron…this was no imp.

It nearly blended in perfectly with the darkness, smiling with fanged, crooked teeth that flashed cracks of white reflections of the moonlight. We strained our eyes to get a better view but his camouflage was so impressive that we could barely assess his features. He was tall and thin like a Guard, but there were no wings to confirm his previous classification. His skin was black and oozy like tar and it appeared to goop down into the soil. His arms were freakishly long and lanky, double jointed with a human hand at each end. Each were complete with demonically sharp fingernails the colors of fiery red and void black.

"Who are you?" Cadence demanded, but the demon chuckled to himself and extended his arm forward like a waving tree branch.

"No one you know," he said slimily, "but I recognize you."

"What was your classification?"

"Doesn't matter. And why would I tell you anyway?"

"What were you doing in the house? What's your mission?"

"Beat me, and I'll tell you," he seethed. "And I promise, that will be no small feat. No one has ever defeated me, in Heaven or on Earth. My name is Lust and it is very nice to meet you, my sacrifices."

With that, the dripping demon launched himself forward.

CHAPTER 10: Lust

"Fan out!" Cadence ordered, reaching behind for his shield. He placed it in the way of Lust's eel-like arm, waiting for impact, but when Lust saw that his intended hit was going to get blocked, he backed off and looked for another opening.

"What do we do now?" Alessa asked. Cadence peered at Lust from behind his raised shield. Lust just stood there and waited, surveying his potential victims.

"I don't think we can harm the field," Cadence said. "But just in case, I want us to take the battle to the hills. Based on how quick he was in house it would be best if we form a perimeter and surround him. Eliminate his chance to escape. Lysander, figure out what he is!"

"Sure thing!" I shouted, accepting my role. "But until we have an idea, be cautious. No reason to see if he's bluffing this early!"

The team didn't respond but they heard me. It was, after all, part of my job to provide strategy. And strategy we needed. Fighting in the darkness was a unique experience for all of us so we needed to tread as carefully as possible. It didn't matter if we could still see, we had to strain our eyes to gaze upon this particular demon, and that meant expending precious drops of angelic pressure toward vision - energy that might be needed to beat him in the end.

And there was no telling what else we would need. The demon had claimed that it wouldn't be easy to beat him, and that his name was Lust. Now, if this was a lie from the start, then it would prove to be meaningless information. But if his words were true, and I would assume this for now...it gave me an inclination as to his former status. But I needed more clues... And why wouldn't it be easy to beat him? His angelic pressure wasn't that intimidating. Actually, it was quite low...

"Marcus, go for it!" I heard Cadence yell out, giving the powerhouse permission to unleash his rage. He had been holding back because we usually needed him for a finishing blow, but this time, he didn't need to hold back. Hearing Cadence's words, Lust finally made a move and headed toward Marcus. Sidewinding like a snake across the ground, Lust suddenly leapt into the air to hit him in the face...but Marcus's arms were longer. So when the Godhand casually swung his fist out, it connected to the demon's face immediately, causing it to stick to Marcus's fist. The rest of Lust's body and limbs whiplashed forward and then went limp. Marcus used his other hand to grab Lust by the throat, getting ready to throw him into the ground. But somehow remembering Cadence's orders about not destroying the field, Marcus hesitated, gathered his strength and proceeded to pitch the lifeless demon far away, over the hill beyond the fields.

"Alessa! We're taking it to the hills!" I called out to her as we took flight. Marcus's pitch had been fast so there was no way we were going to catch up to Lust before he landed, but even so, when we made it over the hill, what we saw was ridiculous.

Lust was on his feet, smiling and shaking his head, standing with his hands on his hips like we were late to an old reunion. Marcus didn't even wait. He dropped down to the ground, stomped forward and punched Lust mercilessly with a hard right hook. Lust dropped instantly and didn't get back up, his tar-like body splashing on the blackened grass.

"Well, that was easy," Farah commented. "Anticlimactic."

"Not over," Marcus grunted, and we stared in horror as Lust climbed to his feet, grunting the whole way up.

"Sorry guys," he chuckled, "but we might be out here all night."

Catching us off guard, he sped past us and went straight for Farah. Farah screamed like she was getting murdered and turned to zip away, but he reached out and managed to grab part of her armor. He wasted no time in pulling her toward him, right into his sludgy body which began to suck her in like quicksand.

"Ew-Ew-Ew-Ew," she cried out as she struggled to get out of the muck, her fingers struggling to pierce through the stretchy goo. "This is soooooo gross!"

"Farah! Hold on!" Cadence yelled out. He threw his shield at Lust. Lust turned around and the shield slammed into his back, somehow being sucked in faster than Farah currently was. By now, Farah had managed to unsheathe her tiny sword and was hacking away in a panic, but she was losing strength. Irritated, Lust wrenched the sword from her hand and inspected it while Farah pouted and started punching his body from the inside.

"I love a toothpick after a good meal," he said, licking his lips and scratching his teeth with Farah's blade. Marcus bounded at the mess called Lust and fired off a punch once more, but at the last second, Lust jumped up, and Marcus's fist caught Farah in the face.

The hit knocked her unconscious on contact.

Marcus stepped back in shock as more sludge shot out from Lust and hit Marcus's breastplate, pulling him in with its muddy substance. Marcus kept his feet firmly on the ground, and did his best to fight against it like it was a game of tug of war.

But Marcus wasn't one to take losing lightly, and he turned, draped the muck over his shoulder, and pulled with the force of 10 semi-trucks. Lust yelped out in surprise and was dragged off his feet, falling onto his back with flailing arms. Amos, who had been waiting for his moment, jumped in, and comically stomped on Lust's face with all the force he could muster, eventually bouncing up and down like he was on a trampoline and was determined to reach maximum height. Lust went limp again and the sludge drooped off of Marcus, and with a sickening splat, spit out Farah. Farah woke up as soon as she was free and half-shuddered, half-cried.

"That was horrible," she said, taking a gulp. "Don't go in there, guys."

"What was it like?" I asked her. She stared at me in disbelief.

"What does it matter? He's finished."

"Nope," Lust said from where he lay, unexpectedly springing to his feet. "Not yet."

"Get him away from me!" Farah shrieked, running behind Amos. Marcus was fuming and Cadence was keeping his distance, still waiting to know what Lust was.

"Where is my shield?" Cadence whined and I fought back a chuckle. That armament was like family to him.

"yUmMy," the demon said, his voice getting echoey and strange. "GoOd sHiELd."

"Lysander, tell me something!" Cadence cried to me. I shook my head.

"I have no clue!"

"Well don't just stand there and watch! Think harder!"

I decided to cast my gaze upwards to the sky, fixing it on the hazy, dim blue moon. While I made an extra effort to concentrate, my friends engaged Lust in combat for the fourth time, going for an all-out beating at this point. I put my faith in their bravery and strength, refusing to watch and beginning to analyze what clues I now had.

He was nearly impossible to knock unconscious. And when it seemed like we had beaten him comatose, he just got back up, which meant he either had a fluctuating demonic pressure, or somehow...an unlimited supply. His body was made out of a sludgy substance that moved on its own and could absorb not only other spiritual beings but objects as well. This was brand new territory, and we didn't have a classification like this in Heaven...so what was he? Or at least, what had he been before?

I couldn't use Iron as a basis. Sure, he had been a Guard, but on Earth he had been turned into an imp, despite having been Lucifer's general in Heaven. Therefore, his size had nothing to do with his current state. Could Lust be a Guard? Maybe...but his defense wasn't good, though his ability to reset to a previous state was impressive. Was that a form of defense?

Perhaps it was better to rule out what he wasn't.

Okay, he was definitely not an Archangel. Or at least, I suspected he wasn't. Satan had been an Archangel and his power had been much too great for us to handle, so I ruled that out. Lust wasn't strong at all.

Glory? No...there were no clues suggesting that classification. Godhand? Definitely not. His strength was even inferior to mine. Was he a Messenger? Did he have a tactical mind like I did? Possibly... How about a Faithful? Hmmm....Farah was a Faithful, and she was able to perform some impressive feats. I had once seen her stand still and take a beating by a Guard, feeling no pain whatsoever. Could Lust be a Faithful, perverted and changed to this state? If so, how were we going to beat a former Faithful when his faith in God was gone? Would his abilities now be tied into faith in Satan? Or himself?

I was getting confused, and it was getting harder to decipher him. Not to mention that the battle was going on for far too long. I came out of my thoughts to see the score and so far they had knocked out Lust on eight different occasions. Four more since I had stopped watching. Messenger, he was not. So, it was down to Faithful or Guard...and I needed a way to find out...

At this point I saw that Lust was trying to absorb Amos, who was practically begging Marcus to stop punching Lust in the face and start helping him to get free. Cadence and Farah were holding on to Amos's arms, straining to pull him loose.

I made a judgment call.

Creeping up slowly behind their fiasco, I mustered up some courage, ran to Lust's back and flew into his spine.

The sludge welcomed me the moment I touched his slimy skin and clutched at my angelic body like the stars did when I raced through them. Lust wasn't that big, so I didn't think it would take long to search through him, and only a second had passed when I looked up through the muck and saw the shield, Cadence's shield, resting just below his left shoulder, to the right of Amos's arm. I grabbed the armament and tried wiggling my way out, but I was stuck. I called out to the others to come help me too but by now my voice was muffled and weak. Apparently, I hadn't factored in Lust's demonic presence weakening my angelic one so quickly.

But thankfully, Farah saw my legs kicking out from Lust's shoulder blades after a minute or so and she flew around to help me. Since Lust was concentrating on absorbing a Godhand, he completely ignored my escape, and she was able to wrestle me out with minimal effort.

Disgusted and tired, I walked around Lust to his front. Amos was now almost halfway in. Marcus and Cadence were losing strength and barely keeping him out, but I didn't care. I had risked being absorbed for a purpose.

I focused my angelic pressure, took about half of it, and put it into my arms. Clutching the shield, I tightened my grip, reached back, and slammed it as hard as I could into Lust's face. The shield's force caused his head to whip around in a sickening twist, and he fell sloppily to the grass, out for the ninth time.

Amos stumbled out intact and wiped the sludge off his armor, accepting a terrified Farah into his embrace as they consoled each other over the horror they had experienced inside of Lust's body. Cadence, Marcus, and I sat on the grass, catching our breath as we waited for Lust to regenerate.

"I was so scared!" Amos cried out. Farah nestled her face into his shoulder.

"I'm not even supposed to be crying!" she wept as her angelic pressure flickered. "But I don't care! It was so horrible!"

"Did you figure out what he was?" Cadence asked me casually as if he was wondering what my opinion was on a movie we had just watched.

"Not yet," I sighed, clutching his shield like a teddy bear.

"Can I have that back?"

"Not yet. I need it. It's vital in discovering his classification."

"Okay."

"We're not doing too great, are we?" I chuckled, looking over at my Guard friend. He yawned and shrugged his shoulders.

"Could be worse. We're all conscious. That's a plus."

"It looks like the intervals are getting longer," I sighed.

"What intervals?"

"Between Lust waking up. When he was first knocked out, it was barely a minute. Now it's going on three."

"Is that significant?"

"Very…" I said. "But I wanted to confirm."

"So what have you narrowed it down to?"

"He's either a Guard or a Faithful."

"And what do we do if he's either?"

"If he's a Guard, then we'll just have to keep beating him down until he wears out, or maybe Farah can get enough faith to put him down with one of her knockout punches."

"And if he's a Faithful?"

"That's the scary part," I admitted. "What do you do to a former Faithful when faith is no longer a factor? Demons don't have faith in God, so what can we do? Have him waver over Satan? Make him question his own current state? Not likely."

"I see the dilemma…but we'll figure it out."

"Easier said than done."

"We have no other options. I'm thinking of sending Farah over to Alessa, to ask her for a favor in taking this guy out for us."

"Don't we need her here?" I asked, afraid of losing our angel with the most faith.

"What choice do we have? Lust is not staying down."

"Fine," I sighed. "But send Marcus. Farah might be able to knock him out. It doesn't matter what her angelic pressure reads. It's her faith that strengthens her. But Marcus…he's famished."

"No," the Godhand said flatly, shifting over in the grass to face us. "I stay."

"No," Cadence insisted. "You're going. Just follow orders."

Marcus huffed and stood up to leave, just as Lust yawned.

"Whew, that was rough," Lust whispered as he whipped back to his feet like nothing had happened. Marcus murmured under his breath and took off toward the house as we climbed steadily to our battle positions. I picked up the shield and rushed Lust before we made a plan, reaching out to hit his face with it again, but Lust saw it coming and grabbed the shield, wrestling it from me easily. I still hadn't recovered from escaping his absorption earlier and his effortless overpowering of me was proof enough. I stared at him dumbfounded as he waved the shield over my head.

"No more of that," he said as he got ready to put it back into his body.

"What difference does it make?" I spat at him. "I'll get it back in a moment."

"Oh really?" he said, believing my pretense. Cadence and Farah glanced at me like I was crazy while Amos fought back a laugh.

"I'll take that shield and knock you over and over until there's nothing left of you!" I yelled at him, going for my best Alessa impression. Lust scowled at my words and raised the shield at my head.

"I don't think so, little one," he said threateningly. "Only if you're awake can you get it."

"Yeah, right," I said, calling him out. "You can't throw that shield for the life of you."

"Watch me."

I gave a fake yelp and turned my back to him, attempting to escape while he threw the shield at my head. The shield barely left his hand when it plopped down awkwardly to the ground. Cadence swooped in, rolled, grabbed his precious weapon, stood up in one quick motion, and uppercut Lust in the face with all his might. Lust dropped like a tree that had just been axed.

"Whew," I said. "That was insane!"

"What was that?" Cadence asked, putting his shield back into its holster. "You were acting strange."

"Goading him into throwing it, that's all," I replied, chuckling. "Now we know he's a Faithful – or was a Faithful."

"Strange way to find out...figured that a true Guard would be able to throw a shield huh?"

"You could say that."

"So, congratulations. We can defeat him now, right? Got a plan?"

"Um. That would be a no."

Cadence laughed and we both stopped short as we heard a groan to our side. Lust was already on the move and it was as disheartening as ever. How was he up again so soon?

"Let's get back to work," I sighed as we moved further away from Lust. Even when they had beaten him while he was down, he just got back up like he had woken up from a good night's rest.

"I thought he was supposed to be easy!" we heard a voice cry out as an angel came from behind the hill. Alessa was striding onto the battlefield, and she was not happy.

"Did you pray as soon as Marcus arrived?" Cadence asked but then scowled at the face she was making. Alessa looked like she was going to slap him.

"NO! This isn't a pizza delivery service. You don't just put in an order and it comes when you want it. No. No! NO! When Marcus told me what you wanted, I refused and decided to see the situation for myself."

"Geez, Alessa. What about the family?"

"Marcus stayed back with them. He's tired."

"You were supposed to stay behind."

"And you're supposed to be making good decisions! Are you going to ask for God to intervene whenever we're in a bind? I thought this guy was going to be easy!"

"Well, he's not. We knocked him out nine times and he's gotten back up each time without fail. Besides, what does it matter how many times we pray? Shouldn't we ask for his help whenever we need it?"

"Ten times," I interjected.

"What?" Cadence said towards me in confusion.

"We knocked him down ten times."

"He doesn't look so tough," Alessa muttered, scrunching her face up in disgust.

"Don't let his looks fool you."

Lust remained still as Alessa walked up to him, until she was about a foot away, and glared at him intensely. Lust started grinning, waiting for Alessa to hit him so he could grab her, when his eyes suddenly shot open wide in horror. We followed the path of his gaze and were in shock at the source of his fear.

Standing on the hill behind us was Abel.

Abel watched us with wide eyes, looking back and forth at us in shock as his mouth moved on its own. We forgot all about Lust.

"Why is he here?" Farah cried out nervously. Amos immediately dropped in front of him, ready to keep him safe. Cadence was glaring at Alessa furiously.

"What is Abel doing here?! I thought Marcus was watching them!"

"I think the more important question," I said, "is...can he see us?"

Abel's eyes were moving frantically but they stopped at specific points, points where we were individually standing, as if he could literally see us there on the hill. His mouth started moving faster when he finally focused on Lust, who was beginning to cringe like he had eaten some rotten food.

"NO PRAYER!" Lust screamed out in rage and ran at Abel. Amos met him at the pass and tackled him in mid-flight, keeping Lust away from the boy and chucking him into the ground. All I could hear were Abel's last words.

"GOD SAVE US ALL!" he cried out, pointing his hand directly at Lust. Lust shrieked like he was on fire, stood up, and pushed Amos away with abnormal strength. Amos stood back as Lust clutched his own head, screaming and weeping angrily. He glared at Abel for only a second, who was standing tall and strong on the hill, his face clenched and filled with confidence. Lust gnashed his teeth at him, and without a word, ran away in the opposite direction of the house. He ran so fast, no one suggested a chase, and for a minute, nothing but silence washed over us.

Abel remained still on the hill, but since Lust had left, his face softened and his eyes wandered, no longer locking on any certain position.

"He's wondering where we went," I concluded at last, seeing him fidget in his pajamas.

"What just happened?" Cadence demanded, periodically glancing at the path Lust had taken in his escape. The group assembled in front of the boy, who was still unaware of our presence. It looked like he was considering heading back home.

"Abel happened," I said matter-of-factly. "He defeated the demon."

"No," Alessa corrected. "God did...but, it was because of Abel's prayer. You're right in that sense."

"So that's what Raphael meant," I said in awe. "The power of prayer that the humans possess. The boy showed us an example of it."

"Lust will report this," Cadence reminded us. "The demons won't take this lightly. They'll be back, and probably stronger than before."

"What does it matter?" I said happily, wanting to pick Abel up and give him a swing on my arms. "With the humans praying, they won't be able to touch them or us."

"You're right," Farah said. "It's like I'm always saying. You just need to trust God and it will all work out!"

"Right!" I said, with a chipper voice for once, and we all started laughing at my awkward attempt. But I didn't care. Our first real demon had been defeated, and we weren't too overzealous or proud to give God or Abel the credit either. It just didn't matter. The side of good had won, and we were ecstatic.

But of course, no matter how in tune I was with my tactical mind on the battlefield, I became inattentive to it when I was comfortable, and comfortable I was. Already I had a notion tickling the back of my neck, yanking at my leg, trying to tell me something important.

But I dismissed it as soon as it came.

And stupidly happy, I remained.

CHAPTER 11: Contingency Plans

"Satan himself would have been defeated if he were there," Farah gushed as Cadence sighed obnoxiously.

"Can you two pay attention? That was last week."

"Not over it yet," I laughed and Farah joined in. Ever since Abel had seen glimpses of us on the hill and increased his prayer life, we had been especially excited, almost boisterous. To put it bluntly, it was grinding Cadence's nerves.

"I haven't heard you talking about a situation over and over like that since the island."

"And it won't be the last!" Farah chipped in. We all burst out laughing again. The only one besides Cadence who wasn't laughing was Marcus. When we had escorted Abel back to the house, we had found Marcus standing in the middle of the field, scratching his head. When we asked him why he hadn't watched Abel, he basically said that he had seen Abel leave, and tried to follow, but he couldn't remember anything after that. We had at first been alarmed, but then chalked it up to a demon having an influence over him, but when it happened again two days later, while we were in the middle of a conversation, we got concerned. No one knew what Marcus was going through, and since he was a man of few words, we didn't know how to help. Recently, we'd been keeping the incident in the back of our minds, refusing to discuss what was happening for we had no solution. We weren't even sure if it was real or if we would be blowing something out of proportion.

"In any case," Cadence spoke up louder, "we have to put a system in place to keep a watch over the house and the family. It's not enough being present anymore. Lust nearly defeated us that night and although we're all excited over how great Abel's prayer was and the results it produced, we have to prepare for the possibility that it won't happen the next time. We need a plan."

"Cadence brought the idea up to me so that I could ask God about it," Alessa continued for him, "and I vouch for this plan myself. Naturally, we'll have to put it to a vote."

I raised my eyebrows in concern. He had already talked to Alessa about it? And Alessa didn't say that God had any input on the matter. With her endorsing this idea ahead of time and then prepping us for the vote by vocalizing her support...was that swaying our vote? Being a little deceptive? Maybe I was just overreacting...but I'd been suspicious of Alessa and her interactions with God before. No. I thought. I can't begin to dissect the motives of my teammates. This is how Vergil fell. This is how we would all fall. I must stick with a unified mentality.

"The plan is as follows," Cadence stated. "We'll have shifts spread over the 24 hour period. Since there are six of us, this amounts to 4 hours each. During your shift, you will be actively patrolling the grounds, keeping a mental log of any suspicious activity and watching Cain and Abel, ensuring their safety."

"What about Adam and Eve?" Farah asked.

"I'm sure by now you've noticed a few other angels flying around the property at different times during the day. We haven't taken the opportunity to introduce ourselves formally yet, but we can assume they are Adam's, Eve's and the other children's guardian angels. The first thing the shifts will do is free us up so we can meet and greet the other angels when we're off duty. Since there's six of us, we have a great advantage over individually assigned angels."

"Could we help each other if we wanted?"

"Of course," Cadence smiled. "As long as you accept responsibility for what happens on your shift. And all of us have to remain close by. Unfortunately, there will be no trips to Heaven while we're on this tour. We're to remain on the premises."

"Don't you just love him when he's all authoritative?" Alessa chuckled. Cadence glared at her from the corner of his eyes. He was probably wondering if she was joking or not.

"With that being said," Cadence continued, "if anyone has a different idea or plan in mind, there's no reason why we can't implement that one instead. I'm up for fresh ideas."

"Vote," Marcus grunted and we all mulled over our decisions. Only thirty seconds passed.

In the end, it was unanimous. Not only did the idea make sense, but no one had a better one.

And thus we truly began our twenty year stretch...

At first, it was exciting, sitting in the house as the family had dinner, watching Cain and Abel play. Sure, we tended to favor Abel a little more but that was only because he had saved us from Lust. Cain was loved dearly as well, and he actually reminded me of Marcus in a lot of ways. He was a commendably hard worker, and despite the minor hiccup with his father that first night at the dinner table, he was very respectful. Still, the rest of him remained much of a mystery as he rarely voiced his opinion, even in private. He spoke so little that we could only imagine what he was thinking - since we couldn't read minds.

But as days turned to years and little interrupted the flow of monotony, we soon got complacent, waiting for a little excitement. The days began to run into each other and we learned their habits far too quickly. Farming, shepherding, raising children and fixing or expanding on the house were all time-consuming projects that ate up their very lives. And as the boys grew, their work days got longer, not because of required necessity, but because of their excitement in newfound knowledge and joy in their expertise. By the end of fifteen years, a lot had changed, and yet...so little.

Indeed, we managed to introduce ourselves to the other guardian angels, hurriedly zipping around the farm, and they were happy for the company, but because they were only in pairs or they had a job to do alone, they mostly kept to themselves.

Adam and Eve bore more children, one each year, and spent their leisurely mornings raising them in the reverence of God, though I did notice that the more children Adam had, the less he told of his time in the Garden of Eden. I'm not sure if it was because his time there was becoming a distant memory or if he was growing tired of the same stories and was focusing more, instead, on the present. Eve usually had her hands full with the children while the boys worked outside, and it didn't take long for the two fields that once ran alongside the house to become surrounded by seven, reaching miles and miles away in fertile land begging to be nourished and plowed.

Cadence, Alessa, and Farah stayed the same as far as I could tell. Since there were no demon ambushes, not even imps since the night Lust had attacked, there was little talk of strategy. No more votes or serious meetings. We just did our job, and made sure we habitually followed our shift's instructions. Cadence did get back into old habits when he wasn't on duty, often staring into the sun and lying amongst the grass. Alessa kept on talking and in more recent years had begun stressing how we couldn't turn into the island all over again - that we had to keep speaking to one another and having fun.

Fun was still there, but it didn't have the same zest it had boasted before, as we were focused more on when our next shift was rather than the free time that surrounded it. With her friends taking a more stoic and increasingly lonely approach to leisure, Farah took it upon herself to have her own fun. She was as crazy as always, taking it upon herself every day to test her might on the flaming sword. She even became friends with the Cherubims that guarded it, after many visits of course. In the beginning, Marcus went with her, desperately attempting to win the contest over who could touch the blade first, but with each passing year, his condition, whatever it was, got a little bit worse. Spells of momentary absence doubled from one year to the next and though they lasted no more than a couple minutes, we were all secretly concerned.

But we didn't talk about it.

Because it would have ruined the magic.

That magical cohesiveness that kept Team Six revered and well known throughout Heaven's host. That child-like connection to each other and our God.

To question our imperfections...our weaknesses...to us it meant failure, a breakdown, an abrupt end to the potential so many saw in us but not we ourselves. The longer we ignored the problem, the worse it got, but the easier it was to maintain our peaceful illusion that everything was okay.

Even Farah, with all her great faith, fell to this belief – when she stopped asking Marcus to join her in her escapades...and went on her own, leaving behind her powerful partner. Marcus never complained, but I caught him sometimes when he was on duty, searching through his mental database when he was supposed to be keeping watch – something he never used to do when he had fun with Farah. With nothing to look forward to, with no exciting activities after work to anticipate, he now found entertainment from within, closing himself off from us and even more frightening, reminding me more and more of a potential Absent.

He did stay minimally aware, and not in complete neglect of his duty, evidenced by his head movement in Cain's or Abel's direction whenever he sensed an angel nearby. But his actions were alarming just the same...

And I didn't tell Cadence.

Because I hadn't been the best guardian either. With boredom taking over, and my strategic mind sleeping, I was determined to find a project worth holding onto, and found one I did. Dusting off some old memories, I replayed all of our experiences and battles, recorded in my mental database – a horrible instrument for someone who harbors feelings for the past as much as I did. And I found that complacency and lack of motivation tends to bring up old habits.

At first I searched for Vergil only when it was my time off.

No one cared because not a single demon had been sighted in over a decade. We had all gotten lax with the rules in our own way so no one protested when I began venturing far past our borders. What they didn't know was that eventually my exploits extended to the other side of the Earth. It was a stupid and dangerous decision. I could have been ambushed and completely destroyed, but not a soul showed itself.

Not a soul, angel or demon.

I started calling out to Vergil without shame, journeying through the ocean, dark caverns and the Earth's mantle, waterfalls and volcanoes, canyons and clouds...but I saw no sign of his existence. I began to get frustrated. How could I not find where Satan and his army were? Not one demon? How were they so good at hiding?

I became so obsessed with finding not just Vergil but any demon, that I started trailing off the property during my shift. Not too far, but enough that if a demon had a second with Cain or Abel, they could win. When I finally realized how bad I had gotten, I started forcing myself to stay on campus, searching the database for clues.

It was like the island in its own way.

And it wasn't the humans' fault.

It was ours.

We had forgotten about how strong we were collectively and how weak we were individually. We were becoming too familiar with the superficial humor and over-the-top actions. Sure, we had been together since the beginning, but how much did we really know about each other? Going into Alessa's house had been a shock. What else was in Alessa's mind? What did Cadence think about when he was lying in the grass? What scared Farah and made her waver in her faith? Who was Marcus beyond his few words? My Lord, who was Amos? Since he had been accepted, I had barely gotten to know him, and yet, he was the only one that faithfully spent each hour, duty or not, with the boys - treating them like they were his own children. And for some reason, we stayed away from the Godhand...

"HEY! WHERE ARE YOU GOING!?" Abel cried out to Cain who was going past the first set of hills near the house. I snapped to and assessed the situation, but I realized there was no danger. Abel just wanted to talk.

"I'm done with my work!" Cain called back. "I don't feel like building anything and I want to be alone!"

"But that's all you ever want to do."

"And since when have you cared?" Cain snapped back at him. I perked up, standing up and flexing my wings. It'd been years since Cain had talked to any family member like that. Sure, he mumbled some questionable words in his sleep, but I had chalked it up to dreams. Nothing to worry about. But based on the flush of his face now and the tremble of his fists, he was very passionate about what he wanted to say.

"I cared since last night," Abel replied. That had been Farah's shift. I had no clue what had happened.

"Isn't it terrible that you didn't care since then?"

"No...I do care," Abel said, searching for the right words. "I've always cared...but I mean, I want to talk to you and convince you to stay."

"Abel, I'm going."

"But Father said to leave the Garden alone. A flaming sword is there to keep people away, not invite them in. You could be killed."

"I've spent years thinking about this, and I've waited for a sign, an answer to my curiosity, and I can't wait anymore. I'm not backing down. I have to go."

"Can I come with you?"

"No. Stay on the property."

"Why can't I go?"

"Because if I die, I don't want to hurt Father and Mother any more. One death will hurt enough."

"Why don't we try my way, Cain?"

"And what's that?" the man said, turning to face his brother. It was a rare occurrence in which Cain gave Abel his undivided attention. Abel wasn't about to disappoint.

"I've thought about the Garden too, Cain. You're not alone in this."

"And what have you discovered?" Cain asked, a twinge of impatience already coating his words.

"I asked God about it in prayer, and He hasn't given me an answer. But I believe that if we offer up a sacrifice to Him, maybe He'll find favor with us, and answer our request."

"And that would work? We've offered sacrifices before."

"Yes, but this is different. It's like fasting. Sure, you could fast for your health, but if you fast for God, and a specific purpose, there's a greater chance you'll receive an answer."

"You and God must talk often," Cain said casually. Abel shifted nervously.

"Quite a bit. Don't you?"

"No," Cain said flatly. "We don't talk much anymore. But that doesn't mean I still don't love and respect Him...do you really think a sacrifice would work?"

"Definitely."

"Then...I guess we'll try it your way."

"So you won't go to the Garden?"

"Not if I have a greater chance of getting in with this burnt offering."

"Then it's settled! Let's work together and reach our goal!"

"Are you going to talk the whole time?"

"Part of the deal, my brother," Abel laughed warmly as he placed an arm over Cain's shoulders. They started walking back to the house, detailing their plan. I was just getting ready to pursue when Amos crashed in front of me and placed a hand on my chest.

"Shift change!" he bellowed happily, a goofy grin covering his face.

"Already?" I asked, looking up at the sun.

"Why? Something interesting happen today?"

"The boys are trying to find a way inside the Garden. Abel's proposed a burnt offering to God - gain some favor."

"Yeah, I heard Cain mention it to Abel last night. It's good to see them talking."

"I thought last night was Farah's shift."

"Oh, I was there too, yapping up a storm. Farah didn't mind. She enjoys my company."

"Two peas in a pod," I chuckled as I watched the boys descend the hill.

"Do you think a burnt offering will work?" Amos asked as we began hovering over them.

"Not sure," I admitted. "I've seen Adam perform them. God would come out of the clouds and speak with him like they were back in the Garden. The children would watch and hear nothing but Eve probably could. She usually had a smile on her face. All in all, the idea isn't bad. I think it could work."

"Who was it that started that whole system anyway? Offerings…"

"It's not really a system, like he just gives an offering and God is guaranteed to appear. No, I would think of Alessa and her Glory classification. While an offering doesn't ensure an answer, it probably increases the chances."

"Yeah, but who started it? God? Or Adam?"

"God. The first animal sacrifices were to clothe Adam and Eve in the Garden. That's what I've heard from Isaiah, Adam's guardian angel."

"I see..."

"I don't think the boys can get in trouble from it, if that's what's worrying you. They aren't exactly children anymore. I'm sure you've noticed."

"All I see is when I first met them..." Amos said, getting choked up. "I know I'm just an angel...but I really like to think of them as my boys." A warm smile swept across my face.

"You're a good guy, Amos."

"I try, Lysander. Thank you. Hey, I got a question for ya. Have you talked to Cadence lately?"

"Not recently. The group hasn't had a reason to congregate since that beam almost fell on Abel."

"There shouldn't have to be a reason. Should just come from the heart."

"I understand what you're saying. It's just, we've been fractured lately. Not sure why."

"When Raphael mentioned cracks all them years ago, he wasn't joking, you know. I saw them too. But since I'm the new guy, I didn't think it was my place to comment."

"You've been with us for fifteen Earth years," I laughed. "I think you have tenure."

"Well, if you don't mind me saying...I think you spend too much time chasing shadows when we don't have a clue what happened to that friend of yours. Cadence is so worried over making a bad decision that he thinks he should have all the say in a vote, and no one's talking about Marcus. There's something truly wrong but folks are staying silent."

"So Marcus, Cadence, and I are the problem?"

"In a manner of speaking? Yes. Alessa's a little short-tempered but she means well, and Farah just gets bored so she makes her own games. Not much much of an issue there though they should be speaking up about Marcus too. My problem? Well, I should've said all this before."

"You know I go looking for Vergil?"

"I do," Amos said solemnly. "And it would be stupid to think the others aren't aware too. Now, I don't remember this fellow too well, but if I recall, he joined Lucifer of his own free will. And it looked like you were over him. Why pick up the search again?"

"Because Cadence and I don't talk like we used to," I said, looking down at the grass. "Sure, I love the whole group, but Cadence and I had a connection. Lately, he's been looking at me more like a weapon, not a friend, and since there's no battle, there's no point in me being around. He'd rather lie in the grass."

"That's a sad outlook…you should go speak your mind. It's my shift so you got the opportunity."

"We'll get this squared away," I promised. "We still have five more years until we can choose another tour or assignment. I don't want us to get worse before then."

"Good, and please bring up Marcus. I mean, it feels like he's in a nursing home and we never visit, the way we keep our distance."

"I will," I said ashamedly, folding my wings behind me. Amos nodded in my direction and followed Abel and Cain to the house while I took a different route. Finding Cadence was easy since he never left the property and he had long ago found the perfect hill for lounging, teeming with an abundance of bedded grass and dandelions. With more than twelve hours until his next shift, he was deep into his next "nap," not really sleeping, but he might as well have been. I decided to make a grand entrance.

Positioning myself a mile above him, I aimed for his stomach and sat in the air. I glanced down and confirmed my trajectory before I shot down like a nuclear missile, keeping my speed at a briskly paced 500 miles per hour.

I crashed into his abdomen hard, sending his limbs out in reflex and filling his eyes with a mixture of fear and agony. I bent down and smiled warmly, giving him a wave of my hand. He roared and pushed me off, ready to punch my face in, but he stopped when he saw me standing there innocently, waiting for the attack.

"You're not scared of me, are you?" I asked. I had already rehearsed what I was going to say so I should have been able to keep talking, but I stopped. The thought had never occurred to me until now...not that he was scared per se, but that we had never sparred because he thought that I could figure him out tactically. But again, I was probably just over-thinking it. What reason would I have to fight my friend?

"What are you doing, Lysander?" he said firmly, calming down. "That was rude."

"Considering I just sat on your stomach with the force of a tornado, that was pretty polite of you to say."

"What's gotten into you lately?"

"More like us," I replied. "Why don't we talk anymore?"

"You sound like Alessa."

"Then you know things are bad." Cadence couldn't help laughing at that, slowly brushing himself off and standing up at full attention.

"I'm going to get you back for that someday," Cadence chuckled more to himself than me. "We have years left."

"Yes, five more years as a matter of fact," I said, "and those five years could be the end of Team Six."

The conversation had suddenly gotten serious, which was what I needed. If I didn't initiate this discussion right away I could get distracted and never get around to it.

"What are you talking about?" he gruffed, sitting back down on the grass and rubbing his stomach. Apparently, he hadn't recovered yet.

"We've been here fifteen years. When was the last time we spent time together as a family?"

"We have shifts. We haven't been together because we have a job to do."

"And that's the issue. Despite this long reprieve from battle and the demons, we're worse off. Isn't that strange? If anything, we should be getting stronger."

"What do you suggest?"

"Can't we do a shift – with all six of us?"

"We voted, and agreed on it as a group. The shifts stay as they are."

"Just because it sounds like a good idea and it works at one point, doesn't mean it should be law and stay that way forever. Think about it, Cadence. We have a twenty year tour. Not their lifetime. Twenty years. Even God is letting us know that every so often we have to reevaluate the policies and decisions that have been put into place, that we need to be ever changing and growing. This isn't to cause discord, but to further solidify us as a group."

"The shifts are working fine. Think about it. No demons have showed up."

"But it's not perfect. We should be stronger than this. What if the demons aren't coming because they want us to stay on this course?"

"So what do you want me to do?"

"Call a meeting – to discuss new ideas, and when a couple are on the table, we vote on them."

"And if the shift idea stays?"

"Then it stays. But at least you'll know where everyone stands. No one tip-toeing around you and talking behind your back because you're starting to take this leadership role too seriously."

Cadence's eyes shot to me on that comment, and I met them with great concern in mine. His gaze shifted to worry for a second.

"You think I'm too serious? Okay, so what should I be?"

"You were a great leader when the burden of the job wasn't at the forefront of your mind. Seriously, you may think this sounds crazy, but the lazy, nonchalant Cadence was the best leader this group ever had."

"I don't understand. How was that helping? You actually want me to be lazy?"

"You were lazy but that didn't mean you didn't intervene and step up to your role when it was needed. We only needed the leader Cadence at certain times and inherently you realized this. But you're so worried all the time now, going over scenarios and what-ifs when that's supposed to be my job. I'm the over-analytical one, not you. Don't you see the problem? You're turning into me. Me, Cadence."

Cadence chuckled a little but maintained his rigid stance, contemplating my plea of reason.

"We are all pieces to the same puzzle," I said. "If you're part of the border, why are you trying to fit in the middle? You don't belong there."

"So I shouldn't worry about the future?"

"No. Just be yourself. Clear your mind, so that when it's time for you to step up, you can, and you'll be rested enough to make the best decision possible - instead of relying on the past and half-baked ideas."

"I'm not the only one who dwells on the past," he said, turning to me now that he had the upper hand. I could see his jaw tighten, his countenance becoming colder. "If you think I haven't seen you flying to the other side of the world, you're more naive than I thought."

"I'm not hiding anything," I admitted. "So I did. But I've realized my mistakes and have remained on the grounds for the past six months."

"That's not good enough, Lysander," he sighed. "It doesn't change the fact that you left Cain and Abel alone. They could have been attacked. And for what? Vergil?"

He said the name like he was stepping on a bug. The disgust in his voice made me feel uneasy and only further confirmed Amos's suspicions. Cadence wasn't the same. No matter what he thought of my and Vergil's relationship, he would never have expressed such disdain so openly, because I was his friend, and he knew how much finding him meant to me. Sure, I still had hope for the lost Archangel, but the more years that went by, the more realistic I got, and the stronger I became. I had had a relapse lately but at least my search was no longer an unhealthy obsession. But Cadence failed to see this progress in me and he was being vocal about it. As the leader, he knew how to talk to each of us, how to get the best from us...so who was this cold Cadence before me?

"That's over now," I said assuredly. "I'm done searching the Earth."

"But not the database," he said, looking at me with disgust. "Almost sixteen years and you're still obsessed."

"And if we lost Alessa? You wouldn't do the same?"

"That's different. Alessa didn't stab me in the back...or the front."

"What wrong with you?" I snapped at him and we both stepped closer to each other.

"You're unstable," Cadence yelled at me. "I gave you time to get over it, but you're taking too long! What are we going to do if Vergil does show up? How can we trust you?!"

"You will let me talk to him like you promised," I said, choking back my feelings. "And if that doesn't work, we put him down."

"You say that so casually!" he said, throwing up his arms. "Like you can do it at a moment's notice! Like flipping a switch! Are you kidding me? This is deep within you. A stronghold that has to be removed. I mean, c'mon Lysander, what if we never find Vergil? What then..."

Cadence was so appalled by my behavior that he looked up to face the sky, his hands on his hips as he thought about what to say next. And I just stood there, nervously figuring out what to say. Cadence had never spoken to me in this manner and I didn't know how to react. He had always been my greatest ally, my most trusted confidant. What was happening? I couldn't lose him and Vergil...what would that do to me...

"Okay, you're right," Cadence said finally. "You're done searching for now...at least physically - so as long as you stay on the grounds, we'll leave it at that."

But the damage had been done. The words had been said, and I found myself unable to speak to him candidly. I was too afraid of being hurt. Of feeling that betrayal again...the only difference was that this time it wasn't a physical sword spearing through me, but words, piercing my spirit. I fought his words back, trying to keep them at bay, to not let them taint me and burrow deep, sending me further into myself.

"Also," Cadence added, "I didn't want to talk about this as a group, but...Marcus is in bad shape. Sure, it only happens so often, but him shutting down like that...it's not good."

"Right," I muttered weakly, ready to move on to a different subject. And we did need to start talking about Marcus.

"So, I was thinking…maybe you could be his wingman. Whenever it's his shift, you can accompany him, but keep your distance. We won't take him off duty, but we'll keep an eye on him. What do you think?"

Cadence's eyes were so hopeful, and sure that I would agree. But I couldn't do it. I couldn't agree with this angel, my friend, over what he was implying.

"That's wrong," I said adamantly, gaining my composure and clearing my throat. "Marcus – he needs us. We should…pull our resources together and figure out what's wrong with him before it gets worse. He doesn't say much, and I've been thinking lately that just because he's a Godhand, doesn't mean he has to speak only a couple words at a time. Amos talks normal enough and he's the same classification. Why can't Marcus? There's obviously a problem somewhere."

"I hadn't thought of that…"

"We have to solve this. For him. He doesn't say much, and he might not be able to tell us everything, but we can sit down with him and figure it out together. In the meantime, we carry on as normal until our next vote. I, nor anyone else, should babysit him. It shows we don't trust him, and Farah already leaves him behind in her adventures. Giving him a chaperone will only hurt him."

"This isn't about hurting him. I know his pride will be wounded but Raphael…"

"Don't twist our mentor's words," I snapped at him, taking my turn to be appalled. "This has nothing to do with that lesson. If you put a second angel on his shift, you will crush him. Do you hear me? Marcus will lose trust in us and you because we will have shown that we don't think he's reliable."

"Sounds like you have all the answers," he said coolly.

"You used to think so," I replied, finding my strength. "You used to come to me and talk about what's wrong. Now, you carry the weight on your shoulders alone. I think that's what Marcus meant all those years ago when he said 'pride' to you and I. You've been full of pride because you want to carry the world on your shoulders and you actually have the audacity to think you can…and I, I've been selfish…I liked having Vergil around because I was superior to him socially. I was accepted. And when he was banished, I tried to fill that void. I didn't want to be the socially awkward one again, but you know what? That's something I have to deal with, and figure out. And funny enough, I can't do it alone! I need you all by my side or I'll never get any practice on getting socially stronger! Since the war I've been trying everything else, thinking I'm stronger than I am, trying to prove myself in battle because it's the only time I can shine – basically putting a covering over the problem itself. We were given this guardianship, and you know what? It's exactly what we needed. Because it forced us to confront our own inner demons."

"If you don't like my idea," Cadence said, gritting his teeth and getting into my face. "Then get Alessa to do it. That's an order."

I clenched my fist, ready to hit him legitimately, when I heard a chuckle beside us. Cadence and I turned in unison to see a scout demon, small and ugly, standing below us. We hadn't even sensed it getting so close.

"If I were a larger demon," it chuckled again, "I would've had a couple of angels in my pocket."

Cadence reached out to grab its throat, but the demon backflipped and kept his distance, raising his hands in the air.

"Sorry, pal. Already heard from Iron about that grip of yours. And there's no need for the animosity – I'm here to talk."

"Demons don't like to talk," Cadence said assertively. "They like to hit you when you least expect it. I have to say – fifteen years. That's dedication."

"Too bad I can't say the same for you," he giggled. "I loved watching the two of you bicker."

"Say your piece, demon," I said abruptly, trying to be cool and firm.

"Don't be so worried. I'm not here under pretense. If you just do a quick scan, you'll notice that we have done no harm to your precious humans or your teammates."

We performed his suggestion internally and confirmed his words.

"Then why are you here?" Cadence demanded. "Why hasn't a demon shown himself in so long?"

"I have a message," it smiled. "My master Satan would like to send a test your way and see how much you have improved since Heaven."

"Who is it?" I demanded.

"Rufus," the demon said happily, squeaking on every syllable. "He's a lot stronger than when you faced him last and he wants to settle the score. If you pass this test, then Satan vows to leave this generation of humans alone, about thirty more years of peace. Otherwise, he plans on killing them all. You don't think he's been sitting in the grass all these years, do you?"

The demon looked squarely at Cadence who scowled at him and sighed.

"And when is this supposed to happen?"

"Tomorrow," the demon said. "Whether you like it or not. Rufus is coming to wipe this place out. He just wanted to give you a heads-up so you wouldn't have an unfair disadvantage. He said, 'give them a day.'"

"I guess Rufus must have been training pretty hard," Cadence said. "But we'll be ready for him."

"Before you go, I have a question," I asked the demon. Cadence gave me a strange look. "Do you know where the angel formerly known as Vergil is?"

"Of course," the demon spoke. "Since you're stuck on these grounds, you wouldn't know about it, but there's a battle about to start over in the east. Michael, Raphael and other angels are about to fight there. Vergil has been requested to attend."

"About to start...you wouldn't mean by tomorrow, would you?"

"Why yes I would. It's supposed to start at the same time as your fight with Rufus, in fact. Not only does Rufus want to avenge his former loss to you, but Satan doesn't want your team in the east with all the problems you've caused him in Heaven. So, the choice is yours. You can leave the grounds and see what happens to your precious humans when Rufus shows, or stay and defend them. Either way, you're fighting, so have fun!"

The demon seemed to sink into the grass, and before we could ask him another question, he disappeared.

"So that's how they do it," Cadence said to himself. "I wondered how they blended so well with the shadows. It's like they go invisible...which means there really could have been demons here this whole time."

"So there's a battle off to the east," I whispered to myself. And Vergil would be there. Already I could feel those old unhealthy thoughts enter my mind.

"Let's get everyone together," Cadence said to me. "We'll have the meeting near Cain and Abel so we won't disrupt our duties."

"Good idea," I said, finding it ironic that it was another demonic threat that was bringing us closer together again.

It didn't take long for us to gather for our first meeting in years and I could feel the excitement in the air. We were about to do battle, and not with just anyone: Rufus – whom we had fought our first battle against as a team. And this time we had Amos to help. It didn't matter how strong Rufus had gotten since we last met, the general sense was that we were determined to win.

"Is there a way to confirm this battle in the east?" Farah asked as we sat to the side of the house. Cain and Abel were nearby, discussing how their father always built altars, ensuring that they get it right on the first try.

"I asked God about it," Alessa confirmed. "It's real."

"And Vergil will be there," Cadence said out loud, obviously seeing how I and the others would react.

"You've been looking for him for so long," Alessa said to me. "You must be conflicted."

"No," I said assuredly. "My place is here. I'm satisfied with knowing Vergil is out there. I was about to lose my mind – thinking maybe he had gotten turned into a rock or something."

"Why's that?" Farah asked, but I dismissed her quickly with a wave of my hand. Cadence chuckled at how easily I was handling the topic.

"I think what no one is asking is if we should go to that battle," Amos spoke up. "If Satan doesn't want us to be there, then shouldn't we go?"

"Not necessarily," Alessa said. "This message wasn't relayed to us through a Messenger angel so it's probably not for us to decide. And remember that we have a guardianship to complete. Imagine if we went to the battle and Satan sent a squad of demons to attack and slaughter the humans? No...we stay. We have to."

"She's right," Farah agreed. "I wish I could go though. Maybe we don't all have to be here! Maybe I can go to the battle...and Lysander too! He could get his chance with Vergil!"

"No," I said again. "I want to be here for Team Six. And we really can't afford to have any missing members. The demons are generally stronger than us, and Rufus may have gained some weird new ability since we last saw him, just like Lust did. I'd rather not take the chance. We're all needed - all six of us."

"Can a demon even kill a human?" Farah chimed in. Alessa glared at her.

"Farah, we're staying. No point in discussing it further."

"Hmph," Farah said, crossing her arms and plopping down onto the grass.

"So, I guess we plan," Cadence said. "If we're staying, we have to prepare for Rufus. He apparently thinks he can win, and it would do us well to not underestimate him. So let's hear it – what do we know?"

"He's a Glory," I said. "And though we can count on God staying off his side, we don't know what a Glory turns into when they're a demon - what abilities they gain. It will be very difficult to strategize until we can see him tomorrow."

"You figured out what he was before," Cadence said. "Lust too. So you're the key. Tomorrow, we'll keep you in the background and let you analyze the battle until you come up with a way for us to win. The rest of the team will cautiously attack, searching for weak points."

"I'll do my best," I said. "But that means we can't plan much until then and we don't want to lose any members during the fight. I think we should have Alessa and Marcus stay with me during the initial part of the battle until I can assess the situation properly. We'll be productive. Alessa can pray for assistance while Marcus waits for our signal. It's safe to say that Rufus won't fall for the same thing twice."

"Good, then I guess this meeting is adjourned. We'll just make sure to follow Lysander's lead tomorrow and we'll be fine. In the meantime, Amos, you can continue watching the boys and the rest of us will prepare ourselves mentally."

The prospect of working together again was getting me excited and I was hoping that after the meeting, we would hang out and have some more fun, but unfortunately, the group silently went their separate ways, leaving Amos and I alone. Barely a good-bye was said as we watched them leave.

"Well that was fun," Amos said as he yawned and stretched against the house.

"We're fighting tomorrow," I sighed. "And sadly, it's going to be different."

"How so?"

"Because we're not as confident. And my talk with Cadence didn't go as well as I had hoped."

"Did he listen to you?"

"He heard me. I'm just not sure how much stuck, how much he accepted."

"As long as he heard you, he'll come around. C'mon, let's see what the boys are up to."

We left the house and hurried over to Cain and Abel, who were fervently gathering their precious altar materials: plates of brass, wood, and particular stones. From the sheer amount of raw material, it was apparent they intended to build two altars. And this required a great deal of scavenging, but it didn't matter to them. They were actually enjoying each other's company, and it was the first time I had seen such happiness cross both of their faces. The cheesy grins, excited conversation, and bouts of play between them – it gave me a warm feeling on the inside, a hope for what was to come, and I smiled unabashedly at the sight, for if they were to survive this world, they would unequivocally need each other.

More than anything...

CHAPTER 12: Completion

"Then you put the wood on top like this," Abel said. "The largest piece of wood should be in the middle because that's where we're going to put the portions of meat. Have you gotten yours?"

"Yes," Cain said monotonously. Yesterday, he had been so excited to build the altar that he had smiled at least three times. Now he was as gloomy as ever, helping Abel half-heartedly as if his mind was preoccupied with other things.

"Excellent, "Abel said and touched the stones on both of the altars, making sure their respective walls were intact. "I think we did a better job than Father ever has. It must have to do with us working together."

"Yours looks a little neater, I think," Cain commented, rubbing his arms. The sky was crowded with more clouds than usual so a gray overcast blanketed most of the sunlight, making a cold front blow through and chill the air. Based on his clothing, Cain hadn't prepared for this, while Abel was in his signature shepherd attire as always, rain or shine.

"Then take my altar," Abel said. "It doesn't matter which one I take. As long as they're both prepared properly."

"No, it doesn't matter. You go ahead."

"Okay, well, I'm ready whenever you are."

"Then I guess we better set up." Cain sighed as he stooped down and rummaged through a sack by his feet. Abel did the same, making sure he didn't forget anything. His meat was already waiting on a piece of wood, cleaned and separated proportionally. He placed the meat on the altar carefully, including the kidneys and the fat that was on them and the caul above the liver. It took him fifteen minutes to demonstrate for Cain.

And he had all the time he needed. Adam, Eve and the other children were currently off tending to one of the other fields, trying to grow a new vegetable while Cain and Abel stayed behind. Being grown adults, they didn't need to be watched over and therefore were trusted to tend to the flock and the farm without supervision. Plus they had us there as well. Every member of Team Six was in attendance to this event - if for no other reason but the chance to hear God's voice again.

"Consider yourselves blessed," Amos declared, breaking our captivation in the brothers' task.

"Why is that, Amos?" Cadence asked him.

"Because I saw Abel kill the goat personally. I have to say. It's not pretty. It's nothing like when we get stabbed by a sword. There's a mess involved."

"Then I owe the Lord a thanks," Cadence said as we watched on.

"Cain, what are you doing?" Abel asked, pointing to the contents of Cain's sack. On his altar, Cain was placing various fruits, arranging them neatly on the middle plank.

"The first fruits," he said coolly. A worried look appeared on Abel's face.

"That's not what Father meant when he said that."

"Listen, these are my first fruits. The best of my crop. You're a shepherd. I'm a tiller. That's how this goes."

"Father always says to use one of the sheep, or a goat if we must."

"Father says a lot of things - that we have no proof of. I'm following his instructions, Abel. What difference does it make if I kill a sheep? Do you really want to give me one of yours? How does that make it my offering when it comes from you?"

"I don't know...but I think we should stick to how Father does it. I'll give you one if you want."

"How about this? You do it your way, and I'll do it mine, and we'll see what happens, okay?"

"Okay," Abel agreed weakly as Cain began to set the fire. Within ten minutes, the fire was set on both altars and the meat and fruit were ablaze, the smoke rising from the middle of the rectangular structures and going up to the heavens slowly, as if climbing layers of air. Cain's fruit was consumed almost immediately, roasting and transforming into black curls. Abel's offering took significantly longer, but Cain waited patiently for it to be finished. When it was, we heard the rumble.

That wonderful, familiar rumble.

Looking for the source, angel and human watched in awe as the clouds parted and the sunlight shone brighter than ever, illuminating Abel's altar.

Cain was in awe.

It was apparent he had never seen a basic manifestation of God, let alone what would follow. Before he could ask Abel what was happening, a voice boomed across the land, knocking Cain onto his butt. He scurried to his feet and grabbed his brother's shirt, who was welcoming God's arrival with excited anticipation.

"Well done, Abel," God said audibly, his voice calm and soothing, filling the sky. I prayed silently for a quick trip into His presence - I didn't care who saw me.

"Thank You, Lord," Abel replied humbly, bowing his head. Cain, who hadn't heard a word, looked at his brother frantically.

"Did God just talk to you, or you were just saying thank you?"

"He spoke," Abel said lowly. Cain looked over at his altar, still basked in darkness. He pursed his lips and looked back to the sky in frustration.

"Why are You not accepting my offering? No...Abel, ask Him about the Garden."

"No," Abel said to his brother in a hushed tone. "You ask Him. Now that I am in God's presence, I can't bring myself to do it. You have to."

"Just ask Him, Abel."

"I won't."

"Fine. God...why didn't You accept my sacrifice?"

God didn't answer him. Instead, the sun began to cease its illumination and withdraw from the altars. As soon as Cain realized that God was leaving, he began to get angry - his sudden fascination washed over with rage as he scowled at the sky. Without warning, a second boom cracked like a whip across the plains and Cain wiped the anger from his brow.

"Why art thou wroth?" God said, saying no name, but we and Abel all knew it was directed to Cain. Cain practically hid behind his brother, his face sunken and scared.

"And why is thy countenance fallen?" God asked. "If thou doest well, shalt thou not be accepted? And if thou doest not well, sin lieth at the door. And unto thee shall be his desire, and thou shalt rule over him."

As the firstborn of Adam's children, Cain was to inherit much of the land and many blessings when Adam eventually died. But that didn't mean his heritage was invincible. He was obligated to do his part in life...and with God, or else face the consequences. As an angel that had survived the war in Heaven, I knew this all too well. But what I couldn't understand was why Cain was so angry. Didn't he admit that he had been taking a chance by offering fruit? Now that God didn't accept his offering, shouldn't he bear his correction like he had with his parents in the past and move on?

Cain didn't answer God's questions, instead waiting solemnly behind Abel for Him to say more. When He didn't, and it was apparent that Cain was adamant in keeping his mouth shut, we felt God's presence leave, vanishing as quick as a breeze. Cain sensed the change in the air and turned to his accepted brother.

"I heard Him," Cain said. "Did you hear Him when He spoke to me?"

"I did," Abel said sheepishly. "I told you it wouldn't work. You should've used one of the lambs."

"He finally spoke to me," Cain said to himself, ignoring his brother. "And all He did was scold."

"He wasn't going to scold you, but you asked Him why your offering wasn't accepted and He addressed you."

"The first time He spoke to me, and it was out of disgust."

"No, that wasn't it..."

"I don't think He rejected my offering because I offered fruit. I think it was because of you," Cain said, staring into Abel's eyes.

"You can't possibly believe that," Abel said. Cain shrugged him off. Shaking his head, Cain walked off back toward the house, leaving Abel to look at the two altars and wonder where he should start in disassembling them. We finally breathed over the heated event.

"Abel did the right thing," I said. "He followed the instructions his father taught him. Cain knew to do the same. I'm unsure why he didn't."

"So, do you think Cain knew what to do, but refused to do it," Alessa asked, "or did he really believe he could get by with fruit?"

"Hard to say," Cadence replied. "Cain sounded genuine in his explanation, and it's not like God openly denied him. It sounded more like when Adam explains the difference between dropping the seeds or planting them into the soil. It's stern, but outlined with care."

"Time?" Marcus asked, and we looked up at the sun.

"A half hour to go," I said. "Then Rufus arrives."

"What are we going to do about the boys?" Amos asked. Bewilderment crossed our faces. No one had thought of that.

"I don't like the idea of one of us staying behind," I said. "That's the whole point of us not going to that battle in the east. We need our collective strength. But if we had to choose, I would say that Amos, you should stay back with the boys."

"But," Cadence trailed off, "what about Mar-"

"No," I said firmly, glaring at him. "It has to be Amos." I was sure Cadence wouldn't challenge me outright in front of the group. "Amos is powerful enough to keep any demon that tries to sneak up on him at bay. And no offense Amos, but when Marcus gets revved up, he's stronger than you are. This has nothing to do with keeping the original five."

"Didn't cross my mind," he laughed. "Besides, I like guarding the boys."

"Then it's settled."

"I have a question," Farah spoke up. "Did the demon mention where Rufus will show up?"

"No," I said, "so I was thinking we should head over to the hills where we fought Lust and wait for him there. It's far enough to keep him away from Cain and Abel, but close enough to the house in case he shows up there and we have to rush over."

"Sounds like a plan," Cadence said, glaring at me strangely. "Let's go."

We waved good-bye to Amos and glided toward the hills, but as soon as we got to the tips of the first set, we felt it.

A demonic pressure.

Coming from behind us...

Facing the source, we saw a shadowy figure standing in the middle of Abel's field, standing sideways from us, and facing where the sheep normally grazed. We could see through any kind of weather so his physical features should not have been shrouded, but they were - almost as if the sun were creating waves of smoldering heat in the air. The hot currents blurred our vision, enabling the demon to stand tall and formidable, as if no ambush, no attack could faze him. He was completely confident in his abilities. I saw him lift his head to the sky slowly, as if praying to God, and he clenched his fists tight. I fought to see him through the demonic pressure creating the staggering heat wave, the intimidating vacuum.

We approached cautiously, ready for him to attack, for that was Rufus's way, but he didn't move, and he waited for us to approach, the ground around him beginning to erupt into rings of flames that attached themselves to the ground but yet didn't burn it. To be honest, I was starting to get very afraid.

"Do you think it's the escort?" I asked. "The one who brought us from the island to Heaven? I mean, we can't see who it is. He might have joined Lucifer's side in the end."

"No chance," Alessa said. "This demon is different. But be careful. You know how their physical body means nothing."

"Who are you?" Cadence demanded. The demon dropped his head down to his chest. I almost heard sobbing coming from where he stood.

"Have you forgotten me already?" the demon lamented, sadness and concern echoing in our ears. We all perked up in curiosity, fighting through the waves of heat and venturing steadily closer, forgetting that we were to do battle.

The demon remained facing sideways from us, staring at the sun when he spoke again.

"You know…" he said ominously, "I've always loved this sun. I do not see it often enough, but when I do, it reminds me so much of before. You see, I looked into the light once, but it was so bright, it burned me, and cast me hopelessly into darkness…I was blind…but now I see."

I contemplated his words as the heat began to clear. And when we were able to see him better, he was far different from the other demons we had seen. He was not so hideous and grotesque. In truth, he was very much like us in basic structure. However, there were some distinctions. His skin was cracked like Satan's had been, and glowed a hot red, but the cracks traced along him like veins rather than skin imperfections. And the red glow emanating from him was more like a tan rather than his true pigmentation. Sharp, strange markings and tattoos covered his arms and back, wrapping around them violently, resembling chains. His hair was spiked in the manner of horns, and his face moved strangely, as if it had a life of its own, producing an afterimage whenever he moved. He was quite unique from Satan, Lust and the demon scouts, but his demonic pressure declared it all – he was no less dangerous than they.

Still, I couldn't deny the lump in my throat when I heard his forlorn voice, and recognized the accent of his speech. I knew who stood before us, but I could say nothing, for no words were needed. No matter the conversation that would inevitably ensue, hearts would be shed and despair would be spilled onto that field.

Vergil...what did you become? Just because you were fooled into betraying us? What was your name now? Now that you could not be saved so easily? Would you recognize me and feel the same way I felt towards you? Have you been waiting for this day but never had the heart or the chance to visit? Had Lucifer been preventing our reunion, forbidding our unity? Could you live with what you've become a little bit longer to hear me pour out my heart? Would you see your reflection in my eyes? Could I bear to look at mine in yours?

"Verg-" I began to say but Cadence cut me off with a hand to my chest.

"Choose your words carefully. We have no idea what he's capable of, and remember, he was an Archangel."

"Cadence, you promised I could talk to him first," I said, my voice beginning to crack over finally seeing him. After so long, after so much searching, here he was, standing right before my eyes. I couldn't let him leave - not before I'd said my piece.

"Can't you sense it?" Cadence snapped at me. "He's dangerous!"

"It's...funny," Vergil said languidly, closing his eyes and scrunching up his face. "So funny...how so many of my comrades have changed. Their visages disfigured – heights altered, turned into monsters and yet...I remain, for the most part...intact...why wouldn't I be transformed?"

No one said anything to his sorrowful monologue. We stared at him intensely but he refused to look our way, his hands staring at him in the face as he examined them. His wings, veined in black and red, extended powerfully from his back.

"Why must I be reminded of my former state? Why do I still have my wings? So many demons have lost theirs! Why must I be a demon...that still resembles an angel? What a cruel joke...that God would make me this way..."

"Don't blame God!" Alessa cried out suddenly, pointing at him accusingly. "You chose your path. We fought for you, but you made the decision. The only reason you're filled with regret is because you lost!"

Vergil faced us at last, intentionally revealing his lean and angular countenance. His eyes were piercing and full of hate, and it was when I saw his eyes that I realized just how far he had fallen. In Heaven, regardless of his Archangel status and how much power had flowed from his being, he had had an innocence upon his face, revealed by his eyes. Behind his impressive angelic pressure, he had been a gentle giant, happy to just fight alongside his fellow angels. But now, I couldn't even see a glimpse, an inkling of what he had been. His sun-fire eyes raged, consuming all that he was. He could not see his reflection, what he was, in my eyes. Hate veiled them and all he knew...

"Regret?" he chuckled, his voice becoming less like Vergil's and more like his demonic counterparts' - hoarse and gritty. "What regret?"

"Vergil, I want to talk," I said, but Cadence grabbed my arm. I yanked it away from him and kept walking toward my friend, maintaining a safe distance. Not that this mattered. Being a former Archangel, he could probably take me out before I was even aware of it.

"What can we possibly talk about?" he asked. I was taken aback. This lean, toned being before me threw me off. His words were laced with superiority and the very aura around him was stifling. I had always imagined that when we met, I would be confronting the old Vergil.

"I want to take you home," I said, and the demon laughed heartily.

"Home?" he chuckled, his red skin rippling like water. "Wait…you're serious."

"Very," I said. "Come back to the group. We're Team Six, remember?"

"It looks like you already found a replacement."

"No. Never. We just needed an extra member to help pick up the slack. And if you come home with us, we'll change our name to Team Seven."

"Hey, that's God's number of completion, isn't it?" Vergil chuckled, an eerie smile emerging from his lips. "We would all be reunited, wouldn't we?"

"Without question! I know it seems impossible, but that's only because it has never been attempted before. There's no reason why if you repent and ask for forgiveness that God couldn't change you back."

"Forgiveness? Why? I don't think I made the wrong decision. Your teammate said it herself. I'm angry because we lost the war, not because we regret our choices."

"You don't believe that," I said, feeling myself losing him all over again. "Stop thinking like Satan and his demons, and consider what I'm saying. You can be saved, Vergil."

"And then what? I go back to Heaven? Sing His praises and watch children all day?"

"If you want…"

Vergil laughed again and stretched out his neck. The waves of heat that had dissipated were beginning to form again.

"Lysander, you are a good friend, and I appreciate your kindness, but you're still as credulous and naïve as they come. We are in the aftermath of a war, Lysander. A war. And I want you to hear what I have to say next without taking it lightly, because when I kill you…and your friends over there…I want you to understand why I did it."

His words were so cold and strange that I stopped talking and waited for him to continue. Cadence and the others stood back and watched in shock, waiting for me to come to my senses.

"Do you know why Lust came to the house that night?" Vergil asked, and waited for an answer.

"No. He was chased away by Abel's prayers before we could find out."

"He was a scout - just a more powerful one than those others you've already seen. I had no clue that your team would be there when he entered the house. Imagine his surprise when he saw you all – Team Six, standing idly by inside. The team I had come from. The team he had heard so much about. He wasn't supposed to fight you, just perform some reconnaissance, but he couldn't resist testing his power…he was pretty disappointed in his loss…though I was ecstatic to learn you were all in good health."

"You were happy to see us?"

"Let me finish," he said. "Now, I could've fought you the next day, but I remembered your teamwork, and I knew not to take you lightly, especially with the experience you'd acquired in my absence. So out of admiration and respect, I waited. And waited, for years, and I was so delighted to see that there were more cracks in the legendary Team Six than I had thought. It felt good to know I wasn't the only flaw. But I won't get into detail about that. That's not the point. The point...is all about my first question. Do you know why Lust was asked to be there that night?"

"To inspect us?"

"No," Vergil laughed. "That is wrong, old friend. See, Lust was there to check out Cain and Abel."

The gravity of his words brought me back to attention, and I stepped away from him in horror.

"Why would you want to harm them?" I said slowly. "I don't understand...you can't be serious..."

"Of course I am," he said casually. "Cain and Abel have always been my target. I just decided to wait for the perfect moment."

"So the demon lied to us yesterday. Rufus isn't coming. And there is no battle to the east."

"No, Rufus isn't coming, but it wasn't a complete lie. The Battle of the East is well underway as we speak. It's been set up so there's no interference in my mission. You see, Heaven trusts your team. Sure, you couldn't stop Lucifer, but he was the head of the resistance in Heaven. No one actually expected you to win. The fact that you chased him after experiencing his demonic pressure was impressive in and of itself, even to us demons. There are not many humans in the world, Lysander. And they are very important to God's plans...so we realized that if we outright attacked them, and didn't provide some kind of distraction, Michael and the others would come to your aid. The Battle of the East is serving as that distraction and now that they're far away, fighting to apprehend Satan once and for all, I am free to resolve this problem altogether. This has been a plan in the making for a long time. And it's always been about Cain and Abel. Always. Adam and Eve have too many memories of God and the Garden, but Cain and Abel? To them it's all hearsay. And I plan to use that to my advantage."

"This was all a ploy?"

"Of course it is. Michael and the others are too busy to help you now. Not that you would need it in most cases...see, you should be honored. No one takes your group lightly. And this is why Rufus isn't coming. He wanted to, but let's be honest, he would've failed. I, on the other hand, know your specialties, how you work together, and how you try to hide your weaknesses. I'm the best demon for the job."

"Vergil...you've changed," I said to him in a whisper. I could feel my angelic pressure fluctuate, my emotions overwhelming my will to stand. What had happened to him? How could he say these things so easily?

"Changed, Lysander?" Vergil chuckled. "No...I think I'm being more honest than I've ever been. Do you really think I didn't know what I was doing in Heaven? I tried to play both sides the best I could, my friend. And when it looked inevitable that Lucifer would emerge the victor, I took his side. How was I supposed to know that God would intervene in such a manner? After being absent for so long?"

"You...you needed my help," I said. "Socially..."

"You fell for that too?" Vergil guffawed. "This is hilarious! If I needed lessons in social skills, why would I go to the most awkward of them all for advice? Has that never occurred to you? No, Lysander, I stuck to you because you were the softest. You were so weak and pitiful that I knew you would vouch for me, even if I chose Lucifer and he lost the war. I'm an Archangel! Not some lowly Messenger, or a defective Guard, a sick Faithful, or a poor excuse for a Godhand...I never needed you. None of you!"

Vergil's eyes went ablaze as he pointed to each of us in rage, but I couldn't...I couldn't believe his words. I just refused to believe that this was the same Vergil who had raced me through the stars and saved me from Boris in the Fellowship Hall. I wouldn't accept it...

"I don't believe any of that," I said, my jaw firm. "I refuse to believe it!"

"I don't care," he said coldly. "I just have this to say. If there was some chance of me getting back into Heaven, then yes, I would have 'repented and returned home' but I see no hope for that, so what's the point in pretending anymore? I'm just going to carry out my mission and go to my rightful home."

"You're brainwashed...you-you're being controlled."

"Do you think Satan would send me here if there was the slightest chance I would change my mind? I am one of his most trusted generals. I helped form this plan myself and I volunteered to sever our ties. I could be at the Battle of the East right now but I chose to reveal myself to you, so that you may see how completely useless and pathetic you truly are. How nothing you do will ever accomplish a thing! Mark my words. I will win today."

"We won't allow you to kill them," I said to him, fighting back a breakdown. "We are their guardian angels."

"Kill them?" Vergil said in surprise. "No. No. That's only if I absolutely have to. You're not getting it. I don't want them dead just because I'm a demon. We're smarter than that. No, I want them to be on our side. I want to persuade them to stop following God, and follow Satan or an idol, or anything else, just not God. You saw what Abel did to Lust. We can't have that, and killing them all is meaningless if God just creates another species we have to learn about...but if we turn them from their Creator...now that is a plan. We can destroy His creations internally, render their prayers useless, increase our power and therefore decreasing yours, causing God agony and suffering over His fallen humans. And in the meantime, we plan for our next big move, continuing the cycle until all of Heaven has fallen at our feet or

God wipes his precious humans himself from the very face of the Earth because too many have decided to join our army. Now how is that for a plan? I know you're all about them, so you can appreciate where I'm coming from."

"You're a monster," I breathed to him. Even though I barely believed the words that were coming out of my mouth, I could not deny the alarming revelation that was resonating throughout my mind – that it didn't matter if Vergil was brainwashed or not, I couldn't let him carry out this heinous act.

"You're not the Vergil I know!" I screamed. "This…demonic body of yours is tainting you…messing up your head. But I don't care! If I have to stop you, I'll do what I must!"

"Don't blame me. Blame God. He gave me this form."

"I've heard enough," Cadence said, pushing me back. "Vergil, if you don't leave, we're going to fight you. This is the only courtesy I can extend."

"Cadence, Cadence, Cadence," Vergil laughed in his face. "I see the fear all over you. You don't know how this will end, do you?"

"Neither do you. But I'm ready to find out."

"I'll make sure to keep you all conscious enough to watch the final act," Vergil seethed and glided backward a few yards. The movement was so graceful and natural, I barely realized when he had taken flight and when he had stopped. He stood rigidly on the grass and pulled out his sword - a sharp, scimitar-shaped blade with jagged edges. It blazed as red as his eyes and gave off an aura that begged for blood and spiritual decomposition.

This was really happening…

How could this be happening? Wasn't our reunion supposed to be a joyous occasion?

"Vergil!" I cried out abruptly. "It's not our fault, or God's, or those boys' that you didn't make it! It was in your heart, and yours alone!

You made the decision to go with Lucifer. If you just realize this, maybe there's a way we can help you!"

"You can help me by standing still," he replied calmly, and disappeared from our sight, leaving the atmosphere silent and still.

Cadence turned to me immediately.

"Same plan. Different demon. Are you up for this? Can you assess the situation and come up with a strategy?"

"Yes. Yes," I huffed, trying to maintain my composure. Cadence grabbed his shield while Farah unsheathed her sword. Alessa started praying without a cue and Marcus waited, looking around for the invisible Archangel.

The silence was eerily soothing, and the stillness was slowing making us lose our edge. Cadence waited patiently, steadying his shield close to his chest. I desperately tried coming up with scenarios, options to explore, tactical plans to implement, but my mind was foggy. Why couldn't Vergil just listen to me? Why was he driven to carry out Satan's plans so fervently? Didn't he realize that he could deviate from Satan's orders? He had to have free will...

"Lysander!" Cadence cried out, breaking my concentration. I had shut my eyes in the silence and now Vergil had appeared behind us. Without hesitation, he plunged his sword into Alessa's back, severing the link between her and God and cutting her prayer short. Vergil immediately kicked Alessa off his sword and waited for Marcus to hit him. Marcus had leapt forward upon seeing the Archangel reappear and was determined to put an end to the battle as soon as possible. He aimed a hard-hitting blow at Vergil's face, and strangely, the Archangel accepted it with open arms, letting it hit him square in the nose. Marcus stared in horror as Vergil punched him back, sending the Godhand flying across the field and through the house - and into Amos.

"What do we do?" Cadence cried out to me, frozen in fear. His words finally wriggled their way into me and I unsheathed my sword, but Vergil ignored my stance and walked past me like I didn't even matter. The gesture was so infuriating that I swung at his back, determined to clip his wings. Vergil turned at the last second and grabbed my sword, putting my arms to a halt. He smiled my way and, with an insult – decided to let go, allowing me to swing at him again. I tried a second time and he simply batted it aside with his bare palm. With his other hand, he reached out, and I yelped in surprise as he placed an index finger on my forehead.

"You're so weak," he stressed, and pushed me backwards with barely an effort. The force sent me sprawling to the ground and my sword out of my hands. Vergil swooped down and picked it up, turned around and aimed at Cadence who was sprinting our way. Vergil laughed and chucked the sword at him casually. Cadence managed to raise his shield in time, but the power with which Vergil threw it was too strong. The sword ripped through the shield like it was made of paper and plunged well into Cadence's abdomen. Cadence staggered back under the blow, right into Vergil's personal blade. I didn't even see Vergil move behind him.

Farah tried to rush in and punch Vergil, but he quickly flew around Cadence and held him close, using my friend as a shield. Cadence attempted to reach behind him but with two swords sticking through him, he had already lost a significant amount of energy. Before he could even reach halfway to Vergil's face, his arms suddenly went limp. Farah shuffled left to right in the air, waiting for an opening, as I stayed motionless on the ground, watching Cadence's eyes begin to lose their vigor. What was I doing? Why was I so afraid?

"Can anyone give me a challenge?" Vergil mused loudly for all to hear. "Is this the best Team Six can do without me? Remember, I plan on turning the children to our cause. Has anyone forgotten?"

"Stay still and let me hit you!" Farah called out to him. "I'll stop you for sure!" Vergil flashed her a grin.

"I said I wanted a challenge. Not play in a game of chance!"

Amos and Marcus answered the call, tackling him to the ground from behind and proceeding to pound on him with all their might.

Cadence crashed into the grass, his eyes closed and his body lifeless. I nervously crawled over to him and pulled the swords out, watching the rest of my friends continue the fight.

Farah rushed in, seeing that Vergil was now stuck under the Godhands' barrage. And her chance arrived when Vergil unexpectedly struck back at the Godhands from underneath the beating. He lashed out and grabbed Amos and Marcus by the throats, holding one of them in each respective hand. Farah swooped between them without hesitation and began punching Vergil in the face repeatedly with all her might…but there was no effect. He continued to squeeze Marcus's and Amos's throats as if Farah were nothing but a fly and the Godhands' fists slamming into his arms were nothing but air. He squeezed harder and I watched in horror as their angelic pressure waned, and their bodies stopped moving. When they struggled no more, he thrust them to the ground like he was casting two garbage bags aside. Still conscious, but in dire need of some energy, the two Godhands watched in rage as Vergil ended our last hope - swinging at Farah once, and putting her down for good…

"You can tell her what happened when she wakes up," Vergil relayed to us. "I don't need her getting a random burst of strength."

"Vergil, stop this," I cried, leaping forward. Vergil caught my wrist in mid-air and shook me out of my attack like he was beating a rug. My vision became blurry as I tried to kick him in the face. I missed again.

"Stop pestering me," he stated and punched me in the stomach. I crumpled to the grass with an "oof" and didn't get back up.

"Somebody stop him," Amos rasped as Vergil strode toward the house. Cain and Abel were just coming from behind it, the last of the altar's materials put to the side.

"Why can't you get rid of all of it?" Cain yelled at his brother as Abel kept walking to the sheep pen.

"Cain, I can't talk about this right now. They have to be fed."

"Then tell me why you're leaving the altar's remains by the side of the house!"

"Father might need them in the future."

"That's the point. If you leave them there, he's going to ask why they're there, and we can't lie about it. We're going to have to tell him why we built the altars in the first place and what happened afterwards! He'll learn I offered fruit to God instead of meat, and that I planned on going to the Garden!"

"It would take me another hour to get rid of it all," Abel retorted, "and I have to tend to the flock. Why don't you clean it up?"

"My job actually puts food on the table," Cain snapped. "I don't have time to be cleaning up. Besides, I got nothing out of it. God liked your offering, not mine."

"God would have accepted your offering if you had done it properly."

"Then build me another altar and prepare a lamb for me."

"No, I told you I have to tend to the sheep."

"If I'm going to get in trouble for the altar being there, I might as well get the knowledge I want. I need to know how to get past the flaming sword."

"Cain, I don't have time."

"Well, make time!" Cain yelled, grabbing his brother's arms and shaking him. "Let the sheep go hungry!"

"I won't do it! Let me be!" Abel cried out, getting loose and pushing his brother aside. Cain was shocked at his meek sibling's display of strength and he proceeded to push him back. Abel almost stumbled over a rock but caught himself at the last second. I thought he was going to turn around and fight his older brother, but instead he started running to the pasture - where we were lying, writhing in agony. Cain pursued him and reached out to grab his younger brother's robe, but Abel reached the gate fence before Cain could take hold and, grabbing his cane, pivoted and cracked it against the crown of Cain's head. Cain yelped more in surprise than pain, and nursed his forehead nervously, wincing at the throbbing ache and wiping the blood that poured from his wound onto the grass. Abel dropped his cane and went to his brother's side out of concern, asking to inspect the wound, but Cain pushed him away and ran off toward the house, stumbling the whole way. Abel remained where he was in solitude, staring at the path his brother had taken, wondering if he should have handled the situation differently...

Cain's blood was beginning to dry on the wood of Abel's cane at this point, and I tried not to let my curiosity get the best of me. Was that crimson flow their version of angelic pressure? Was that their energy? Their life? The moment Cain had been wounded, the blood had started to seep through his skin, and he had been noticeably hurt. It was pretty similar to what happened to us when we were wounded, except the humans' "pain" was able to manifest itself in a different way.

A chuckle from Vergil abruptly broke my concentration and I struggled to climb to my feet out of instinct. He was still nearby and I had to do something. It didn't matter if he hadn't made a move yet, he surely intended to, and once again, I was the only one with enough angelic pressure to move. I had to ensure that what happened in the Garden of Eden was a one-time event. There was to be no more tainting. No more innocence lost...and it was up to me. I looked over at Cadence who was trying to stand too but his wounds were too great. Whatever power Vergil possessed, it was paralyzing. Like Cadence, I was able to get to my feet and even take a couple of steps in the house's direction, but that was all. I fell over, my angelic body refusing to obey as I ended up on my stomach in the grass. Cadence was soon to follow.

Stuck on the ground, we were helpless to intervene as Vergil shimmered into view and glided over to Cain. The elder brother was ignoring his wound and beginning to clean up the altar, removing the stones one by one and walking them over into the next field. It was only temporary but they would escape Adam's notice and could be properly disposed of later.

Vergil slid over and leaned into Cain's ear, whispering.

And Cain didn't respond at first…but soon, his mind was racing, and his body temperature rose at an alarming rate as his eyes fell on the large stone in his hand. I could see them widen at the thoughts Vergil was placing in his head, bidding him to taint his relationship with God. Cain thought about Vergil's suggestions for a few minutes, tossing the stone back and forth, before deciding it was a crazy idea.

But Vergil wasn't about to give up. He continued talking to Cain as the young man continued to clean up the altar, and soon, it was obvious that something Vergil had said, was sticking. Cain picked up another large stone and looked off into the distance at his brother. After a few minutes went by, he started walking, stone still in hand.

I couldn't take it anymore.

Overcome with agony, I sprawled out and began crawling forward in the grass, trying to shuffle over to where Abel was leading the sheep into the pasture. Cain was openly carrying the stone in his hand, and it wasn't yet noticed by his brother. I groaned a little too loudly at how fast he was moving compared to me and Vergil glared at me for a moment. I thought he was going to come over and finish me off, but he smiled and strangely called out into the air.

"Okay! Have your fun!"

As I pondered his bizarre saying, small demon scouts came from all directions and sides, becoming visible before our eyes, emerging from the soil, the grass, and the roof of the house. They cackled and squealed in delight as they began punching and kicking the six of us without remorse…even Farah's lifeless body. Alessa was unable to talk, but she grunted something as a few imp demons began kicking her sides. She had to be trying to pray. Undoubtedly, the pain wasn't helping. Normally, the demon imps' weak attacks would do nothing, but with our angelic pressures at such low levels, their blows were increasing in strength and becoming more deadly with each passing moment.

And I couldn't afford to go unconscious. Not now. Not with what was about to happen. Because deep down, I believed Vergil – that no harm would come to either of the boys, and he would just try his best to turn them to the demons' side…but that was a lie. Sure, if there was a chance of Abel converting, perhaps they would both be kept safe, but he had hurt Lust, and became a threat to Satan's agenda…and all as a little boy. What could happen if he was allowed to grow? To cultivate and nurture his relationship with God? For a demon, it was just unacceptable, and I prayed that Vergil hadn't thought of this…

But Cain…Cain had potential. Not that he was evil…but he was misguided and troubled and had enough darkness within him for the devil to manipulate. And so, Cain crept up on his brother, who was just getting ready to shear one of the sheep. He raised the rock over his head, paused only to confirm the trajectory, and struck him. The sheep ran at the sudden movement, bleating frantically and scaring the other sheep into a frenzy. But no help would come to answer their cries…

At first, Cain stopped after the initial blow, frozen in disbelief over what he had done. But when Abel began to cry out in pain, and especially to call out for help, Cain decided he was already past the point of no return…

I could not watch as Cain brutally killed his brother...

But I could hear Vergil's laughs, even beyond the sickening thuds, echoing along the hills for the entire spiritual realm to hear, and when it was done, Cain could not move. His hands were shaking, his breathing rapid and shallow…Vergil turned to us for closure.

"It is done, my friends," he said cheerfully, picking up and sheathing his blade. "God will either destroy or banish Cain now, and should he be left alive, we will welcome him into our embrace. Abel is dead, and the outlook could not be more satisfying…now, I have to say some last words."

He glided over to us and stooped down, looking directly at me.

"This does not end with Abel. After Cain has received our tutelage and is deemed ready, we will send him out to kill the rest. You know, ensure that Adam doesn't have any more offspring of Abel's caliber. You see, we can't usually kill the humans outright, but as you just witnessed, we can surely persuade..."

"Vergil," I choked as the imp demons left our sides. "Cain won't."

"If he refuses us, then we will kill him," he said proudly. My mind was starting to get more hazy, my eyes heavy.

"But you can't..."

"Ah. That's right. I did say we can't kill them...but that's only for those with God's blessing or protection. Annoyances like Abel have to be killed by other humans via manipulation. Recluses like Cain, however, are another story. There is no salvation for him now. He's just become discarded trash, recycled for our master Satan's use. Should he try to repent and change his ways, we'll destroy him before any kind of redemption is complete, before any protection is given to him."

"I don't believe that..."

"Shhh," he said to me. "Save your strength. Because this is what Satan has authorized me to do: from now on, I'll be your guardian demon. Doesn't that sound exciting? Whenever you're on the Earth, I'll be watching each move you make, study every word that comes out of your mouth, and when you least expect it, I will strike, and ruin you all over again. I won't knock you unconscious, but I will torment you for eternity, until either the human race is gone or you lose your minds. So you see, in a way, we'll be together! Isn't this what you wanted, Lysander? Team Seven has been created! We're complete!"

Vergil laughed maniacally and patted me on the head – the taps carried out with just enough strength to sap the last of my energy.

"Be good now," he mused. "I'll be watching."

And with those words, I wept to the point of exhaustion, causing my angelic pressure to give out, and my mind to go unconscious for an unknown amount of time...

CHAPTER 13: Research and Development

"Even with a plan, we would have still lost," I said to the group. We were standing inside Alessa's house. It had been two days since Cain had killed Abel, and we were back in Heaven, resting after our traumatic experience. We had been unconscious for half a day and when we woke up we had been dropped off at Alessa's house with a written message from Raphael stating that he figured this is what we would have wanted. He knew us well, because with the death of Abel still fresh in the angel population's mind, we weren't ready to go outside and face the crowd. That also meant ignoring the Throne Room which was located in the city core, and since we hadn't been in God's presence in years, we needed to see Him – if anything, to be revitalized. The only way we could manage that without running into our fellow angels was to go to Alessa's house, apparently one big empty room where God came in regularly to fill the space. For the first day or so we just kept silent, sitting in various spots of the house with nothing but our mental databases for company. But there were too many questions floating amongst us, and one of them only I could answer.

"He was too strong," I assured them, standing up and looking at my brooding teammates. "A plan wouldn't have made a difference."

"No time to come up with one, I guess," Farah said, still weeping over the results of our blunder. Having been knocked unconscious due to Vergil's might alone, she was the only one who hadn't seen what Cain did to Abel, and she had been the last one to wake up. Only God's healing presence had brought her back, and not to good news. She had come out of her rest anxious and full of questions, but we were too distraught to answer her right away. Eventually she settled down and waited. Little by little, we relayed the ending of our fight with Vergil. She took it better than we had, but then again, she didn't have all the pictures to go with the story.

"Lysander was frozen," Cadence stated flatly, climbing to his feet. "We were fighting blind, and it got us nowhere."

"How was I supposed to know we would be fighting Vergil, and not Rufus?" I yelled at him, taking the initiative. "We were all caught off guard."

"It doesn't matter! You offered no advice! No options! You might as well have gone to the Battle of the East after all!"

"It's not all my fault that we lost," I said vehemently. "And besides, you promised me that I could talk to him. I said my piece. And now that I know who he is, and what he stands for, I can counter him."

"I don't want to hear it...now you're ready to face him? We had to lose Abel for you to realize that Vergil's on the wrong team? What do we have to lose for you to come up with a plan to beat him? The human race?"

"I know you're upset, but this affront isn't solving anything."

"Lysander's right," Alessa said, stepping in front of Cadence. "We all failed, as a team. No one's to blame. I think seeing Vergil like that threw us all off."

"It doesn't matter," Cadence stressed. "Abel's gone. After fifteen years of guardianship, we failed. We spent all that time, waiting for that day to arrive and when it came, we failed miserably, like it was all meaningless..."

Cadence didn't say another word, walking out of the house and slamming the door. I didn't blame his harsh words. He had to have dwelled on our upcoming demonic attack every night since Lust had showed up. The weight of this loss, the first test in our protection of Adam's children, would haunt him for many days to come, but for the first time in my life, I wasn't ready to mourn the past. I was poised for action, and whether it was the appropriate moment or not, I couldn't shake this feeling.

I had been a complete fool.

And Vergil had capitalized on this from the beginning. To think that I had spent countless hours in the mental database looking for ways to bring him back to Heaven, staring at the globe in Raphael's hall, neglecting my friends, shunning basic companionship and putting everyone I cared about in danger...all for him to practically spit in my face and laugh, making light of my kindness, compassion, and love...

And yet he always would be family to me. No matter how terrible he had treated me, deep down I still believed that it hadn't all been a ruse, but I couldn't hold on to that belief anymore. There was too much at stake and I had to be responsible for my actions. Cadence was furious, but he had still given me my chance to save Vergil. For that, I was thankful and I would repay him many times over in exchange. As for Vergil...sometimes even family needed tough love...

"Should we follow him?" Farah asked. Alessa shook her head.

"He needs to think about the decisions he made. From our previous conversations, he was confident we would make it through the whole tour, regardless of any conflict."

"Well, I'm ready for action," I said suddenly, and she looked at me like I was an Absent speaking for the first time.

"You sure find bravery in the oddest moments," she said, raising an eyebrow. "The Battle of the East is still raging on as we speak, and you want to jump in?"

"No, not the Battle. We weren't asked to fight in it, so I don't want to interfere."

"Then what action are you implying?"

"Cain. We may have lost Abel, but our guardianship of Cain can still persist. We can prevent Satan from infecting him with his doctrine."

"Satan is busy, and until the Battle is over, Cain will be left alone. There's no threat to him yet. Besides, our job is finished."

"What do you mean? We're still his guardians, right?"

"Are you insane? We lost those privileges. Coming to Heaven wasn't meant to be a quick trip for some healing and rest. I already asked God about it. Cain is being reassigned."

"To whom?"

"Not sure. It's on a volunteer basis. Since Cain's status has changed due to the murder he committed, he needs a new guardian. I'm not sure who's going to ask for that job though."

"Is the posting at the Mission Center?"

"Probably."

"Then that's where I'm headed."

"What?!" Farah exclaimed. "You're not taking it, are you? Just to see Vergil again?"

"I never said I was signing up for it. I'm curious about the details."

"What's going on?" Amos asked out of concern, putting his hand on my shoulder. "You looking to get yourself hurt?"

"This isn't about Vergil. At least not in the way you think."

"I don't understand," the big angel said. "If anyone signs up for watching Cain, it should be me. I still got love for the kid regardless of what he's done. I remember when he used to put his head under water in a bucket and hold his breath, trying to beat his best record. He thought the Garden of Eden was under water and he'd have to swim down to find it! HA! I tell you, he was full of adventure."

"No, Amos," I said firmly. "I have to take a look at the listing first. Promise me you won't sign up for it until then."

"Uh, well, I guess…"

"Got a plan in motion?" Alessa asked, but I shrugged it off.

"Maybe, but I have to clear my head. Make sure I'm doing this to actually take Vergil out and not because I want to save him…I'm heading out. And I would appreciate it if I did this alone. You understand."

Farah began to speak but Marcus patted her head to silence her. The last thing I saw as I closed the door was her grabbing his wrist and judo-flipping him over her shoulder onto Alessa's bare floor. I stifled a laugh, cleared my throat and then sighed heavily, forcing my thoughts to stay on a serious track.

I couldn't be around them, not now. Vergil had said I was weak, and didn't hesitate to completely humiliate and degrade us. He manipulated Abel's death. Ruined our morale. Fractured Cadence's resolve. And he showed no remorse for my compassion, no consideration. It was unforgivable...and yet, I forgave him, though I didn't want to. Holding a grudge would get me no closer to having a unified team again.

Still, his actions...could not be forgotten.

And I believed his threats. There was no doubt that Vergil would keep watch until we returned to Earth and make good on his promises, destroying any assignments we were given. Not only would we lose faith in our teamwork, but soon we would get pessimistic, used to failure. He had to be stopped, and soon. But until the right moment presented itself, I was forced to wait and plan ahead. Something I should have done properly from the start: have a contingency plan in place to take him down, as well as one to save him, just in case - because I knew more than anyone how powerful Vergil really was, and seeing him in his demonic form, it was apparent his pressure had only increased. If we were going to save the rest of the human race, I had to do the unthinkable.

I had to defeat an Archangel.

But I had to be patient...and in Heaven, this was possible...

I made my way first to the Archive Building, because I had been neglecting it for far too long. Out of all of the buildings in Heaven, I should have spent my hours here and not gazing at a holographic globe, for this was specifically a place for research, and I was sure I would find the valuable answers I needed, right here.

It was like a town hall in structure, with massive, stone pillars in the shape of spirals waiting by the entrance and creaky wooden doors swaying at the forefront. Why in Heaven there were creaky doors, or even wooden ones, was a mystery in itself, but I saved this contemplation for a future endeavor - there were presently more important things to consider.

The inside of the building was like a library. Books hung on the shelves in immaculate condition, unable to tear or rip. Cased in gold or diamond respectively, they gave off an inviting aura to the room, reflecting their shine off the red carpet that rolled down a long, polished corridor. An angel was sitting at a corner desk at the entrance, with stacks of books and papers to the side. A large angel, with shoulders too big and wide for his body. His arms were as skinny as broomsticks though, and the rest of his frame was fat. I didn't know what to make of him, but he greeted me warmly and I waved back shyly. When I got over my initial timidity, I felt a rush of warmth surge through my being as I realized how glad I was to see a smiling angel wave my way. It was good to be back in Heaven! Here, I had no enemies, and therefore, there was no reason to fear.

"Can I help you?" the angel asked, rubbing his eyes. "The selection is infinite."

"I guess so," I mused. "How does this place work?"

"Like the buildings near the city, or your homes, your mind is the key. You simply think of a book or event you would like to view and start flying down the hall. You are literally transported to the right section. When you are done, imagine yourself back at the entrance, and there you are."

"Has anyone tried navigating this place manually?" I queried, making a mental note to view the backside of the building when I left. It must stretch out for light years.

"I have," he laughed. "And they closed the building down to look for me. Didn't see much of the war to tell you the truth. I was lost somewhere between Shakespeare and the Psalms of David. I especially enjoy Psalm 119 when it says -"

"-Excuse me?"

"Oh, right...future, secrets...yadda, yadda, yadda...forget I said anything, okay? That's not for you to know."

"I don't understand."

"This place," he said in awe, "is a physical infinite database. All of the knowledge and information found in your mental database is right here, and more. All you have to do is find it, or know what you're looking for."

"You're saying...there's knowledge in here that's not programmed into us?"

"That's right. Fascinating, isn't it? There is risk in taking a leisurely stroll down a random aisle, but you could end up learning about a historical person who hasn't even been born yet, an event in God's plans, intricate details about your past, what life was like before you were born, or even the awesome secrets of the future! Just pray you can find your way back...once you decide to go it manually, the teleport feature is shut off and the building quickly turns into a labyrinth. I believe it's a security measure to prevent tampering with the future, but if you're willing to dig deep, you might get away with some precious gems."

"It's no wonder I never met you," I laughed. "You must be here literally all the time."

"It's true...I don't get too many visitors and I get awfully bored. When some company does arrive, it's usually high ranking angels, here to look up a direct file on God's orders. A few come of their own free will, but they tend to run away after my explanation of the place. Who knew excitement could cause such turmoil..."

"It's not all fun and games," I admitted. "But I could definitely find myself getting lost in here. Back on the island, I was too scared of turning Absent to dig deep into the database, but here...I could get lost and be quite content with it."

"A kindred spirit," he said warmly. "My name is Ethan."

"Lysander," I said, extending a hand for him to shake. He took it and shook it like he would never get the opportunity again. "Ethan, if you don't mind me asking, what classification are you?"

"Godhand," he chortled. "I've been slacking."

"Your classification never ceases to amaze me," I chuckled. "I know a couple of Godhands. The three of you are all so different."

"It's because of our physique, which changes based on how we use it. Let's take me for example...I'm fat from the waist down because I sit and read all day. My arms are skinny because all they do is turn pages and reach for books, and my shoulders are big because I shrug a lot. I tend to do it when I'm engrossed in a good story or reading about current events."

"I take it you haven't heard the latest news..."

"About Cain and Abel? Awful, but I don't blame the team watching them. Facing an Archangel must be tough."

"That's actually why I'm here. I'm doing some investigation in how to take one down permanently."

"Why would that interest you?"

"I'm actually part of the team that fought Vergil. I'm from Team Six."

"Wow!" he said, leaning forward to inspect me. "A local legend right before my eyes!"

"Please...I don't think I can take any of that right now. The most legendary thing I've ever done was sulk for five days."

"Sorry, I understand how difficult that must have been...well, if you're trying to do some specific research, I would head to the Present Room."

"Present, like gifts?"

"No, like THE Present. What we are living at this current moment. Just concentrate on the name 'Present Room' and head down the hall.

You'll get there automatically. The room serves as a holographic projector. It's programmed to play what's currently happening on Earth by default, but it can also play events that you've lived through, or experiences on Earth from the humans' perspective."

"Any footage on humans seeing demons? That might give me a clue to Satan's location."

"No, not yet anyway. Remember, there's not too many humans on the Earth. They've barely begun to spread out."

"Right. Okay...what if I want to find footage on Vergil specifically?"

"There will only be recordings of when he was in Heaven or what you experienced with him on Earth. Unfortunately, information like that on the demons, as far as their locations and strategies goes, is not easily accessed. If we did, there would be no Battle of the East. If you are desperate for those answers, it will require a manual trip."

"Got it. Thank you."

"If you need assistance, just call for me!" he waved. I concentrated on 'Present Room.' When I finally felt safe traveling, I headed down the hall. I barely took a step forward when my eyes closed involuntarily. I felt something lift me up like an air current and, as I struggled to open my eyes, I was whisked away, with a suction noise popping behind me. When I was able to open them again, I was in a massive flat circle that was etched into the marble floor. It extended about a football field wide. Surrounding me were seven skyscraper-sized bookcases, filled with books bigger than I was! A holographic orb similar to the globe in Raphael's hall descended from the ceiling and stopped just above my head.

"Please make your request," Ethan's voice resounded off the walls. I glanced from side to side but saw no one.

"Ethan?" I called out, wondering where he was, when the orb expanded without warning, filling the entire circle. Before my eyes, a replay of my conversation with Ethan was played out, reciting it word for word, body language and all. I realized that the voice from earlier had only been a recording.

"Stop," I said and the orb retracted, cutting off the scene and going back to normal. I had to think...what should I see first?

"Adam," I said, thinking I would go to the beginning. Since Lucifer had been in the Garden, perhaps the demons' headquarters were near it. The holographic orb descended and I was back in the Garden of Eden, except this time, I could see a conversation God was having with Adam. Adam was sitting up against a tree, looking intensely into the eyes of what I knew to be a couple of bears. The bears didn't move, just looked at Adam dumb-founded, blinking periodically. Adam scratched his chin and sat up after a second, looking to the sky.

"Bear," he declared, and the bears exited to the left amongst a row of lush, leafy bushes, making way for a pair of eagles. The eagles landed gently in front of Adam, who already had an answer.

"Eagle," he said and the birds left, allowing two dogs to bounce happily forward. Adam continued to name the animals and this went on for about fifteen minutes before Adam looked up to the sky without even glancing at his next assignment.

"Lord, why don't I have a companion?"

The sun brightened a little through the trees and Adam smirked.

"You wanted me to notice that I was alone, didn't You?"

"Very well, Adam," God's voice rang out across the sky and I saw Adam's eyes begin to get heavy. He slumped down on the tree until his back was completely on the ground, and he fell asleep.

"Stop," I said, and the footage was cut short. That was too far in the past. But it didn't mean that I hadn't learned anything. God was teaching Adam the importance of having others by his side. This was a lesson I made a mental note of for myself, because if any kind of plan was going to work against Vergil, everyone from Team Six would have to be involved. I still needed them.

"Adam and Eve banished," I said, changing gears. I was transported to the flaming sword, a mile away from its position. Looking to the left I saw Anton and Synon stretching their limbs and preparing for duty. To the right stood Adam and Eve, holding each other and sobbing uncontrollably. A rumble was heard and Adam stopped his weeping. Like us, he understood it meant God was approaching, and that sometimes it wasn't a good thing.

"Woman," God said to Eve, and she lifted her head. "I will greatly multiply thy sorrow and thy conception; in sorrow thou shalt bring forth children; and thy desire shall be to thy husband, and he shall rule over thee."

Eve bowed her head in silence, sobbing lightly. With her taking the first step in disobedience, it seemed like her husband would assume the role as leader rather than having a more equal partnership like in the Garden. Even though it was not supposed to be that way. Maybe God gave Adam the lead because he sinned last. This was only speculation...but it did confirm for me that Cadence shouldn't be the sole decider of our fates. He was our leader, but not our commander or dictator.

"Adam," God continued, "Because thou hast hearkened unto the voice of thy wife, and hast eaten of the tree, of which I commanded thee, saying, Thou shalt not eat of it: cursed is the ground for thy sake; in sorrow shalt thou eat of it all the days of thy life; Thorns also and thistles shall it bring forth to thee; and thou shalt eat the herb of the field..."

So that was why the land was dying. With it no longer being kept up by God, it was now subject to the forces and elements of nature. And the land near the Garden not only had the rays of the sun to contend with, but the flames of the sword as well.

"In the sweat of thy face shalt thou eat bread," God continued, "till thou return unto the ground; for out of it wast thou taken: for dust thou art, and unto dust shalt thou return."

Hence the purpose for all of the hard labor they were doing. No wonder they continued to expand. With food not readily available, and more children on the way, they had to constantly increase their crop intake or face starvation. But this information still gave me little to work with, though I was beginning to form an idea…

"Stop," I said. "Who is the next son of Adam and Eve, after Cain?"

In order for the plan forming in my mind to work, I would need a brother of Cain. Someone he could closely identify with. I could use a sister, but he never gave them much thought growing up.

The orb expanded and I was taken inside their house. Adam, Eve, and a large group of their daughters, all different ages, were looking into a makeshift bassinet. I hovered over them to take a look and saw a baby boy, sleeping soundly and breathing lightly. Adam looked over at his wife, who was fighting back tears, and rubbed the back of her neck, pulling her close to him.

"You name him," Adam whispered to her. "Whatever you like."

She stared down at the baby boy and tried to say the name but it wouldn't escape her lips. She started to choke up and began to cry. One of her daughters came over and rubbed her back. A couple of them joined her in her sorrow.

"It's okay, Eve," Adam said solemnly. "Take your time."

"We will name him Seth," she said through her sobs, "for God has appointed me another seed instead of Abel, whom Cain slew."

"Stop," I said. I asked the orb for the Earth date: twenty more years had passed since our encounter with Vergil. Plenty of years for Seth to gain the demons' attention, especially if he took after his brother Abel.

"What happened to Cain after he killed Abel?" I asked, and the orb revealed the rolling hills near the house. Cain was running as fast as he could, refusing to look behind him as a rumble continued to grow in strength across the sky. Cain was so terrified that he didn't watch where he was going, and he tripped over a rock sticking out of the ground. He was about a mile from the Garden of Eden; a few more hills remained in his path.

"Where is Abel thy brother?" God asked him, cutting him off at the pass with His thunderous voice. Cain looked up and stumbled to his feet.

"I know not! Am I my brother's keeper?" he shouted at God.

"What hast thou done?" God questioned, His voice full of concern. "The voice of thy brother's blood crieth unto me from the ground. And now art thou cursed from the Earth, which hath opened her mouth to receive thy brother's blood from thy hand."

"No," Cain began to weep, "I don't want to be cursed."

"When thou tillest the ground," God said, "it shall not henceforth yield unto thee her strength; a fugitive and a vagabond shalt thou be in the Earth."

"NO!" Cain screamed, weeping bitterly between bouts of shouting at God, "How will I eat? How will I survive? Tilling the ground is all I know! My punishment is greater than I can bear! Behold, thou hast driven me out this day from the face of the Earth; and from thy face shall I be hid; and I shall be a fugitive and a vagabond in the Earth; and it shall come to pass, that every one that findeth me shall slay me!"

Cain pounded his fists into the grass, clutching the grass and ripping it from the ground.

"I might as well be an animal. A sacrifice! When my father finds out what I've done...my mother...my siblings...they'll kill me!"

"Therefore whosoever slayeth Cain," the Lord said, "vengeance shall be taken on him sevenfold."

At the word "sevenfold," the sky darkened and a flash of lightning shot out and struck the side of Cain's face. Cain cried out suddenly in pain and nursed his face as he fell to his knees. The lightning had struck the opposite cheek from which Abel had struck him with his cane.

"A mark," God said, "for thy safety."

Cain was furious, and though God left as soon as the mark had been planted, Cain shouted and spat at the sky, screaming wildly for God to come back. I could only watch so much.

"Stop," I sighed. It could take years searching for the right plan.

"Hey," Ethan said, appearing in front of one of the bookcases. "I'm sorry to disturb you, but there's someone at the entrance for you."

"Who is it?"

"Don't know."

"What do they look like?"

"I think you should just come with me. She gave me this look when I told her you couldn't be disturbed – like she was going to burn the building down."

"Alessa," I whispered. I could only imagine the threats poor Ethan had endured before he acquiesced.

"Thank you," I said. "Let's go." I stepped out of the circle and concentrated with Ethan on returning to the Archive Building's entrance. It looked like further research would have to wait. When we reappeared in the lobby, Alessa was waiting by the counter, leaning into it and tapping at a fast rate.

"What are you doing here?" she immediately demanded, but I brushed her off.

"I said I needed to be alone."

"Doesn't matter now," Alessa said. "Cadence has a plan – to get Vergil."

"He does? What is it?"

"He's calling a meeting. We're all to show up and vote on it."

"Okay," I said, "but I think we should speak up and say whatever's on our minds before we go to a vote. From the sounds of it, you already know what he plans to do."

"I have some idea," she grinned and we headed off to his mansion. Okay, not really mansion. It was more like a skyscraper, tall and lanky just like him. It boasted only a few pieces of furniture and only the first floor was hospitable. To be more precise, there was only the first floor. The rest of the building was completely hollow, with no floors or rooms or anything, but it did boast an interactive training room that I had yet to use. Alessa and I walked into the open front door to see that we were the last to arrive. The rest of Team Six were sprawled on the furniture, waiting patiently for us.

"I grabbed Lysander," Alessa announced. Cadence nodded in reply, lounging on one of his sofas. He stood up and waved us over to where the rest of the group stood. They all looked like they were in trouble and weren't really speaking to each other.

"Has anyone taken Cain's position?" I asked them collectively and Farah yawned.

"I went by the Mission Center to ask about it an hour ago. No one's claimed it yet."

"Why were you over there?"

"Because." Cadence spoke up. "She was trying to fill it."

"What? Why?" I asked in shock. She shrugged her shoulders and looked down at the floor.

"Because I wanted a shot at Vergil," she said, her jaw tight and shoulders tense.

"Alone?"

"Why not? We're not acting like a team anymore."

"How true that is…"

"Hey!" Cadence said sharply. "We are still a team! I don't know what's gotten into everyone lately, but we're having this meeting to do exactly that - be a team!"

"Why don't you have the meeting?" Farah shouted at him. "I don't understand why you would force me back here! I wanted that shot at him. I can beat him and you know it! He knows it! I was the only one he knocked unconscious!"

"Farah," Amos said. "Let's hear him out."

"Fine," she huffed, crossing her little arms, "but it better be good."

"Vergil wouldn't expect us to return to Earth so soon," Cadence began, "so I think this is a good opportunity to take the offensive and catch him off guard while he's distracted. I've done some digging, and there's word that he's in the Battle of the East, fighting alongside Satan. I say we go down to the Battle, catch him off guard…"

"…and die," I said flatly. Cadence glared at me and grit his teeth.

"Have something to say, Lysander?"

"Yes. Your plan is dumb."

"Oooooooo," Farah mused, punching her fist out playfully. "Lysander vs. Cadence."

"Showdown," Marcus grunted and Farah giggled. Cadence ignored them.

"Do you have a better one?"

"I do actually," I said. "I did some thinking on the flight here and I've figured it all out. There's some details that need ironing out but the framework is set."

"Oh, so you just have a plan ready to go?"

"Yes, and it's better than a suicide mission. Going to the Battle of the East could result just as badly for our side as theirs. We'd be in the way, trying to face off against several high ranking demons just to find

Vergil. We might not even make it to him, be too exhausted to cause any real damage. Not to mention that if we do catch Vergil off guard, which isn't likely, he'll probably destroy us anyways. Cadence, if you listen to me, and everyone follows my lead, we can beat Vergil. I guarantee it."

"So you want to be the leader now?"

"No. Never," I said. "I'm just doing what I always do. Tactics."

"Then what's your master plan?"

"I can't explain it all because I don't want it accidentally slipping out around any demons, but I am asking for trust."

"Trust? And what exactly would this trust entail?"

"You signing up to be Cain's guardian," I said, smiling a little too widely. "A five year tour."

The silence in the room was as dead as space, but I was confident in my plan. Sure, it wasn't all together, but the moment Cadence had spouted off his ridiculous idea, I forced myself to come up with something quick, and the seed that had come forth was all I needed. With Cadence doing a five year tour, I would have about a year to perfect it – without him getting in the way.

"Five years? With Cain?!" Cadence shouted. "Why? What am I going to do there?"

"Nothing. Just wait for my signal."

"Your signal."

"Yes."

"No."

"It's essential," I said. "You have to be the one to do it."

"Why?"

"I have my reasons. It has to be you. Just put your pride aside and trust me."

Cadence strode over and slapped me across the face, causing my head to turn to the side, and I tried, Lord I tried, not to hit him back. I turned my head back to see his finger pointing in my face.

"Stop saying I'm full of pride," he barked at me.

"Okay," I said, clearing my throat. "If you won't sign up for the guardianship willingly, then how about I challenge you for it?"

"You want to fight me for it?" Cadence snapped. "So what's the condition? You win, I have to be Cain's guardian angel?"

"Yes."

"And what happens if I win?"

"I quit the team," I said. "And I'll be out of your way for good."

"But…" Cadence cracked up at this. He hadn't expected me to make such a bold statement, but I had to put it all on the line. I had to save Cadence from himself, while I still could. My fear hadn't done Vergil any good, and neither would it help Cadence. Blindly following his increasingly insane orders would lead to our destruction in the end. I had to stop it now, and defeat Vergil in the process.

"You want this," I said to him, trying to get him angry again. "Unless you want to step down and make me the leader."

"No," Cadence said, his fear and antagonism returning. "I'll accept your challenge. But remember, you chose these conditions."

"Yes I did," I said as I spread my wings out wide and stretched out my arms. I had to end it as quickly as possible. Drawing out the fight in Cadence's own house wasn't going to increase my chances.

Cadence unlocked his shield and held it by his side.

"First one to go unconscious or say they give up loses," he said. "No defense system."

"Doesn't matter to me," I said, going over the scenario. "Your move."

Cadence threw his shield at me as I unsheathed my sword and used its face to block the attack. With the shield dropping to the floor, I headed for the ceiling. Cadence looked at me while he retrieved his armament, wondering what I was planning, but I was confident he'd fall for it. Cadence climbed slowly, shield in one hand and a sword in the next. I fought down the urge to run and headed straight for him. With my wings tucked behind me I sped at him like a bullet, with my sword out in front of me like I was jousting. He dodged my straight shot and took a swing at my passing legs. He barely missed and I turned around immediately, my back toward the floor below. He swung at me fervently, our swords clashing, the clanking noise echoing off of the walls. I knew that, because he was a Guard, he would win a battle of strength. Not only did he basically have more power, but his defense was top notch. Nothing short of a crippling blow would suffice. All other strikes might as well be paper cuts.

"You're losing pressure," he said casually as he attempted a stab at my left arm. I parried it and flew past him, pretending to go for his back. He blocked it easily and I floated upwards, keeping my back to the ceiling and my face firmly towards him.

"Getting some fresh air?" he asked and cocked back his arm for another shield throw. Here it was…

The shield flew straight at me and I blocked it with the face of my sword again, but as it fell back down, free-falling to Cadence below, I placed all my angelic pressure into my right arm, clutching my sword with every ounce of strength I could spare without losing flight. When the shield was a couple of feet from his waiting arms, I threw my sword at him like a fired bullet. The sword met the shield just as he caught it, and the amount of force I had put into it sent the blade plunging through the shield, all the way to the hilt. Carrying the shield with it, the sword fired into Cadence's chest like a sledgehammer and sent him reeling backward to the floor. I made my quick descent, meeting Cadence's body as he hit the tiles, and grabbed the sword from his shock-vibrating hands and thrust it into his side. Cadence roared in agony as I took the sword out and placed it at his neck. Glaring at me through hurt eyes, he reluctantly tapped the floor.

It was a risky move, but I had won.

"I didn't think you'd try such a cheap trick," he grunted as Alessa helped him to his feet. "I guess you and Vergil like the same techniques." I ignored his attempt to hurt my feelings, for I was sure his were ablaze. One of us needed to keep our head cool.

"That's exactly why my plan will defeat him. He'll never see it coming. Now go and sign up." My voice held no remorse. "I'll let you know what the signal is in time."

"I'll have to leave as soon as I sign up," he said, wincing at his wounds. "Shouldn't you tell me the signal now?"

"Nope. Wait for it."

"Fine," he groaned and hobbled to the door, clutching his side. "So how did you figure out how to beat me? Just curious."

"Your shield," I replied. "It's a beautiful instrument, but you're so used to using it that it's also a crutch - it's hard for you to fight without it. You placed so much attention on catching it that you didn't see me gathering my angelic pressure for one last hurrah. As for the move Vergil used...I chose it because it suited me best at the moment...not because I wanted to insult you."

Cadence didn't respond but waved a half-hearted goodbye to the group. No one said a word as he left, and within a second, he was gone. Gone to complete a five year guardianship with a murderer.

All according to plan.

"Alessa, I have to talk to you," I said, "but everyone should hear what I have to say."

"What is it?" she asked. She was still in shock over my victory and Cadence's departure. It was all happening so fast, a surreal fog had clouded the room. I tried not to stop and notice it, in fear that I would forget my instructions for her.

"You are the acting leader until Cadence returns," I said. She was surprised, but after seeing how hard I had fought for Cadence to follow my lead, she questioned my declaration gracefully.

"Why me? I thought you just fought him for..."

"No. That was to get him to sign up for Cain. I don't want to be the leader, especially since I'm leaving the team."

"What?" Farah exclaimed, coming to my side. "Then what was the point of the fight?"

"Just trust me," I laughed. "If this is going to work, I need all of you on board. So, Alessa, do you accept?"

"Sure," she said sheepishly. "But what do I do?"

"Just keep everyone together. Promote that good old-fashioned unity you love so much. Keep the group strong and healthy. In the meantime, keep a close watch on Cadence's angelic signature. When you sense Cadence rushing into battle on Earth, I want you to bring Team Six and be ready for a difficult fight."

"Okay," she said, unsure of her job. "I'll do it."

"What do I do?" Farah asked.

"Farah, stay with Alessa. Don't go looking for Vergil. The same goes for Marcus and Amos. All of you are to stay put until Alessa knows it's time to go down."

"And what about you?" Amos asked. "Are you going down to Earth?" I sighed heavily.

"Unfortunately, but I'll be fine. Just make sure you all tend to your assignments, okay?"

"Sure," Amos said and Marcus grunted. I smiled at them all, and turned toward the door. I was sure they would follow my lead, and I left before they could ask me more. It was essential that their final thoughts of me were solely about my request and not worry over my safety.

To ensure the plan went perfectly, I would need their collective strength.

And their trust…

CHAPTER 14: Wise as Serpents

"But I'm his guardian," the Guard told me. Apparently, he hadn't been listening to my explanation as thoroughly as I had thought.

"I know," I said, leaning against the house. Back on Earth, there was no way an imp demon hadn't seen me and reported my arrival to Vergil. Every second I spent on the planet by myself was one second closer to my mission becoming unraveled and myself becoming subject to extreme pain... "How long have you been guarding Seth?"

"Over twenty years," the Guard said.

"And what's happened in that time? Any demons? Scouts?"

"Nothing."

"Do you know why? It's because most of them are off in that Battle of the East, still fighting for dominance."

"But I have to stay vigilant," he said. "No offense, but what happened with you and Team Six...I don't want that to happen to Seth."

"Me neither," I said, "but think about it. There were six of us, and there's only one of you. Do you really think you're ready to fight an Archangel?"

"Of course not, but I have faith that God will keep us safe."

"All I'm asking is that you take that faith and apply it to another matter."

"But what you suggest is very dangerous. Very, very, dangerous."

"It's been on Seth's mind since he was old enough to understand the story of Cain and Abel. And he's seen some of his sisters move to the east of the Garden personally. He's curious. One day he's going to investigate, whether you like it or not."

"But if Cain killed Abel all those years ago, what's to stop him from doing the same to Seth?"

"Cain was distraught over what he did, and he's been struggling with it ever since. He won't harm Seth. Besides, if there is a way Seth can reconcile with his brother, wouldn't that be an important blow to the demons? Their plan is to indoctrinate Cain and his people. That's a whole new threat that no one's concentrating on. A rekindling of the two families could put an end to it before it has room to take off."

"I see what you're saying…but where do I come in? Seth can go any time of his own free will."

"Increase your angelic pressure to its maximum level tomorrow morning at 8. Seth is following in Abel's footsteps, and he's sensitive to the spiritual realm. Have him follow you over the hills toward the Garden of Eden."

"You're not thinking of having him try to break in, are you?"

"No. But it will be neutral ground. Have him on the first hill beyond the Garden, heading toward the east"

"And you think this will work?"

"Confident."

"I hope you're right. It's putting Seth into some serious danger."

"Victor, he's in danger every day."

"Well said. Okay, I'll be there."

I left the house quickly, flying out towards the hills where Seth and Cain were to supposedly meet. It was the only way. I traveled until I was in the middle of the hilly valley, out of earshot of the Cherubims near Eden and Victor. I didn't need them to see this…

"HEY! DEMON SCOUTS!" I shouted out. At first, there was no response but I remembered when we had fought Vergil. Those scouts were hiding everywhere, camouflaged in everything you could think of. "C'MON, I KNOW YOU'RE HERE!"

One demon scout flickered into view, right at my feet. He chuckled and pointed at me as I rolled my eyes. I bent down so I wouldn't have to voice my message so loudly.

"We need to talk," I said. "I have a message for Vergil."

"For Vergil?" the imp demon said in shock. "Are you looking for trouble?"

"In a sense. I devised a plan to defeat Vergil once and for all, but I need the coward to actually show himself."

"That's bold of you," he said. "Why didn't you just pretend to be on his side and then stab him in the back?"

"Because that would be lying and besides, Vergil's smarter than that. It wouldn't work."

"No. I guess it wouldn't."

"Tell him I'll have Seth with me tomorrow morning at 8, in this valley. I told his guardian angel that Seth wants to make amends with Cain, which is true, but we're pushing the meeting along, you could say. However, I need Cain here in order for that to happen. I want to get Cain back into God's good graces but he needs to see Seth for anything to occur. You see the benefits for both of us. Vergil wants Seth dead. I want Cain to repent. This is an opportunity for both of us to fight over something we want."

"Well, I'll be curious to see who wins. I'll gladly pass the message along right away."

"Thank you," I said, and he vanished before my eyes, probably scurrying along the grass to his master.

The plans had progressed faster than expected, but that didn't matter. It was better to be safe than sorry. In the hours before our second meeting on Earth, I would search the database, making sure my plans were adequate, because this was it. Vergil was going to be furious once he figured out what I had in store and I couldn't wait for it all to unfold.

I made sure to say an extra prayer when morning arrived, asking God for His blessing and for Him to swiftly end the Battle of the East; and for Him to protect Seth, Cain and all the humans from the demons' clutches.

By the prayer's end, I could see Victor coming over the hill, with a confused but intrigued Seth following behind. Victor was at full strength, and looking out across the hills frantically, like he was a demon magnet. I laughed at his anxiety and asked him to tone it down and save it in case we had trouble.

Seth waited with us, sensing a change in the atmosphere, wondering what was going on. At a little past 8, looking like they had stepped out of a dream, we saw Cain and Vergil coming over the hill. Vergil was leading Cain the same way Victor had led Seth, and when the two brothers saw each other, their eyes widened in surprise. Neither said a word as they both moved closer but still kept a healthy distance.

"Cain, what are you doing here?" Seth asked, his shepherd's clothing causing a stir in his older brother. Cain took a gulp.

"I could ask you the same, brother."

"I always wanted to meet you."

"How do you know it's me?"

"Mother talks about you a lot...what you looked like, what a great son you were...I know what you did, but I always felt like I had to see you for myself. I just didn't think it would be so soon."

"Neither did I. I would like to see the family sometimes but...you know what I did. I can't ever return."

"That doesn't mean we can't have a relationship," Seth said. "Of course there will be boundaries, but we can see what we can do. Nothing is impossible with God!"

"This is disgusting," Vergil commented, speaking over the brothers' conversation. I turned my attention to him.

"How are you, Vergil? Isn't this interesting? Brothers meeting one another..."

"You seem quite smug," Vergil said, looking bored. I noticed he didn't bother making a grand entrance this time. "So what's your master plan?"

"It's already in place," I said quickly. "Where's Cadence?"

"Unconscious. What? Did you think that by having him become Cain's guardian, he'd become immune all of a sudden?"

"No...but I thought he would get stronger somehow..." I trailed off. "So how's the Battle of the East going?"

"Lysander, why are you trying to make small talk? What's your game? Are you stalling for Michael to arrive or something?"

"No. Nothing like that. As a matter of fact, my plan is already taking place," I waved a hand at the two brothers. They were still at a distance from each other, but they were laughing now, and speaking candidly as if they had grown up together. In actuality, I had never seen Cain look so happy to see a family member. He was older now, with a gray beard, and had a tilt to his walk, but now that tiredness was beginning to shake loose from his bones. He was beginning to feed off of his brother's vitality and remember a distant time when his mind had been at peace. That peace – the memory of it soothed him. It had to, for I knew myself how it felt. I had felt it upon my return to Heaven, and I was determined to get a slice of it on Earth.

"So they get some bonding time," Vergil said. "So what?"

"I thought it was strange that even when Cain murdered Abel, he was still given a guardianship," I said. "I figured that this was a great testament to the fact that he wasn't lost. I figured that by getting him and Seth together, I could bring him back into the fold, clear his name with his family, and convince him to turn to God."

"Oh," Vergil said. "Not bad...but that's not much of an endgame. I mean, all I have to do is this..."

"Lysander…" Victor warned me from a distance, but I waved him down. I left Vergil to his tricks. He leaned into Cain, whispering his evil, discussing how easy it would be to kill his brother. No witnesses. But Cain's eyes said it all. His murdering days were done. And as they widened, his lips pursed and a scowl grew across his face. He clenched his fists and Seth, seeing the display, began to take a step back. Victor was by his side in a second.

"Demon! I know your voice!!!" Cain shouted, and clutched his head. "I won't. I won't kill him!"

At these words, Seth began to step back further and Cain started pounding the ground in a rage. Vergil kept up his verbal assault, trying to soothe him, convince him it was the best thing to do, but I was right. Being on God's list meant there was hope. Something Vergil didn't have, and this infuriated him.

"What are you doing, Lysander?" Vergil shouted at me, taking a step forward as Cain began to calm down.

"Ruining your plans," I replied, "but I'm just getting started."

"Oh, are you?" Vergil mused, turning back to Cain and unsheathing his sword. "And does your plan include his death?"

"I don't want you to kill him," I said adamantly. "Just let Cain have his relationship with Seth. Let the human beings go. Fight your battles with us and leave them out of it."

"See that's the thing," Vergil spat at me. "We're not doing too well against you angels collectively. So forgive me, but we have to use the humans. Otherwise this Battle will be lost too."

"Then why can't you just put down your blade and come back? Why do you have to follow Satan?"

"What do you care?"

"Because I am, and always will be your friend," I said. "When it comes to salvation, nothing but relationship matters. Nothing. I relied on you so much when we were in Heaven and you didn't even know it.

I needed each of you – to help me, console me, save me, and that's fine, because that's what friends are for...but when you left, it broke my heart...because I couldn't believe life would just continue normally without the ones I'd been with from the beginning. But it did...and I've gotten stronger. I see now...none of us can save you. I can't even save me. Only God can help me, define me, give me purpose and victory in all that I do. When each of my friends deserted me, all I had was God to lift me up, and I realized that whatever mission I failed, I had God to answer to, not the others. And because of that, I have to take responsibility and do what I must. I feel for you, but if it was in your heart to serve God completely, you would've been saved. Period. God is full of compassion, and we judge Him for His decisions when we, as angels, demons, and humans, kill and fight each other for pettier reasons! The bottom line...is that if we perish, we are to blame, no one else. And I won't perish for you. So no more sympathy. No more sorrow. I cannot hold back any longer on you, for you are now my enemy and nothing more. And you decided that. You forced my hand. So when I found myself before God, alone and friendless, I embraced the gift He gave me, and with that tactical power, I will utterly defeat you today."

"No, Lysander. Not today," he laughed, and with a swiping motion, he cut Cain's throat. I closed my eyes for a second, to push back the wave of emotions struggling to break me, but I stuck to my plan. I had hoped it wouldn't come to this. I had hoped that Cain and Seth would be permanently reunited. But it appeared that we would have to do it the hard way.

I didn't want this part of the plan to happen...

But unbeknownst to Vergil, it was a part...

I opened my eyes, and I saw Cadence...hovering over Vergil. With wings spread and glowing with a force and brilliance as powerful as the sun, he poised over him, with his sword aimed downward, ready to strike. Vergil glanced up and saw him, but he couldn't move his body. A power, greater than each of us, kept him still, and no strength he possessed could break him free. In the last second, he looked at me, with hateful, fired-up eyes, wondering what was about to happen, trying to hold back the fear that quivered at the surface of his lips. And in reply, I whispered only one thing.

"Sevenfold."

And as the word left my mouth and drifted on my breath, Cadence struck. With the impact of a solar flare, Cadence slashed straight through Vergil. I couldn't see the details, but the spiritual explosion rocked the physical world. The hills shook like they were at the epicenter of an earthquake and the tectonic plates beneath were rumbling violently. Amongst the quaking and the blinding light, Vergil screamed, his pain soaring far beyond anything he had ever felt before.

God's curse upon Cain...was that anyone who took his life would be avenged sevenfold. Which meant...that as Cain's guardian angel, Cadence had just struck Vergil with seven times his maximum angelic pressure...

And that had to hurt. A lot.

Vergil had been a fool to think that this curse, this decree by God, applied only to the humans. As if he could casually take a human's life, one of God's creations, without consequence. How arrogant he was...

The whole valley was lit up under Cadence's power and when the light cleared, Vergil was on his knees, coughing and clutching the crown of his head where Cadence had struck. Cadence, with his God-given power now gone, wasn't glowing anymore, but that didn't mean he was about to stop. He struck Vergil over and over, hacking away at his demonic pressure until Vergil had to push him away with his own two hands. The wounded Archangel staggered to his feet and I caught Cadence in my arms, welcoming my friend back to the battlefield.

"You knew this would happen!" Cadence said excitedly, looking back at me. "You knew all along!"

"Don't get too excited yet. It's not over," I said. "I wish I could've used Marcus or Amos, but with Marcus's problem, I didn't know if he would lock up. There was also no way to tell if that power would deplete all of an angel's pressure. And we need all the Godhand power we can get, no offense."

"None taken!" Cadence laughed. "That was incredible!"

"You look well," I said and he patted me on the back.

"I'm sorry, Lysander. For everything. I hope you can forgive me."

"We'll have plenty of time to talk later. Heads up!"

Vergil rocketed toward us and tried to punch me in the face but Cadence met it with his shield at the last second, slapping Vergil's hand away. Vergil looked at his fist in surprise and Cadence decked him across the face with his armament, sending him rolling down the hill.

"I can't believe I just did that," Cadence laughed. I tried not to join in his excitement. I had to keep a clear head.

"Victor!" I yelled to him. "Get Seth out of here! We'll finish this!"

"Okay!" he shouted back, not wasting a minute in getting away. "Be safe!"

Vergil shot up from the bottom of the hill, enraged, staring at us like we were ants fighting a god.

"Do you think this is over?" he demanded, sounding frantic. "I have plenty of power left."

"Yes," I said, "but from what I can sense, it's been cut in half. I'll take half an Archangel any day."

"You can't win!" he roared - and then Marcus fell on top of him. Vergil cried out in rage as he was slammed into the grass below. Amos, Farah, and Alessa floated down, laughing hysterically.

"Sorry about that," Farah hiccupped, trying to stop crying. "It's not supposed to be funny. Marcus blacked out when we were descending and he kind of just fell down. I made sure I positioned him on top of whoever that is you're fighting."

"It worked out perfectly," I said. "He hit Vergil square on the head."

"You're fighting Vergil!?" she exclaimed in awe. "WOW! That doesn't feel like it's Vergil!"

"Correction. We're beating Vergil," I said confidently as, down below, Vergil threw Marcus off of him. "But listen, we have to work together from here on out. Just because he's in a weakened state doesn't mean we should take this blessing for granted."

"Right," Farah said, squeezing one of her biceps. Amos and Alessa nodded, waiting for my next order and patting Cadence on the back at the same time.

"Alessa," I said. "I want to try something new with you. Engage Vergil in battle, but pray while you fight. Amos will back you up. Farah, tend to Marcus. Cadence, you and I are going to wait and assess."

"Sure thing," Cadence said, watching as Alessa nervously unsheathed her sword.

"Don't be scared," Farah shouted to her. "Get your faith up!"

Alessa flew at Vergil who met her head on. But before his fist connected to her face, she ducked under it, keeping her sword parallel to the ground and slicing through Vergil's midsection as she passed by him. Vergil spun around so fast I barely saw him do it, but Amos had already used his body as a shield and enabled Alessa to escape. Marcus woke up and quickly joined in the action, stopping Vergil from hitting Amos by grabbing Vergil's cocked-back hand. Amos responded with a punch of his own and Alessa swooped in again for a slash. This continued on for a few minutes but I was quickly beginning to see a problem.

"Looks like part three of the plan is going to have to go into effect," I muttered. Cadence and Farah, who were standing next to me, looked over in surprise.

"How many parts are there?" Farah asked. "And why do we need them? They're doing great."

"No, they're not," I said firmly.

"They're getting tired," Cadence said and I nodded.

"Yes. Vergil still has a massive amount of energy, and though we have two things to our advantage, it won't last long. As an Archangel, he's never experienced pain like this. To have his pressure cut in half must be scaring him which is why his attacks had been sloppy ever since Cadence swooped in. But he's gaining confidence with each passing second. Also, his demonic pressure is going down, but much too slowly. Our friends will tire and level out with him before he reaches zero. That's not good."

"So what do we do?"

"We bring in Farah," I smiled. "I think it's time we see what you can really do."

"That's what I'm saying," she piped up. "Tell me the plan."

"Okay,' I said, then I whispered the plan as quickly as possible into her ear. After hearing it in full, she nodded and took off into space. Cadence chuckled as we continued to watch.

"So when do we jump in?"

"The last possible second," I said. "Oh, and while we're at it. I'm sorry for saying some hurtful things myself."

"No, Lysander," he said. "I was in the wrong. Any plan I had wouldn't have gotten us this far."

"We'll see," I said. "We're not out of this yet...so what did you experience over in Cain's camp that got you so optimistic?"

"I had plenty of time to think," he said. "And it's depressing over there. I can understand why Cain was so eager to reconcile with Seth. There was nothing for him in that city."

"Perhaps it's not too late for his family. Maybe when this is..."

I was interrupted as a loud smack cracked across the valley. Vergil had gotten a good hit in on Amos and the Godhand was falling fast.

With only two instead of three to contend with, Vergil was gaining confidence by the second.

"You ready?" I asked Cadence. "Because we have to go now!"

As Vergil reached for an elusive Alessa, I zipped in front of him, hovered up quickly and kicked him in the face. It didn't hurt him, but he was furious with all I had done so far, so he ignored Marcus and Alessa completely, in order to get me. Vergil almost wrapped his hand around my ankle when Cadence appeared and slammed him backwards with his shield. I didn't look back. I took to the skies, rocketing up with all my strength.

I heard more loud smacks below and soon after, the sound of Vergil calling as he chased after me. Using a massive amount of energy, he caught up far too quickly, and at first I was afraid my strategy wouldn't work, but he missed an important grab of my leg at the last millisecond and I sped upward once more. It was funny how it reminded me of our race in the past, flying to the Throne Room, through the stars…and now I was trying to get away, to avoid being angelically murdered.

I slowed down just enough for him to catch up by about a foot and, with that calculation carried out, I gave my speed one last boost. Clearing Earth's atmosphere, I came to a full stop, and Vergil, with his bloodlust screaming from his eyes and throat, reached forward to end my life.

But his fist did nothing.

Because it hit a wall…an invisible barrier specially made for demons…

I had taken a chance on this, and it was only after much speculation and database searching that I had come to this conclusion – that unless God allowed it, the demons were stuck on Earth. For why would a demon ever want to go back to Heaven? And even if they did, it would only be to ruin the place. Surely God had a contingency plan for this, and there were probably a few demons that had tried to break through the barrier on occasion. But Vergil, in all his anger, had forgotten about it, and that was good. Because I needed him to be momentarily off guard.

Farah zipped past me as I waved goodbye to my old friend, and she slammed into Vergil's breastplate with her little body and held on with all her might. I had told Farah her part in my plan early enough that she had enough time to not only get into the atmosphere, but to also gather her faith – her greatest strength.

And now, Farah was pushing an Archangel down to the Earth at neck-breaking speeds, scaring Vergil out of his mind for his demonic pressure had gotten quite low already. I could've had her punch his lights out, but we had to make sure he stayed down. And besides, she had been training for this.

The target: the flaming sword of Eden.

Pushing, pushing, pushing, she rocketed down like a shooting star, until Vergil saw where she was headed. He fought back at the last second, expending the last of his energy to push her away, but it was too late. They hit the end of the sword with an explosion rivaling that of Cadence's. Anton and Synon shrieked in fear and ran toward the hills as lights of all colors shot out into the sky and across the valley, riding the winds like invisible roller coasters.

Farah emerged almost immediately, rushing toward us like she had done this a million times, yelling out of complete thrill and joy.

"GUYS! I TOUCHED IT!" she screamed. The end of her sentence was washed out by another flash explosion. She was swept forward and Cadence caught her.

The six of us stood in the dead valley, waiting for Vergil to emerge, but there were at least three more explosions that followed before we saw any sign of him.

Finally, we spotted him. Unable to stay on his feet, he crawled like a toddler, falling flat onto his face and getting back up again, only to fall once more. He did this continuously, reaching for us, but his body was flickering wildly. I could already sense it. He would be done in a matter of minutes. His dwindling pressure was on a steep decline and the end of the line was near. Eventually, he fell over onto his back and lay there, breathing heavily. The flaming sword shone a little brighter than usual, but then it went back to normal, allowing us to see his defeat in all its glory.

Anton and Synon began wildly screaming at us about our crazy spectacle, but when they saw us hovered over our foe, they quieted down. We surrounded the fallen Archangel in a circle, keeping a foot or so away from him in case he tried anything.

"It looks like this is it, Vergil," I said. "We've won, old friend."

"Stop," he began laughing, coughing and closing his eyes. "Just stop...stop calling me Vergil. My name is Pride..."

"No. I won't," I said. "I'll remember you as God created you."

"So righteous now..." he groaned and chuckled.

"Goodbye Vergil," Cadence said. Vergil's eyes shot open and he glared at Cadence. The red on his body flickered like lights. As he continued to stare at Cadence, the lights began to burst into flames until his skin looked almost ablaze. He was using the last of his demonic pressure to send a message.

"Now...do you really think this is over, Cadence? No...this is a beginning. You were nothing before...only I knew your potential. But now they will come. All of them. All six of them. They will hunt you, and put you down like dogs. You will see everyone you know suffer. You will diiiiiiiiiiiiiiiiiiiiiiiiiiiiiiiiieeeeeeeeeeeeee."

With his last breath, Vergil closed his eyes, and the flames went out.

And darkness...covered his face like a shroud.

We stood there silently, the breeze feeling cool against our bodies and the quiet giving us a much needed respite. I waved to Anton and Synon.

"If you don't mind, we'll tell you the whole story a little later."

"Don't care," Anton replied. "Just go."

"Go get some rest and come back!" Synon replied. Anton slapped a hand on one of his foreheads. Amos picked up Vergil's lifeless body.

"What do we do with him?" he asked.

"Bring him to the deepest part of the ocean," I said, "and leave him floating there. From the damage his body's taken, it will be a very long time before he wakes up. I left a message with Raphael to send a clean-up crew to that location. They'll know what to do with him. "

"Okay. I'll dispose of him immediately."

"So what now?" Alessa asked me. We were all in good health and had just had an incredible victory. Honestly, I was quite tired.

"Ask Cadence," I laughed. "He's the leader. I'm done being in charge, forever."

The group looked to Cadence for the answer to Alessa's question and Cadence gave a content smile.

"We go home," he declared.

And it was the best decision he'd ever made.

CHAPTER 15: Harmless as Doves

"NO! NO! NO!" Marcus bellowed. "She cheated!"

I shook my head in disbelief as Farah crept up behind him, struggling not to giggle. We were in the solar system to the right of Raphael's hall, playing a game of galaxy tag. One of the rules was that we weren't supposed to hide in stars because their light was so bright, it was hard for us to see through them. Marcus was confident that Farah had flown through one right when he was about to grab her. It would have been the first time he would have caught someone, and the first time he would have finally been on the other end of the game and got to see what it was like. You see, he was it.

He was always it.

Even when it was a random draw, he somehow ended up being it. Only God knew the answers to such mysteries…

"Guess who!" Farah squealed as she covered Marcus's eyes from behind him. Marcus roared.

"LYSANDER!"

"I'm right here," I said flatly. With eyes still covered, he grabbed me and pulled me close.

"No. HELP."

"Oh!" I said. I went behind him and pulled Farah off his head. She giggled as I held her in my arms.

"Okay," Marcus said, turning around. "Now hold. Tight. I punch."

"Whoa!" I said, letting her go. Farah zipped around his head like a fly and he swatted at her lazily.

"Is anyone going to come looking for us?" Alessa cried, showing up with Cadence. "Seriously, I've been hiding in the same spot for an hour."

"There were some complications," I replied as Marcus roared again.

"CHEAT!"

"If you want me to," Farah giggled.

"NO! I HATE THAT GAME!" Marcus bellowed. "YOU CHEATED!"

"Wow," Alessa said. "I'm impressed."

"I think he filled his quota for the year," Farah giggled again. Marcus swung at her. She flipped upside down and floated out of harm's way.

"You didn't cheat, did you?" I asked her. She scowled at me. "A moon is not the same as a star, so no, I did not cheat."

"I think we have to revise the rules," I muttered. Just then, we heard someone calling from Raphael's doorway. We looked over in the distance to see Raphael calling for me to go and see him.

"Well, it's been fun," I said. "I'll meet you all at the Café."

"See ya! You better be there too!" Alessa declared. Cadence smiled and waved at me. I noticed his smile was warmer than usual.

"Bye!" Farah waved. Marcus tried to punch her in the back of the head. She caught his arm and judo-flipped him again, leaving him floating in a somersault. As I left the group, I overheard someone ask how Amos could be so good at the game when he's as big as a house, and I just had to laugh the entire flight to Raphael.

"Had fun?" he asked as I stepped into the familiar territory.

"Tried. But we were bonding, and that counts."

"Good. Good," he said. "Is it too soon to talk about Vergil?"

"Talk about him all you want!" I laughed. "After all, I kind of helped take him down."

"Kind of? You orchestrated the whole thing."

"I'm trying to live up to your old lessons on pride."

"Good," he chuckled. "I didn't want to hear your lame story on how you executed the plan anyway." I followed him down the hall, walking slowly as we talked.

"So are you okay, Lysander? Honestly."

"Perfect. I think I'm finally free of that burden."

"It's part of growing up."

"I imagine so."

"Do you know what else is a part of growing up?"

"I'm already scared."

"Responsibilities," he said, pointing forward. "Ulysses, can you come forward?"

I looked ahead and watched as a tall and toned angel in a long white robe stepped out from where Raphael's global room was. He shyly looked at us and then back down at the floor, biting his lip.

"Nice to meet you, Ulysses," I called out to him. He looked up and smiled warmly, stepping toward us and reaching out a hand. I took it and shook it firmly and genuinely.

"And nice to see you again, Lysander," he said. "You're different from how I remember you...stronger I think."

"We've met?" I asked, very bewildered.

"Ulysses was on the island with you," Raphael explained. "He remembers your time together. He has been in Heaven since the war, but he just never had the courage to step forward and introduce himself formally to you."

"On the island?"

"You sat next to me for three hours," Ulysses said shyly. "And I remember hearing you talk to the shroud about Heaven and how you didn't want to leave without your friends. Those words stayed with me…and eventually, I was able to fight through."

"You were Absent?"

"Unfortunately, yes…but the fact that you stayed with me, even for that little bit of time, made me want more than to just be lost in the mental database. I realized that…I needed a friend like you…"

"Well, you got one!" I replied, shaking his hand again. "My friends are headed to the Café as we speak. Want to join?"

"Of course!" Ulysses replied and I turned to Raphael.

"Is that all?" I asked. He laughed.

"Yes. You don't have to be a mentor or anything. Just show him a good time. Oh yes, and he also happens to be an Archangel. Hope you don't mind."

"Raphael, I don't mind one bit. If anything, I probably need him just as much as he needs me," I said, patting my mentor on the shoulder. I snapped my hand back as soon as I realized what I was doing, remembering that Raphael didn't like to be touched, and turned quickly to my new Archangel friend. "Ulysses, you've just become friends with the coolest Messenger in Heaven. Let me show you the sights!"

Ulysses followed me happily as I ranted on and gave him advice, asked him if he liked arm wrestling competitions, and told him not to mind Marcus if he challenged him to a fight. I informed him to not be afraid to yell back at Alessa, to occasionally accept one of Amos's hugs and to never, ever, ever accept a challenge from Farah. Finally, I told him that we had a great leader who just loved to be woken up by a cannonball on the stomach…

Fun was about to ensue, and Ulysses had no idea.

I was just there for the ride.

And so, I stopped worrying and decided to shut off my over-analytical mind for a little while, just to enjoy myself…

I didn't care about demons or Satan, the raging Battle of the East, or why the Café was somehow better than the Fellowship Hall all of a sudden. I forgot all about bickering and arguments, grudges, betrayals, and the war in Heaven. I left shyness, worry, fear, and depression to the side. My Lord, I forgot about Vergil, and for the first time in my life, I completely went absent...of negativity. I was going to have some much deserved fun with the greatest group an angel could ask for and enjoy new adventures with my latest friend Ulysses. I was going to race through the stars and laugh at Alessa's house, beat Marcus in an eating competition, and try to survive the black hole with Farah. I was determined to make Raphael laugh at a joke by next year and to personally pray more than ever before.

I was going to have fun.

Because everything was right, perfect, and restored...and I had all the time in the world to worry about those things I had no control over.

But for now?

For now, I was on a very long vacation.

And I figured that sometimes...

Sometimes...immortality can equal eternal bliss...

But just sometimes....

Angels and the Ark

Book III

"But he that is greatest among you shall be your servant. And whosoever shall exalt himself shall be abased; and he that shall humble himself shall be exalted.

—Matthew 23:11-12

"Even a child is known by his doings, whether his work be pure, and whether it be right."

—Proverbs 20:11

Prologue

Before the creation of the Earth,

God created the islands.

Small testing grounds that new angels were taken to after birth.

Those that passed their tests were allowed into Heaven.

Others...became the Absent: angels who couldn't handle the pressure, and therefore found solace only in their mental databases—the internal encyclopedia given to all angels when they are created.

One particular group of angels passed the tests and entered Heaven, just as war began.

They were Cadence—the Guard, and their leader,

Lysander—the messenger, the tactician,

Alessa—the Glory, with an inseparable connection to God,

Marcus, the Godhand, the muscle,

Vergil, the Archangel,

And Farah, the Faithful.

Together, they created a formidable team that fought against the charismatic Lucifer and his army of angels. Unfortunately, before the war was over, Vergil was persuaded by Lucifer's words, and in the end, he betrayed his teammates.

Lucifer and his army were banished from Heaven...along with Vergil.

Vergil was gone, however, he was not forgotten. Though human begins were soon revealed to the angels, and guardianships were developed, Lysander couldn't accept his friend's fate—believing that Vergil could still be saved...

As Lysander began to neglect his guardianship duties in order to search for answers, Team Six begins to fracture amidst the growing demon threat.

Mistrust and uncertainty starts to affect their friendships.

Marcus begins to lose consciousness on occasion and no one knows why.

Cadence—over fear of losing his friends, begins to make decisions that just creates more problems. Alessa is not getting the answers they need from God.

And when Vergil finally appears, Team Six is broken. Cain and Abel are murdered under their watch, and they are defeated in battle.

A former archangel is too much for them to handle.

But Lysander is not ready to give up. While most of Heaven's angels are on Earth, fighting the demons in the great Battle of the East, Lysander prepares to face Vergil one more time.

He creates a master plan, and Team Six executes it beautifully. Team Six defeats the archangel Vergil—boosting their morale, and gaining even more respect in Heaven.

But there is little time to celebrate.

Before losing consciousness, Vergil tells them of six other demons—stronger than he—that will soon come to hunt them down.

The Battle of the East has still not been concluded.

And as the war between angel and demon intensifies, man is caught in the middle.

Team Six has a lot of work to do.

If they have any hope of surviving the incoming flood...

Chapter 1 – Reflection

Without a reflection, I'm not sure how I can examine my flaws.

The humans can do it every day, and sometimes, they're not even trying to see who they really are. It just happens.

While heading down to the stream to wash their clothes, or evaluating their land after a torrential downpour, they catch a glimpse—in a puddle, in the stream itself—their reflection is always there to greet them, speaking in volumes of their current condition. They never keep going with the task that they set out to do.

They always stop, even if it's for a moment.

The vain might run their fingers through their hair or wipe the grime from their face. Those that lost loved ones—either through sickness or worse—just stare back at themselves, wondering when the sorrow in their eyes would cease to exist. When their eyes would sparkle and shine again, and match the forced smile coming from their pursed lips.

I imagine that my visage must have looked similar to them—those filled with sorrow.

But once again, I have no reflection. So there's no way for me to know for sure.

My friends could tell me, if I asked. But I was tired of asking questions. Lately, I haven't liked the answers.

"Your face is going to get stuck like that!" Farah screamed behind me. I flew up about a foot up into the air and hunched forward, so that her fist would catch the surface of the bronze shield strapped onto my back. Though there was little force behind her punch, I propelled myself forward anyway, falling down to the row of abandoned houses below. I could hear her suck her teeth above me, but I stifled a chuckle. I was sure she knew what I was doing.

I crashed into one of the houses, located on the third ring of Heaven. My eyes were closed, but I knew immediately when I hit the gold floor. It rippled on impact, like I had landed onto a waterbed. I yawned and stretched out my limbs. I turned my face onto its side and laid there on the floor, closing my eyes and waiting for Alessa to inevitably ruin my rest.

On cue, a slender hand grabbed the back of my collar and yanked me to my feet. Alessa's face was scrunched up and she was scowling so hard that her eyebrows looked like they were going to fuse together. I bit my lip to cut off a laugh, but it was too late. A small chirp escaped my lips, and she cocked back a fist to hit me in the face. I didn't budge. I just waited for it. Who knows? Maybe I would get another three second nap in.

But she didn't hit me.

She didn't even yell.

Her face softened, and her body relaxed as she let go of me. I just stared at her as she studied me. I looked around me absentmindedly, examining the bare walls and floors. They were all made of gold, and they shone magnificently, but for some reason, it was like the hue had been dimmed. They didn't shine as brightly as they once had. *Would I see my reflection in their shiny surface?* The thought bounced off the walls of my mind, but before I could dwell further on the matter, I already had my answer. Of course, it wasn't the one I wanted.

I was a spirit. So the answer was a resounding no. I was invisible to all but other spirits. *But wasn't all of Heaven spiritual? Wasn't it the same composition? So why couldn't I see my face in the rivers? Why did God leave this out?*

"Snap...*out of it*," Alessa said in disgust. "What is wrong with you?"

"I'd rather not talk about it," I said, as I heard the voices of my other teammates flying down to rendezvous with us.

"So when?"

"When what?"

"When do you want to talk about what's going on?"

"Um…how about when cell phones are created on Earth." We had all talked about that particular invention in depth many times. Lysander had discovered the concept while delving into his database and he was thinking about coming up with a version for Heaven. Though we could talk to one another at any time, regardless of distance, it was only when God allowed it. Otherwise, we had to wait until we were in each other's presence, or wait for a messenger to give us some news. An angel's version of a cell phone would come in handy, but I wasn't sure what to think of Lysander's idea. Everything was spiritual. We couldn't just create human technology, and most of all, God had not created such a device or method for us. If it was necessary, it would be in Heaven already.

And I wasn't about to start trying to create things that God didn't want us to have. That's how discontent began. That was how angels began thinking that they didn't need God, and started questioning why he wasn't just giving us everything we wanted from the beginning. That was how war broke out in Heaven.

I had a job to do…well, I *had* a job to do. Either way, I was going to do what I was designed to do. Anything else was either counterproductive or detrimental to God's plans.

"Cell phones?" Alessa scoffed. "That's when you're ready to talk? Do you have any idea how long from now that is?"

"Exactly," I winked at her. I tried to flash her a smile, but she wasn't buying it. She just crossed her arms across her grey and purple armor. Her face remained expressionless as the others arrived, gliding down around us.

"What's going on?" Farah asked, her tiny wings flitting so fast that I could barely see them move. She was small and petite, as most Faithful were, but she was certainly more rambunctious than any I had ever met. Even though she had the same dragonfly wings and long, lightning green hair as other members of her class, she was recognizable all throughout Heaven for her fiery spirit and insane strength. The Faithful's power lied in their faith in God, and Farah had more than enough for our entire team. She might punch you in the arm as hard as she could and it could barely register a feeling, but don't you dare make fun of her for it. The next punch will send you into the next century.

"Cadence is having another one of his moments," Alessa sighed.

"He's probably too hurt from that punch I gave to his back," Farah said, bobbing her head up and down. I kept my mouth shut.

"No, he's just trying to get out this training session."

"I'm confused, did the training begin?" Lysander said, scratching his head.

"*Thank you!*" I exclaimed, throwing my hands up in the air. "That's what I'm wondering! We've been sparring for an hour, but there's no direction. We might as well just be flailing at the air."

"I was," Marcus huffed, crossing his arms across his massive Godhand chest. "Farah so fast I got whiplash. Neck hurt like Lysander's."

"What are you talking about now?" Lysander raised an eyebrow at him. Marcus pointed at the messenger angel slowly, as if he was about to declare death upon him.

"Your neck hurt...because your head...BIG."

Lysander just sighed and closed his eyes, but Farah fell onto her back, holding her stomach as she cackled. A smug smile came upon Marcus' face as he stretched out the palm of his right hand toward Alessa.

"What?" she asked, just staring at it. "You want a cookie or something?"

"It's high-five," Marcus said, with his hand still out. "You take your—yes. Yes, I want cookie." Alessa rolled her eyes, and I couldn't help but chuckle. I wish I hadn't, because their attention was immediately drawn back to me.

"So it's my leadership that you have a problem with?" Alessa asked me. Before she even finished her sentence, the room fell deathly silent. I didn't take my gaze off of her.

"You are a fine leader," I said. "Many of your ideas have boosted the morale of the team. That's more than I've done. I'm happy with what you've done. I just think that if we're going to have a sparring session, we should know what we're supposed to be focusing on."

"I would give the leadership back to you whenever you like," she said in a small voice. I just shook my head.

"I don't want it. Not after what I did."

"Did what?" Lysander asked me, placing a hand on my shoulder. "Cadence, don't tell me you're talking about Vergil again. We went over this. I thought you understood that the only reason I fought you and implemented that plan was because it was the only way to beat him. I wouldn't have used you otherwise."

"I should have listened to your input and followed your lead from the beginning."

"I was all over the place," he sighed. "There was no reason to trust me."

"Well, Alessa's doing a fine job," I said, my eyes still fixed upon hers.

"No," she said, bowing her head and rubbing her arm. "You're right about what you said earlier. There's no direction. I have no clue what I'm doing. I'm just going with whatever pops into my head."

"At least you're keeping us all together."

"Hey," Lysander said, "where is Amos anyways? He said that he was going to be late, but he should have been here by now."

"The rivers," Marcus gruffed. "Amos still at rivers...probably."

"What's he doing there?" I asked, but Marcus just shrugged his shoulders.

"He needs one of us," Alessa said, rubbing her forehead. "I just received the message from God."

"Just one of us?" Farah replied. "Not all of us?"

"No. Just one."

"Then I'll go," I spoke up, already beginning to stretch out my wings. "I'll talk to him."

"And then you'll be back?" Alessa asked, her eyes pleading.

"I'm not sure."

"We'll wait for you."

"No, no," I said, giving her a smile. "Go on without me. Have fun."

"Fun isn't going to fix this," she said. "We have to work this out. What we did down there on Earth all those years ago...we defeated an archangel. *An archangel in demon form*, Cadence. No one in Heaven has done that yet, not even Michael. From the little bit that we hear, the Battle of the East is still raging on, and it shows no signs of stopping. They *need* us, but we're not going anywhere until we get clearance from Raphael."

"And that's not going to happen," Lysander said, "until we're all working as a unit again. That includes all of us. Not most."

"I'm not ready to go back into battle," I said.

"But why?" Lysander asked me, seeking understanding. I could see him searching my face, analyzing my body language for signs of my problems, but none would appear. Besides Marcus, I was the most reserved out of them all. I had to be. Though no one had ever said it, I *was the leader.*

Even with Alessa taking the reins temporarily, I knew that I would be forced to step up again one day, and I wasn't ready for that. I would fight it as long as possible, because I wasn't going to be responsible for the loss of anyone else, ever again, whether it was angel, demon, or human.

Sure, Alessa was doing well with the team—everyone was laughing again, and there were times in which it felt like the old days, but we were still in Heaven, where no harm could come to us. There were no wars or opposition. There was just peace and majestic beauty. Not a single reminder of the blood and violence galaxies away. With so many years having passed, I'm surprised that they remembered Earth at all, and that they were so eager to go back.

Didn't they remember the Garden of Eden? Cain and Abel? How strong and powerful Vergil was? We had defeated him, but according to Vergil, there were more coming for our heads, and those demons would stop at nothing to get to us, even if it meant destroying the lives of every human we came across...every angel we got close to. We could never again be guardian angels without a gigantic target on us.

Since the islands, for every victory, there were also profound losses. And with each loss, the weight grew heavier upon my shoulders. I didn't want to take my team for granted, but their jobs were focused and narrow when it came to carrying out missions.

Lysander, my tern-winged, tactical friend, got to stay back in battle and watch. He rarely participated, and therefore, there was a disconnect between what he saw was happening and what it *felt* like.

Alessa was a Glory, and therefore, she was always in communication with God. No matter what happened, her faith could not waver, for our Master was always right by her side. She couldn't see past his radiant light into the darkness that flooded the hearts of demon and man.

Farah's faith was borderline blinding. Though it was her greatest strength, it was also a horrible weakness. She couldn't relate to the suffering she witnessed. She was only affected when her own shortcomings rose to the surface.

Marcus was mighty and strong, but his mind was simple. He only thought of one thing at a time, so how could he ever know what a leader had to mull over? Amos was no different.

They just didn't know what it was like, and I didn't hold it against them. I knew that they were waiting for me, wondering when I would finally come to my senses, but that was the problem. I could see all too clear. There would be much suffering before there was relief. Our team had a great record, but only when one looked at the win column.

"Why aren't you ready for battle?" Lysander said again, and I turned to him with what I could only guess were weary and exhausted eyes.

"Because there's too much at stake," I said. He shook his head. He didn't understand. I continued. "When I was Cain's guardian…I saw just how much we were alike. Not that I had a propensity to violence, but that we both carried the burdens of those around us. In the land of Nod, there was little order. He was a father to all, and yet respected by none. His people would press him for a decision in matters, yelling in his face how he was to be a provider, but then, behind their back, they would curse his name, wondering why they couldn't enjoy the fertile land that the descendants of Seth enjoyed.

"They wanted to kill Seth and his family so bad. They figured, why not? Cain had already killed Abel. But Cain kept them at bay. He denied them. He did the right thing, but the burdens of the people were still too great for him. He would drown his sorrows in wine or flesh, he would rent his clothes and hurt himself. He was troubled until the day he died."

"But we're not pressing you," Alessa replied. "We're here to help. We just need you to trust us."

"It has nothing to do with trust now," I said. "It's just the reality of things. When I'm asked to make a decision, I try to do what's best for everyone involved, but that's not always the case. And when things go bad, I'm the one that has to deal with the choices that were made.

You all perform your jobs wonderfully, but I haven't. I'm a Guard. That's my class, yet all I've done is succeeded in getting you all hurt."

"We're not—"Alessa began, but I cut her off.

"—if we go out there," I said, pointing behind me. "There will be losses. There will be suffering. It's fortunate that after all we've been through so far that we've *only* lost Vergil. I wouldn't be able to take it if I lost any of you…so *no*, I'm not ready for battle. I want to stay here, and be lazy, and eat, and relax, and just have some fun. I don't want to be a leader anymore."

"What are you saying?" Lysander said. "You're going to quit?"

"No, I'm saying that I'm not going to be the leader again. I know you all are waiting for me to take over, but it's not going to happen. Now you can all stay here in Heaven with me, or you can fight. If you leave, I won't stop you. You would all be better warriors under someone else anyways."

"You can't just stay here forever," Farah said. I turned to her.

"I'll try. As long as I don't do anything, I won't be fit for war."

"But they might need us over in the Battle of the East."

"They might, but I won't know for sure."

"We could help turn the war in our favor!"

"Or make it worse."

"Cadence," Alessa said, catching me by surprise and hugging me. "We're not going anywhere without you. We need you."

"Alessa's right," Lysander said, as Marcus nodded. "We're a team, and if that means you need centuries, that's what it's going to take. Besides, I could use a little more time in the Archive Building."

"And what if it takes longer than centuries? What if I never come around?"

"Oh, I doubt that will happen," Farah laughed, slapping me on the butt. With her being so short, it was the furthest up she could reach. "Trouble has a way of finding us."

"Truth," Marcus stated, and I had to chuckle at that.

"But before you start napping for years on end," Alessa said, letting me go, "why don't you carry out your last task. Amos still needs someone to talk to."

"Right," I said. "I will. I'll see you guys later?"

"Of course," Alessa smiled. She was worried about me, and I knew that we would be having another conversation later about what we just talked about, but that was okay. I knew she was just worried about me.

"Bye!" Farah waved to me as I began floating out of the hole I created. The others waved at me as well, and I gave them all a smile. Before they were out my sight, I saw Marcus grab Farah by the head and throw her through one of the side walls. I shook my head and continued on.

The plains were located in the 1st ring of Heaven, right next to the homes of the angels in the 2nd, so it wasn't that far at all, and I could have transported there in a second, but I found myself lazily flying there. My mind wandering as it tended to do.

My thoughts once again turned to Cain. My only sole guardianship. After he had been killed by Vergil, I thought that I would be relieved to be free from my job, but I was actually saddened by it. Even though I was just there to watch him, I felt like maybe my presence would have some kind of effect on him, like a parent watching over a child.

But it wasn't so.

He was haunted by his own internal demons to the bitter end.

And even though he tried to do right by his people, he didn't have the effect I had hoped he would on them. I returned to the Land of

Nod only once after Cain's death, and it was the last time I had gone to Earth since.

They were all unorganized and unsure of what to do next. Leaders were elected. Families were restructured. Some moved from Nod, some stayed. But one common denominator was present. That fact that not one was ready to adopt the philosophies of Cain.

Not one sought to adhere to his wishes of maintaining peace and order with their surrounding neighbors and each other. Before I left for good, I saw a boy, only eleven, talking with his father by their tent.

The boy had asked him, with sand blowing into his eyes, if they should be nice to their neighbors like Cain wanted. After all, they had been nice to *them*, and there were no signs of hostility. In fact, there might even be hope of forming some kind of truce. Imagine the possibilities! The people of Nod could indulge in their relatives' fertile lands and eat of their crop while they helped with the workload or provided other services.

His father turned to the boy, slapped him hard across the cheek, and told him to spit those thoughts out of his head right away, especially if he wanted to keep all of his teeth. When the boy quieted down from his sobbing, his father stooped down to his level, looked him in the eye, and said:

"We can't act on the word of a murderer."

And there it was.

The final word.

It didn't matter if Cain's notions were right or wrong, all that mattered was what *he had done in the past.*

Once I heard those words, I knew I couldn't return to Earth. Because I knew it was only a matter of time before I was shunned just like Cain had been. I've seen Michael, Gabriel, Raphael and the other leaders of Heaven. They had no friends. No teammates. No personal time. It was just the job. That's what being a leader got you.

Suffering and Loneliness.

I still had my friends, I could still relax in the fields of the 1st ring and enjoy my mansion in the 2nd. I could laugh and play and eat until my spirit began to waver at the fellowship hall. I hadn't lost those privileges yet, and if I continued down the path my friends wanted of me...all of those wonderful things would be taken away.

What was the new phrase Alessa had learned from the mental database?

Ah yes. That's what it was.

I'm not having it.

Chapter 2 – Beside the Still Waters

Amos was sitting in the grass with his legs crossed, gazing into the stream a few inches in front of him. It wasn't hard to find him since Heaven had been quite empty lately, and he *was* a Godhand. I could see his massive frame and bald head shining from a mile away.

I'm sure he noticed me approaching, but he didn't look up. He just stared into the river, contemplating. I sat down next to him and waited for him to speak first. If Alessa had gotten a message from God that Amos needed someone, then it had to be serious. I just hoped that I was the right angel for the job.

"It's so peaceful here," Amos said, sticking a finger into the water. I looked around me and took in Heaven's wonders. The shooting stars weren't moving as fast at the moment, and so I was able to see their brilliance in more detail. The black hole in the distance was spiraling slowly as well, and I could barely see it from where I sat.

Heaven's buildings and mountains were shining so brightly that even the black hole couldn't take their light. The grass beneath me tickled my fingers as a cool breeze rubbed our backs. I smiled and turned to the Godhand.

"But are you peaceful?" I asked. Look at me. I was already getting into that *mode* again—where I would listen to the plights of my friends and seek out a solution. As long as the solution didn't involve perusing the mental database. Was that why I was the unofficial leader of Team Six? Because I found myself trying to solve the problems of others?

"I don't know, brother," Amos replied, reaching out to pat me on the back with his meaty hand. "I can't stop thinking about things lately. I should probably take on another guardianship. Keep myself busy."

"What was the last one you had?"

"Enoch," he said. "God had me and this other angel named Tora watch over him. Since the humans have been living for so long now, I figured that it would keep me occupied for a long time."

"Well, at least you're back with us now," I said. He turned to me with a saddened expression.

"The reason I wanted such a long guardianship is *because* I didn't want to come back. Wasn't looking forward to what I knew I had to do."

"What do you mean? Did something terrible happen to Enoch?"

"No, no," he said, shaking his head. "Enoch is more than fine. Matter of fact, God just took him one day."

"Took him," I chuckled. "What does that mean?"

"I don't know. One moment he was there, just going for a walk, and a second later, he vanished, like he had never existed. I was out of sorts, Cade. I thought a demon had gotten past me and killed him somehow. Never got over what happened between Cain and Abel."

"I don't think any of us have…but you said God took Enoch?"

"Yeah, a messenger had to tell me. Of course it was Dan delivering the news, so it took a few minutes for him to actually explain. I got no clue what God is doing with Enoch right now. All I know is that he's no longer under my care. I've been hoping that it's not something I did. You know, like I wasn't the right guardian."

"I'm sure it had nothing to do with you," I said, placing a hand on his shoulder. "I've heard a couple of things about Enoch up here in Heaven. I heard he was really close to God, and that's rare these days. Maybe God just decided to prepare him for something greater. You remember Abel. He was just a little boy when he defeated that demon on our behalf. Maybe God knows that he needs certain humans to help with the Battle of the East."

"Perhaps," Amos smiled. Then he let out a loud guffaw. "Cade, you really know how to make an angel feel special, don't ya?"

"I'm just here to help," I said, giving him a big smile.

"Well, since we're talking privately, I might as well be up front with you. I'm going to be leaving Team Six." His words didn't surprise me at all. And I couldn't blame him. We were just a bunch of individuals still holding onto the hope that we could be a team again. This moment was inevitable, and I was sure that it wouldn't be the last.

"What are you going to do instead?" I asked calmly. His jaw dropped in shock.

"You're not upset?"

"Not at all. I completely understand."

"It's just that we're not moving forward, Cade. If you think about it, we're kind of moving backwards. Not saying that the battle with Vergil or losing Abel wasn't traumatic. No angel in Heaven would say otherwise, but time is moving quick, and the humans need us. We were made to help them, and that's what I intend on doing."

"Don't worry about us," I said, looking back to the shooting stars. "We'll figure it all out eventually. You do what you have to."

"Can I give you some advice?"

"Sure."

"Don't give up on yourself. Even if you don't feel like it, and you think you'll do a horrible job...you owe it to the rest of Team Six to try and make it work."

"But I could get another human killed in the process," I winced, looking at him face to face. "Or one of them could be captured or knocked unconscious for years. I don't want that on my conscience."

"Then take it slow. Think about going to the Battle of the East. You don't have to lead. Just help out there. You all are too talented to be sitting here."

"Look who's talking," I laughed.

"Just think about it, boss," he replied, and I shook my head.

"Not anymore, Amos. Not the boss anymore." He winked at me and then stood to his feet. "I think I'll go to the Mission Center and see what's available. Care to join me?"

"No, thanks," I said. "I think I'll stay right here for a little bit. Some angel might come out of nowhere and help me sort out the mess in my head."

"Stranger things have happened," he said. And then he was off, taking flight with his massive wings. I watched him as he headed out over the houses, the mountains and into the core of Heaven where all the major buildings stood. I thought about lying down in the grass, but I knew it wouldn't solve anything.

As soon as I got back up, I would be no closer to feeling better. Maybe I just needed to talk more with the group. Have a little more fun. Who knows? Maybe I would find a new role for myself within the team, and Alessa might step up even further. Just because she did things that I disagreed with, it didn't mean that what she was doing was wrong.

My eyes wandered around the majestic view in front of me, and I found myself looking back at the black hole. A twinkle of light flashed from its midst, and I sat up in confusion. I frowned as I squinted my eyes, trying to figure out what it was when the twinkle reappeared. *What was that?*

Then it went off *again*, and a second one blinked right after it, bigger than the first. I stood to my feet and decided to investigate.

It wasn't every day you saw flickers of light coming *from* a black hole.

As I flew closer to the anomaly, the sounds of giggles and laughter brushed past my ear. I recognized the sources instantly, and my thoughts were confirmed as soon as they came into view.

Farah and Marcus were playing again, but this time, they were using the city-wide black hole as their plaything. Was there anything that they didn't mess with?

Marcus threw Farah into the midst of the darkness. She threw up her hands in the air just as she hit the center, and she instantly disappeared, her laughter being drowned out. I could feel its gravity tug at my angelic body, but I stayed my ground. Marcus crossed his arms and looked at me.

"She be back," he said. "I think."

"Is this the first time you threw her in?" I asked, waiting anxiously for Farah to return, but the black hole just kept on spinning, and sucking in the little light that Heaven allowed to be siphoned away.

"First," Marcus confirmed. "But Farah strong. She make it."

"Didn't Lysander tell you two why this thing is here?" I sighed, reaching behind me to unstrap my shield from my back. I had no clue what I would be able to do with it, but I figured that if Farah didn't come back in a few minutes, I had to do *something*.

"Why here?" Marcus asked, pointing to the black hole.

"It's there in case Heaven is attacked in the future. Though God is able to keep the demons out, there's no telling what they might cook up. This black hole isn't like the others around the universe. It could destroy our spiritual bodies. And you just threw Farah right in the middle!"

"WHOOOOOOOO!" Farah cried out as she went spiraling between and then past us. We turned to see where she was going to end up falling, but with a quick twitch of her wings, she righted her trajectory, forcing herself upright. A big grin was planted on her face.

"Guys," she gasped with joy. "This," she said, pointing to the black hole, "is the best thing I have ever experienced. I'm serious. That was better than touching the sword by the Garden of Eden."

"You shouldn't have even been touching that either," I sighed, closing my eyes. Marcus pounded his chest once in approval, and then he gave Farah an enthusiastic high-five. The force behind his hand was so massive that it created an echo from the slap. Farah screamed on impact, and I couldn't tell if it was out of excitement or agony.

"Wow, that was fun!" she yelled, looking over at me. I guess it was excitement. "Cadence, are you going to try it?"

"Me?" I scoffed. "No, thank you. Did Lysander tell you two why this black hole is here?"

"Yeah, yeah," she said, waving me off. "Many times. But that just made me want to play with it more. I thought this was just an ordinary thing, so I never thought twice about it before. But now! I owe Lysander a great big thanks!"

"How did you even survive that thing?"

She placed both of her fists on the sides of her hips and raised her chin proudly.

"Faith," she and I both said at the exact moment. Farah scowled at me.

"If you already know, why are you asking then?"

"Farah, you know, you can't just keep living so dangerously. One day your faith…um—"

"—I know you're not about to say what I think you are."

"Never mind."

"I miss," Marcus said, scratching his forehead. Farah turned to him.

"Cadence was *about to say* that my faith was going to run out at some point."

Marcus glanced over at me and gave me the craziest 'yeah, right' look I've ever seen, pursing his lips and tilting his head down diagonally.

"You crazy," he said, and I just raised an eyebrow.

"You really have been around Alessa for too long."

"And us not enough," Farah said, zipping behind me and shoving me forward. I tried to hit her with my shield in protest, but it only caught her hair. She darted out the way and frowned. "Hey! I'm trying to help!"

"By throwing me into a black hole?"

"Um, yes. It's amazing."

"I might be destroyed!"

"Oh, you're immortal. Stop being a baby."

"Yeah," Marcus retorted. "Don't be Lysander."

"I'm not going in there," I said, putting my shield up so that my eyes were barely able to see above the curve. "I'm not even supposed to be here right now. I just wanted to know what in the world would be crazy enough to be hanging around here."

"Or maybe you *are* supposed to be here," Farah winked at me. "Did you think of that?"

"I don't follow."

"I think it's time for a lesson in some faith. You know what faith is."

"Yes," I groaned, as she began pacing back in forth in mid-air.

"Now, faith is relying on something that we cannot see," she said, completely ignoring me. "But it's more than belief. It requires action, and that is the part I believe you are lacking. The action. You think we are great warriors and we have great talent and potential, but you're not willing to let us show you what we can really do. Instead of being our leader and guiding us into how we can best utilize our abilities, you're treating us like children."

"*Children*," Marcus spat out with a blank face. I raised an eyebrow at him as Farah continued.

"We are all equal in this team, it just so happens that your contribution to our collective is delegation and guidance. That doesn't make you better than us. It doesn't mean that we can't share the burdens with you, but it does depend on how much you're willing to share. How much you're willing to trust us, and yourself.

"Stop thinking about the bad and focus on the all the good you've accomplished. Stop second guessing yourself and trust us to pick up the slack when you're having a bad day or making a mistake."

Farah let out a big sigh and clutched her stomach as Marcus began clapping profusely. I blinked and crossed my arms.

"Well, Farah, I've never heard you speak like that before."

"I wrote it and memorized it myself," she beamed, showing me her full set of teeth. "You think I can just say stuff like that off the top of my head?"

"But all you need is....never mind," I laughed, as she pointed at me in smiled.

"Ah, there you go!" she said, nodding her head. "You were going to say faith, weren't you?"

"Maybe," I snickered. Farah began dancing around me, and Marcus soon joined her. His face was blank, but his arms were flailing wildly as Farah chanted in a sing-song voice: "*He was going to say faith! He was going to say faith!*" I tried not to laugh.

"So Marcus," I said, following him with my eyes as he circled me. "Did you help with that speech?"

"Yes," he grunted, still throwing his arms everywhere and nearly hitting me in the face. "I wrote...children."

"The part about how I was treating you all like children?"

"No, just the word 'children,'" Farah giggled, throwing her arms around like Marcus, and *still circling me.*

"I'm sorry if I came off like that," I said, bowing my head. "But I hear what you're saying. Maybe I shouldn't be so negative. I mean, like you said, not all of my decisions were bad…I guess I should have just listened to Lysander more back when he was making his plan."

"*We got your back! We got your back!*" Farah began singing.

"Can you guys stop that?" I laughed half-heartedly, trying to swing at Farah. She dodged it, stuck out her tongue and then halted a few yards in front of me. Marcus stood next to her.

"Well, let's see if you truly learned the whole lesson!" she declared. Marcus gave a hard nod. "You may be willing to trust us, but do you trust yourself?"

"I'm good," I said, but pursed her lips in reply. She was unconvinced.

"Prove your faith then. Take that precious shield of yours, and throw it into the black hole behind us."

"Yeah, I'm not doing that," I said, turning to leave. "Good day, you two."

"Hey!" Farah cried out as Marcus grabbed my shoulders and spun me around to face them once more. "You're not getting out of this that easily!"

"I am not chucking my shield into that thing. I was born with this shield. Every guard only gets *one.*"

"Oh, you can get another one. Just make it out of one of those buildings in the 3rd ring."

"Those aren't the same. I can feel the difference. Besides, with that material, any angel could just reshape my shield into whatever they want. How's that going to work in battle?"

"Well, we're not going to be fighting against any angels for real."

"Says the one who fought a number of them that were in Lucifer's army."

"That was a one-time thing. There's not going to be another battle up here."

"Then why is the black hole there behind you?"

"Decoration?" she tried to give me, shrugging her shoulders.

"I'm not throwing my shield in there," I said adamantly. She sighed and folded her hands together.

"Cadence, you have to let go sometimes. I know that shield is near and dear to you, but you can't hold onto it forever. It's not going to break. It's not going to leave you."

I stared at her for a moment, hugging the shield to my chest. Then I gave a big sigh.

"You're saying the shield is like you all."

"That's exactly what I'm saying," she said, bouncing her head up and down. I sighed again and looked down at it. It wasn't impressive to look at, and it was just made of bronze, not gold or diamond or krillic. It was actually a pretty crappy shield, but it was mine.

Still...Farah had a point. I couldn't protect my shield no more than I could my friends. I had to trust in their durability, as well as the defensive tool in my hand.

And so, I cocked back my arm. Marcus and Farah flew out of the way, and then I threw the shield into the black hole as hard as I could.

It was sucked up instantly, and I took a deep breath once the deed was done.

Farah and Marcus came to my sides. Farah placed a hand on my forearm.

"I'm proud of you," she said. "I know that was hard for you."

"More than you know."

"And just watch. It's going to come right back."

"How?" Marcus asked, staring ahead with us.

"What do you mean, 'how?'" Farah chuckled. "It's going to come back at any moment."

"It shield," he replied. "Not boomerang."

"Oh yeah," she muttered, scratching her head.

My eyes widened and I glared down at her.

"Oops," she said, keeping her eyes facing forward.

"What did you think?!" I shouted. "That there was someone on the other side who would throw it back at me?"

"I thought that the black hole would just spit it out."

"You thought the non-sentient anomaly that literally sucks in everything around it, including light, AND our own angelic bodies if we let it…*was just going to spit it back out*!"

"You have to have faith," she said.

And I lost it.

I screamed and began chasing after her as fast as I could.

If she had so much faith, she should have stopped running and held still.

Have a little faith that I *wasn't* going to throw her back in to get my shield.

Chapter 3 – Rent Asunder

"It was my only one," I sighed as Marcus and Farah sat next to me in mid-air. Marcus patted my back hard.

"There are others."

"You know, I was thinking about our problem," Farah said, standing up in the air. "I'm thinking that I might go in there and retrieve it."

"Bad idea," Marcus replied.

"Why?" she exclaimed, but I just shook my head.

"Farah, that shield has probably been obliterated into a billion molecules by now and dispersed throughout the entire thing. You would have to somehow spot every single 'piece' and then put it all together. Even then, I'm not sure if that would work."

"You have to have a little faith!" Farah shouted, placing both fists on her hips.

"Sometimes it's not all about faith," I said, staring straight ahead. "Sometimes it's about being smart, and not putting yourself into a situation you may not come out of."

"I can do it," she retorted. I just turned my head to look at her.

"And what about the Absent?" I asked. Her face immediately fell. "I'm sure they had plenty of faith while searching through their mental database. I'm sure they were certain that they would find God, but all they ended up doing was losing themselves, into a black hole of their own. They might be able to find the pieces, but we both know that the odds are so low that we don't even bother waiting for their consciousness to return. All these Earth years have passed, and we forget that there are *still* angels on those islands."

"Goodness," Farah said, scowling at me. "That explanation almost made me Absent."

"Same," Marcus nodded. She gave me a smirk.

"But you know what, Cadence? I'm not Absent. And I'm not afraid of any black holes either."

"Don't be reckless," I said, but she was already sizing up her light-sucking opponent.

"When have you ever known me to be that?" she asked, and then she darted forward, toward the black hole. I jumped up to my feet.

"Farah, wait!" I shouted, reaching out to grab her, but she was able to spiral forward in mid-air, dodging my attempt, and she flew straight into the hole. I barely had time to think. I flew in right after her.

It's hard to describe the sensation. It's similar to being in God's presence in a way. Usually, when you were with God, you literally became one with his light, but it wasn't that you were necessarily absorbed. It felt like the light itself came to you, attaching itself to every atom of your being and fusing with it until you were literally nothing but light. Then you were integrated into God himself.

But this…it felt like my body was instantly ripped apart, and all at once. I had no time to assess what I could sense when I was divided. I couldn't see, hear, smell, taste, or touch. I couldn't move, and every piece of me was tossed around like I was in a tornado.

All I could do was reason, but even then, my thoughts had been divided as well, and with each passing second, it was getting harder and harder. The name "Farah" would enter my mind, and then it was snatched away from me, and I was given something new to ponder.

I remember that I was starting to feel distant at one point, and I wasn't sure how much time had passed while I was inside. It was like I didn't exist for a few minutes, and then suddenly, a clear thought of consciousness would come to the forefront, reminding me that I was a sentient being. When I lost myself for a third time, and then came back, I was terrified.

Because I had had this feeling before.

Scattered thoughts and the loss of self.

Unsure of what to do or where to go.

Just existing.

Just breathing.

No one knew of my existence but me.

No one would acknowledge who I was because I didn't even know myself.

I screamed.

Wait...I SCREAMED.

With my mouth somehow intact, I began climbing through the hurricane with my will, fighting against the pull of the black hole's oppressive will and weighted strength. I fought. I fought. I fought. Until finally, I was thrown out the other side, nearly slamming into Marcus' midsection. He caught me before I hit him, and he turned me upright. If I could sweat, I'm sure I would have been.

"How long was I gone?" I gasped, though it was impossible for me to be out of breath.

"Few second," he replied, and I found myself hugging him. He gently pushed me away. "What wrong?"

"That was horrible," I said, rubbing my forehead. "Wait, where's Farah?"

"Don't know," he said, looking toward the black hole. I turned and stared at the phenomenon in horror. *She was still inside.* The realization hit me hard, and I felt a waver in my angelic pressure.

"How are we going to save her?" I asked him, but he just crossed his arms in reply.

"We don't," he said firmly. "She save herself. Between her...and God now."

"But she needs help!" I yelled at him. Immediately, I heard a sucking sound, and Farah came flying forward, laughing like the black hole had just told the greatest joke in the entire world. Marcus didn't even try to catch her speeding body. He let her go, and she went flying past us and out into the galaxy, howling in delight the entire time. Marcus poked me in the chest.

"You one needs help," he said. "Not her. Save self."

I stared at him in awe after hearing his words. Was this what Farah was trying to explain to me earlier? That all I had to worry about was myself when it came to most matters? That when we were together, working as a team, it was my job to delegate, but otherwise, I was to allow them to do what they all did best. Just as they would trust in my delegation and commands, I had to trust them to get the job done, and deviate from my orders if for some reason, they saw a better path...

But that couldn't be how it was supposed to be. God was cut and dry, black and white, one way or the other. Lucifer and his army had gone against God, and they weren't given a second chance. So that meant that was how God was, right? So shouldn't I be the same when it came to my team?

Then again...when Lysander had gone against my wishes, it resulted in our team defeating Vergil, which wouldn't have happened otherwise. I had been beyond furious that he had defied me, fought me...forced me into a guardianship with Cain.

There were times on Earth in which I didn't think we could even be friends again, and I wasn't sure how that would work out with both of us being a part of Heaven. There were even a couple days when I thought that God might kick Lysander out of Heaven for his insubordination...

But then Cain died.

And as his guardian, I was transported right above his killer to enact vengeance. For Cain had been placed with a mark that said that anyone who harmed him, the same would be enacted upon the aggressor sevenfold. And for those couple of seconds, when I was encased in that radiant light and power, I realized that not only did Lysander's plan work, but God had approved of it. It all wouldn't have worked out so beautifully otherwise.

Which meant...God was either neutral, or in agreement with Lysander when it came to disobeying me.

And I didn't know what to think of that.

It was obvious I still had a lot of learning to do about God and what he wanted of me, but my options were limited. I had the Throne Room, but it was a place to recharge and bask in his glory. I didn't learn anything new about God specifically.

And then there was the mental database.

Which might as well have been no option at all.

I wouldn't go back into the recesses of my mind. Not again.

"Ready to go back in?" Farah asked with a giggle, appearing next to me.

"Oh, no," I said, looking down at her. "It's all yours."

"That was fun, wasn't it?"

"Um," I said, frowning. "What was it like in there for you?"

"I was just being thrown all over the place. But I was aware of each piece. I could reform whenever I wanted."

"How is that possible?"

"I don't know," she said, shrugging her shoulders. "Maybe it's because I'm a Faithful. You know how we are all super weak. If it wasn't for our faith, there would barely be anything keeping us together. With that kind of weakness, you have to be more attuned to yourself and the world around you. I know my limitations."

"And what are those?"

"That I have none!" she laughed in my face. I smiled and Marcus gave out a big guffaw.

"I'll take your word for it," I said. "So what are your limitations, Marcus?" I asked, turning to face him, but he just stared back at me with a blank expression. I poked him in the shoulder, but I ended up pushing him backwards in the process. I turned to Farah in alarm.

"What's wrong with him?"

"He's been doing that for a while now, remember?" she said quietly. We watched as he floated onto his back, his face still as frozen as a statue. It was only then that the memories began flooding back to me.

Times on Earth as guardians of Cain and Abel.

Marcus being late to his shifts.

Amos saying that Marcus needed help. Watching him suddenly go idle in the middle of a sparring session. I had been so focused on my own problems that I hadn't dwelled on his. They would be right in front of my face, but the issue was habitually thrown to the side. Marcus was so quiet normally that I hadn't placed much thought in what might really be going on with him.

"We kept saying that we'll talk about it, but no one ever does," Farah replied as we continued to watch Marcus spin upside down. "I try talking to him, but he won't tell me. He's too stubborn. He thinks that if he tells me what's going on, I'll look down on him or take it easy on him when we fight. It's funny. By not telling me, that's exactly what I've been doing. I don't know what to do, Cadence."

"Since we don't have any jobs or guardianships at the moment, maybe we should find out once and for all."

"That might take a stroll through the mental database," she said, and I winced. "I know how you hate going through that."

"I might make an exception for Marcus," I said, wondering if I could actually go through with it. "But we might as well do this now before we're called to battle or something."

"Amos was the first one to mention that something was wrong with Marcus. Maybe we should ask him what he noticed over all this time. I know the two of them were close."

"Might be impossible at the moment," I sighed. "Amos left Team Six."

"WHAT?" Marcus shouted, still in mid-spin. He flailed his arms and legs wildly until he was standing upright. "WHY LEAVE?!"

"He doesn't think we're much of a team right now," I explained reluctantly. "And he thinks he'll enjoy himself more taking on a guardianship."

"He no goodbye," Marcus frowned, crossing his arms.

"So we're Team Five now?" Farah groaned. "Again? For such a well-known team in Heaven, we sure can't keep new members."

"We do have some problems to work out," I said, looking back at Marcus. "And before we start adding more members again, we should probably take care of ourselves."

"What mean?" Marcus scowled at me. "You talk of me, right?"

"We're worried about you," Farah said. Marcus pointed to me.

"He not. He ignore."

"What?" I asked him. "What do you mean?"

"I come for help. You not bother. You say no bother."

I bowed my head in shame as my teammates looked at me. I remembered those moments, but I had been trying to work out my own issues. Besides, I thought that Marcus was just going to ask me to play a game or something, not tell me about what happened to him when he 'shutdown.'"

"Is this true?" Farah asked, and I nodded. "Cadence, you're our leader!"

"I don't know if I want to be," I said. "I'm not sure I'm qualified."

"Okay, well, that's fine if you don't want to lead anymore. Alessa can take over for now, but you have to at least listen to your own teammates! I thought we were a family. If Marcus came to you asking for help, his shutdown problem could have been resolved years ago!"

"Okay, okay," I said with a chuckle. "Well, the important thing is that we're going to take care of it now. Better now than later."

"Yeah, let's not let another few decades go by."

"Marcus," I said, turning to him. "Do you want to tell us what's going on?"

"Not here," he said, glancing over at Farah. Farah groaned and rolled her eyes.

"I'm not going to look down on you," she said, but he shook his head adamantly.

"No, tell Cadence only. Not you."

"Fine," she sighed. "You two go off somewhere and work it out. I'm going to play around with the black hole some more."

"We'll be back," I said. I nodded to Marcus, and we began taking off. When we were out of earshot from Farah, I had to ask him: "Where are we headed?" Marcus gave me a curt smile.

"My house," he said. I had no clue what that entailed. None of us had ever been to his mansion, and from we learned about all of the angels in Heaven, each house was specifically designed to mirror its owner in some way. I could only imagine what Marcus' might be.

Chapter 4 – Broken Home

We traveled to his house slowly, and I was about to ask Marcus why we weren't picking up the pace when he glanced back at me.

"How Earth?" he asked to my surprise. Was he going slow on purpose for some small talk?

"I'm not sure, I haven't been there recently."

"What heard?" he asked. I tried to recall the bits and pieces I heard from my fellow angels when I wasn't enveloped in my own thoughts.

"It's all about the Battle of the East at this point," I said. "Most of the demons and the angels are fighting for dominance of the Earth, and the humans are basically left alone. There are still guardianships in place, but that's diminishing in number from what I've heard. More troops are being ordered to the frontlines."

"Humans alone?"

"I know it sounds bad, but think about it. The demons need their best fighting the angels. Michael, Gabriel, Raphael…they're all at the Battle. So, there's no way that the demons are going to send someone of Vergil's caliber to poke at a few humans. The humans should be fine. I fear more for what will happen if the angels happen to lose this Battle."

"Won't lose," Marcus declared. "Too strong. More numbers."

"I hope you're right."

"Humans need us," he said, turning to face me. It was then that I realized we had arrived at Marcus' house, but he wasn't ready to take me in yet. I took a peek past him to the mansion on the large piece of rock below.

It was enormous, and fitting of a Godhand. Painted in blood red, the mansion looked like a fortress, complete with castle-like towers and stone bricks infused with krillic in liquid form, acting as a type of mortar. It was bold, but not frilly or extravagant. It didn't speak of majesty, but strength. Even without going inside yet, I thought it represented Marcus precisely.

"In a way, this is a great test for the humans," I said to him. "Think about it. Without influence by demon or angel, they are able to show God how they really are. They can reveal their true nature."

"Or go Absent," he said. The words hit me in the stomach. Would that be the default? To become so lost searching for God or the Devil that they would basically lose themselves? Just existing but not living as so many angels still did on the islands? I didn't want to believe it.

"It's different," I said, still trying to believe that I was having an argument with Marcus. "The humans have experienced the spiritual world. They'll remember us. They won't be lost."

"God did same," he said, crossing his arms over his massive chest. "We forgot. We go Absent."

He was right. God had given us his love and light upon creation, but then we were cast to the islands, where we had to find out who we were and what we were really made of. Since the humans could live for many, many years, how long would it take before they also forgot? Would they tell their children? Or would stories of the Garden of Eden, direct conversations with God, and the angels and demons that fought for their souls—all be lost. Would we become nothing more than fables and myths?

"That doesn't mean all of the humans will fall," I said. "Like with the angels, there will always be someone that will have a relationship with God."

"Maybe," he said. "Come. Continue inside."

I followed him, eager to hear what he had to say next. Maybe he needed time to sift through his thoughts. When we hit the island's edge and stood in the grass, Marcus placed his hands on the short but formidable steel frame that was his door. He pushed at it, to the point that I heard him grunt, and the door pushed forward, not to the sides. It was as if it had no hinges.

Once the door had moved forward a few yards, it went over to the left a few feet as if it was on an invisible track, and then it stayed there. Marcus walked in the house and I followed. As soon as we were out the doorway, the door moved again on its invisible track until it blocked the opening behind us.

I took a look around me. The floors were checkered in black and red, and the walls and ceiling were bare and white. The area seemed to stretch on for miles and I just placed my hands on my hips.

"This place is huge," I said to him, but he held up a hand for me to stop.

"No move," he ordered, and I chuckled.

"Why?"

"For safety," he said. "I...unpack."

"Unpack? What does that—"

And then it sounded like an explosion went off all around us. I ducked and reached behind me for my shield, but of course, it wasn't there anymore. I grunted and opened an eye. My jaw dropped as I saw a bookshelf, the height of a small house, crash into the floor in front of us. Then another came down at our left, then our right, and then more in succession slammed down onto the checkered pavement behind those. Slowly, the entire mansion was filled with bookshelves, each with thousands of books, all embroidered in a myriad of colors on the wooden planks in which they sat.

Marcus pushed at the one in front of us, and it slid backwards. None of the books shook or even threatened to fall off the shelves. A red couch fell from the ceiling, and then another right across from it, giving us a place to sit. In the distance, I could still here more bookshelves falling and crashing by one another. Marcus waved me to follow him, and he went over to sit on one of the couches. I sat on the one across from him in awe, still picking up the sounds of construction.

"That's better," Marcus said, leaning back onto the couch. His voice was so clear and his words were so enunciated that it was like he had transformed in my eyes. Not in body, but in essence. Even his eyes had gained new vitality.

"What is going on around here?" I asked him in awe.

"I unloaded as much of my mind as I could," Marcus replied. "I wish I could create some food here, but it's regulated to the Fellowship Halls. I guess it's for the best. If I could make it here, I would probably never leave!" He laughed as I continued to stare at him in shock. This was a completely different Marcus. I never imagined that we could have such a clear conversation.

"So this is...from inside your mind?"

"As much as my mental database as I can possibly take out," he said with a chuckle. "It's a lot, but I'm sure you know that it's not even close to everything. Centuries of history, technology, concepts...this is the only place I can do it. My home. It's the only place where I can think clearly. Though even that's been getting more and more difficult."

"So you're...you're..."

"I'm not dumb at all," he said, flashing me a grin. "I'm not some brute with no intelligence. I'm not mindless and I actually have a lot to say. It's just that I can't speak like I want to outside this place. My mental database prohibits me."

"What's wrong with it? Were you Absent?"

"No," he said, shaking his head and leaning over. "I've never been Absent. That would mean that I lost myself searching through the database. With me, it's the opposite, I lose myself because too much is coming at me. I don't know why I was designed this way, or why I'm flawed, but my mind is getting more and more flooded with every Earth day. I gain more information, but at the same time, I lose the ability to express. I see the other Godhands, and they aren't like that at all, so I don't know what's wrong with me."

"New information? Like what?"

"Little things. Insignificant things. I've gone to the Throne Room and asked God about it but I get little answers. From my time dwelling on the matter, I think I'm being prepared for something. I...maybe someday I'll be given secrets or something, and I'll be forbidden to tell anyone unless God allows it. Maybe my shutdown will be permanent someday."

"So that's what's been happening," I said, putting a hand to my chin. "So whenever your brain is starting to get flooded, you shutdown...are you aware of yourself when it happens?"

"I am. I just can't say anything or move."

"I don't know why God would allow this."

"There's a lot we might not understand or agree with, but it doesn't mean it's random, or it's not for the greater good."

"Aren't you afraid? From what it sounds like...unless we find a solution to your problem, you're not going to be able to interact with anything. No more fighting. No Team Six. No more food. All of the things that you enjoy—they won't be there anymore."

"That's why I've been trying to talk to you," Marcus replied. "Because I'm trying to spend time with everyone before it's too late, and you're the only one I haven't gotten to hang out with."

My angelic pressure flickered when I heard those words. I had no idea what he had been going through, but I should have at least listened. This was horrible. Not only did we lose Amos, but we were going to lose Marcus too. Team Six down to four...what was the point of all of this? Why was God allowing this to happen? After all we had accomplished, how was our team's destruction going to be our end? I couldn't accept it.

"We're going to find a way to stop this eventual shutdown," I said, clasping my hands together firmly. "There's got to be a way."

"I've talked to many angels," Marcus said. "And I've done much research. There's no one else with what I have. But I don't want you to feel sorry for me, Cadence. I've had a lot of time to think about this, and I truly think that it is what God wants. Imagine the secrets I could be entrusted with! Think of how much trust God has in me by giving them!"

"No, no," I said. "If God trusted you with these so-called secrets, then he wouldn't take away your ability to speak."

"Perhaps it's a failsafe. What if the demons win against us? They might be able to get information out of us somehow. If I can't even speak or feel, how will they break me?"

"We already have an Archives Building, so there's no need to entrust a ton of secrets to one Godhead, and you're assuming that those demons could even get to you. Think about it, we haven't been down to Earth in so long…and it's gotten to the point that you won't even be able to battle now. The only way they can get you is if they're able to break into Heaven, and that's impossible. They're confined to the Earth."

"That's the same thought I had when we were fighting our own brothers and sisters, among the homes that were built for us, and the fields we once played in. I thought, 'this is impossible.' When Abel was murdered, I thought that too. Just when I think I can't be surprised anymore, I am."

"That doesn't mean we have to just give in to your condition though."

"Why not? You have." I stared at him, my eyes steady onto his. He refused to turn away. "I know you are hurt by what happened, but it was a one-time deal. Just because you lost your way once, and you made some decisions that weren't the best, that doesn't mean *you* have to shut down and stop being our leader. Take what happened into consideration and learn from it. Move on. We need you."

"Funny you say that," I replied, "considering you're ready to shutdown yourself."

"My situation is different. I have no control over what's—"

"Shut up," I said, and then I gave him a smile. "Okay, I get it. I've been moody and unsure of myself. Alright, so I'm afraid of making another decision that will get us hurt, but that doesn't mean you get to just shut down too. We need you, Marcus."

"What are you saying?"

"I'm saying that we're going to look for a way for you to escape the shutdown. If we can't find a solution, so be it. But we're not going to lose you. Not if I can help it. Have you talked to Lysander yet?"

"No, but I—"

"—then that's what we're doing. He's probably at the Archive Building too, which would be perfect for what we need.

"But I've accepted what—"

"—this is happening," I said adamantly, rising to my feet. "We're getting you together. And we're getting the team together, which includes myself. We're not going to let you go." Marcus stared at me for a moment, and then I saw his angelic pressure flicker. He gave me a smile.

"Thank you," he said, and then another explosion sounded off in the distance. I watched as the bookshelves began slowly rising to the ceiling with their cargo intact. "Whether you like it or not, Cadence," Marcus continued as the bookshelves rose. "We need you. And the whole you. Not pieces. The same goes with humanity. They need us, whether they realize it or not. Otherwise, they'll just accept their fate."

"So," I smirked. "You knew that telling me about your situation would get me motivated? You tricked me?"

"Not at all," he said. "No trickery. I really have come to terms with my condition, and I don't have the faith that Farah does. I don't think I'll be cured of this, but at the same time, I'm excited to see the old Cadence emerge—and try to change my mind."

The bookshelves and the couches disappeared in a flash of light, and once again, we were standing in a bare room, with only the checkered floor beneath us for decoration.

"Are you sure you don't want to stay here a little while longer?" I asked him. He shook his head and pounded a fist to his chest.

"Not baby," Marcus said firmly. "We go."

"I won't treat you like one," I said. "And I'm sorry if I have in the past. From here on out, no matter what happens, we're in this together. I'm hoping that we can get to know each other more."

"Yes," he said, and that was all. I grinned, and then we headed for the door. As Marcus grabbed the ring handle and pulled it away from the entrance frame, I thought about all he had said. It was funny. The more I thought about my problems, the more of a hole I dug myself into, but the moment it seemed like I was going to lose one of my friends forever, I immediately jumped right back out. They truly were everything to me. My family. My friends. My teammates.

And they needed me just as much as I needed them. We were all flawed, but together, we were a powerhouse. Still…I wonder if they would feel the same way about me if they knew the truth. If they knew what I had done…

I couldn't dwell on it now though, not when we had already accomplished so much, and Marcus' faith in a cure had been renewed. I needed to be there for my team, and I would worry about the past later. I would tell them everything.

But in my own time.

Chapter 5 – By the Renewing of Your Mind

"My friends!" Lysander shouted, as we entered the Present Room of the Archive Building. I had never been there before, but it was undeniably Lysander's favorite place in all of Heaven. It was a large room with a marble floor and several bookcases that were as tall as buildings on the sides. The major feature though, was the holographic orb that one could use from the center of the room. It was able to replay events on Earth, show images, and provide a great deal of information right from the comforts of Heaven. Lysander had fallen in love with it, but I was not one to dwell on the past for too long. As we entered, I wondered just how far back Lysander had been looking recently. I would be lying if I said that I didn't still feel a little bit of apprehension toward him for our altercations earlier, but I was trying to let that go.

"Do you do anything else in your spare time?" I laughed.

"Nope," Marcus answered for him, crossing his arms, as he liked to do.

"What brings you here?" Lysander asked. "Did you get my message?"

"No, we didn't," I said. "What's going on?"

"I've asked Ulysses to gather our team together and meet here. Through my research, I might have found something that could turn the Battle of the East in our favor."

"Really? What is it?"

"I would rather wait until everyone is here, but I think we're going to have to go back to Earth and check this out."

"I see," I said, turning to Marcus. He nodded at me with a clenched jaw. I got the message. If there was an important mission coming, we needed the whole team. Marcus was still having his 'blackouts,' but preserving the humans and defeating the demons came first. And we might not have time to deal with Marcus' problem and Lysander's new discovery simultaneously. I knew that there would be risks involved. I could easily tell Alessa and the others what was going on with Marcus and everyone would agree unanimously that Marcus had to stay in Heaven, but what would that do to Marcus?

He knew the risks, and yet he wanted to go through with the mission regardless. I decided to trust his judgment on this one, and keep what he told me to myself.

"How is Ulysses doing?" I asked instead. Lysander waved to the holographic orb up above and it began to descend. Whatever he wanted to talk about, he needed to show us visually.

"Excellent," he said. "He's been teaching me a lot."

"About what?" I asked. Ulysses was a former Absent that had recently found himself and was allowed into Heaven. He had replaced Vergil in Lysander's life, but he was still too unsure of himself to commit to any missions or even our Team. I wasn't sure when he would be ready to join us, if ever. He was a nice guy. I just didn't know him. Besides, he hadn't even been to Earth yet.

"He's been teaching me about the islands and the Absent," Lysander said.

"Oh?" I said. Marcus reached out to tap me on the shoulder. When I looked his way, he threw a thumb behind him. I looked to see Alessa and Farah walking into the room from behind a bookcase.

"This place gives me the creeps," Farah replied. I noticed Alessa's hardened face soften as soon as she saw that I was present for the meeting.

"You give me the creeps," Lysander muttered from the center of the room. Farah put a hand to her chest like she was appalled and Lysander stuck a tongue out at her.

"That's because you *are* the creeps," she grinned. "The definition of the word."

"What is the definition?" Lysander responded inquisitively.

"Oh, forget it," Farah sighed. "You win." Lysander chuckled as Marcus nodded in approval. I didn't blame Farah for letting the fight go. Talking to Lysander was like having a conversation with a vocal encyclopedia that wouldn't stop until it had revealed everything on its pages. Farah probably figured that it was better to put an end to the verbal sparring before Lysander got too worked up.

"I thought you would be too busy for us," Alessa said to me, placing a hand on my shoulder. "It's good to see you."

"And you," I smiled, reaching out and giving her a hug. When we parted, I continued looking into her eyes. "I'm sorry I've been such a...knucklehead lately."

"SEE LYSANDER?" Marcus shouted to him while pointing at me. "He knucklehead. NOT ME! TOLD YOU!" Lysander looked at him in confusion.

"What are you—oh, that. Wow, Marcus. That was centuries ago."

"I smart," Marcus said, tapping his forehead. I found myself nodding at the statement. Then I turned back to Alessa.

"I've been doing a lot of thinking," I said to her, though it was loud enough for everyone to hear. "And I want more responsibility again. I don't want to be a leader full-time, but maybe we could both do it together for a little bit. At least until I can get my bearings. How does that sound?"

"Awesome!" Alessa practically squealed. "Oh my goodness, Cadence. Being a leader is *awful*." She gasped and put a hand to her mouth as she scanned the room. "Um," she said, removing her hand. "Not that you all were difficult."

"Hey!" Ulysses shouted, flying into the room from behind us. "I couldn't find Marcus and—oh hey! You two made it here? That's great. I was looking for you two."

"Good to see you again, Ulysses," I said, extending a hand out to him. He shook it eagerly and stared at me like I was glowing. And I didn't know why. Surely Lysander had told him of our time together and of my failures. What was so special about me?

"It doesn't get old talking with you," he said, shaking my hand harder. His bright eyes were wide and full of vitality. "I can't wait for the day to join the team and see what I'm made of. I just need a little more time to prepare. I don't want to disappoint you."

"I'm sure you won't," I chuckled nervously, slowly taking my hand away. Ulysses let go and strolled over to Lysander and stood next to him, facing all of us.

"Is that everyone?" Ulysses asked his friend. Lysander nodded and looked up at the suspended holographic sphere.

"Earth, please," he said to it, and the sphere was suddenly filled in with colors. A mix of blue, green, white and brown swirled around in the middle like it was in the midst of a tornado, and it exploded, splattering along the walls of the hologram, and then spreading out intelligently, with each color running into its proper spot. Within seconds, the holographic sphere had been filled in, and a representation of Earth was before us. Farah began clapping excitedly.

"Do it again!" she shouted.

"Unfortunately, we have work to do," Lysander stated, crossing his arms and still staring up at the display. "The reason I called you here is because Ulysses and I may have discovered something that will change the war."

"Oh?" Alessa asked, looking over at me, seeing how I was to respond. I was just as curious as she was.

"Ulysses and I have been spending a great deal of time discussing the Absent and what it's like to truly lose yourself within the flow of information. What happens? Is it just a bunch of images running through your mind? A jumble of thoughts like too many people screaming, so that you are unable to decipher the words? Ulysses has explained to me that it's actually neither. A proper allegory would be floating in the midst of an ocean that has no beginning and no end. You're just slowly swimming forward, experiencing a new thought or concept, and then you move on to the next, without any hope of finding your consciousness and the real world again."

"Then how did you get back?" Farah asked Ulysses. He nodded nervously.

"It wasn't easy," Ulysses said. "I think the difference between me and many others was that I kept swimming. I don't know if it's because I'm an Archangel that I was able to sift through the information faster, but I didn't give up. It's easy to get lost in one concept or thought for a long period of time, but I didn't stop, even when something interested me. I needed to find God."

"We believe," Lysander continued for him," that time for the Absent is kind of like how it is for us here in Heaven compared to the humans. There is no real concept of it to hold onto. This means that there could be an Absent who decides to dwell on why the sky is blue, for example, but they don't realize how much time is passing before they continue swimming. To them, it may feel like seconds, when in reality, its many, many Earth years. Also, there is no way to measure how close one is to the proverbial shore when they are swimming."

"But what does the Absent have to do with the Battle to the East?" I asked. "You're not thinking of trying to get all of the Absent on the islands to come out of their stupor and join us, are you?"

"No," Lysander said, shaking his head profusely. "That would take too long. But it did get me thinking about things the Absent have seen, and how it's possible, that some of them have even seen the future. And I don't mean concepts as we know them like blenders or cars or names of future countries. I'm thinking that some of them are so far into their mental database that they are able to tap into levels we can't even fathom.

"Take this archive building, for example. It is essentially a gigantic mental database, and I've been told that if one is willing to search through it deep enough, they could find information on the future. They will definitely get lost, and they may not get out in time for the information they find to be relevant, but still, think of the possibilities!"

"So..." I groaned. "Let me get this straight. You're trying to get a glimpse into the future and how the Battle to the East turns out...so that we can intervene, knowing how to end it?"

"Something like that, but since the Battle to the East has already been going on for so long, it wouldn't make sense for me to go searching through the archives. By the time I got back out—if at all— the battle would probably be over. But that doesn't mean we can't be proactive and find clues that will help us achieve victory."

"I don't follow."

"I've been going deep into the mental database again," Ulysses declared proudly and we all looked to Lysander in astonishment.

"What is *wrong* with you?" I found myself saying, but then I stopped myself from saying anything more. What Lysander was having Ulysses do was insane, but I felt like I had no place to speak. Lysander had discovered a way to beat Vergil. What if he had a way to end the Battle to the East as well?

"He was an *Absent*," Alessa stressed, taking a step forward. "He just got to Heaven recently, and already you're risking him going back? What if he goes Absent again here in Heaven? Do you have any idea what that will do to morale when the other angels come back and see that?"

"We've been taking it slow," Lysander winced. "And I figured that since he went Absent once and made it out, he'll be able to recognize the warning signs ahead of time."

"What are the warning signs?" Alessa asked Ulysses, but the archangel shrugged his shoulders.

"I honestly have no idea," he said. "It's like a feeling. It's hard to describe."

"Lysander, you can't do this," she said, turning back to him. "He's an angel, not one of your projects."

"I'm sorry," he said, throwing up his hands. "But...um, it did help!"

"How?"

"I, uh," Lysander pointed at the representation of Earth. "We've been studying the Earth in particular because it is the demons' jail in a sense. They can't leave the barriers, and Heaven has yet to find where they are hiding. I know that they're spiritual, but being that we are of the same composition, we should still be able to see them. For example, Lucifer has yet to show himself in the battle. Well, if he's not there, then where is he? It got us thinking."

"We've been scouting out the Earth while we researched," Ulysses said to my surprise. "We did some exploring and tests, and we think that the majority of the demons are hiding under the ocean."

"The ocean," I echoed, contemplating the words. "But the ocean has been searched."

"This is true," Lysander said, "to the very bottom. But when I go over reports and I talk to the angels that have scouted at the bottom, their stories are all the same. They say how they swam around quickly, and then they all left as soon as possible. This is because the water is another physical deterrent for us. The deeper we go, the more the liquid affects our spiritual composition, applying a pressure on it that threatens to break and completely obliterate it."

"We fly through the stars," Alessa said. "Sure, we are affected by their energy, or the gravity along planets, but it is a weak pull. Nothing serious."

"The ocean deep gets stronger the further down we go," Lysander responded, "and think about the stars and planets we pass by. We never stick around long enough to see what exactly happens. From my tests, I can tell you that the gravity gets stronger the longer you stay around the planets, and the energy of the stars begin to drain your angelic pressure."

"So what are you saying?" I asked. "That the demons are down there?"

"No," Farah gasped. We all looked down at her. "They are further down."

"Wait," I asked. "Further?"

"Farah knows what I'm talking about," Lysander laughed. "After all, she loves to play with black holes. The ocean deep is certainly not even close to that kind of power, but it has a similar effect on us. We stay down there long enough, and we are torn apart.

"But we must remember that the demons are also stronger than us. It's not inconceivable to think that they would have an easier time putting themselves back together, especially the stronger ones like Lucifer. Perhaps the imp demons have to stay on the Earth surface, but the headquarters of the demons has to be down below."

"We have a theory," Ulysses continued on. "We think that the demons are broken apart, and with their consciousness intact, they take their pieces or—what was it, Lysander?"

"Particles."

"—particles," Ulysses said, "and they travel below the ocean, the mantle, and into the Earth's core."

"We've confirmed that no one has been to the core," Lysander said. "Not a single angel. Part of this is because of the effect the ocean deep has on our bodies, and another is the great deal of barriers keeping us at bay, but I believe, that if we are able to split apart, we would theoretically be able to travel past the invisible barriers, into the Earth's core, and ultimately, right into the demons' headquarters. We could end the Battle to the East, and the war as soon as tonight."

Chapter 6 – To Arms

"You haven't gone there, have you?" I asked.

"No," Lysander replied, "but we're certain that's where the demons are hiding. We haven't done too much scouting at the ocean's deep because we didn't want to attract too much attention, but we were able to get past one invisible barrier using the particle separation method. Knowing how to do that alone is a great discovery."

"So what do you propose? That we take an army to their doorstep?"

"Ideally, yes," he smiled weakly, "but I know that's not going to happen."

"Then what?" He just stared at me with pleading eyes, and I could feel my fists clenching on their own. I grit my teeth. "No," I said flatly. He took a step toward me.

"Cadence, this is a golden opportunity, and everyone else is busy. Even Raphael and Michael are at the Battle, trying to figure out a way to win. We have an opportunity to cut off the head of the snake."

"What does that even mean?"

"I taught that phrase to him," Alessa said. "Um, it's like, you're taking out the leader so that the rest of the army will fall, because there's no leadership."

"We are in no condition to take on Lucifer alone," I said. "Let alone a great deal of other demons and former archangels. It will be a massacre."

"I don't want to fight them," Lysander said. "I just want to confirm that the headquarters is there. Once we have proof, we can bring an army there instead of just fighting back and forth on the surface."

"We are not a Special Ops group," I said. "We have been left out of the fighting for a reason. If we go down there, we're going to be destroyed. Not even Farah can speak to the contrary."

"Um," she squeaked. "I don't think you know me."

"Are you seriously thinking of going through with this?" I asked her. She shrugged her shoulders at me. I turned to the rest of them. "This sounds reasonable to you all?"

"We've been left out of the fighting because of you," Lysander said quietly, but loud enough for us to all hear. "We've been waiting for you to get your courage and confidence back, so that we can go back out there and make a difference." His voice grew louder. "We have a chance to end this never ending war once and for all, and I think it's worth the risk.

"If we're taken captive or destroyed, then so be it. But how great would it be if we're right? If the headquarters is down there and we can subdue the demons once and for all? It would be good not just for us, but the humans as well. I've watched footage of the Battle to the East here in the holographic room. It's senseless. There is no gain, and yet everything to lose."

"We don't know what to expect down there," I said. "And we would have to prepare for something like that. Would Ulysses be coming with us on this suicide mission?"

"No," Lysander said, but I shook my head.

"He would have to," I said. "Because we would need back-up, and more than just us. Ulysses, are you ready to fight? Have you even sparred with anyone? Or has it all been research?"

"Just research," he said meekly.

"You might have to take on the Devil himself," I snapped. "And a number of our former brothers and sisters. They will smell the anxiety on you and try to exploit it. They will try to sway you to their side with sweet words and then they will stab you in the back when you least expect it. And that's just you." I turned to Lysander. "You're saying that we'll have to split apart and then put ourselves back together again on the other side, but how long will that take? How many of us are ready for that?"

"I've done it a couple times," Lysander said, but I wasn't finished.

"In the ocean?" I demanded to know.

"Yes."

"What about the black hole?"

"No," he said, wondering where I was going with my line of questioning.

"There's no guarantee that we'll all be able to come back together. We might get lost, just like the Absent do within their minds. Farah will probably be okay, but the rest of us have no training in traveling as particles. What if the trip to the core takes years in such a small form? What if it's not there at all? What if we're attacked as soon as we get there? Don't you think the demons will notice if they see our team go to the ocean's bottom and begin pulling ourselves apart? They know who we are!"

"And that's why they'll be afraid," he said, with a fire in his eyes. I had seen that same fire before, back when he challenged me in my own house. I wasn't ready to relive that memory. My fists became unclenched, and I sighed heavily, glaring at my friend with such intensity that I thought he was going to lunge forward and engage me in battle at any moment. But that didn't happen. He waited for me to continue speaking, but I had said my peace. There was nothing left to say. Once Lysander had his mind set on something, it was hard to change it.

"Talk to your leader," I said, throwing a thumb toward Alessa. "But count me out. If you can come up with some kind of argument that will convince me, then fine. But otherwise, you'll find me in the plains, doing what I'm actually good at."

"Don't be like that," Lysander said, the fire in his eyes dying out. "We need you, Cadence. Whether you like it or not, your decisions are what helps us to succeed when we're in the midst of battle."

"No, it's your tactics," I said, bowing my head. "I just know what questions to ask you to get your mind racing. You're still the one to figure out the solutions to our problems. Maybe you should be the leader of the team."

"No, not at all," he said. "I'm not fit. And without you asking those questions, how would I be able to do my job? We're a team. A cohesive unit. We all help to complete one another."

"Or you are all complete, and I am still broken," I said to them, raising my head. "Perhaps you should consider finding another leader that will agree to go with you on your suicide mission, but not me. And it would be silly of you to not at least consider what I'm saying. Look for someone else to lead you, and take you to higher heights."

And with that being said, I walked away from them. It wasn't that Lysander's plan didn't sound interesting, but the risk was in fact, too great. If the demons' headquarters was in the Earth's core, then it had to be a covert mission. Something for the likes of Raphael, who was used to espionage, but not us. We were a misfit band of angels that had been fortunate to still be conscious. I wasn't in the mood to tempt God any further.

I stepped outside the Archive building and went down the steps, but I didn't take flight. Instead I sat down into the short grass and stared off into the distance, not really taking in the sights, but contemplating on what the answer to Lysander's proposed plan was.

We should probably tell one of the higher-ups. But they were busy, and there was none in Heaven at the moment. We couldn't go to the Battle to the East without getting caught up in the conflict, and God already knew what was going on, and even where the demons were.

Did that mean we shouldn't go? Knowing that God knew and he didn't order anyone to go there? Or was he once again letting us sort it all out for ourselves? Without guidance?

I grunted in frustration. What I wouldn't give for a little clarity. But whenever I went to the Throne Room, I was infused with love and joy, not direction. I had to figure that out for myself, and I wasn't too confident in my actions. How was I going to get better? How was I going to be able to make the right decisions without anyone telling me what they were? What was the point of just messing up and failing over and over? I didn't like how it felt. But what would I accomplish by just staying still and lying in the grass? It was all so frustrating.

"Hey," Alessa said from behind me. I didn't turn around, and she sat in the grass beside me. "What are you thinking about?"

"Lysander's plan mostly," I said.

"And how insane it is?"

"Of course," I chuckled, turning to face her. She wiped the hair from her eyes and smiled back. "Alessa, please tell me I'm not the crazy one. You see how we can't go through with this, don't you?"

"I don't know," she sighed, turning to face forward. "We've accomplished some pretty impressive things in the past. With the help of God, of course."

"Have you asked God about all of this? If we should go with Lysander's plan?"

"All I got was one sentence: 'Do not stay idle.'"

"As cryptic as always," I laughed. "A push forward, but into what direction, we have no clue."

"But at least we know of a certainty that he wants us to do *something.*"

"That's true," I said, bowing my head between my knees. "But it's difficult. Knowing what to do exactly. Even when we take a step out on faith, it doesn't mean it's the right path. You know I lost my shield?"

"I was going to ask you about that," she chuckled. "When I walked into the holographic room and saw your back, I wasn't sure it was you at first. I'm so used to seeing it on you. What happened to it?"

"I threw it into the black hole," I said with a grin. "Farah asked me to do it on faith."

"Ha, well that was stupid."

"Well, yeah, I know that now."

"Farah's the only one I know that can do what Farah does."

"Yeah, I shouldn't have done it," I said with amusement, raising my head and staring off into the horizon. "But I know better now."

"Exactly," she said, patting my back. "And that's how it goes. You take the most educated step of faith in a direction and see where it takes you. And then in the future, you'll be more educated—to take another blind step of faith. No matter how much knowledge you have about a situation, it's still a guess. Who knows what will happen? That's Lysander's problem, you know."

"What's that?" I asked, facing her.

"He can't accept the fact that he can't control his future. Even though the whole ordeal with Vergil is over, he still wants to ensure that nothing like that happens again. He also wants to lessen the damage to his fellow angels, and so he gets obsessive at times. Out of all of us, he has the greatest risk of going Absent in Heaven, simply because he can't just let life happen."

"Let life happen? Is that what you do?"

"It's all I can do," she said, throwing up her hands. "I have complete access to God, but he is never the one to initiate the conversation. I have to be the one to ask him a question or make a statement. Sometimes he responds, and sometimes he doesn't, but when he does, it's hardly ever a clear cut answer. And it's not because he wants to see me suffer while I'm figuring out the mystery. I know he's not like that because I feel his presence every time I go home or to the Throne Room. Anyone who feels his love *knows* he's not like that. But he's not going to let me stay a baby forever either. He wants to see me grow, and learn. He wants to see me make decisions and see where it takes me, and having no fear because he is always with me. That's the thing, Cadence. If we can always see the future, then in a sense, we don't *need* God anymore."

"I see what you mean," I said, nodding in agreement. "What God loves to see is that we trust him. That when we make a decision, even if it's the wrong one—there is always a way to escape, and a hope, as long as we trust him and know that he will not let us die."

"We might suffer," she said. "But we will not die unless we choose it."

"So...I should—" I was cut off as a flash of light suddenly blinded me. I closed my eyes as I heard Alessa cry out in surprise, and in the next second, I heard a loud crash, and then a sound similar to that of a small explosion. A gust of wind flew past us, and we leapt to our feet, unsure of what had just happened. When the light had first hit me, I thought it was God, taking me into his arms, but it wasn't. The unsettling noises that followed only put a fear within me. Alessa grabbed my forearm and I opened my eyes, following her gaze.

Hundreds of small meteors, all encased in blinding light, were falling from above and crashing into the buildings below one after the other, destroying homes, mansions, Fellowship Halls, and the Mission Center. Only the Throne Room escaped destruction as the meteors that hit its sides just fell down to the ground below in a slump.

I took in the display in horror, watching one meteor after the other slowly decimate my home, and I found myself clenching my fists in rage, wondering who had the audacity to attack it. It could only be the demons, but how they had escaped the invisible barriers around Earth and came here was—did they do it by using Lysander's method? Of separating themselves and passing through it? Were they bringing the fight to our doorstep even now?

I heard footsteps behind me and the rest of our team stepped out, staring out in awe.

"What is happening?" Farah cried out in agony, as Marcus wrapped one arm around her to console her. I stretched out my wings, preparing to take flight as soon as the meteor shower was over. But as I stared at each meteor closely, my eyes began to adjust to the blinding light, and little by little, I was able to see what was hiding underneath.

They weren't meteors at all.

They were angels.

Our brothers and sisters.

I took off and headed for the closest falling meteor, ignoring Alessa's cries behind me. I put myself in the trajectory's way, and braced for impact. When it hit my midsection, I nearly lost all consciousness from the blow, and I suddenly wished I still had my shield, but there was little time to dwell on the past.

The meteor pushed me forward, sending me to the ground below, but then two hands pressed up against my back and pushed the other way. I glanced behind me, out of the corner of my eye, and saw the Godhand of our team, Marcus, using his strength to slow our descent.

With him helping, we were able to stop the momentum, and the light suddenly died out. The angel nearly fell out my arms, but I caught him. I didn't know his name, but his armor was cracked, and his face was worn and sunken. From the steady pulse of his angelic body, I could tell that he had been unconscious for a while.

"Angels," Marcus stated, and I nodded at him. He took off, trying to catch more angels from crashing into the buildings. Having already been unconscious, more damage to their bodies would just extend the time until they were awake. And we needed answers *now*.

"Why are angels falling into Heaven?" Alessa asked, appearing next to me. I frowned and studied the angel in my arms further.

"I don't know," I said. "But tell the others to steel their minds. We're going to help out with the damage around us first, but afterwards, we're heading straight to Earth.

Chapter 7 – Steel

Not one of the angels were conscious, but we still kept moving forward, picking up our fallen and bringing them to our mansions. We laid them down to rest and moved on to the next site for more, while keeping a watchful eye on the sky above. I waited for the demons to come at any moment, but they never arrived. That was okay. I would be seeing them soon enough.

Though I hadn't said anything to my team about wanting to be a leader again, I became one, and once again, it was unofficially. Before I even realized what I was doing, I was giving orders and delegating, putting them into cautious battle formations while they helped the wounded, and having them report to me anything they thought of that could help the situation.

Heaven was our home, but it was also so much more. It was our sanctuary. After Lucifer and his army had been banished in one fell swoop, there was not a single thought of Heaven being attacked. Not a one. Deep down, we all believed that it was impossible, as if God had placed an impenetrable barrier around it, as strong as the Almighty himself.

And now our resolve had been shaken. Though it had been angels falling from the skies, and not demons, it was still felt like an attack. At the very least, our siblings had suffered at the hands of the demons. And suddenly, I didn't feel the need to lay on the grass and wait for change. I was ready for battle. I was ready for war.

I only hoped that I would make the right decisions—ones that would keep our team whole.

"Should we get Amos to come with us?" Farah asked. I glanced over at her as we flew toward the Mission Center.

"No, let him be," I said. "Besides, he may have already went back to Earth. For now, we'll work with what we have. Ulysses, how are you holding up?"

"I don't know," he replied truthfully from behind me. I didn't pry any further on that matter.

"Just keep helping our fallen. If things turn into a fight for some reason, just let us handle it."

"Okay," he said weakly. He wasn't ready for battle. And I wasn't sure if I was either.

The Mission Center had been damaged the least so we left that site for last. Besides us, there had been a thousand other angels in Heaven. We were the only ones left behind in the Battle to the East. A thousand may sound like a lot, but it felt like a handful. It had taken so many trips back and forth to our mansions and making sure each unconscious was okay that we were beginning to feel weary. It had been a long time since we had been alert, and now it showed no signs of stopping. I hoped I wouldn't make a mistake because of it.

"Down there," Lysander said, pointing to the entrance of the Mission Center below. To our surprise and delight, Raphael was standing there, with another angel lying on her back. We descended and Raphael examined us one by one.

"Please don't tell me you're tired already," he muttered. I couldn't help but laugh.

"Nice to see you too, Raphael," I said. "What's going on here?"

"Why are you here?" Lysander interrupted before Raphael could speak. Lysander yelped and instinctively grabbed his face and backed away.

"We were hit hard on Earth," he said, his eyes squinting for some reason. "I had a few troops under my command when a few former Archangels and some Godhand caught us by surprise. We fought back, but they overwhelmed us. We've already lost so many angels to the demons that I decided that we should all fly back to Heaven to recover. Nearly all of my angels were so hurt that they lost consciousness when we were nearly here. By the time we arrived, they were free-falling. It's a miracle that we made it back at all. From my count, thirty-four are unaccounted for."

He fell silent after saying that, and we waited for him to continue. Raphael was one of the strongest angels I knew emotionally, but even he had to pause when thinking of the horrors he had witnessed, and the angels he had lost. I didn't ask why he left the thirty-four behind. I knew he had his reasons, and yet, those same reasons would probably haunt him for years to come.

"We're losing," he said finally, staring at us one by one. "There's no way to say it other than that. The demons are cutting us down, troop by troop, little by little. There's not much else we can do. They're going to take the Earth at this rate."

"We can't allow that to happen," Alessa said, and Raphael crossed his arms.

"I'm glad you said that. Because for me, this is only a pit stop. I'm here to take you to the Battle to the East. I don't care if you're ready. We need you. Is that understood?" He glared at me when he said the last part, and I simply nodded toward him. He just kept staring.

"We might have a better way," Lysander stated. Raphael sighed.

"Fine. What is it?"

"We've discovered that if you go to the bottom of the ocean, and allow it to affect your angelic pressure, your body will eventually break apart. While in the broken state, you can travel through the invisible barriers, the mantle, and eventually hit the Earth's core. I think that's where the demons are hiding. If we go there and attack them, we could end the war altogether."

Raphael stared at him with a blank expression, then he turned to me.

"So Lysander has finally lost it, huh?" He said it so matter-of-factly that I snickered, and Farah burst out laughing.

"I'm serious!" Lysander stated, but Raphael glared back at him with weary eyes.

"That's not going to happen right now. Maybe if you had come up with this plan a decade ago, sure. But right now, we're trying to keep the demons at bay. We're on the defense."

"But if we just spare—"

"—there's no one to spare!" Raphael shouted, and we all winced. "Every angel that could even attempt a mission like that is busy keeping our army afloat. The most I could offer you are angels with far less experience and strength, but the problem is, we would only get one shot at the kind of mission you're speaking of. If we fail once, then the demons will either move their headquarters or increase their defenses, making it even harder in the future."

"What if we ditch the Battle to the East and go there instead?" Lysander asked.

"Can't do it because if the Battle to the East officially ends, where will their heavy hitters go? Right back to their headquarters. In which case, it will be even harder to succeed. If what you're saying is true, our best course of action right now is to keep them occupied at the Battle while we figure out a viable way to get to their headquarters. In order to do that, we have to free up some of our powerhouses first, and that means the Battle has to go a little more in our favor. We're doing so badly at this point that their heavy hitters will soon leave and just let the peons finish us off."

"So we help out with the Battle to free some angels up, and then we hit the headquarters?"

"Yes," Raphael said firmly. "That's the only way."

"Then let's go," Lysander said, flexing his wings.

"Calm down, butterfly. We need a plan."

"Why are we losing so badly?" I asked, and Raphael shook his head.

"I don't know," he said. "But there hasn't been a point in which we were ahead. We've been slowly losing ground with every passing year."

"Are the demons getting stronger somehow?"

"I don't think so."

"Well they must be doing something right." Raphael squinted his eyes and stared straight through me. I tried not to look at him for too long. Raphael muttered something under his breath and then began to hover above the ground.

"If any of you have any suggestions, I'm open to them. Now let's head out." Raphael took flight at full speed and we had no time to question his orders. It was time to get to the battlefield.

The flight back to Earth was not like the journeys we had in the past. Before, we would take our time, sightseeing and playing with the stars and the planets, but we had a war to get too, and I wondered how long it would be before I could take in God's masterpieces again. Everything became a blur as we sped past, a blend of colors and slight gravity pulls from the planets we rocketed by.

When he came upon planet Earth, I was in shock over how much angelic and demonic pressure I felt coming from its atmosphere. We had barely passed Mars and my body began shaking uncontrollably. My flight pattern began to waver and I nearly stumbled off course. Raphael looked back at us. Out of the corner of my eye, I saw Alessa bump into Marcus.

"You will adjust soon," Raphael said. "It's just a shock from being away for so long. There is a lot of fighting happening."

"And I take it we're going to the middle of it?" Lysander asked. Raphael didn't respond. He faced forward and kept moving. It was like a blur, flying over the plains and the erected cities, new worlds created at the hands of the humans. We didn't have to time to examine them and admire the architecture, nor could we get a reprieve to examine their faces, in order to determine how they were doing without their angelic counterparts. We simply headed for war.

When came to a valley of mountains, covered in snow and fog. Snow fell softly, creating a tranquil ambience that almost put me at ease. It was the clashing of swords and the cries of the wounded that ensured I didn't feel too comfortable. As a low hanging cloud passed from our view, we were able to catch a glimpse of the ensuing battle, and my eyes couldn't help but widen. There had to be a million angels and demons at war with each other, fighting all at once.

Angels fell by the hundreds. Some were able to gain their composure and fly back up for another bout, but most disappeared into the fog below. The demons fell by the tens, and many of them didn't stay down. They gained up on our brothers and sisters with their gaining numbers, slashing at wings and armors with no mercy, cackling as they watched their former comrades quiver and lose consciousness. I could only watch in horror as an angel came sky-rocketing toward us, his back at our faces.

Marcus wasted no time. He sped forward and caught him in mid-flight. Carrying the fallen angel in his arms, he presented it to Raphael. Raphael snapped his fingers and a messenger angel came over to retrieve him, taking him back to Heaven or whatever passed for their version of a hospital.

"Come," Raphael said calmly, waving us to the left, just as a cloud covered up the battlefield from our sight.

"Shouldn't we go out there?" Farah cried, but Raphael put a finger to his lips.

"Not yet. Be patient."

"I don't know how you could be so calm," Lysander said, and Raphael just glared at him for a second.

"Don't make me regret bringing you," he said through clenched teeth. "Now keep your mouth shut and follow me." Raphael took a sudden dive downward and we followed suit, spiraling into a narrow, circular tunnel. Suddenly, he took righted himself and went forward, heading into another tunnel after the same fashion. We traveled for ten miles, and then there were no more tunnels to take. We reached the outside and ended up in a hidden valley, surrounded by snow-capped mountain walls on all sides. In the middle of the valley below were about a thousand angels, talking among each other excitedly. From a simple glance, I could tell that there were many high-ranking officials there.

"This must be the headquarters," Lysander whispered. Alessa smacked him upside his head.

"Thank you," Raphael sighed heavily. "Seriously, why would you say that out loud? What if we had been followed?"

"No follow," Marcus said, placing a hand to his chest. "I would crush."

"Uh-huh," Raphael said as we headed to the snow covered flat land below. Once our feet hit the ground, a couple intimidating angels strode forward with arms crossed.

"Took you long enough," Gabriel said, with a twinkle of amusement in his eye. He was the messenger of all messengers.

"Reinforcements?" Michael said, his arms crossed over his massive breastplate armor. He was huge but he was surely not a Godhand. An archangel of the highest order, he was God's general, and an artist of war. If Michael was there, and we were still losing, I wasn't sure what good Team Six could do.

"A few," Raphael sighed, waving his hand toward us. "Made it back to Heaven…barely. What's the word here?"

"Not good," Gabriel said, his long white hair nearly blending in with the snowfall. "The demons' morale is high, and they are beginning to target our Glories. With each one we lose, the less prayer and assistance that is requested of God. Not to mention that our fighters are weary in general. For only being a third of Heaven, you would think we have the advantage, but not so."

"It's because the demons are stronger than we are," I found myself saying. "Their bodies are tied to the Earth in a way we have yet to figure out."

"This is Cadence?" Michael asked, pointing at me. When Raphael nodded, he took a step forward and placed a meaty hand on my shoulder. "We have heard much about you and your team. How you were able to defeat Vergil was impressive."

"That wasn't me," I replied.

"It wasn't?"

"Lysander was the one to—"

"Ah, Lysander," he said, his hand still on my shoulder. "A member of your team helped with the tactics. That doesn't take away from what you've done though. Without your leadership, Team Six wouldn't have gotten that far. Lysander wouldn't have grown to the point that he could use such tactics."

"I hardly think—"

"Don't be so modest," he said, with a smile in his eyes. "You defeated an Archangel. That is no easy feat. You have my admiration." I glanced back at my team and gave them a weak smile. They were all shaking their heads at me.

"Um, thanks," I said with a sigh. "But it might have been a one-time deal. I'm not sure how much help we will be here."

"What did I just tell you about being modest?" Michael chuckled, removing his hand from me. I awkwardly stood upright. I hadn't noticed how far he had been pressing down upon me and causing my knees to bend.

"We'll need to use you right away," Gabriel said. "We think the left quadrant is where we'll have you go. Raphael can show you the way, if that's okay with you." He turned to Raphael who just nodded wearily.

"When do we leave?" I asked, and Michael scowled.

"Hold on," he said. "Raphael, did you make sure you weren't followed before coming here?"

"At the end," he huffed.

"Did you start scanning for followers while you were in the tunnels or before?"

"Tunnels," he winced. "I'm sorry. I'm at my limits. I didn't think. But why do you ask?"

"I sense…" A shriek pierced the air and a collective gasp sounded off throughout the valley. A demon appeared from the tunnels, popping out so fast it was as if he had been shot from it like a cannon. With a halberd in hand, he hovered above us and scanned the area. Once he recognized Michael, he smiled wide. From behind him, we could hear the shrieks and squeals of more demons right behind him. From what I could tell, the demon before us was a messenger…which was the last thing we needed.

"They just found this place," Gabriel said hurriedly. "They wouldn't have had time to relay the message to the others. Team Six, it looks like you have your mission."

"Got it," I said, getting ready to take flight. A delicate hand slapped me on the back. I turned to see a smiling Alessa, grinning from ear to ear.

"Tag," she said. "You're the leader now."

I smiled back. And then we got to work.

Chapter 8 – Like Riding a Bike

The skinny demon tried to run away, but I was already upon him. I grabbed his wings and pulled him back from the tunnel. Holding him tight, I let Marcus finish him off with a punch to the face. Once that demon was unconscious, I turned to my team quickly.

"We have to clear them out. Marcus, that's your job." Marcus nodded and then he stretched his fists outward. Flying forward through the tunnel, he smashed into demon after demon, clogging up the passageway while sending them back from where they came from. The rest of us flew behind him slowly, making sure that none got past him. Once we hit the exit, Marcus kept flying upwards while he burst out like confetti, taking out the demon scraps as quick as possible. I unsheathed my sword from my hip and gripped it tight.

A demon came from behind me and I turned with my right hand stretched outward. At the last second, I realized that I wasn't holding a shield and I swung my sword up to parry, but it was too late. The blade was already past my defensive stance. Thankfully, Alessa kicked him in the head at the very last second, sending him spiraling to the side.

"That was close!" she yelled as I blinked rapidly.

"Sorry!" Farah said as she flew to my side. Lysander and Marcus came to my side as the demons above us slowed their assault. Now that we were together, they could see the enemy before them.

And they were afraid.

For in their minds, we weren't ordinary angels. At this point in the battle, Michael, Gabriel and the others hadn't really shown themselves on the battlefield, and certainly not to the grunts of the demon world. So to see us...those that had fought against Lucifer, who had defeated the Archangel, Vergil...it must have been a scary sight to behold. I took their moment of hesitation and fear to delegate.

"Listen up," I said, trying not to notice Alessa smiling after I said it. "Our job is to get this tunnel looking ordinary and inconspicuous again. In order to do that, we'll need to clear out this whole area for miles. That's a lot of demons, but we can do this easily, especially with all we've been through. I trust all of you to do what you've got to do. If you have a question, I'm here, but otherwise, use your best judgment. Lysander, go in battle, but stay back as much as possible in case you have anything to relate to me. Marcus will stay by your side as protection. Alessa, I want you to contact God and ask for his express assistance. I don't care if you're using up a prayer. If we don't clear this area out, the war could be lost. And Farah?"

"Yes, sir?" she said innocently.

"I want you to go out there and shine," I said with a smile.

"You want me to go all out?" she said, with a gleam in her eye.

"Wreck everyone."

"But…but you don't like it when I'm reckless."

"You can get reckless today. We need that crazy, insane faith of yours."

"REALLY?!" she said, clapping her hands together. "I can—" She stopped and turned her neck backwards, giving the demons above us the scariest glare I've ever seen in my life. It was almost like I could see literal fire in her eyes. She glared at one demon in particular and rubbed her hands together. "Oh…" she chuckled mischievously. "Oh, you're going to get it." The demon's eyes went wide and he began floating backwards, getting ready to make his mistake.

"Go," I laughed and she sped toward the demon so fast that I didn't even see her move. A second later, all I could hear was the demon crying and the mad cackling of Farah as she smashed into one enemy at a time like it was a pinball game. I turned to the others.

"I don't need to say be careful," I said. "Because I already know that we're going to come out of this victorious. Let's get this done."

Marcus roared, causing me to close one eye and wince. He then barreled upwards and got to work. Lysander followed close behind him, taking out the scraps. I engaged a couple demons to my right, parrying their blows and slashing through them. One of them nearly got a clean cut at my head, but then he was suddenly struck by a bolt of lightning. I didn't even see what became of him afterwards. One moment he was there, and in the next, he was gone. I turned around to see Alessa hovering in mid-air with the palms of her hands pressed tight against one another. With her head bowed and her eyes closed, he was engaged in deep prayer, and it must have been answered for lightning bolts were erupting from the sky a rate that was increasing by the second, hitting demons left and right with deadly accuracy. Any demon that happened to be near her were hit with two bolts and soon they began leaving her alone altogether.

It only took an hour to clear out the area for five miles, but I wasn't done yet. I could still hear the cries of our fellow angels close to us. Marcus, Farah, Alessa and Lysander came to my side, and the five of us stood next to each other in a line, watching as the cloud before us began to move off to the side, revealing the horrific battle we had witnessed earlier. Except now, there were even less angels in attendance. I looked from left, and then to my right.

They were all looking at me for answers. And I already had them.

"Let's go until there's not a demon left," I said, and that was all they need to hear. They flew forward with a speed that left my hair blowing back in the wind. I followed close behind.

Farah wasted no time. She went into the heart of the battle and performed an uppercut through a group of seven demons, all ganging up on a helpless Godhand, wounded and weary. The group of demons were thrown off guard and she began punching them without mercy. Other demons nearby tried grabbing her, and one even succeeded, but a kick to his face ensured that he didn't have a grip for long. She zipped back and forth like she was a gnat, so tiny and so quick that they could barely catch her movements, while simultaneously, she had the strength of a Godhand. For every failed grab or punch, a demon fell, and soon they began coming at her by the dozens. Still, she didn't let up.

I turned my attention away from her. She would be okay.

I slashed my way through a number of demons. Over time, it was so many that I had long lost count. And eventually, I was barely aware of my actions anymore. Occasionally I would glance over and see how my teammates were doing, but it didn't take long before any worries I had were completely gone. I was on automatic, hacking and slashing, destroying and smashing. Some demons tried to catch me by surprise, but I was a Guard. Defense was my job, and so trying to catch me off guard (excuse my pun), was a waste of time.

A Godhand stood before me and I came to, but then a lightning bolt ruptured through him. My gaze lost its luster, and I continued on. Wave after wave they came, and wave after wave they failed. Until a shout grasped at my attention.

"ARCHANGEL!" someone cried out, and I blinked, coming out of my stupor. I looked around me, and I noticed that we had freed up many of our angel soldiers. Where once there was only the five of us standing side by side, there were now hundreds, their morale having been increased by our assistance. They gripped their swords and shields tightly and they had a look on their faces that showed both confidence and determination. I smiled and looked forward. The Archangel that had been spoken of was in the distance. I could feel his angelic pressure from where I stood.

"For you," Farah said as she appeared to my right, placing a shield into my hand. "It's not much, but you'll be more comfortable." I smiled and thanked her. I looked over the shield. It was a standard shield, fashioned out of diamond. It wouldn't hold up under the continuous attacks of an Archangel, but a couple would do. A couple was far better than none.

"Any ideas how we go about this?" I asked Lysander. He had a hand cupped over his chin and he was glaring at the Archangel in the distance with a scowl.

"He's trying to intimidate us at the moment. There is no reason for him to stay so far away like that. And I realized that this was one big show once the demon soldiers all backed off. If they were smart, the Archangel would have just showed up in the battle like we did. Actually, that would have been a lot scarier."

"Agreed," I chuckled. "But even so, this is an Archangel. What should we do about him?"

"Intimidate him right back," Lysander said with a smile. "Why don't you go out there and greet him. One on one."

"You've certainly outdone yourself with that one," I laughed. "That's a terrible idea."

"We've got your back. You might take a hit or two though."

"I can handle that," I said, stretching out my neck. I began floating forward slowly, past the fog and the low clouds until I came upon him. I couldn't recognize who he had been back in Heaven, but it didn't matter. The energy emanating from him was so impressive that I almost lost my composure. My right hand wanted to instinctively raise the shield in front of my body, but I fought the urge. Still, I made sure that I didn't get too close. I remembered Vergil's speed all too well.

He glared at me and clenched his jaw. It was obvious he was offended that I had come to him alone, but I didn't care. It was all playing right into Lysander's plan, whatever that was. All I knew was that I trusted him. No matter what anyone thought, he was the one that had the experience under his belt. He was the one that had defeated an Archangel, and so it would be stupid of me not to listen to his advice, even if I was in danger.

"You come to me alone?" the Archangel gruffed, his massive fists clenched at his sides. His face was hideous, and I couldn't make out any of his facial features like his nose, mouth or eyes. I wasn't even sure how he had just spoken to me. It was as if someone had taken a gigantic hand and wiped his face diagonally to the right, bringing all his facial features with it. His body was like Vergil's. Big yet toned. Rippling with fire and heat and anger. There were large spikes sticking out of the skin of his forearms, and his breastplate was cut off at the sleeves. He wore a loincloth, but nothing else below, showing off his huge legs and feet, singed by fires I had never experienced.

I thought of what Lysander said. Of how the demons were more than likely living in the Earth's core, and how it was probably affecting them the same way the stars and ocean did for us. Though they were spirit in composition, their time below the Earth had taken its toll on their bodies.

"Why waste the manpower?" I asked him, keeping my chin held high. He grunted or laughed, I wasn't sure.

"You are just a guard," he said, and this time, I laughed.

"And you are but an Archangel."

"That is why you should be afraid."

"No, I'm not," I said confidently. "Because I've already defeated one of your kind. I'm sure you remember Vergil."

"Ah yes, him," he said. It was only then that I remembered Vergil's location—the bottom of the ocean...and close to the Earth's core. Had he been taken back to the demon's headquarters by now? Would he even be strong enough to endure the trip?

"Is something wrong?" the Archangel asked, and I gave him a smile.

"I was just thinking about how much we've learned from our battles with him, and how we can use it against you now."

"And how will you do that?" he asked. Based on the way his arms relaxed, I could tell he was trying to put me into a false sense of security. He wanted me to think that he had no intention of attacking me, when nothing could be further from the truth.

"Archangels are very powerful, but they are not invincible. Vergil's defeat proved that. You all have pools of spiritual energy just like the rest of us, which means that you can hit a point where you can reach zero and go unconscious. You can be defeated, it just takes a lot of hits on you to do it."

"And how will a lowly Guard do such a thing? You're not even designed for offense."

"Haven't you figured it out by now?" I laughed, having figured out Lysander's plan myself. "I'm the distraction while the rest of them get in place."

"WHAT?!" he shouted, and I shook my head as a hundred angels came from his sides and behind him. He turned to attack but I had already sprinted forward and slammed my shield into his already deformed face. It didn't hurt him, but he was already so enraged at me that I took all his attention. As the other angels began slashing at every inch of his body, he punched my shield. On the third hit, his fist crashed through and reached for my throat. I backed away from his flailing fingers and Farah zipped in front of me. She grabbed his hand with her tiny one and squeezed, causing the Archangel to wince and cringe at the strange sensation shooting through his body. She let go and he swung at her, but she was already behind him, kicking him in the back of his head. He growled at the pain and swung again, but she was too fast for him, moving like flashes of light around him.

It took an hour. A long, painstaking hour, but eventually he fell. We had lost nearly three dozen angels at his hand alone, but it was far less than it would have been if we hadn't worked together. I didn't even want to think about what could have happened.

Farah was knocked out on Marcus' shoulder, sleeping soundly from all the energy she had exerted. Alessa's eyes looked sunken and weary, and Lysander was all smiles, examining the fallen Archangel's body the best he could from a distance. Raphael and five other angels I hadn't seen before, all dressed in black armor, came to take the Archangel off our hands. He nodded at me and began flying away but I quickly grabbed his forearm.

"Don't take him to the bottom of the ocean," I whispered to him. "There has to be another place."

"We'll figure it out," he said, giving me a rare grin. "We've got it covered. Your team get some rest. Hmm. I knew bringing you out here was a good decision."

"Is that why we couldn't go to the battle beforehand? We were your trump?"

"Don't get proud now," he scowled at me. Then he gave me a wink and took off before I could say anything else. I looked around me and saw the angels heading off in different directions. I felt a wave of panic come over me, but then a meaty hand pressed down on my shoulder. I knew who it was without looking behind me.

"This was huge for us," Michael said as I turned around. He removed the weight off of me. "Thank you for your assistance."

"It wasn't me," I said. "It was all of us. But thank you all the same. I have to ask though, why is everyone going off in different directions? Shouldn't we all be sticking together?"

"Everyone has been assigned valleys similar to the one you were at with us earlier. They have other officers to report to. Don't worry, they haven't gone far. Should a single demon show his face, we'll know."

"And what if they show their face somewhere else on the Earth?"

"Not likely," he said. "Make no mistake. Most of the demons are still here. Just not nearby. They have an army similar to us about a hundred miles away from us. Given the speed in which we can all fly, you know that's not very far. They have their own valleys and crevices in the mountains east of here."

"So we can assume that they have their own base of operations similar to what you have."

"Of course, but that's a lot of demons to get through before you get there, and we're not ready for that. Slow and steady."

"No disrespect, but perhaps slow and steady is what nearly lost us the battle. We may need to try more drastic measures."

"You mean a kamikaze mission?"

"Maybe," I said, as Lysander tapped me on the shoulder. I flew slightly to the side to give him room to join us in the conversation.

"I was studying the battlefield while we were fighting," Lysander said to Michael. "And I've come to the conclusion that there has to be an ulterior motive at work here. The demons are a lot smarter than we give them credit for. That was evident to me with how they handled Cain and Abel long ago. Yet, here today, it was just wave after wave, as if they were throwing away their soldiers. Even the Archangel was a throwaway."

"What makes you say that?" Michael asked in concern.

"Because he was ugly."

"Okay," he said, unconvinced.

"No, listen. I don't know why this is, but you can determine how strong a demon is by their relative beauty. I'm not saying they are beauty, but the way their physique, scars, tattoos, and all that...the way they are placed...they tell a story of sorts. It's like a painting. And the uglier the painting, the weaker the demon. My old friend, Vergil, for example—he looked nothing like the one today. And we know scout demons by their misshapen ugly features. They are small and ugly. I'm not saying the Archangel today wasn't powerful, but as far as Archangels go, he was one of their weakest."

"What are you talking about?" Michael scoffed. "Why would they be throwaways? They are winning here. What reason would they have to just give us their weakest?"

"Why not?" I said, going with Lysander's theory, though I wasn't sure of it myself. "If their weakest can defeat us, why not send them out? They can save their best for any surprises we may have coming their way."

"Not to mention," Lysander said, "it might all be a distraction. One very long distraction. Vergil wasn't here at the Battle of the East.

He was on Adam's farm, trying to change the course of humanity and history all at once. How have the humans been?"

"They are fine," Michael said. "The demons rarely bother them. All of their resources are sent here."

"Or is that just an illusion? Maybe they have already planted the seeds within the humans, and now they are simply letting them grow into what they want them to be."

"To what end?"

"They have already proven that they can beat us one on one," I said, glancing at Lysander. "And they know how powerful we can become when humans help us. They may be covering all of their bases. Distract us here, affect the humans covertly, and then when they are sure everything has gone in their favor, they'll send the heavy hitters to finish us off."

"Goodness," Gabriel said, appearing from above them. He swooped in and stood next to Michael in mid-air. "Perhaps you're right."

"You were listening the whole time?" Michael asked, shaking his head. "Why do you do that?"

"Because you try to keep secrets from me," Gabriel said, giving him a smile. "And I don't like it. But never mind that," he said, turning back to me and Lysander. "We've been keeping a close eye on the humans, and we've yet to see anything out of the ordinary. They are just progressing naturally, without any influence by demon or angel."

"And that is how angels became absent," I said. "They had no guide. And that is only if the demons are not subtly affecting them. Either way, we need the humans on our side. It's a win-win. If we help them, then they might be able to help us in the war with prayer. If we learn that they are doing fine on their own, and they are not being affected by the demons, then at least we can have the comfort of knowing that the demons aren't using them, and then we can divert our energy elsewhere."

"We don't have a lot of extra manpower."

"We know the humans," Farah said, interrupting the conversation. "We were even guardians once." Alessa punched her in the arm.

"Yeah, and that didn't turn out great," she whispered.

"You would want to investigate this?" Gabriel asked me. I shrugged my shoulders.

"If Lysander thinks it's worth looking into, it probably is."

"After what you did today, we could really use you here."

"Even with this mission, it doesn't mean we can't come back if need be and help. At least we'll be closer since we'll be on Earth."

"And if you determine that the humans need our help, what then? Let's say you're right. The demons are secretly using the demons. That means that you will be facing the best they've got, and I'm sure they won't face you head on either. They will take you by surprise, and after what's happened to Vergil, they will not let you go. Is that a risk you're willing to take?"

"Not doing anything could be worse," I said, turning to Alessa. "We can't stay idle and expect things to change."

"Then I wish you the best," Gabriel sighed. "I hope your concerns are for nothing. Be safe and pray for assistance."

"We will," I said, nodding toward him and Michael. We parted from their presence and began flying away from the battleground, heading to somewhere. We weren't sure what direction to go in, but the first humans we came across—we would start there.

"Gabriel's right, you know," Lysander said to me as we flew on. "If the humans are the demons' secret weapon, then we're probably not going to come out of this unscathed."

"What else is new?" I muttered, and he laughed.

"By the way, thanks for agreeing with me back there. I could tell by the tone in your voice that you weren't sure."

"You haven't given me a reason not to trust you," I said, facing forward.

"It doesn't mean I'll never be wrong," he said after a moment of silence.

"I know," I said, facing him. "But when you are, I'll be there to clean up the mess. I just hope you'll do the same for me."

"Of course," he said. "That's what a team does."

Chapter 9 – Some Guy Named Noah

After an hour of seeing no signs of life, we decided to head toward a more familiar location.

Adam and Eve's farm.

Strangely though, it was desolate. The house was still there, but it was unkempt and ruined, having been eaten by termites and other bugs. Spiders were now the owners and they had no mind to make the place presentable. The land was filled with rocks and the dirt almost had a rusty color to it. We stood before the house and worked through a number of scenarios, wondering why Adam's descendants would leave and why.

"Perhaps there is better soil elsewhere," Lysander suggested. It was a good an excuse as any. We began leaving the area when we heard shouts nearby. With urgency, we headed in that direction and came across a couple of middle-aged men fighting over a dead rabbit. They were pulling at it on both ends, spitting at one another and gnashing their teeth together angrily. I took out my sword and waved the team forward, signaling them to inspect the area. Images of Cain and Abel flashed through my mind, and there was an uneasy feeling in my spirit. The first humans we came across, and they were fighting. What were the odds? Were the demons really affecting everyone this much while were off fighting a battle that meant nothing? How bad would it be in the cities? Where there were much large populations?

We spread out around the two men and examined the area, but we could find no traces of demons at all. It didn't make any sense. Maybe the demon had run off in a hurry. But wouldn't we have sensed its spiritual pressure?

I called everyone back to my side.

"Let's keep watching these two," I said. "If the demon did run away, then they will begin to calm down. They won't keep this up without influence."

"Good idea," Lysander said, and so I knew it indeed was a good one. We stood nearby and watched with our swords at the ready. But no demons came. And the fighting didn't stop. One of the men expressed that he was tired of the other's "antics," and so he slapped him across the face with his free hand. The victim of the slap was sent reeling, clutching his face as he stumbled backwards. The man who slapped him shielded the rabbit with his arms, keeping it close to his chest, and then he ran off, nearly stumbling over his own feet.

We didn't give chase. Instead we watched the slapped man as he watched his food being carried off in the distance. The man didn't give chase either, but he was fuming. His fists were clenched tight and he grit his teeth hard. Even when he turned around and began walking in the opposite direction, his anger didn't subside.

We followed him, as he walked over the hills near Adam and Eve's house. Except he didn't head for what I knew to be the city of Nod. Instead, he went southwest, to a land that I was not familiar with. And to my horror, the first man that he came across, who was on his own travels and minding his business—the slapped man hit the traveler in the face, sending him into the dirt and clumps of grass. His knapsack exploded open and his supplies spilled out. The slapped man kicked the traveler once in the stomach, and then he began to go through the supplies, taking as much as he could carry in his bosom. Tin cups, parcels of paper, various fruit and even the traveler's clothes.

The slapped man took it all, leaving the traveler on his knees, cursing the ground and pounding it with his calloused fists. I found myself shaking my head at the sight of it all.

"No demons were near here," Lysander said. "None that I could see at least."

"It doesn't make sense," Farah whispered. "Why would that man hit someone like that, without a demon's influence?"

"Maybe the demon's influence have gotten stronger," Lysander suggested. "Maybe it lingers on them for a while, even after they have left the humans' presence."

"But how is that possible?" I asked, turning to face him. Out of the corner of my eye, I saw the traveler pick up his empty knapsack, brush it off, and then began heading back to where he came from, probably to replenish his lost goods.

"No clue," Lysander said. "It's all theories at the moment. No concrete evidence."

"Well, you might as well tell us," Alessa sighed. "I asked God about it all. He said that he is watching the Battle of the East."

"So he didn't answer your questions?"

"No," she said, shaking her head. She folded her hands together and cast her eyes to the side. "If past experience is any indication, I would say it means we're about to walk into something that we should have no part in."

"What do you mean?" Farah asked. Alessa pursed her lips.

"When it's a simple question like what God's favorite color is or what music does he like listening to, I get straight answers. But when I start delving into current situations, the answers begin getting more cryptic. Usually it's in parables or mysterious phrases. And when I want to know about the future? Well, he either misdirects me, changes the subject or says he won't answer at all. That's the scariest to me. When he doesn't even want to talk about the situation. It usually means that something bad is about to happen."

"I think of it as an opportunity to learn," Lysander replied, but I just sighed heavily.

"Learning can be difficult," I said. "And sometimes you have to repeat the lesson over and over before you get the point. If we're about to walk into a lesson of sorts, I can't say that I'm completely looking forward to it. The last time we got into trouble, we had to fight an Archangel."

"We came out on top."

"That's open to interpretation," I replied. He just stared at me with a blank expression, and left the conversation at that. Marcus placed a hand on my shoulder.

"No point. Argue," he said. "Let's go."

"Did anyone else pick up on that?" Farah asked, cupping her hand against her ear.

"What?" Alessa asked, and Farah put a finger to her lips.

"That's the third time I heard someone mention that name."

"There's no one around," I sighed, but she scowled at me and shook her head, placing her hands at her hips.

"The traveler muttered the name, and I heard two more say it in the distance. If you weren't so busy yapping, you would have heard it too."

"Okay, what name?" I chuckled.

"Something named Noah," she replied. "The traveler mentioned something about Noah having food."

"Might as well follow the traveler then," I said, unsure of my own order. "We're here to see how the demons are affecting the humans so we might as well get some more information."

"And what if Michael is right?" Lysander asked. "What if the humans aren't being controlled by the demons and it's all about the Battle of the East?"

"Then we'll head back there," I replied. "Simple as that."

We took flight and caught up to the traveler easily. He hadn't gotten far. But what we were surprised to see was the construct in the distance. I was under the assumption that Noah was a city of some kind, a place where he could buy wares. But there was no city. Just a very, very large boat in a barren valley. I heard Marcus mutter under his breath something about an "ark." About a mile away to the north from the ark was a tree line that extended into a forest, stretching on as far as I could see. Based on the number of hewn trees surrounding the ark, it was safe to assume that that's what it was being created out of.

The Ark was gigantic, and nearly as big as a city in width. Its height was taller than the highest building I had seen, and nearly reached the height of the structures I had seen in Heaven. Hundreds of people were working on the Ark simultaneously, hammering and applying more wood, reinforcing the exterior or cutting down more trees along the edge of the forest.

"It's beautiful," Farah said, crossing her arms. "I wish I could push it over."

"No one's pushing over anything," I laughed. She sighed and bowed her head in disappointment.

"What's the point of this?" Alessa scoffed. "Protection?"

"I suppose," Lysander began, "that with an ark such as that, you could keep a great number of people at bay. And after seeing what happened to the traveler, I don't blame them."

"But why an ark?" Alessa asked. "Why not a city with large walls?"

"Nod had walls," I said, watching the people work down below. "Didn't make a difference. If someone wanted to get in bad enough, they would find a way."

"Okay, but it still doesn't explain the boat concept. There's no water nearby to put it on. We know that there are bodies of water, but do the people? Has anyone even ventured out far enough to find one?"

"I would imagine so," I said, pointing down below. "Whoever had the idea of building this had to have seen the edge of their world."

The people quieted down below, as if something within them had sounded an alarm, letting them know that they had to cease their speaking. They put down their tools and left them in the dirt next to where they had worked. One by one, they marched to the front of the ark and waited. For what, I could not tell. Not without entering the ark and seeing for myself. I considered it, but I wasn't one to go looking after knowledge. It wasn't any of my business. Instinctively I reached behind me and placed a flat hand on Lysander's chest. I barely caught him from heading down.

"Let's see what's going on first," I chuckled. "There could be danger."

"Right," he laughed. "Danger."

We made our way to the front of the Ark so that we could see what was taking away everyone's attention. At the front of the Ark was a man that appeared to be wiser beyond his years. Though he didn't look old, his demeanor was that of someone that possessed a great deal of experience in the matters of the world. He stood before the people, with no podium or stage to put him higher than the rest. Only those in the first few rows of the crowd would be able to see him face to face. The rest would have to be content with his voice.

Still in the air, we watched the young/old man as he scanned the people. He took a deep sigh and then he smiled with his eyes.

"Dinner is almost ready," he said, and the crowd began cheering and pumping a fist in the air. The young/old man chuckled and shook his head. A teenager in the front of the crowd shouted above the ruckus.

"How much longer, Noah?" he asked, and suddenly, the young/old man gained more of my attention. This was Noah? Not a city. Not the ark, but a man? And to have so much food as to feed such a large amount of people...how was this possible? Even in Nod, a place that boasted a large community—they still went hungry. Did the workers on the Ark help him gather food?

"As soon as I am finished," Noah said with a smile. The crowd quieted down and waited for him to continue. "Men and women, I don't consider myself an eloquent speaker, but speak I must do. Once again, before I begin, I must thank you for all the great work that you have done on the Ark."

"Who else is going to give us bountiful feasts in exchange for a little labor?" a man shouted from the middle of the crowd and a couple men chuckled in response.

"I realize," Noah continued, "that food is scarce, as it always has been from the days of our forefathers. But the Lord has been gracious, and has blessed me with a great supply in which I can use to barter for your services."

"We don't care what sorcery you use," the young teenager in front replied. "As long as we get fed." Noah stopped and stared at the boy, longer than what was deemed normal. Even from where I hovered, I could see the concern in Noah's eyes. The man knew deep down that the teenager was plotting something sinister, and perhaps he wasn't alone in his intentions. I believed Noah when he said that God had given him the food, but how many men would believe it? Especially if they were those like the descendants of Cain—those that denied God and eventually refused his existence altogether. They would surely think that Noah had gotten his bounty through ill means. Perhaps he had overtaken a city somehow. It didn't matter. If the men in the crowd wanted to overtake the ark once it was completed, in order to secure both living quarters and Noah's endless supply of food, they could probably do it. As long as God didn't intervene, that is.

"Just give us the daily speech," an old man with salt and peppered long hair said from a few yards away. "We're starving."

"Of course," Noah said humbly. He took another sigh and then lifted his head high to look into the eyes of his fellow men. "I know that none of you believe the words I have to say, but that doesn't mean I will stop trying. Before it is too late, I ask that you at least consider my words."

"Go on," the old man said again, and Noah nodded toward him.

"The wickedness of man has brought forth the wrath of God," Noah said as a few yawns was heard from the back of the crowd. "In the beginning, we had a paradise of our own, but through our disobedience, we were cast out. However, even then, we were not left to the cold. The Lord stayed with us, as long as we communed with him in turn. Should we choose to follow our own way, and our devious heart, the Lord will not hear our prayers. He will not commune with us in the way our souls desire. As the years have gone by, the world has become quiet. Few still pray to the Lord, and worst, they have even begun to turn against their fellow man. It is thought that without God, man can at least find the decency to treat one another with love and respect. But history has shown us that this is not so.

"We are selfish and jealous creatures, and as time has passed, we have only gotten worst. We have gained God's attention, but not in a good way. He has seen our evil and how we desire only the destruction of all of his creations. In that regard, he has answered our silent pleas for annihilation. He will send the rain. The sky will weep, and the tears will fall upon the earth, giving us more water than we could ever want...that we *will* ever want. Those that have not found favor in the sight of the Lord will perish. I do not wish this, but it will be done. There is nothing that can—"

"That was it, right?" a man with dirty brown hair snapped from the crowd. "We can eat now?"

"I'm not finished."

"You've never gone this long before. Why can't we eat?"

"I need to tell you about—"

"We need to hear from the champion!" someone cried out, and the crowd began cheering.

"Yes, the champion," someone else cried.

"YES! HE IS HERE!" another shouted. "LET HIM SPEAK, NOAH!"

Noah took a deep breath and scanned the crowd. Then from the middle of them, a tall man began making his way to the front. The people in front of him parted gladly, giving him the space to walk toward Noah. He had long braided hair and his shirt and pants were torn and baggy, yet it was apparent that he was a hard worker, just based on the size of his massive frame. If Noah was afraid, he did not show it.

"I take it you are the champion," Noah said. The champion stood before him and nodded once. Then he turned to the people to address them. Noah made no move to stop him.

"If you don't know me by now," the champion shouted, "then you must not be from around here!" The crowd cheered as he laughed and then continued. "My name is Aloof, and I came here to listen to the words of this man behind me. I heard of the work he offered to those who are willing, and the food he would give you in exchange. Now that I have put my hands upon his ark and listened to his words, I must say this. He is wrong."

The crowd gave a curt shout of approval and then waited for the champion to continue.

"This man has been preaching for decades. My children remember his cries of sky water from when they were barely able to walk. Now they have wives and children, and they try to shield their family's ears from his ramblings. You know as well as I that there is no rain. No sky water. We simply use him for his food, and that is all.

"However, even that isn't the main reason I came today. I'm here because I've heard grumblings among the villages. I heard that some have begun to entertain Noah's ramblings and consider his words. This is foolish. You have heard the whispers as our father Cain heard them long ago. The words of the dark ones. The angels that were banished from Heaven."

"What?" I asked, turning to Lysander. "Have you heard about this?"

"No," Lysander whispered. "But it makes sense. If God can directly talk to humans, why not demons?"

"But that's God," I said. "And we can't talk to the humans directly."

"Not that we've ever tried that hard," Alessa said. "I don't think we ever really thought about it, considering that we don't want to interfere in their lives. The demons have nothing to lose though."

"So the demons *are* spreading their influence," I said as I turned back to hear the champion.

"Even if God could still hear us," the champion replied, "why would we want his grace? Think of the tools we've gained through the fallen's whispers. The pockets of food we've discovered. Think of how similar we are to them. We have nothing in common with God, but we do with the fallen, and they will keep us strong and protected, as they all have. Don't even think about listening to this man's crazy words. God doesn't even think of him. Otherwise the sky water would have come.

"All you have to worry about is enjoying the pleasures of this life and listening to the fallen's words. They are only looking out for us."

"Excuse me," Noah interjected. "But I'm confused. Why would the demons help you?"

"Because they want to get back to Heaven," the champion said, glancing back at him for only a second. "When we die, we will be sent to Hell, and over time, we will amass an army, to one day take over Heaven. The only thing that holds us back from storming God's palace now is the flesh that surrounds our spiritual bodies. Once that is shed, we'll be able to work with the demons directly."

"That's insane!" Noah shouted and the crowd murmured among themselves.

"No more crazy than sky water. No…it makes a lot more sense. At least we periodically get messages from the demons. God remains silent and angry. If we are to believe your words, then what you're really saying is that God is seeking to destroy us all because we won't follow him and beg for his mercies. Why would I want to serve one such as him?"

"You don't know him," Noah snapped back. "How could you? You don't even seek to understand him. You simply demand sustenance and pleasure without having to show any love in return. If you can't even treat your fellow man well, how can God trust you with the blessings he has for you?"

"And what about you, Noah?" the champion scoffed. "What blessings has God promised you?"

"Life," Noah said with a smile. "Life after the rain."

"You smile, but you would not be smug if my men and I were to attack you now and take the ark for ourselves. It is mostly completed. There is no reason that we would need you now."

"You could try," Noah said confidently, "but you may be surprised by what happens."

"His confidence disgusts me," the champion declared to the people. Then he turned back to the older man that dared to question him. "Your days are numbered, Noah. Be mindful of this."

"Such is man on this earth," Noah replied, and the champion scoffed. With a wave of his hand he began shepherding the people away from the ark and back to their homes, even as many of them grumbled over the meal they had just missed out on. When they were all gone, which took a lot longer than I expected, a family of seven came from behind Noah. It appeared that they had come out of some secret compartment in the ark but I wasn't paying attention at that moment. Three men and four women stood behind Noah and watched what he watched, waiting for the man to speak. It was apparent by their intrigued faces that unlike the crowd that was just before him, they were willing to listen to his words.

"We should have been out here with you, Father," one of the men said. A tall young man with disheveled dark hair and a smooth disposition. He was stocky and wore his tunic tight. He looked very strong and I found it curious that he hadn't been outside as well. If not to work, but at least to defend Noah.

"Do not worry, my son," Noah replied. "God protects me."

"He would protect us as well," his son replied. "There's no reason why we can't all be out here."

"Let's not tempt the Lord," Noah said, turning to face them for the first time. He greeted them with a warm smile and extended his arms out for a hug. His family reciprocated the gesture and they gave each other a great embrace. "I do not want to see any of you get hurt," Noah said, his neck nestled into the neck of the eldest woman. I assumed it was his wife. "Our mission here is almost finished."

"And so is their boiling," one of his other sons replied. "The lid is soon to be knocked off and the water will spill."

"I've always loved your metaphors, Ham," Noah chuckled. "And I'm sure you're right. They will try to take the ark sooner than later. I have no doubts that they are planning as we speak. But we must not worry. The Lord has seen us through this far, and he has provided us with everything we need. The end is near, but for us, it is just the beginning."

"And what if they are right, and we are wrong?" his last son asked, short in stature but strong in build.

"Wrong?" Noah asked, blinking rapidly. "What do you mean?"

"They speak of the fallen—those that offer eternal life in exchange for their allegiance. We are offered the same by the Lord. How do we know what is right and what is false?"

"The Lord has provided for us our whole lives."

"And these fallen have provided for them."

"Not enough it would seem if they come to us for a quick meal."

"Regardless, the message sounds the same."

"I have no doubts, son. And you will soon see why."

"I hope, Father...I hope."

I turned to look at my team and they all had the same puzzled looks on their faces that I had. The fallen? Demons talking to humans? What were they saying that could convince so many people to their side?

"I can see how this is possible," Lysander said. Our attention turned to him. "Think about it. The angels aren't intervening in the lives of the humans because we not only want them to grow on their own, but we're also quite busy with the Battle of the East. Also, God has proven that he wants us to mature for the most part on our own which means if he has spoken to anyone, it's not often. It's very possible that the people may not even consider God at all, especially if they are constantly bombarded by demon influence."

"Do you think they are praying to demons?" Alessa whispered, looking down at her hands. "I mean...would that give the demons strength? Like Abel's prayers helped us long ago?"

"It's possible," Lysander stated. "And if so, I would surmise that's why our Battle of the East isn't going so well."

"We have to tell Michael and the others," I said. "And quickly."

"Go fast," Marcus stated. We took off fast, sure that Noah's family would be safe, and uncertain that we would be able to stop any demons in the vicinity if they weren't. If the demons were gaining their strength from the prayers of the humans, then we wouldn't have much of a chance. We weren't too proud to realize our limitations, our strengths and weaknesses...I had learned that lesson all too well—of what happens when you are blind to your shortcomings.

"Um...that's not good," I heard Farah say ahead of me. I halted my flight and lifted my head to see what she saw. If Farah was wavering in confidence, then I already knew that it was a bad situation.

And indeed it was.

Two archangels hovered in our path, gripping a long sword in each of their hands. Their frames were chiseled and their muscles were like rock. The tattoos that branded their skin seared into their "flesh" continuously, as if they were constantly being branded but the seal wouldn't take. They were both stone-faced and ready for our approach, and I couldn't help but feel a sense of dread welling up within me. In that moment I knew for sure that we had found out the secret to the demons' recent strength, and the archangels before us were going to make sure that it stayed that way.

"This is where it ends for you all," the Archangel on the right of us said.

For once, it sounded like a demon was telling the truth.

Chapter 10 – Not a Fan

We have come up against great opposition so many times already, and in each of those times, I was never afraid as much as I was now. There was not just one archangel but two before us, and neither one of them was an old friend. I could already tell that there would be no reasoning with them, and I wasn't sure what plan we could concoct that could defeat both. Nothing short of giving it all we had.

Basically…a kamikaze attack. One that had no hope of actual victory, but enough to cause some kind of damage. The equivalent of a disrespectful slap to the face. A spit on the shoes. A meaningless and hopeless act of defiance.

"So should I take a crack at them?" Farah asked me, and I shook my head no. Attacking them head on was foolish and pointless. As long as they didn't intend to destroy us outright, we had a chance. I just had to wait for the right opportunity, and maybe give Lysander a little more time to get that mind of his reeling. In order to do that, patience was the key.

"So we're just going to accept our fate?" Alessa asked me in disbelief. I could see the disgust in her eyes as the thought of surrender. But to me it wasn't giving up. It was survival.

"We're at your mercy," I said to the Archangels, and they looked at me in shock. I didn't think their stone faces were capable of such expressions. The one on the left scoffed at me.

"Why are you surrendering? Aren't you Team Six? The ones who defeated Vergil?"

"That we are," I said with a smile. Lysander looked at me and we exchanged glances. He smiled back, for he knew that based on the archangel's reaction, we were gaining a little more footing. Sure, they would still apprehend us, but paranoia would now settle into their minds. They would wonder how the team that defeated an archangel could just give up so casually. They would wonder what we were planning. Perhaps that paranoia would lead them into making a mistake.

"I don't understand," he said, but I simply shrugged my shoulders.

"We are too weak," Alessa said with a grin, catching on to the plan. Farah looked at us like we were crazy.

"Speak for yourselves," she muttered and Marcus grunted in her direction.

"I weak," he moaned, rubbing his massive forearms. "I so weak. I cold. I feel like Faithful." Farah gave him a look of concern but Marcus just pouted at her and continued to lay on the charade thick. The archangels were really concerned at this point, looking back at one another and wondering what to do next. The distraction was all I needed.

"GO NOW!" I shouted, pushing Farah in the direction of our superiors. I knew it would be a long flight, but she was the quickest out of all of us, and I could hold the archangels back for a little bit. I could take some hits.

"Stay here!" Lysander cried out to Alessa, who was beginning to follow Farah. She got the message and stayed behind with us. Marcus had already engaged with one of the Archangels and they had their fingers locked into a power struggle. It was obvious that the Archangel he fought was still unsure about us, as he did not yet tap into his full power. I further used this to my advantage.

"Now you'll see what we can do," I said in a deep voice, unsheathing my shield from its straps. My wings expanded and I floated toward the other Archangel slowly. Alessa and Lysander advancing with me from behind with maniacal looks on their faces.

Alessa stuck first. Having already put a prayer in, a lightning bolt shot through his body from above, making his body shudder and quiver under the shock. I bashed my shield square into his face, but he didn't move. And it was then...that he realized the truth. I could hear him chuckle from behind the cover of my shield.

"Go!" I shouted to the team as I dove toward the earth below. Alessa and Lysander quickly followed behind and Marcus used every ounce of his strength to push his Archangel back. He had to use up so many energy that when he followed his flight was shaky and he was diving faster than us merely because he didn't have the strength to keep himself upright.

I knew the situation wasn't good. But as many teams as possible had to survive the ordeal. There was no guarantee that Farah wouldn't come up against other adversaries on the way back. And so with that in mind, I decided to take one for the team.

I wasn't feeling like a leader lately, and though the last day had been great as far as making the right decisions, I knew it couldn't last. Perhaps I should have kept up the faith, but my strength was still low, my resolve still waning. I don't know if I was the best one to make the sacrifice out of the five of us, but it didn't matter at that point. The decision was made.

"Get back to Gabriel," I said as I halted my descent, tucked my wings underneath me and then shot upwards with my shield right in front. I didn't hear my teammates acknowledge my order, but I had no time to further attempt confirmation.

To the Archangel's surprise, I slammed into his stomach and subsequently plowed into the second Archangel's body, who happened to be right behind him. I shot upwards with all the energy I could muster up, knowing it wouldn't last. And once they were over the initial shock of my little maneuver, they switched to the offensive.

They both slid off of my shield as if they were made of water. It was so smooth and slick that I didn't even notice their movement until it was too late. I tried to stop my ascent but I was already greeted with two hard fists into my sides. I could feel my angelic pressure fluctuate as I was instantly made immobile. One of the Archangels caught me and held me in his arms before I could fall. The other examined me meticulously as he held my half-cracked shield in one of his gargantuan hands.

It all happened so fast. It was sad and pathetic. For me to keep them at bay for barely a couple seconds. I craned my neck as far as I could back toward my teammates and saw that they had disappeared from my sight. It didn't mean the Archangels couldn't catch them if they wanted to though, and so I groaned and tried my best to wretch myself from his grip.

He kept me close to his chest, barely flexing at all to keep me stationary. Eventually I gave in, and waited for what was next. They began flying in the opposite direction of the Battle of the East, and that both soothed and unnerved me.

"Where are we going?" I asked them, but they gave no reply. We flew in silence as I assessed my strength. It wasn't enough to break out, even if I tried my hardest. Only God could save me now.

We came upon a canyon bathed in red. The rocks were so bright and emblazoned that it looked like each stone had bathed in lava, yet their composition was so soft to behold that it looked like it was all made of sand. With the sun shining like a spotlight in the middle of the canyon, it created a dead yet beautiful landscape. One that I would have stopped to admire under different circumstances.

We flew even further down, past the cliff faces and giant rock faces, weaving through jagged, tall and fragile structures, made of stacked boulders and eroded mountainside. As we passed by, I cast my eyes in front of me as the Archangel still held me in his arms, and I saw that there were hundreds of angels being held captive in the canyon walls. They banged their fists and cried out for deliverance, but it was as if they were hitting up against invisible walls. My brow furrowed as I thought of how it was all possible, when one of the Archangels threw me on top of one of the jagged rocks—one that was near an empty hole in the canyon wall.

"What happens now?" I asked, trying to stand tall, but they were no longer afraid of me. The great Cadence was just another angel when all was said and done. They were probably asking themselves of what really happened to Vergil, for the team that had stood before them could not have been the victors.

"Go into that cell," the tallest Archangel said as his partner flew off, probably to check on the other inmates. I glared at the Archangel before me for a moment, and then I turned toward the hole in the canyon. I stretched my hands straight out before me and they bumped up against an invisible wall, just like the ones that were in the Garden of Eden. I made a fist and punched it lightly. There was no way I could just walk in.

"I can't," I said, beginning to turn back to the Archangel, but he didn't allow it. He grabbed the back of my head with one of his powerful hands, and nearly shoved my head into the wall.

"It's because you still have some energy left," he said, shoving an inch closer. He was gripping my head so tight that it was beginning to affect me spiritually. I could feel my body getting weaker. My vision was starting to get hazy. "Right before you go unconscious, and your angelic body is at its weakest, I need you to pull your spirit apart. Force your particles to go through the wall and then solidify."

It's like the black hole, my thoughts cried out. Or it was like Lysander said—it was how the demons were able to go into the Earth's core. If it was their way of going in and out of their headquarters, then they had to be experts at the process while it was a concept still foreign to most angels. Why would we practice such a thing? The only one I knew that did it for fun was Farah, and even if she was able to replicate the process at will, she certainly couldn't go into the demonic headquarters herself and take them all down, no matter how great her faith was.

As sad as it was, I was starting to learn that there was a difference between blind faith and reality. One could hope all they wanted for a situation to change, believing that God was in control and that he would alter one's life as soon as he felt ready...when the opposite couldn't be more true.

He's been ready. He's outside of the confines of time and space.

He's waiting for us to make a move.

To make mistakes and learn lessons, to pick ourselves back up and keep on trying...then he would step in, knowing that we were stronger and better than before. And because we had gone through the suffering, knowing that God was waiting for us at the other end, we were more powerful than ever before, through and through.

So in actuality...the more that I thought about it...maybe Farah did have the strength to take down Hell. Or maybe she just had to learn a few more things. Why I had forgotten all of this? That in order to grow and mature, you had to face the fear, not ignore it and hope it went away.

Why was this coming to me now?

"Now," the Archangel growled as he shoved my face *into* the invisible wall. It didn't hurt, but it was an unsettling feeling nevertheless. I could literally feel my face break apart, like a cloud opening up to let the rain fall. I could feel half my body seep into the other side, but the Archangel still had to help me do it. I was stuck in the sensation and the moment, trying to fight against his grip still, right down to the very last second. When I finally made it to the other side, my body solidified instantly, and I stumbled onto the soft sand-like floor. I pivoted awkwardly and ran at the invisible wall, but I ended up slamming my face into it and I fell back onto my butt. The Archangel outside scoffed once, gave me a sly grin, and then disappeared from my sight.

I ran up to the wall and pressed my cheek up against the wall, trying to see where he went, but he must have moved quickly. All I saw was an empty canyon. I couldn't even hear the cries of my brothers and sisters near me. I punched the invisible wall once, but there was no sign of damage. It was the island all over again, except this time there was no magnificent views. There was only rust colored rocks and a slowly descending sun from the corner of my eye.

I sighed and turned around.

And I nearly jumped at what I saw before me.

"Hello," he said, his body only half-revealed in the light coming from my rock cell's entrance. He was sitting on the floor several yards away with his legs tucked into his chest. He was leaning his arms over his knees and his head was hunched down, as if he was weary from a long journey. I stayed where I was. Did all the cells have two inmates? And if so, for what reason? Were there not enough cells?

"Didn't think I would ever see you here," the mysterious being replied from the shadows. From what I could see, he was clothed in tattered leather and rags. He wore a hood over his head, and the one hand that was illuminated in the sunlight was cracked and calloused. There were tattoos on the back of his hand, but they weren't glowing like they did with the demons. Could it be that there was a human before me?

"You don't even remember me," the stranger laughed under his breath. "Of course you wouldn't."

"Who are you?" I asked him, taking only one step forward. Once again, I felt naked without my shield.

"Abdiel," he replied. A name that sounded familiar, but the association was so distant, he could have whispered anything and my brain would have cried out for recognition.

"That's an angel's name," I said, realizing at least that much.

"It was," he muttered. I didn't like the way he said that.

"Are you a demon?" I asked, and he let out a heavy sigh.

"I am," he said, dropping his arms to his sides and then slowly rising to his feet. "Does that mean we can't be friends?"

"I'm friends with no demon," I replied, but he responded with a snort.

"You angels were all friends with demons at one point. Just because the surface of the lake did not reflect the deep, it doesn't mean the waters weren't murky."

"Why are you in this cell with me?" I asked, trying to get to the point. "Are you here to keep me weak? So that I can't escape?"

"Not at all," he scoffed, his voice sounding less gruff now that he was standing up. "If you get weak, then you can leave the walls that hold you here. They don't want that." He stepped into the light further, toward me, and I saw that he appeared young. His face was soft and babyish in composition. His hair was cut short but ruffled, and only one sole tattoo—a bright red chain—stretched across his face. His silver eyes looked at me with sorrow behind him, and his stance was not one of hostility. He was thin but not frail. His clothes were indeed tattered and ripped. Having seen many demons, I had to admit that I hadn't seen one like him before.

He was a demon, but the way he looked…it was as if he had not fully transformed.

I shook my head at the notion. *That's what they want you to think*, I thought. *That he's not as dangerous. They had to have chosen him for some reason. He wouldn't be in this cell because he had gone against Lucifer.*

"Cadence…" he said, his voice nearly cracking once my name escaped his lips. "You really don't remember me?"

"I don't," I said truthfully, scanning his eyes. "I'm sorry…but who are you?"

"I'm your biggest fan," he said with a curt smile. It quickly disappeared as I scowled at him. "Well, not anymore," he replied. "I don't know if anyone could be after what happened."

"I don't know what you're talking about," I said, very much confused.

"Angels don't lie," he said, his jaw clenching. He was starting to get frustrated, but I seriously didn't know why.

"I'm not lying. I don't know you."

"Why don't you search your mental database?" he asked me, and I hesitated to respond.

"What's the matter?" he snapped. "Afraid I'll attack you?"

"That's—"

"—I know that's not the reason," he shouted at me angrily. He turned around quickly and went back to the wall at the end of the cell. He put his back to it and then plopped down onto his butt, putting himself back into the position I found him in. "When was the last time you even went in there?"

"The mental database?"

"Yes."

"What does it matter?"

"It matters a lot," he said, his voice calmer now. "Because if you're still aware of the reason, it means that you actually care about what happened back then. It means you have remorse...and it probably explains why you're not a demon...like I am."

"Abdiel, I—"

"We were on the island together," he said finally, looking up to face me. With his body falling between light and darkness in the cell, one of his silver eyes were visible, staring straight into me, while the other remained hidden in the shadows. "You and me...we were part of the first group. You remember that, don't you?"

"I do," I whispered. It was starting to come back to me, though I was afraid of what might happen if it all flooded into my mind. I had suppressed so much...I had neglected the mental database for so long that I wasn't used to concepts and memories outside of what I allowed. I stayed in the moment while hoping for a brighter future. That was who I was now.

But not always.

"We were inseparable," he said. "At first it was just you and me before others started appearing. Back then you weren't afraid of the database. You did everything you could to reach God again, even it was at the expense of all of us."

"I didn't mean for all of that to happen."

"But it did, old friend...and here we are. Reunited."

"They put you in my cell, didn't they? To get information on what's happening with the angels."

"What do they care about that? The demons are winning through and through. Don't just assume I'm a monster because I'm on the other side. I told them that I wanted to tear you apart personally, but that's not the case. Me and several others...we're not like the rest. We're just trying to earn our way back into Heaven however we can. I said that I would hurt you but I really want to help you. Considering our history, I know that we can work well together."

"You want to get back to Heaven?"

"The only way is to turn the tide of this war," he said, standing to his feet. "And I know that you can make a difference. You can lead others into doing anything when you're at your most persuasive."

"Abdiel, I know you're sore from the islands, but I really don't remember everything that—"

"I went Absent," he declared loudly. "You pushed me into your beliefs so strongly that I went too far in the database. And when I was finally able to come out of it and I made it to Heaven, I was barely there a few days before I was banished to Hell. It's not fair, Cadence."

"I never asked anyone to go as far as they could in the database."

"Yes you did!" Abdiel scoffed. "You might not have said it explicitly, but you did. You would tell us how God is still out there, and the answers would be found in the database. You kept us tethered to you while we searched frantically, all of us seeking to fill that small hole in our spirits. You told us what to do, but you never searched all the way yourself. You had others do it because you were afraid. I think that deep down you knew the risks of going in too far. And you knew that if you went Absent, you may never find God. You were selfish, Cadence. You got back to God alright, but at our expense."

"No one had to listen to me."

"What were we supposed to do? You were the first on the island. You were the one who had survived outside of God's presence the most. We trusted you with our eternal lives and you used us for your personal gain. I don't care how righteous and holy you may claim to be, it's wrong, and even though God might not be casting you into Hell this very moment, you will pay for what you done. I'm sure of it."

"See," I said, trying not to break. "You do want revenge against me. How can I trust you?"

"Revenge?" he scoffed. "I want equality! I want to help you now so that you can help me later. I want to get back into Heaven and you're the only one that could vouch for me. You owe me a chance, at least. At least that much after what you've done."

"I'm not the bad guy," I said quickly. "What happened back then was terrible, but I was just going off of what I knew. I didn't know that we would lose so many…"

"If you're not sure, then it's best to keep your mouth shut and observe."

"A little too late now, don't you think?"

"Not for redemption," he said, walking back toward me. I could see that he was hurt. His lips were quivering and his body was shaking wildly. "We can both redeem ourselves. You might not want to admit it, but you have a stake in this too. Not being able to access the mental database over the guilt you have…that's not good. God gave us that resource for a reason, and you'll never be the leader you can be without it."

"I don't know," I replied, unsure of what to make of him. Abdiel extended a hand out for me to shake, and I stared at it anxiously.

"I'm all you've got," he said. "If we don't work together, we're both stuck here."

"Maybe that's for the best."

"Then it will be just like the islands," he said, as if mirroring my thoughts from earlier. "And we all know what happened there. You're not as strong as you think. None of us are. We may be spiritual and immortal, but we are not invincible. Once in a while, the former Archangels take us out of our cells to watch one of the other angels break. It's the most terrifying thing you've ever seen. Watching someone beg to go Absent, just so that they didn't have to be alone anymore. The actually *beg* the demons on the knowledge of how to go Absent. If we don't work together, I wonder how long before it will be us out there, tearing at the Archangels' garments, trying to lose our minds."

Chapter 11 – My Enemy and My Friend

I wasn't sure of what to think about our reunion. For all intents and purposes, we were enemies, and yet, we had once been good friends. Abdiel was the type of angel that wanted to please, and it didn't matter who, as long as everyone was happy with him. Being that I was the only angel on our island at the time, he made sure that was happy through and through.

And if that meant going deep into the recesses of the mental databases, even beyond places that I was willing to go...well...he was going to do it.

I didn't mean to hurt him. To be honest, I admired his tenacity. How he was able to forego all fear and just dive right in—it was a quality I envied in him. Yet that same quality also helped to cast him out of Heaven...

I don't know if it was my fault, or what percentage of the blame I was to take, but I did feel guilty, because deep down, I knew that I wasn't completely innocent. To this very day, I used my team to overshadow my shortcomings, and while someone could look at me and say that it was a result of my great leadership, I saw it them as a shield. My team...they performed brilliantly, and oftentimes, I believed that it wasn't because of me.

Funny enough, I shined best when I was just another member, being used in Lysander's plan to defeat Vergil. That was my greatest moment, and I hadn't delegated a thing.

So what was I to do now?

Act like a leader and sacrifice myself for the potential good of them all? Or look out for myself and work with Abdiel? I knew that there was absolutely no reason to trust him. And it wasn't just because he was a demon.

He had motive to betray me. The demons were winning—they just needed to know the location of Heaven's generals (which I would surely end up bringing him to), and he was being too friendly for my taste. But what choice did I have? If there was anything I was learning recently, it was that staying idle wasn't going to make my problems go away.

I ignored Abdiel and the others on the island and now here he was, back in my life. I had ignored Marcus' cries for help and now he was in danger of shutting down. I had ignored my teammates' cries and who knows what we could have accomplished if I had just taken the initiative. I was tired of sleeping, tired of waiting, and tired of waiting for the solutions to come to me.

I was going to go out and find them.

"Let's go," I said suddenly, taking his hand and shaking it vigorously. His eyes widened in shock as he let out a small chuckle.

"What changed your mind so quickly?"

"I'm trying to make things right."

"You're willing to put your trust in a demon?"

"No," I said quickly, hopefully not too quickly. "I'm still watching you, but I realize that we need each other in order to get out of here. If I stay here, I know that the angels will lose the war. Unless God intervenes, of course."

"And by going," he finished for me, "you have the opportunity to shift the battle in your favor."

"Hopefully," I said, turning to face the outside. "Now how do we get out of here?"

"It's going to be rough for you," Abdiel replied.

"What do you mean?"

"Demons have practiced phasing in and out of the barriers, but the angels have not. I'll have to weaken you further just to get you outside."

"And then what? Carry me back to the frontlines? Fight against a host of Archangels by yourself?"

"Not fight. Run."

"What were you as an angel? What was your class?"

"Messenger."

I winced at the answer, not because I had a disdain for Messengers, but because it seemed like that particular class was the one coming back to haunt me the most. What was that about?

"Messengers can't outrun Archangels," I replied matter-of-factly.

"That doesn't matter. Most of the Archangels aren't here right now. They're out retrieving others for the cells. I might only have to dodge one, and if we do it quietly, it should go smooth."

"They should have known that you could do this though," I scoffed. "They had to have known before they threw you in this cell."

"Demons have a signature," Abdiel replied, walking up to the invisible wall and looking around the canyon. "We're all monitored by Lucifer and his most trusted advisors. Even if I escape, they know where I am at all times. That's why I need your help too. I can't do this on my own because I'll fail."

"But if I take you to my superiors, then Lucifer will know their location."

"Not if we only stay there for a bit. As long as we don't linger. No more than ten minutes I say. Lucifer will think that we're back on the move."

"I can't guarantee that will happen. Once Michael and the others see you, they'll imprison and interrogate you. You might be trading one prison for another."

"But that's where you come in," he said, turning to smile at me. "You'll be able to tell them that I'm on your side."

I nodded slowly and he went back to looking outside. After a minute had passed, he backed away.

"I think the coast is clear," he said. "We have to move now though. Are you ready for this?"

"Just get it done," I sighed, and he punched me in the face, as hard as he could. I reeled backwards into the invisible wall as my head bobbed up and down.

"That was hard," I muttered, and he winced at the sight of me.

"Sorry, I just want to get this over with."

"Just do it."

Abdiel kept hitting me in the face, over and over until I could feel myself beginning to lose unconscious. I concentrated as hard as I could on the wall at my back, willing myself to break apart and fall outside.

I closed my eyes and continued concentrating as Abdiel pushed me forward, shoving me further and further into the wall. When I was through, my body re-materialized immediately on its own, but I didn't have the strength to fly. Falling headfirst toward the canyon floor, my wings quivered and fought for uplift but I was too weary.

But suddenly a hand grabbed my foot, and my descent ended. Abdiel threw me up into the air so that I was upright and then he grabbed my hand and took off, past my imprisoned brothers and sisters and out of the canyon as fast as he could. The way he moved...it wasn't graceful, but it was alarmingly quick. He had the speed of a flea, so quick that one moment you saw it, and in the next it was long gone.

"Where do we go from here?" he shouted and I was barely able to open my eyes. The last thing I saw before I went unconscious was a small angel headbutting Abdiel in the face.

    * *   *

Abdiel was fighting when I awoke, and for a second I thought it was with an Archangel. I shot up to my feet, using my wings to propel me. I was surprised to find that I was no longer in the air but back on the ground and in the dirt. Thankfully, it wasn't back at the canyon, but even so, I could hear the frustrations of Abdiel coming from a mile away.

I flew over to his location quickly and gasped upon seeing my team.

They were beating him up like he was Lucifer himself, and Abdiel was just on the ground, screaming for them to stop. I intervened immediately, running into the midst of their scuffle and breaking it up.

"Hey!" Farah cried out as I pushed her aside. "What's wrong?"

"Leave him alone!" I ordered them all. I could see Lysander raising his eyebrows in surprise as Alessa crossed her arms and scowled. She was going to need a good explanation on this one.

"He demon," Marcus stated, crossing his massive arms as well. "He had you."

"He did," I explained as their eyes came down upon the writhing Abdiel, groaning and attempting to climb to his feet. "But it wasn't what it looked like. He was taking me to safety, not to the enemy."

"I don't understand," Alessa said.

"I was captured by the former Archangels," I said. "And I was thrown in a prison with Abdiel. We used to know each other, a long time ago. He's a friend. He helped me escape."

"Vergil was a friend," Lysander said quickly. I could only imagine how much of a hypocrite I looked like. Not long ago, I had gotten on him for defending a demon, and now here I was, doing the same.

"Vergil betrayed us," Farah shouted, her little voice barely causing an echo. "He got Cain and Abel killed, and he was part of our team! Why should we trust him?" she said, pointing at Abdiel. "He's a demon for a reason. He's *outside* of Heaven, so what did he do that was so wrong, huh?"

"He said that he chose the wrong side," I explained. "He made a mistake."

"God doesn't make mistakes," Alessa said adamantly. I could tell by the serious expression on her face that she was very concerned for my mental well-being.

"That was Vergil's story too," Lysander said. "That he chose wrong but he wasn't thinking."

"Just because Vergil lied about that," I said. "It doesn't mean Abdiel is."

"He's a demon," Lysander said, repeating the mantra of my team. It was only then I truly began to understand Lysander's previous frustrations. They were so stuck on the current status of Abdiel that they couldn't see through to who he was. But then again...could I? Was I right to trust him? Even now?

"How do you know him?" Alessa asked—the question I had been dreading since the start of the conversation, but Abdiel jumped in before I could stammer out a reply.

"We met before the fall of Lucifer," he said, not entirely a lie, but certainly avoiding the truth. "Cadence wasn't very talkative then, but he was good company. We became friends but after the war in Heaven...we were separated."

"I never heard of you," Alessa said. Marcus nodded in agreement.

"Must have been a quick friendship," Lysander muttered and I shot a reply to him.

"So was yours and Vergil's," I said. Lysander didn't respond.

"So what is he doing here?" Alessa asked, and I turned to her, ready to relay the crazy information.

"He wants to help us turn this war around. He's going to give us intelligence that will help us defeat the demons."

"Mm-hmm," Lysander said. "And what intelligence might that be? You might as well say it now."

"But then what assurances do I have that I won't be thrown in prison," Abdiel replied.

"You have to give us something."

"The demon headquarters...it's located at the core of the Earth, and to go there, you have to phase through the earth's crust and mantle."

"We knew that already."

"But not until recently," I said. "And Abdiel confirms it."

"Or Lucifer suspects that we would have already figured it out by now. Give us something else."

"Um," Abdiel stammered. "The demons are using the humans to assist with the war. By eliminating your prayers, they are essentially making your army weaker. There is a link between the angels and humans that we don't yet understand, but we do know that it has a powerful effect on the spiritual realm. Their prayers weaken us and strengthen you."

"Again, something we already know."

"Yes," I said. "*We* know, but again, it's just speculation to everyone else. If this is all information that we know about then why aren't the angels as a whole using it to their advantage?"

"What is wrong with you?" Alessa asked suddenly. I was taken aback.

"What do you mean?"

"This isn't like you. You're usually so cautious...you would never be so reckless as to take a demon to the angels' headquarters, let alone trust or defend one. What changed? How strong is the relationship between you and him?"

"He feels responsible," Abdiel said suddenly, and all eyes fell on him.

"Explain," Marcus said.

"I was undecided between Lucifer and God when things were heating up in Heaven. And so I asked for his advice. He told me to go with what I thought was best, regardless of how others felt about the decision. And so I did. I chose Lucifer, and I chose wrong. I didn't know he was a lunatic, and I was punished along with all those that wanted to tear Heaven down and cause violence and conflict. When we were in the canyon, Cadence told me that he felt guilty. That he should have persuaded me to stay more neutral or with God at that point…see how things play out. And so, he's trying to make amends now. He has no reason to trust me, but he's doing his best to try. I don't expect any of you to trust me…and I actually want you to watch me from here on out. Then you'll see that I'm not going to harm you."

"Fine," Alessa said, looking at me with a hardened gaze. "But he's your responsibility."

"Of course," I said, and she took off into the air. Lysander, Farah, and Marcus followed her without a word, doing their own introspective thinking on who and what Abdiel was. I was as confused as ever. Abdiel had *lied* to gain my teammates' trust, and he had done it so easily and simply that it was disturbing. Could he be fooling me as well? Or was it just a little lie to get us past my team's interrogation? Either way, a queasy feeling was beginning to form in the pit of my being, and I was suddenly more anxious than before.

"They don't know, do they?" he said, breaking my thoughts. I turned to him with a puzzled look on my face. "They don't know what you did to all those angels back on the island." He turned to face me and he shook his head, as if scolding me for my wrong-doing.

"It's okay," he said. "Your secret is safe with me."

Chapter 12 – Safe Secrets

"I don't know what to think," Raphael sighed as he rubbed the back of his neck. Lysander had gone on ahead and made sure to request their superiors so that they could all meet at a neutral location. No one was about to reveal to Abdiel where their base of operations was on Earth.

So after the message had been sent, we waited a neutral location, about 200 miles from where Michael and the others delegated. It didn't take long before Raphael came from the skies and looked down on Abdiel like he was a weed in the midst of his garden. Without a word, he motioned for the demon to go with him.

They only flew a few miles away, but I still couldn't hear them. All I could do was watch as they talked candidly, neither one of them making gestures with their hands or having identifiable expressions on their faces. After ten minutes had passed, Raphael came back to us, and surprisingly, he left Abdiel alone—to wait, and to wonder.

"Is his story true?" Lysander asked. "He's trying to defect to our side?"

"That can never be verified without decades of service," Raphael sighed, turning to me. "You really put a dilemma on our doorstep. I wasn't expecting this."

"Neither was I."

"Yet you believe him enough to bring him here. You could have just left."

"Not really. He helped me escape."

"That makes him all the more suspicious in my book."

"I used to know him," I winced. "And he wasn't a bad person before. Just confused."

"There are a lot of demons out there that were confused. But God separated them for a reason. Either they were only feigning confusion, or they were neutral, which is almost just as bad. Neutral means you're looking for a side to win before you make a decision. You can't rely on those type of people."

"What advantage does he gain from being with us now? We're losing."

"Losing, but not out yet," Raphael warned. "If he goes back to his superiors with the locations of ours, the war could be over, and Earth will be lost."

"Then we keep him away."

"You say that," Raphael raised an eyebrow. "But it doesn't sound like you're ready to drop him off in Hell either."

"I can stay with him," I said, bolder than I intended. "I'll keep an eye on him."

"Why?" he asked, puzzled. "What do you gain out of this?"

"Why is there anything to gain? I think that if there is some truth to his words, it's worth looking into. Can you imagine if God decided to let those that were confused back into the ranks? You can't deny them if they are suddenly transformed back into angels."

"Maybe, but that's rather unlikely."

"We've been neglectful for far too long," I explained. "And maybe that's why we're losing the battle. The humans...the demons...we are all part of a system. A balance—and one that we are losing. We should look into other ways of winning the war besides railing our beliefs over their heads."

"That would be your job," Raphael sighed, rubbing his forehead. "The truth is, myself, and all the others...we don't have to investigate these theories. We're barely holding on as it is. But if you and Team Six want to take Abdiel around and look into it, feel free."

"Thank you," I said. Raphael just gave me a concerned glance, sighed, and then took off to the skies. I noticed that Abdiel was watching the direction in which he was headed. I turned to my team.

"What do you all want to do about this?"

"You're the leader," Alessa muttered. I shook my head vehemently.

"We're a team," I stressed. "And leader or not, I'm asking for your opinions."

"What exactly are we figuring out here?" Farah asked.

"We need to decide whether to take him along with us or not," Lysander sighed. "While we try to win this war...I assume we're going back to the humans?"

"I think so," I said, and Lysander shook his head.

"We're better off without him. He doesn't add anything to our mission. If anything, he might sabotage it at some point."

"But do we pass this opportunity up? Just let Abdiel go back to Lucifer? What if he really needs our help?"

"Maybe we should," Alessa said suddenly, biting her lip.

"Why?" Marcus asked.

"Because...um, well, because..." she took a deep breath. "There's always been a division between us. Demons and Angels. Us and Them. And that's how it's always going to stay unless we reach out somehow and try to bridge the gap. We're going to be fighting forever until we try something different."

"It could be our downfall," Lysander said ominously. I glanced at him and smiled.

"It wouldn't be the first time we would face such insurmountable odds."

"True," Marcus said, placing a hand on my shoulder. "Marcus with you."

"As am I," Alessa said, giving me a weak smile. "We've overcome a lot together. We can get through this as well."

"Let's do this then!" Farah said, pumping a fist in the air. Lysander shrugged his shoulders and threw up a limp fist as well.

"Alright then," I said. "Abdiel sticks with us for the time being. I'll let him know on what we decided. Afterwards, we head back to Noah's ark. We have work to do."

My team nodded one by one, and then slowly, they began their ascension toward the clouds, leaving me with my feet planted firmly into the ground. Though they all had smiles on their faces, I could see past it. I could see the concern, anxiety and discontent. They were there for me, because I was their leader, but they didn't trust my judgment completely. Their actions were speaking louder than words, but strangely, I wanted their words, their beliefs, their feelings.

I wanted them to be in agreement with me through and through.

"They're leaving?" Abdiel asked as he flew down beside me. I crossed my arms and chuckled.

"No, they're just getting a head start on our mission. So we have a little time to chat."

"I'm coming with you?"

"You are."

"And I take it they aren't too happy about it."

"They are hesitant, as am I. But they aren't unwilling to give you a chance."

"Thank you."

"What happens next will determine a lot," I said, turning to face him. "If you betray us, I hope it's to win the war, because no one will trust demons again afterwards. I hope you realize that."

"Your warning is unwarranted. I have no plans on betraying you. I'm grateful for the opportunity to redeem myself. If I succeed, countless other demons will follow in my footsteps."

"That's the dream," I sighed.

"Can I make a suggestion to you? It's something I was thinking about while I was standing over there waiting."

"Go ahead."

"Your leadership skills...they are lacking."

"Sounds more like an observation than a suggestion."

"No, you didn't let me finish," he laughed. "What I was going to say next is that your leadership could be better with a simple tweak here and there. Do you know why people look up to you in the first place?

"Enlighten me," I chuckled.

"It's because you don't waver. You're like a rock when it comes to adversity. Sure, you might be quaking on the inside, but no one can tell. People like that kind of solidarity. It gives them peace and comfort. So they turn to you for guidance. Must be the fact that you're a Guard or something. Anyways...once they come to you for advice, that's when it begins falling apart. You forget why God is so powerful in his approach to winning people to his side."

"And what's that?"

"His Presence," Abdiel said. "It's His presence that keeps us coming back to him no matter what. He doesn't say much or do much, but we can't forget what it felt like to be around him. None of us can, not even Lucifer. It drives him mad that he won't be able to feel that again. But we can take God's approach, and implement that ourselves."

"What do you mean? I don't understand."

"All you do is bark orders and expect. Expect people to do stuff for you and then come running back for more. I don't know why. I know the real you. You're not some grand leader that everyone thinks you are. But what you do have, and this I can't deny...is your rock-like presence. And that's what you have to use. Say you have a belief in something that's contrary to your little congregation's...don't just bark out orders and expect everyone to fall in line. Why don't you start carrying out your belief yourself, without the expectation of others coming with you, and then...you'll see. They will follow. They will obey. They will believe for themselves because no one told them what to do. It's the psychology of it all."

"So I shouldn't tell them what to do. I should just act, and they will follow?"

"Yeah," Abdiel said. "It's real simple. That's what God does. He just gives us His presence and we follow him blindly. Lucifer gives us his presence and demons follow him without question. You should do the same. It's much better than just telling people what to do. Those under you don't have a sense of ownership when that happens."

"Why are you telling me all this?"

"Because you're going to need your team to go through some hardship," he said darkly. "Make no mistake, I'm on your side, but the demons are still winning. And from what I'm seeing, they're going to win all the way. You better be ready to lead your team out of the darkness and back into the light. You've spent so much time in Heaven that you forgot how hard it is to get back to it when you're on the outside."

"What's coming? What do you know that you're not telling me?"

"That it's already too late," he said. "Noah is but a temporary stumbling block in the grand scheme of things. The end is already here, and your team will look to you for guidance like never before. You have to be ready. And most of all, you have to tell them the truth about the islands. Now. Before it's too late."

"Our relationship is already fragile. They won't follow me any more if I tell them."

"Better than them finding out. I won't tell them, but they will find out at some point. Trust me."

"I've already lost them once. I don't want to lose them again."

"I know the feeling," he replied. "It's exactly how we demons felt when we were cast out of Heaven."

Chapter 13 – Raindrops

"God's love is infinite," Noah cried out to the masses. They listened, but only because of the food he had promised them. I deemed him a wise man after seeing this ploy for the second time. No matter how noble God's creations were, it was only when they were given something that they were willingly to truly listen.

My team and I sat on a cliff, hanging over the mob and the ark below. As our feet dangled over the edge, we scanned their faces, watching for threats among them. None had taken weapons into their hands, but that didn't mean they weren't concealing them. I wouldn't be surprised.

The ark was complete.

And there were a ton of food and animals inside, ripe for the taking.

If two men could destroy each other over a rabbit, what would they do for an entire zoo?

"I've asked you here today because I want to convince you one last time," Noah shouted. "I need you to understand what's at stake. Today marks the beginning of change, and I ask that you reconsider my plea. Cast down your traditions and your beliefs. Serve the one and true God, and join me on the ark."

"It's probably plagued!" someone shouted from the crowd.

"The animals in there would kill us!" another cried.

"You're wasting your breath, Noah!" someone else shouted. Noah sighed but continued his speech.

"It has never rained," he yelled. "I understand that. But that day has arrived. And the rain will not end until the Earth is cleansed. There—" Noah stopped as an older woman patted his back. He turned around to see his wife, concerned and weary. He nodded and faced the crowd once more.

"I have preached this message for decades," he said, his shoulders sunken and his countenance crestfallen. "Perhaps it is time that I cease from speaking and we should just wait to see what happens." Noah walked away from the mob with his wife hand in hand. At first, the crowd just stared at him curiously, and then they began murmuring among themselves, whispering about what was happening.

"You better give us the food you promised!" a woman screamed and the mob's voices began growing in number, raising their fists in the air and shouting until their faces were red and strained. Noah never turned around.

"It's coming," a voice muttered from behind us. I spun my head around to see a imp demon, so small that standing up completely, he was right in my face while I sat. I leapt to my feet and saw that there were hundreds of demons behind him, of all classes and sizes. Strangely, none but the imp in front of me was glancing my way. They were all staring down at the crowd of people below.

"What is going on here?" I shouted, so that the rest of my teammates would hear. I turned to my right to watch Abdiel's expression once he saw his former teammates. To my surprise, his face was that of shock and fear. Lysander scowled as Farah hovered above his head, clenching her little fists.

"We didn't even hear them," Alessa said as she grabbed my forearm.

"What is going on?" I asked the imp. "What are you all doing here?"

"Don't be scared, Cadence," the imp seethed. "We're not here to harm you. We're just here to watch."

"Watch what?" Marcus asked.

"The end of humanity," the imp replied. "There is nothing you can do about it. Look. And see how futile your efforts have been. The Battle of the East was nothing but a distraction, and even to this very hour, your superiors fight in that distant land while here, right now, the outcome of the war is being decided."

I craned my neck, ignoring the demon masses in front of me, and watched the humans below, still yelling at the ark. Noah and his wife had gone inside and closed the hatch, sealing it.

But now the people were beginning to slowly step forward, inching closer to the ark and wondering if they should take it over completely.

They eventually gained confidence, rushing the ark and pounding on its sides with their fists, screaming and shouting for Noah to show himself and give them the food he promised. They continued this for a few minutes.

Until the first raindrop fell.

It hit a middle-aged man in the forehead. And the sensation was so strange that he must have thought someone had spit on him. His eyes became enraged and wide as he began looking from his right to his left, wondering who had the audacity to perform the act. And then he realized that the person in front of him was beginning to look to her left and right as well. Then someone diagonally to his left. Another drop of water hit the first man again, hitting the top of his ear and then running down the lobe.

The rain began to fall.

As if the heavens themselves had opened up, the rain began to fall like a torrential monsoon, drenching the people and causing their clothes to stick tightly to their skin. Any anger they had was now lost. All they could think about now was the fear, and the sudden realization that Noah had been right.

They continued banging their fists against the ark, but it wasn't for the food.

It was for the shelter.

"PLEASE!" they shrieked as they began climbing on top of each other, trying to reach the top of the ark. Some ran away to go back to their villages, in order to procure more weapons and tools to break into the ark, but they quickly found that it was difficult to run through the rapidly-forming mud at their feet.

A burst of laughter from behind me caught my attention.

"What's so funny?" I asked the mob of demons before me. A former Guard stepped forward.

"You've lost," he said. "The demons are stronger naturally. The only advantage you had were the humans, and now they will be destroyed. The only ones who will survive are Noah and his family, and they are no threat to us."

"They are God's elect," I snapped at him.

"So are you," he snapped right back. "And yet, here you are...defeated."

"What happens now?" I asked, taking a step back. My team took their feet off the cliff and hovered in the air. Though it was clear that we were preparing for a quick escape, not one demon moved to stop us.

"Do you think you're safe?" the Guard laughed. "Do you really think that there is anywhere you can go? The battle for Earth has gone in our favor. The best thing you can do is go back to Heaven and wait for our assault."

"Perhaps we will," Lysander said, his eyes locked upon me.

"Run and fly, little angels," an imp replied. "Run and fly while you still can."

"Where should we go?" I asked Abdiel. If there was anywhere the demons couldn't find us, he would know of it. I doubted we would be able to reach Heaven in time. We needed time to lay low until we could make a proper escape.

"We could go for the atmosphere," Farah said, mirroring some of my thoughts. The demons in front of us smiled.

"Try," a former Messenger said. "With the heavens opened up, the skies might not be as restrictive as they once were."

"Where should we go?" I asked Abdiel again, and he chuckled to himself.

"You can come with us to Hell," he said. I glared at him.

"Don't do this," I said. "Don't throw away your opportunity. I thought you said you were on our side."

"I am on your side," he said. "I really am. If you come to Hell willingly, then I can make a deal on your behalf. If we run, we'll never survive."

"Deal," I scoffed. "No such thing will happen."

"It's the only way."

"There has to be another."

"Let me ask you something, brother. If I did something that benefits you...even if it hurts...is it wrong of me?"

"What are you saying?"

"An enemy will tell you about yourself. Friends will keep it a secret."

"No riddles!" I yelled at him. "What are you talking about?" I looked at the demons around us, waiting for Abdiel to continue, and in that moment, I realized that Abdiel was respected among them. Whoever he was...he was not a friend. Of course, I knew this from the start, but there was hope. There was...a possibility that you wouldn't be like the others."

"I will never understand your concept of black and white," Abdiel replied. I glanced once again at the demons near me, noticing that they still didn't move. "Perhaps the light blinds you to see the truth— the world and the universe at large is bathed in darkness. That doesn't mean it's bad. It doesn't mean it's evil. Cadence, whether you realize it or not, I am here to help you. You will survive this day, and you will get stronger from it. Of that, I am sure. "

He turned to my team and gave them a curt smile.

"I think it's time that you learned the truth about my dear friend, Cadence."

Chapter 14 – Washed

"Cadence is not telling you everything," he said, as I scanned the faces of my teammates one by one. They all looked directly into my eyes, and while I didn't see any condemnation within them, they didn't tell Abdiel to be quiet either. For whatever reason, they had deemed his words worthy of their attention, and that hurt more than the sharpest of betrayals. What was it within me that they saw?

"What is he talking about?" Farah asked, and I tried to address her but Abdiel interrupted me. I didn't fight back, and I think...I didn't want to. I knew that my team would have to know the truth at some point and I had always been too afraid to tell them myself. It was never the right time. It was hardly the right place. There was too much to do.

Excuses.

Excuses that kept our relationships on hold—for they could not truly begin to know who I was until they realized the depth of my actions.

"Before you arrived on the islands, I was there, with Cadence," Abdiel explained to my teammates. "You may not remember me, but that's because I was Absent at the time. You have your dear friend, Cadence, to thank for that."

My teammates looked at me with puzzled looks on their faces.

"We didn't know what happened to God," he continued. "We had felt his presence and we needed to be in it once again. Being that Cadence was the first angel on the island, we all looked to him for guidance. Whatever his mission was, we would take on, and whatever he wanted us to do, we would do it without question. That was our downfall.

"Afraid of the mental database and how brutal it was to traverse it, he had us perform the task instead. While he sat back and watched, hoping for God to appear, we lost ourselves. For most of us, we didn't realize it until we were already too far gone—that by the time we found God, only he would receive his presence and his grace. The rest of us wouldn't even be aware."

"Goodness, Cadence," Alessa whispered. "Is that true?"

"As more angels arrived," Abdiel said, ignoring her, "the more we had to carry out his wishes. He's always had a knack for leadership and attracting others to his ideals. Even with very few words, he was still persuasive. He was our calm in the storm, and our rock in the midst of the turbulent sea. He used us, and when that wasn't enough, he began changing our outlook on existence altogether. He began introducing an idea to us that caused far more harm than good. A concept that made so many angels absent and defenseless that I'm sure his actions had a direct consequence on their fall in Heaven."

"What was it?" Farah asked as I stayed silent. I noticed that Marcus could barely keep his eyes off of me.

"It was the idea that God didn't exist," Abdiel said solemnly. "That he never existed in the first place. He came up with the idea that what we felt in the beginning was a solitary event, and that there was no God. It had just been the feeling we all received upon birth. He then said that those who went Absent...probably did so because they came upon the truth. Somewhere in the mental database, they realized that God was non-existent, and the shock was so great that they shut down. We now know that's not true...but the notion was still enough to make the island desolate and void of awareness."

"I was searching for answers," I said suddenly, knowing that I had to say something before my entire image was destroyed. "And I was wracking my brain, trying to understand. I was young, and I was trying to come up with an explanation that made sense."

"Is that why you're so lazy?" Alessa shouted at me, punching me softly in the chest. "Is that why you don't want to lead anything? Because of what you did?!"

"I wasn't sure whether to believe it myself," I muttered. "But it was all I had...I...I realized I was wrong later on but it was too late. So many had already gone Absent…when you all arrived, by then…I was so lonely that I didn't even bother talking about the mental database. At that point I just gave up and all I wanted was others by my side, to talk to and have fun with."

"It's all about you," Lysander said, shaking his head. "It's always about you."

"Lysander, what are—"

"—hey!" Lysander shouted, backing up from me and scowling. "all I'm doing is stating the facts! You never want to go into the mental database to help our causes, you refused to relinquish the leadership role before, you didn't want to step in when we needed you because you were concerned about how you felt, and in the end, you couldn't even tell us the truth…I don't even know who you are."

"I'm the same person," I replied, but Alessa was already shaking her head.

"You're our leader," she said. "But now…I don't even know if you're fit for the team…why would you keep something like that from us? I don't' understand."

"Don't let Abdiel separate us. This day isn't over. We can't let the demons win."

"But it's all true," Lysander shouted. "Everything he's saying is true, isn't it? You didn't deny a thing. And now we're defenseless. We're at the demons' mercy. No matter what we do today, we have lost! We were so focused on winning the battles that we lost the war."

"God could still intervene," I said.

"Doubt," Marcus stated. "They have free will."

"So we just give up?" I asked them. They all refused to give me an answer so I turned to Abdiel. "And you…I thought you were on my side."

"You're right, I am," he said matter-of-factly. "You may not realize it now, but I am giving you exactly what you need. I am sure you will survive this day, Cadence. You are resilient. And now that your team knows the truth and there is nothing to hide, you can truly start becoming the angel that God intended you to be. You can start over."

"Look at them down there," I said, pointing to the increasingly loud mob below. "This is no fresh start."

"But it is a start," he said. "That you can't deny. When we were no longer Absent and found ourselves in Heaven, we weren't given anything. It was a strange new world in which we had to find our way and that new world waited for no one. There were consequences to our actions, as there is now for you. But don't fret. I am sure you will make it."

"You betray me, and yet you say it's for my own good. That's ridiculous."

"You'll see it in the end. "

"Whatever you say," I replied. "The fact is that we're going to fight until we have no energy left."

"No, you might," Alessa said. I couldn't believe my ears. "But I'm smart enough to know when we should retreat."

"What about Vergil?" I scoffed. "What about when we fought him? Weren't those odds worse?"

"We were cornered the first time," Alessa said. "And the second time we had a plan—which is something that we should try to formulate now."

"But Noah...he'll be defenseless."

"God is always in control," she said adamantly. "Even if humanity fades and the angels lose, he has a plan in place for everything. Perhaps this is how it's supposed to be."

"I don't accept that," I said, but then Lysander placed a hand on my shoulder.

"Because you're the one that's feeling the brunt of the responsibility. You think that you've failed everyone, when really, this information we've gotten doesn't change a thing. We've lost. The demons aren't even attacking us right now. That should tell you something."

"Not yet," I muttered, then I turned to Alessa. "So we're just going to leave?"

"That would be best," Abdiel replied, and Farah scoffed at him.

"Yeah, right," she said. "You can leave if you want, but I'm not going anywhere. Even if I have to take down every one of them myself!"

"Farah!" I shouted at her as she took off into the air, heading off into the distance. Surprisingly, not one demon followed after her. "Farah, where are you going?!"

It was only then that I saw it.

In the distance...as tall as a mountain.

The tsunami headed our way, ready to take the ark one way or another. The people below hadn't seen it yet, but they would soon enough. Either way, it was as clear to me as blue skies.

It was over.

"Wait!" I shouted at Farah suddenly, watching as she flew toward the humongous wave. "You can't stop that thing."

"She won't listen to you," Abdiel said confidently. He folded his arms as he stared directly into my eyes. "Not anymore, I'm afraid."

"I'll deal with you later," I snapped at him, and then I took flight, ready to chase after Farah. The demons wouldn't allow it. They leapt on top of me and held me down with their collective might. Lysander, Alessa and Marcus tried to come to my aid, but it was like a wingless fly fighting against a horde of ants. It was nearly impossible to win, let alone escape.

Marcus punched one of the demons in the face when I saw his jaw lock up. His eyes glazed over and suddenly he fell over, his chin resting on top of the shoulders of one of the demons. Without a second thought, the demon threw him over the ledge and into the roaring mob below. I couldn't save him. None of us could.

What was funny was that the demons didn't try to break us down. None of them hit me nor try to wound me. They simply held me down, and forced me to watch as the tsunami got closer.

I suppose it was a fate worse than death.

To see all I worked for be destroyed before my eyes. This wasn't just a group going Absent. This was the death of an entire species, and one that I was responsible for. There would be no greater loss than this, and the weight was already beginning to weigh down upon my heart. I wasn't sure what my place on Earth or Heaven would be after this.

I didn't want to know.

Farah charged the tsunami with both hands stretched outward, as if she were holding an invisible mountain-tall shield in front of her, strong enough and wide enough to halt the incoming flood. But it wasn't so.

Her body hit the waves, and immediately she was engulfed. Her body spiraled out of control and then she disappeared beneath the water.

The people screamed and panicked—some running away from the tsunami and others deciding to take their chances at the ark, pleading one last time for Noah to entreat them. They barely finished their sentences when the water poured over them, like they were pebbles underneath a bubbling brook. The water covered the surface of the land quickly, and soon it appeared as if it had always been that way.

The demons holding me took to the clouds, carrying me with them. Lysander and Alessa screamed at me as the demons keeping them back pressed their faces into the cliff's surface. The water began lapping at their legs and their eyes widened as they too were consumed.

I fought against my spiritual restraints but the demons were far more powerful than I, and I didn't really have the willpower anyways.

"Why am I not down there?!" I screamed, and only Abdiel answered my call. He flew up in front of me and gave me a smile laced in sorrow.

"I don't want to see you like this...but you will overcome."

"You're not Abdiel," I said, and he shook his head.

"Of course I am. I'm the same Abdiel I've always been. The problem is that you are so self-absorbed you can't see past your own nose. You act like I alone caused this flood. I didn't. You act like I betrayed you. How? Because I told your friends the truth? Because really...that's all I did. Look down there."

I glanced down and saw the ark floating, bobbing along the colossal waves. The people that had once pressed against Noah were no longer seen.

"Noah lives," Abdiel said. "The human race is nothing but him and his family now, but just think of the fresh start he has achieved. The morals and values he can bestow. Humanity can start over and for the better! The same can be said for you."

"I don't get it," I said. "I thought the demons wanted Heaven. Why would they not mind if Noah survives?"

"Well, for starters, you have to remember that Noah won't just be left alone. Where before we were all spread out, now we can concentrate all our efforts on him and his family."

"So you're still going to try destroying the human race?"

"Of course," Abdiel replied. "Earth is our home. God's creatures have no place here. Until we find a way in which we can leave this abysmal place, we will fight for it until there's not one of us left."

"If you leave, you'll attack Heaven."

"Don't be silly. We don't care about Heaven anymore. Why would we want to be in a place that's so sterile and never-changing? Why would we want a God that is hardly there? Why would we want to follow someone blindly? At least with Lucifer, as temperamental as he may be, we know what we're getting...which brings me to a question...why don't you join us?"

"Me?" I asked, my eyes blinking rapidly at the sudden question.

"You're an outcast now," he said. "Your team is decimated and the truth is out. You will never, ever be trusted again. Never. Not even with scouting missions. At least with us, you can be yourself, through and through. There's no need to hide who you are."

"Hide who I am?" I scoffed. "What are you talking about?"

"Your selfishness. Your desires to be lazy. You can do whatever you like in Lucifer's kingdom. I would know, after all. For my demon name is Sloth."

"Sloth, huh?" I said, shaking my head. "Well, despite your namesake, you certainly put a lot of effort into destroying my team."

"By uttering a few words? If that's all it took then I should have said the truth a long time ago. Once again you're putting all the blame on me without looking at yourself. That's all you angels do. Become so righteous and holy that pride reigns supreme, and as you know, pride often comes before the fall. I take it you won't join me?"

"Never," I said, and he motioned for the demons behind him to let me go by raising his index finger. They pushed me slightly forward and I turned to face them, only to find that they had already disappeared. Abdiel chuckled.

"So you're going to face me now?" I asked him, and he shook his head.

"I'm not really the fighting type," he said. "To be honest, we just wanted to dismantle your team after what you did to Vergil, and I was the demon for the job. I do want you to come back from this though, so that we can combat each other properly. You angels need to expand your thinking a bit. Too often those in darkness are more aware of their surroundings than those in the light. Puts you at a disadvantage, especially if you have any hope of seeing that light shine. Understand?"

"Yeah," I said, calming down. "I understand perfectly."

"Hmm," he mused. "That's a certainly different attitude than what I've seen all day."

"Maybe I'm coming to terms with what needs to be done, that's all."

"It's all I wanted," Abdiel laughed, then he gave me a curt nod and began descending back toward the Earth backwards. "Take care, Cadence. We'll see each other again soon."

"Yes," I whispered as he vanished from beneath the clouds. "Yes we will."

When I was sure that he had completely taken his leave, I flew down as fast as I could and plunged beneath the turbulent seas with my wings kept tight beneath me.

There were countless bodies.

So many that I wanted to shut my eyes. But I had to search for my teammates. It was possible that one had escaped, and I knew that if there was any chance of atoning for the mistakes I made, it would be through them. Perhaps I was the reason Team Six never aspired to be all it should have been. Perhaps that was why we lost members.

It was because of *my* leadership.

Sure, I could blame it on my teammates, but they were only carrying out my wishes. Whatever consequences came, I was to blame, and now that everything was on the table, I was determined to make it right.

I searched frantically, feeling the tug of the ocean on my spiritual skin, pulling at me as if someone was tugging at my shirt, except in this case it was every pore of my body. I swam deeper, praying that I wouldn't find any demons in the area. But the deeper I swam, the darker it got, and soon I was unable to see anything, no matter how hard I tried.

I was lost in darkness.

Surrounded and wrapped up in its cold embrace.

I never felt so alone then, and for a second, I considered just letting the pull of the water take me, to separate me and spread me out across the ocean however it wished.

But then an answer came, as if it was a reply to an unspoken prayer, a light suddenly shone across the face of the deep, so bright that the darkness fled and receded, going deeper down. It cowered at the light's greatness, and I was so caught off guard that I found myself wading, just taking in the sudden change under the ocean.

I went deeper, feeling invigorated, and knowing that the light was not just that of the sun.

No matter what had just happened, God still cared about me.

He cared about me enough to help me in my task, and that was enough to strengthen my resolve. He really had been watching the entire time, and he knew when I would need him the most. Like always, I had to go through the test. But he was there to help me when I couldn't take another step. I craned my neck from left to right, searching frantically.

I found Marcus!

Floating at the edge of darkness with widened eyes, he remained still. There was no life in his gaze, but I knew that he was still there, somewhere...

I grabbed his meaty hand and pulled him upwards with me.

When we reached the surface, I found myself uncertain on what to do. And as if leaving my current dilemma entirely up to me, the great light vanished in an instant, leaving me floating above the ocean in the meager sunlight. The ark was nowhere to be found.

"What should I do?" I asked aloud, not expecting an answer. Alessa, Lysander and Farah could be under the ocean too, but I knew that the odds weren't likely. Farah was arguably our strongest member and so the demons would more than likely recover her body after the tsunami hit. Alessa and Lysander were already in the clutches of the demons when I was taken from them, and there was no reason to think their situation had changed.

If Abdiel had been telling the truth about him being sent in to overtake Team Six, then it was possible that they would keep my teammates as trophies.

Which means they were being held captive somewhere we didn't have knowledge of...

Or worse...

They were in Hell.

I closed my eyes at the thought, and I considered diving back under, but then Marcus' weight shifted, and I knew that it would be impossible to carry him and go searching at the same time.

I made a choice.

And I prayed it was the right one.

I broke from the ocean's surface and went heavenward.

I feared for my friends' safety, but I knew that I was in no condition to help them yet. If I was going to lead, or even fight again, I would have to take care of myself first.

I wasn't being selfish.

I was being smart.

"Marcus, I'm sorry," I said, as we went beyond the clouds and past Earth's atmosphere. He didn't say anything, and that didn't matter to me. I had a lot of work to do.

With or without his acceptance, I was going to make things right.

Chapter 15 – Baptized

"And that's the end of it," I said to Raphael, sighing as I leaned my back up against the wall. I was sitting in the hall of his home back in Heaven, and it had never felt so foreign to me than it did now. I realized just how little I had visited him of my own volition. In hindsight, I was probably still afraid of my past and the mental database. Innately, I knew that Raphael's hall was a place of knowledge, and it was knowledge that had driven me mad.

Strangely enough, it was Abdiel's imparting of knowledge to my team that had set me free.

"So Abdiel is still out there?"

"Yes," I said. "They all are...how many angels did we..."

"That's irrelevant right now. I want you to take care of yourself first, and then we'll talk about casualties." I looked up at him with a weak smile.

"There was a time in which you would have listed off every detail of what happened out there."

"I suppose there was," he said, crossing his arms. "And I was wrong to do so."

"I can handle it," I said, and he gave me a smirk.

"I admire your bravado and determination, but the facts don't change. You should not have been made into a leader so quickly. We should have trained you, this I admit, but after your team fought against Lucifer and took down Vergil...I thought it was unnecessary, but I suppose we are no different from one another."

"Abdiel thinks that way more than you realize," I muttered.

"What do you mean?"

"He doesn't have a side," I said. "I see that now. He stuck with the demons because they were winning, but he was not unkind to us. He wasn't deceitful…he wasn't evil like we tend to think the demons are. In a sense…he did nothing wrong. Not really."

"We have to use dichotomies to keep the masses championing the good fight," he said. "As gray as the world is, they think in black and white. All they can think about are God's judgments and they forget how often he shows mercy and love. If it was all one way or the other, then why would there be mercy and grace at all? Shouldn't every deed be given its due?"

"I suppose," I said.

"But then," he replied, giving me a smile. "Angels and humans wouldn't be given a second chance—to rise up and become the being God intended you to be all along. It is not until a vessel goes through the fire that they are crafted and made whole."

"If mercy and grace is so important to God…what does that say about the demons who were banished?"

"Perhaps those individuals all needed that to some degree. For someone like Lucifer, he was a bad seed, but for someone like your friend, Abdiel…perhaps he is not lost. He just needed time to reflect. He couldn't have shown the amount of care he did without some level of goodness within him."

"It might have been all deceit."

"He could have torn your team apart from the very beginning with his knowledge, but he wanted to see how we treated one another first. How we spoke to each other and lived. Out of everything said, how we lived is the biggest factor to whether he will join the ranks of the angels again or not. I find it interesting that he revealed all to your team when it didn't matter. Actually, it might have saved you. The demons saw that your team was dismantled and that you were damaged. They were satisfied with your suffering and so they didn't harm you any further, not to mention that Abdiel keeps his rank and gets a pat on the back. I think it turned out very well considering the possible outcomes."

"You think Abdiel is on our side?" I asked, and he sighed.

"I think he's on Abdiel's side for now, until he figures out what he truly needs. I would imagine that if I had been banished from Heaven, I wouldn't be so quick to jump to either side, less I make the wrong decision all over again."

"Then he may be an ally."

"Only time will tell."

"So what happens now?"

"We're taking a look at Marcus," Raphael said, turning around and looking out from his entrance. "Trying to figure out the extent of his…injuries…for lack of a better term. We're also searching for any and all angels we've lost, but resources are limited. We're in no condition to fight. We have noticed that the demons aren't attacking Noah though, and that is good. They are probably preparing for when the waters die down, so that their influence will be felt upon docking. For now, we have a lull in the war, in which we must not take for granted."

"I want to save them," I said, standing slowly to my feet. "I can't sit idly by while they're still out there."

"Are you sure you're ready for responsibility? You've been through a lot."

"I think that I'm ready to start living for once. I'm done slacking. I want to do what I can to win this war."

"I'm uncertain if you are up to the challenge, but it's not like we have much of a choice…fine, I will help you, but we don't have much time. Before I proceed any further, I must ask you, will you do everything I say?"

"Yes," I said boldly. "Make me into a leader."

"Will you always put your team and others before yourself? No matter the sacrifice?"

"Yes."

"And will you accept any and all consequences of your actions on the islands?"

"Yes."

"Don't take this lightly," he said. "Michael and the other leading angels are very concerned over what we've learned, and it's possible that you may be given a low position here in Heaven when this war is finished. A position in which you can be watched. You might not even able to leave Heaven."

"That's fine."

"And your team may never forget what you've done. They may be unable to work with you again, let alone be your friend. Are you ready to face that?"

"I am ready," I said, with a fire in my belly. I clenched my fists tight. "I don't have to hold back anymore. We were a unit, but we weren't complete. I was there, but only physically. I think that if I could show them how much I loved them, and what they meant to me from the beginning, we wouldn't be in this predicament."

"There are no guarantees that anything will go in your favor."

"Either way, I'm fine with it."

"I see," he said, leaning an arm against the arch in the entranceway. "Well, you have persuaded me enough to give you a chance. You will be given a team to manage. Rescue mission."

"Rescue?"

"We don't know where the demons have taken our fallen comrades, but when we do find the location, we will need extraction. It's borderline suicidal, but it's a necessary mission nonetheless. We owe it to the captured to at least attempt a retrieval."

"I'll do it."

"The odds are that you won't come back."

"Then I will get no less than what I deserve...for all the angels that I caused to go Absent."

"I will let you know who they are in a little bit. They will come to you. In the meantime, you are free to travel around Heaven however you choose. "

"Thank you, sir," I said, as I walked past him and then took flight. Lost in a daze, it wasn't until I was almost there that I realized where I was headed.

The rivers.

My usual napping spot. The place where I would rest and daydream, or occasionally, to avoid my team and work altogether.

I stopped in my tracks and hovered in the air.

"No," I said to myself, reversing course and heading into the opposite direction.

Free time, huh?

I flew past the Throne room. I kept going until I reached the second Fellowship hall. Going inside, I heard gasps ring throughout the stadium. I didn't let it bother me. Those that survived needed someone to blame for our great loss, and considering what had been told to every angel in Heaven about me...I was an easy target.

"Excuse me," I shouted, garnering the attention of everyone there. They waited in silence for me to speak.

To make excuses for my actions.

To apologize.

To whine about being treated unfairly.

To say I wasn't to blame.

I did none of those things.

"I need someone to go to the Throne room with me," I said. A chorus of murmurs and widened eyes followed my request. I cleared my throat and spoke up once more. "I want to be with God...but I'm too ashamed to be in his presence alone. I need to get better...but I can't do it alone."

They looked to one another and had silent conversations exchanged between them, visible only by quivers of the eyes and slight movements of the hands. Eventually, one angel, a Messenger, came toward me. He placed a hand on my shoulder, and then he began escorting me outside.

In silence we flew, side by side, and when we reached the Throne room, he opened the doors for me. I sighed and felt God's light wash over me, even from where I stood, and even though I had not yet walked all the way inside. Sensing someone behind me, I turned around.

And the entire host of Heaven was there.

No matter who was to blame or how broken we all were. No matter who we lost and what the future held, we were still a family. Through the good times and through the bad times, we were there for each other.

I could have gone to the Throne room alone and got exactly what I needed.

But I knew they all needed the same thing.

And there was no better way to gain courage for the future and go before the presence of the Lord...

Than doing it together.

I smiled and turned back around, to face the light.

I entered first, because I needed help the most, and then my brothers and sisters followed.

We weren't perfect.

We were a little proud.

And we were very wounded.

But God was going to make it all okay.

I just had to take the first steps...

And keep on stepping...

ANGEL STORY IV

Chapters released monthly starting March 2018 at:

https://www.juliusstclair.com/

My Official Website:

https://www.juliusstclair.com/

Novels by Julius St. Clair:

(Just click on a cover below)

The Sage Saga:

Bundles:

The Seven Sorcerers Saga:

The Angel Story Saga:

The Obsidian Saga:

Witchfall

The Guardians Saga:

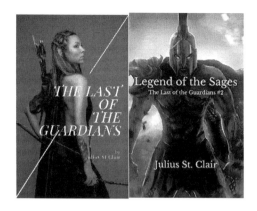

Standalone Novels:

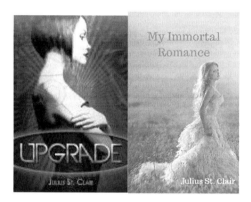

Miniseries:

Short Stories:

Books by Julius St. Clair:

(Just click on a title below to check it out)

THE SAGE SAGA

{A slacker tries to become a warrior for his kingdom while finding love and adventure}

[Now Available for a Discounted Price]

The Last of the Sages (Book 1)

The Sage Academy (Book 1.5)

The Dark Kingdom (Book 2)

Hail to the Queen (Book 3)

Of Heroes and Villains (Book 4)

The Legendary Warrior (Book 5)

End of the Fantasy (Book 6)

Rise of the Sages (Book 7)

Ancient Knights (Book 8)

The Last War (Book 9)

The End of An Era (Book 10)

Hail to the King (Book 11)

The King's Apprentice (Book 12)

Bundles:

The Last of the Sages: The Complete Five Kingdoms Trilogy (Books 1-3)

The Last of the Sages: The Complete Bastion Trilogy (Books 4-6)

The Last of the Sages: The Complete Sorcerers Trilogy (Books 7-9)

The Seven Sorcerers Saga

{A young girl with a troubling past tries to survive the apocalypse on a fantasy world}

The Sorcerer's Ring (Book 1)

The Sorcerer's Dragon (Book 2)

The Sorcerer's Blade (Book 3)

The Angel Story Saga

{An angel wakes up in Heaven as the War between God and Lucifer begins}

End of Angels (Book 1)

Angels of Eden (Book 2)

Angels and the Ark (Book 3)

The Obsidian Saga

{A vengeful teen navigates a world where everyone has been granted up to three wishes}

Obsidian Sky (Book 1)

Fall of the OmegaSlayers (Book 2)

Witchfall

{A conflicted human girl tries to destroy a world of witches while living among them}

Witchfall (Book 1)

The Guardians Saga

{The continuance of James and Catherine's story after the Sage Saga}

The Last of the Guardians (Book 1)

Legend of the Sages (Book 2)

Standalone Novels:

My Immortal Romance – A siren is haunted by her ex-boyfriends in high school

Upgrade – Androids become obsolete in a post-apocalyptic sci-fi world

Miniseries:

The Rest Die Tomorrow (Part 1)

{A narcissistic CEO learns he has eight days to live, long enough to destroy his enemies}

The Rest Die Tomorrow (Part 2)

The Rest Die Tomorrow (Part 3)

The Rest Die Tomorrow (Part 4)

Short Stories:

The Sage Academy (Book 1.5)

Face Punch

Face Punch II

Static Rain

Girl of My Dreams

World War Baby

World War Baby: Day Two

Sanctuary

Join the mailing list for free e-books and future updates!

https://www.juliusstclair.com/

Facebook:

https://www.facebook.com/juliusstclairbooks/

Twitter:

@JuliusStClair

My Official Website:

https://www.juliusstclair.com/

Printed in Great Britain
by Amazon

13399619R00347